Dear Reader,

Have you had your vacation yet? Even if you can't get away for a while, why not take the phone off the hook, banish your family and/or friends for an hour or two, and relax with a long cool drink and one (or all!) of this month's *Scarlet* novels?

Would you like a trip to London and the English countryside? Then let *The Marriage Contract* by Alexandra Jones be your guide. Maybe you want to visit the USA, so why not try Tina Leonard's *Secret Sins* and *A Gambling Man* from Jean Saunders? Or perhaps you'd like a trip back in time? Well, Stacy Brown's *The Errant Bride* can be your time machine. Of course, I enjoyed *all four* books and I hope you'll want to read them all too. So why not stretch that hour or two into three or four?

One of the aspects of my job which is both a joy and a challenge is getting the balance of books right on our schedules. So far, I've been lucky because each of our talented authors has produced a unique *Scarlet* novel for you. Do tell me, though, won't you, if you'd like to see more romantic suspense on our list, or some more sequels, or maybe more books with a sprinkling of humour?

Till next month,

Sally Cooper

SALLY COOPER,
Editor-in-Chief – *Scarlet*

About the Author

Jean Saunders has been writing for thirty years and is the published author of over 70 novels, 600 short stories, numerous articles and five 'How To' books for writers. You may already have read and enjoyed books by Jean under one of her pseudonyms: Rowena Summers, Jean Innes or Sally Blake.

Jean is very involved with writers' organizations such as the Romantic Novelists Association. She is the Chairman of the Southern Writers' conference, has appeared at seminars and conferences, and on radio and television talking about her life as an author.

Married with three adult children and ten grandchildren, travel is listed as one of Jean's major interests and she has visited many countries around the world including the USA.

Other *Scarlet* titles available this month:

SECRET SINS – Tina Leonard
THE ERRANT BRIDE – Stacy Brown
THE MARRIAGE CONTRACT – Alexandra Jones

JEAN SAUNDERS

A GAMBLING MAN

Enquiries to:
Robinson Publishing Ltd
7 Kensington Church Court
London W8 4SP

First published in the UK by Scarlet, 1997

A copy of the British Library Cataloguing in
Publication data is available from the British Library

ISBN 1-85487-949-9

Printed and bound in the EC

10 9 8 7 6 5 4 3 2 1

CHAPTER 1

The flight from England was over at last. Judy unfastened her seatbelt thankfully as the chief stewardess announced that the captain had turned off the engines and the doors would shortly be opened. It had been a long flight, and the plane had been filled to capacity. The window-seat hadn't been such a good idea after all, she reflected, her long legs having been cramped by the narrowness of the seat space.

But peering through the window now, Judy felt her spirits rise. She could see the Los Angeles sky, and it was clear and blue, belying the usual moans of smog and air pollution. It was a glorious day, and it would be even better once she reached the desert . . .

She gave a small smile, remembering her agent's words.

'Don't expect Las Vegas to be the way it once was, Jude. It was a quiet little town when I was there twenty years ago. The desert skies seemed to go on for ever then. Now, well, you'll see for yourself what a boom town it's become.'

1

She had laughed at his mournful face, wondering how someone who always seemed so downbeat could have the capacity to find her such a dream job. Maybe it was his very mournfulness that made people feel sorry for him, and give him a chance . . . but she knew it was more than that. Harry Brady was a smooth and canny operator.

'Harry, I'm not going there just to visit a neat little town, remember? If it wasn't for the casinos and the shows, I wouldn't be going there at all, so I'm certainly not knocking progress. As for blue skies, just to get out of this cold and rainy London will be bonus enough.'

'Well, you call me as soon as you arrive and get settled in, OK? I've faxed Blake Adams to say what plane you'll be on, and he's promised to have everything ready for you.'

More like one of his staff would, thought Judy. She hardly thought the owner of the Sparkling Rocks Hotel and Casino on Las Vegas's famous Strip would be personally concerned with the comfort of a dance choreographer from England, no matter how highly recommended she came.

But shivery thrills ran through her every time the words slid into her mind, just in the knowledge that this was a giant step forward in her career, and she intended to give it everything she had. At twenty-four, she was the youngest choreographer in Harry Brady's theatrical agency but, without bragging, she knew she was also the best.

She'd already worked on some of London's top shows, and her name was beginning to be known in

2

all the right circles. So when Blake Adams had contacted his old buddy, Harry Brady, for the best person on his books to choreograph the British section of an International Show Spectacular in his Las Vegas hotel, Judy had been the natural choice.

'Do you know which line to go to, honey?' the elderly man sitting beside her on the plane asked her now. 'Immigration at LAX can take for ever – '

'I'll be fine,' she assured him. She had enjoyed chatting to him and his wife on the flight, but she didn't want another lengthy conversation now. All she wanted was fresh air . . .

She stood up, hoping this would encourage the couple to move as well, and she didn't miss the way the man sized up her slim figure. The wife noticed it too; with a feeling of relief, Judy saw that it was enough to get her moving.

Ten minutes later she was out of the plane with her holdall and walking along the endless corridors towards Immigration. It wasn't her first trip to America, but it was her first time on the West Coast, and she joined the line in resignation, hoping that the official wouldn't take for ever with his interrogation.

'OK, Miss Hale, you're done,' he told her, after a relatively short time when she'd tried not to feel like a specimen on a slide. 'Have a pleasant stay.'

'Thank you.' Judy gathered up her passport and tickets, cramming the lot into her bag, and resisting the stupid impulse to scuttle away as if she were a criminal.

The baggage hadn't come through on the carousel yet, but in any case hers would go straight through to the Las Vegas boarding area. It was one hassle she didn't have to bother about yet. She made her way to a Red-Top, and quickly ascertained where she should go to get her boarding-pass for the onward flight. Before he gave her the information, he gave her the same kind of puzzled look as the man on the plane.

Self-mockingly, Judy wondered if he was trying to gauge whether or not she was in the movies or on TV, and if he should recognize her face. It wasn't such an unlikely thought. She was tall and slender, with fringed, thick red hair that swung all of a piece around her shoulders. Her features were delicate, her eyes were a wide, clear blue, her mouth full and mobile. She attracted attention even when she didn't want it.

She had been a dancer before she decided she was more comfortable being involved behind the scenes instead of out front, and turned to choreography. She should be used to admiration by now, but she didn't like men who did it so blatantly. She stared the guy out, until he shrugged and gave her the information she needed.

The girl behind the counter of the Las Vegas desk chewed her lip as she studied her computer screen.

'I'm sorry, ma'am, but I don't seem to have you in my computer,' the girl told her eventually.

'But I must be there.' Judy tried to smother the feeling of rising panic at the words. 'My tickets were

4

booked weeks ago, and I have the onward one right here. How can you say I'm not in your computer? Try it again, can you?'

The girl shrugged, and did as she was asked, though they were both aware of the growing line of people behind Judy now. The girl shook her head decisively, but before she could say anything, Judy spoke nervously again.

'Look, there's obviously been some mistake, but if I'm not in the computer already, why can't you just put me in there now? You must see I've got my onward ticket, and all I need is a boarding-pass, right?'

'Wrong, I'm afraid, ma'am. The plane's nearly full. Weekends aren't the best time for a gambling spree to Las Vegas without proper documentation – '

'I'm not going there on a gambling spree – not that it's any of your business,' she muttered beneath her breath.

If she hadn't been getting so alarmed, Judy wouldn't have spoken that way, and she knew it was going to do her no good at all. The girl had a job to do, and she was already turning towards the next person in line behind Judy.

'Can I help you, sir?' she asked, smiling at the tall, good-looking man who was next in line.

'Sure you can, honey. But first of all, wouldn't it save a lot of hassle to do as the lady asks, and just give her a boarding-pass?' he said pleasantly.

Judy was startled to hear the man speak with an educated accent with slight northern overtones. Yorkshire, probably . . . But whoever he was, it

5

was hardly the way to get anything out of this stickler for the rules.

But to her amazement, the girl went several shades of pink. 'If you'll just be patient a moment longer, I'll check that there's a seat available.'

'Good,' the stranger went on coolly. 'We'd all like to get to Vegas tonight if it's not too much to ask. The problem seems simple enough to put right.'

Then, to Judy's amazement after what seemed like a very few details being punched into the computer, the boarding-card was issued. She should be grateful, and so she would have been if she hadn't been so flustered . . .

But far from feeling smug that the counter clerk had been obliged to back down, Judy was annoyed that it had taken a man to put things right so quickly. Male chauvinism hadn't died. It was alive and well, wherever you lived.

The girl would have had to hand over the boarding-pass in the end, anyway. Nobody could dispute the details on the airline ticket, and Judy would far rather have dealt with it all herself, than had the intervention of Mr Macho.

But she thanked the girl and the stranger, and then walked away from the desk quickly.

After all the fuss, there weren't many minutes to spare before the plane was due to leave. But since this was America, people boarded planes like Brits boarded buses, and nobody seemed to be in any great hurry.

She found her seat and sank into it thankfully, more uptight than she realized. After the exhausting flight from London, this had been all she needed . . .

'Do you always cause this much trouble?' came a familiar British voice beside her a few minutes later.

She groaned, tempted not to answer at all. Maybe she could pretend she hadn't noticed anyone fastening the seatbelt in the seat next to her. Maybe she could invent some affliction, like total deafness . . . But of course, he'd know that wasn't the case.

She turned her head slowly and looked into the smiling eyes of the stranger. They were dark brown with hazel flecks in them, in a strong, tanned face. And, oh yes, he was dishy all right, but Judy was in no mood to be impressed.

'Look, I don't want to seem ungracious, and I'm grateful for what you did back there, but I really don't feel like talking,' she said in her own cool English voice.

'That's a pity, Judy, because I was hoping we could take this opportunity to get acquainted before we reach Las Vegas.'

She stared at him. He would have seen her name on her ticket or on the computer screen, of course. But that didn't make them instant buddies . . . and she could probably guess why *he* was going there. With the kind of expensive aura he gave out, he'd probably spend all night at the gaming tables and think nothing of squandering thousands of dollars in the process, whether he won or lost . . .

She censured herself at once for making this swift assessment. Gamblers didn't come ready labelled,

7

and they didn't all look like this guy, or like any of the businessmen on the plane, or the enthusiastic brigade of middle-aged women, off for the weekend with a wad of their husbands' money. It was their business, anyway.

But sometimes gamblers came in the shape of gullible young men who got in too deeply before they realized it . . .

Judy switched her thoughts away from Ricky. She hadn't heard from her brother in months and, cliché though it was, she clung to the thought that no news was good news.

The engines of the plane were already starting up, and her heart gave a small, uncomfortable lurch. In about an hour they would be landing in the gambling centre of the world, exactly where Judy had always vowed she would never be. But fate had an uncanny knack of turning such ideas upside down.

'I guess I'd better come clean, otherwise we're going to be sitting here in stony silence for the entire trip,' came the stranger's voice again.

She turned to him now, her thoughts still uncomfortably on Ricky, whether she wanted them to be or not.

'Well, I don't know who you are, but I've already thanked you for your help. Can we please leave it at that?'

'No can do, I'm afraid – ' he shook his head '– especially as we'll be unable to avoid seeing each other during the next six months.'

She looked at him properly now, her mouth dropping open as a deep suspicion entered her mind. Maybe he hadn't had to look at her name twice to know exactly who she was.

'I'm Blake Adams,' he confirmed, while she was still gathering her wits. 'And I'm sorry our first meeting was such an awkward one.'

At hearing the name, her voice sharpened in embarrassment. 'Well, you could say you're sorry for not introducing yourself at once, instead of making me feel such a fool!'

'Good Lord, the territory really goes with that red hair, just like they say, doesn't it!' he teased her.

She bit her lip, realizing it would take more than a few sharp words to deflate him. And she was doing herself no favours in snapping at him, now that she knew he was her boss.

'I'm afraid it does, and I'm sorry,' she managed to say.

'No, *I*'m sorry,' he answered, to her surprise. 'But I honestly didn't realize it was you until I got to the desk, and then I couldn't resist seeing how you were going to react back there.'

'Well, now you know.'

'Yes, I do. You're a bit of a firecracker, aren't you?'

She might have resented his words if they hadn't been so true. It had been true ever since she was a child, and a quick temper was something she'd always tried to curb. But it wasn't always easy when she found it so hard to tolerate blatant stupidity in others. Which was why she always came down so heavily on Ricky's reckless gambling.

While they had been talking, the plane had taxied on to the runway and taken off, and within minutes the cabin crew were coming round with peanuts and cold drinks for those who wanted them. Things moved quickly on intercity flights.

'I promise you my temperament won't interfere with my work – sir.'

From the sudden sparkle in his eyes she knew she had ruffled him at last.

'For God's sake, get rid of that British stuffiness and relax. You'll find it cuts no ice here. And the name's Blake.'

'I'm sorry. In England we do things differently – as I presume you know.' And she hadn't intended to sound stuffy, nor realized that she had . . .

'Well, neither of us is in England now. And I'd suggest that if you want to get the best out of the girls you're going to work with, you'd better come down off that high horse of yours, elegant though it is.'

It was said so pleasantly that it couldn't have been meant as a threat, but as a compliment it passed right over her head. All the same, she recognized the sense in his words. No choreographer got the best out of her dancers if she didn't have a real rapport with them. Having been a dancer herself, she could see things from both sides of the fence.

And she reminded herself that, as yet, she was a nobody here. Blake Adams had gambled on her because of her agent's enthusiasm for her talents, and she still had to make her mark in Las Vegas.

For the first time since they had met she smiled more naturally at her companion.

'You're absolutely right, of course, and I'm probably suffering the effects of jet-lag. I'm sure I'll be fine after a good night's sleep.'

He put his hand over hers and squeezed it. It might have been the gesture of a Dutch uncle, and she just managed to resist the urge to pull her hand away, since that would *really* have been gauche.

'I suggest that when you've settled in at the hotel, you take a shower or a leisurely bath, and get your head down for a couple of hours. It's the best way to combat jet-lag and gets your body clock used to the time difference, and it's more effective than any way I know.'

'Thanks for the tip,' Judy acknowledged.

She realized that he had somehow managed to turn her hand over so that his thumb was lightly grazing her palm now. He spoke coolly, almost as if unaware that he caressed her skin in that sensual way.

But Judy was intensely aware of it, and tried to ignore the fact that it was sending unwanted ripples of pleasure through her body . . . and from the flickering in those seductive dark eyes, she was pretty damn sure he knew exactly what he was doing.

And the last thing she wanted, or intended, was to form any kind of attachment with Blake Adams . . . Mr Macho Man. In her mind she repeated the scathing name she'd given him at the airport, and quickly removed her hand from his.

'I'm sure I'll be fine.'

'I'm sure you will. But just let me give you a word of friendly advice, Judy. Make sure your cool British reserve doesn't react the other way on you. It could be a real turn-on for some of the studs around town.'

She wasn't sure she liked the advice, but before she could think of a suitable reply he had already turned his attention away from her. He was giving his sexy smile to the stewardess who was leaning towards him now and offering him something from the drinks trolley.

It just showed what kind of man he was, Judy thought. He was so drop-dead gorgeous himself that he thought he only had to smile and any woman would be ready to fall for him. And they probably would . . .

She registered her own thoughts with something like horror. He wasn't *that* gorgeous . . . She watched him covertly out of the corners of her eyes, and knew that, oh yes, he *was*, damn him.

'How about you, ma'am?' the stewardess said, turning to her now. 'Something to drink?'

'Orange juice, please.'

'You're both British, aren't you?' The girl neatly linked them together, and half-filled the plastic glass with ice-cubes before Judy could say that one was enough. 'I have an aunt in Scotland, and I mean to visit her one day.'

'Oh, you should go there if you can. It's a beautiful part of the country,' Judy told her with a smile.

'Are you in show business?' the girl asked her.

'Sort of – ' but Judy quickly sensed the loss of interest when she didn't elaborate.

'Well, I hope you enjoy your stay in Las Vegas, ma'am.'

The girl moved on down the aisle, and Judy could see Blake Adams grinning beside her. She opened the can of orange juice and poured half of it over the ice-cubes.

'What have I said now?' she demanded.

'Well, at the risk of getting you all prickly again, I was just thinking your English understatement is charming and refreshing. I'd forgotten how much I missed it,' he said, disarming her completely.

'I'm not aware that I've understated anything – '

'No? For a woman with your credentials at only twenty-four, I'd say you were definitely in show business, Miss Hale, not merely *sort of*! But don't be too reticent about your credentials, will you? A bit of push never goes amiss in Vegas,' he added. She couldn't be sure if it was meant as advice or a warning. 'Like any show-business centre, it can be a cut-throat town.'

'I'll be sure to remember that,' Judy said, mentally thinking she had to be pushy on the one hand and careful of her cool British reserve on the other . . .

She concentrated on looking out of the window and tried to ignore him, although it was a much smaller plane than the big 747 she'd travelled on from Heathrow, and altogether too intimate, with only two seats on each side of a centre aisle.

They didn't fly at any great height, and once they had left Los Angeles and its sprawling environs, the clear air revealed the colours and shadows of the mountains and desert scenery they were passing over.

As if complying with her need for solitude, and giving her a chance to absorb the changing scenery below them, Blake folded his arms and closed his eyes. And she breathed a sigh of relief that they could

13

stop fencing with one another. It wasn't an auspicious way to begin a new job, and hardly the way she had anticipated meeting her boss.

After a while a drift of feathery clouds obscured the view, and Judy surreptitiously turned her attention to the man sitting beside her instead. In profile he was very handsome, she noted, the kind of guy who probably had half the showgirls in every casino in Las Vegas dreaming about him.

It was more than just good looks, though, and he had those in plenty. Add to them the dynamic quality that went with power and success, the novelty of hearing the educated British accent in a different environment, and that intriguing touch of solid Yorkshire accent that maybe only another Brit would detect so clearly.

It was a combination that was probably a powerful aphrodisiac, and the word was in her head before she could stop it.

As if aware of her scrutiny, Blake opened his eyes languidly. Judy's heart raced, and she felt her face fill with heat at being caught out. The last, the *very* last, thing she wanted was for Blake Adams to think she fancied him.

'Well? Do I pass muster?' he asked.

'I'm sorry. I didn't mean to stare – '

Without warning, he leaned across and kissed her very lightly on her cheek. The slight roughness of his skin brushed hers, and the touch of his mouth was firm. She breathed in the fresh scent of expensive and well-laundered clothes and tantalizing toiletries before she jerked away from him.

14

'Judy, let's get one thing straight. If we're going to be working closely together for the next six months, you'd better cut out this need to keep saying sorry. You've got nothing to be sorry for.'

'All right. I'm –' She caught the glimmer of laughter in his eyes, and her mouth curved into a smile.

'Thank God. I was beginning to think I'd hired one of those stiff-upper-lipped females after all, despite the fact that Harry told me you were the best there is, with a great sense of fun.'

'Harry said that?'

'He did, but I was beginning to doubt the sense of fun until now. Relax, Judy. You're going to the fun capital of the world, so enjoy it!'

She knew it was also referred to as the gambling centre of the world, but she had to agree that for those who enjoyed the gambling and the marvellous shows, it qualified for the other title as well. So many great stars performed in the hotel casinos there: Sinatra and Bassey, Tom Jones and Neil Sedaka, and the incomparable David Copperfield with his magic shows. And the excitement she had felt when she first knew about this job began to surge uppermost into her mind again. All the hiccups along the way couldn't dim her luck.

She realized that Blake was studying her now, and knew that her excitement must be clear to see.

'You're a real loss to the stage, Judy. You have a really beautiful face and figure, and when you smile your whole face lights up.'

She felt herself blush at the unexpected compliment, realizing that in all the time he had been over

15

here, Blake Adams had picked up the uninhibited and disarming way that Americans could pay compliments.

'I gave up dancing professionally several years ago, as I'm sure you already know from Harry,' she told him. 'I've got no wish to go back to it.'

'Well, I agree that there's more to dancing that being on the professional circuit. I'll take you dancing one evening.'

She didn't answer, wondering just how the conversation had got around to such a personal invitation. She hoped he didn't think she had engineered it that way. And it was hardly an invitation. It was a dictum. If Blake Adams said he'd take her dancing, then he'd take her dancing.

Well, not unless she wanted him to, thought Judy. He'd find that here was one woman who didn't immediately fall under his spell. She may have been dazzled by the job and the chance to fulfil a dream, but Blake Adams wasn't part of it.

'We're starting to go down,' he said. Judy refastened her seatbelt, as if to prevent any idea of him helping her.

From his amused smile she knew he was reading her perfectly. Being essentially a private person, it annoyed her, even though she knew it was essential in his line of business to assess people quickly. From the few bits of information her brother Ricky had allowed her to know, she knew there were often ugly incidents in any casino.

But Blake Adams had approved her professional credentials, and that was all he needed to know about

16

her. Her past was her own business, and even though she could still feel a sharp pang whenever she thought of how near she had come to marrying the wrong man, she was thankful now that she had found out in time that he was cheating on her.

'Ready?' Blake asked a short while later, and she knew that there would be no lengthy formalities here as there had been at LAX. The plane had made an easy descent, and the passengers were eager to get into the airport building and be whisked away in taxis to their glittering hotels.

When she stepped outside, the hot dry air of the desert enveloped them at once, and Judy revelled in its heat after the chilly London spring. She followed Blake to the carousel to reclaim her luggage, and while they waited, he put out a call on his mobile phone.

'A car will be here for us in ten minutes,' he said.

'Does everything go so smoothly for you?' she couldn't help asking, marvelling at the way he seemed to get everything he wanted with the minimum of effort.

'Why not? If you want something, you should go ahead and get it if you can. It's not a bad philosophy, especially in this town, Judy.'

'It also sounds a bit ruthless to me,' she commented.

'And *that* sounds all too much like that well-known British reserve to me,' he grinned. 'But give it a week or so, and I'm sure we can change all that.'

He gave her that lazy, sexy look once more, and she felt her heart leap. He had such arrogance and self-assurance, she thought, watching him move towards

17

the carousel as the luggage began to appear on it, and denying her the opportunity for a suitable reply.

But she had to admit that he had the kind of authority that made people step aside to give him room. He stood head and shoulders above most of the other passengers, but it was more than just his handsome appearance and stature and his well-built body that made him stand apart. Plenty of women must be attracted to him.

Hardly understanding why she should be feeling quite so analytical, she assured herself that she had no intention of being added to any list of conquests.

As for her British reserve, well, he must know all about that. But if he had been here for any length of time, which Judy assumed that he must have done, he had inevitably become partly Americanized.

But it wasn't a job requirement for her to do the same. Six months, however wonderful in a dream job, weren't going to change her life in every way, and if he imagined for a single moment that she was going to change one iota of herself because of it, he was in for something of a shock.

CHAPTER 2

The uniformed chauffeur brought the sleek white stretched limo to a halt alongside Blake and Judy. He got out and touched his cap to Blake, opening the rear door for them, then stored Judy's luggage in the trunk.

This was travelling in some style, she thought, breathing in the scent of the luxurious white leather upholstery, and eyeing the phone and TV and the small, well-stocked cocktail cabinet. Though who might bother with such things on a short car journey she couldn't think.

But she was thankful that the back seat was wide enough to avoid the need for contact with the man sitting next to her. The interior of the dark-windowed car held an intimacy of its own, and Judy couldn't resist the half-delicious thought that such a vehicle also had connotations with all the tough-guy movies she had ever seen.

For one wild moment thoughts of the Mafia swept uneasily, yet excitingly, through her head. For all she knew she could be being kidnapped and held to ransom at this very minute . . . She dismissed her crazy imagination as Blake turned to her.

'We'll be there in about thirty minutes, providing the traffic isn't too heavy,' he told her, bringing her back to earth. 'You haven't been to Vegas before, have you?'

'No.'

'Well, don't let it intimidate you. It can be pretty overwhelming at first, but you'll be fine if you remember that it's just another town.'

'Thank you, sir,' Judy answered, as solemnly as if she were being given a tutorial.

Blake laughed and, hardly knowing how it happened, she noticed he had closed the gap between them and slid one arm around her shoulders. She felt the pressure of his fingers on her upper arm through the fabric of her linen jacket, and then one finger slid upwards to caress her cheek.

'You really do prickle, don't you, Judy? I was only giving you some friendly advice, that's all.'

'I'm sorry.' She grinned weakly, realizing she was saying it again. 'And thanks. I'll try to remember that this is just another town – '

But it was almost impossible to deal with such a concept once they had left the usual environs near the airport and were cruising effortlessly towards the most glittering array of buildings Judy had seen in her life. The hotel casinos weren't just convenient places for people to sleep or gamble the night away, but vast edifices ablaze with neon lights, even in the daylight of late afternoon. Names that Judy had only heard or read about leapt into view as they cruised the Strip: Caesar's Palace; The Sands; The Frontier, and so many more. Each one was more spectacular than she could possibly have imagined, and limos and taxis spilled out people in a constant stream at every covered entrance.

Blake was leaning back in the seat now, watching her, and gauging her reaction. 'Is it everything you expected?'

She turned towards him, her eyes wide with amazement and undeniable excitement. There was no way she could hide it now. This was show business on a grand scale, and she smothered her distaste for gambling with the thought of actually working in one of these fabulous places.

'How can you even ask? And how you can call this just another town, I can't think. It's like nowhere I've seen in my life before.'

'It wasn't always like this, though,' Blake told her. 'It was a little one-horse town in the desert until somebody came up with the bright idea of building a hotel and casino. Now it's the wildest, craziest, hottest spot on earth.'

She registered an odd, steely note in his voice, and she spoke in his own terms.

'For somebody who's obviously done pretty well out of it,' she observed without thinking, 'that sounded almost resentful.'

His mouth twisted wryly. 'The other thing to remember in this town is not to believe all you see, Judy. In some ways it's also one of the phoniest places you'll ever come across, so be careful.'

It didn't say much for himself, if he included himself in that statement. But Judy wasn't interested

21

in trying to gauge his hang-ups, if he had any. But why would he, with his money and power . . .? It was a curious statement, though, and one that she put to the back of her mind for the moment.

They were still making slow progress through the congested areas of the downtown casinos, when a huge sign on one of the buildings suddenly caught her attention. The Sparkling Rocks Hotel and Casino was as impressive a complex as any on the Strip, and Judy's heart began to beat more quickly, knowing that this place was to become as familiar to her as Piccadilly Circus . . .

The limo drew up silently beneath the canopied entrance. At once, two young men in green uniforms came to open the rear doors. The chauffeur got out and retrieved Judy's suitcases from the trunk in what seemed like one fluid movement, and placed them on a luggage wagon.

Another clerk in a peaked cap and a striped green waistcoat on which flashed an important badge proclaiming him the Bell Captain, whisked the wagon away at once, and the limo moved on. They were all so efficient it was almost frightening, Judy thought weakly with undisguised admiration.

Once she was out of the air-conditioned limo, the blast of burning heat hit her again, reminding her that this town, for all its glitter and brashness, was still outlandishly in the desert. It was just as though somebody had dumped it there by mistake and then decided to embellish it with all the tawdry luxury in the world.

Judy's linen jacket was starting to cling to her skin, and she longed to peel off all her clothes and take a long luxurious soak in a deep bath. And then do exactly as Blake Adams had suggested – go to bed and temporarily shut out the rest of humanity to fight the jet-lag. Right now it was the most blissful and appealing thought in her head.

'It'll be cooler inside,' she heard Blake say, as she began to feel slightly light-headed. He took her arm and steered her through the crush of people, some trying to get in and some making their way out, with varying expressions on their faces.

She let Blake manoeuvre her through the outer doors and across the deep-carpeted floor of a quiet foyer. Then the doors of the casino opened automatically in front of them, and her eardrums were assaulted by noise.

Having always vowed to keep well away from such places, Judy hadn't really known what to expect, but the overwhelming racket and the dazzling interior of the casino stunned her into silence. Beneath the glittering chandeliers overhead there were rows and rows of flashing slot machines. Men and women took up every available seat in front of them, feeding coins into the machines as if they were starving children.

Every few seconds the sound of bells rang out, proclaiming somebody a winner, and the rush of coins falling into the metal containers of each machine were eagerly scooped up into one of the plastic casino pots.

'It's a little like baptism by fire, I'm afraid,' Blake spoke right into her ear to be heard. 'Don't worry, you'll get used to it. The blackjack and twenty-one

23

tables are much quieter at the far end of the casino, and that's where the serious gamblers head for. But the slots are what many of the weekenders come here for.'

Judy's fascinated gaze had been on the woman staring intently at the whirling icons on the nearest machine, and clearly willing them to stop and make her day . . .

But before she could make any kind of comment, a soft voice spoke beside them.

'Hi, Blake.'

'Hi there. Everything OK?' As he spoke, he smiled at the beautiful girl who had spoken to him. She wore a white, flared silk mini-skirt and the most impossibly high heels Judy had ever seen. She carried a tray of drinks and she paused in the act of gliding towards a group of people at one of the slots.

'Everything's just fine, Blake,' she said, her glance warm and melting. 'See you later?'

'Sure thing.'

Before Judy could wonder if the warmth in his voice was the way he spoke to all his female staff, or was in any way significant, another girl dressed exactly the same as the first came near.

'Hi, Blake. Would you and your companion like a cocktail?'

'Not right now, Maxine, thanks,' he answered.

Judy tore her gaze away from the look in the girl's eyes. She couldn't help wondering if they were all specially chosen for their sexy looks. Or if it was just because Blake was the boss, and the most charismatic thing on two legs . . . and Judy immediately wished the thought had never entered her head.

Blake was walking purposefully towards the reception area now, and as she followed him to the elevators she realized that this was the general entrance. The casino was part of the hotel complex and covered the entire lower level of the building, so that there was no way the arrivals missed out on their first sight of what was on offer.

Judy had had a considerable tussle with her conscience about working here at all, and she was already wondering if she was out of her depth. She hated the very thought of gambling, and here she was, thrust right in the middle of it. And she knew that the worst thing she could do would be to let it show. Her agent had already warned her about it.

You show your sniffy British dislike, Jude, and you'll antagonize everybody from the word go. Just remember who's paying your wages, and paying bloody well.

Harry wouldn't be forgetting it either, since he was getting a generous cut, she thought keenly. But why on earth had he neglected to tell her that Blake was British too! she thought indignantly. Or maybe he thought she'd be dazzled by the thought of working for an American.

Within seconds, it seemed, the elevator had whisked them way up above the casino to the executive floor. Judy had watched the floor numbers on the panel flash by with incredulity, and now the elevator clerk opened the door for them with a flourish.

Did they have clerks for everything? she wondered, and knew she had better check her amazement at this constant pampering, knowing that most of the *grandes dames* who frequented the casinos would expect it. But it had never been Judy Hale's style, and it would take some getting used to.

She followed Blake down an endless corridor, and the silence was so different from the hectic casino below that it was like a welcome haven. She knew she was over-tired and probably overreacting to all she had seen so far, and the fiasco at LAX hadn't done anything to help. By tomorrow, she'd be raring to go . . .

'This is your suite,' Blake told her now, unlocking a door and opening it with a flourish.

Before she could laughingly protest that she hardly rated an entire suite, she was gasping at the opulence of the deep-carpeted room they were entering. It was like something out of *Dynasty* and *Dallas* all rolled into one. The furniture was in the palest Scandinavian style, and clearly very expensive. As well as two white leather easy chairs, there wasn't just one matching sofa, but two. There were flower arrangements on every surface, and the biggest television set Judy had seen.

Magazines and books were systematically arranged on side tables for her convenience. The floor-to-ceiling panoramic window gave a magnificent view of distant mountains. Remembering the usual chaos of her cramped London flat, Judy could only stand and gape. She had her own typewriter, telephone, answering and fax machine. It was too much.

'The bedroom's through here,' Blake went on, opening a second door, through which Judy could see a large bed with white silk covers and the same elegant, pale furniture. Thankfully, she slid her arms out of her linen jacket and dropped it on the bed although, as expected, the suite was blissfully air-conditioned. She noted that her luggage was already in the room.

Blake seemed intent on giving her a mini-tour. As he strode through the bedroom she followed automatically, and they entered the *en-suite* bathroom. It followed the general ambience of the suite, with everything in tasteful, pale colours. There was a stack of huge lemon-coloured towels, and a range of toiletries that hadn't come out of Woolworth's.

'It's too much,' she said at last. 'You surely don't give a suite like this to all your employees!'

'Not all, only to the special ones. Don't underestimate yourself, Judy. You come highly recommended, and I prize the people who do a good job for me.'

'Now you're making me *really* nervous,' she laughed. 'As if all this wasn't enough – ' She waved her arms helplessly.

They were still standing in the scented bathroom, and she was acutely aware of it. None of the accoutrements were personally hers as yet, but she couldn't deny the sense of intimacy in being here with a very desirable man. As if totally unaware of her thoughts, his rested his hands lightly on her shoulders.

'Judy, I believe in giving my people the very best, so don't let it worry you.'

'But I do! I've done nothing to deserve this treatment yet, and you have no idea if I'm going to be an asset or a liability to you.'

She wasn't normally given to bouts of nerves, but she felt nervous now. And not only because of the hectic job schedule ahead of her, and working with a large company of unknown girls . . . but also because Blake Adams's thumbs were softly stroking her upper arms, and the sensation was sending waves of pleasure through her that she hadn't invited.

'You'd be an asset to anybody,' he said, his voice so sensual and full of promised seduction that only an idiot could fail to know it.

She spoke in a low voice. 'Please don't.'

'Don't what? Don't show that I'm already very attracted to you – or don't stop?' he teased her. 'Don't forget I'm fully aware of the English habit of denying their own feelings.'

She felt her face burn. Besides, as far as she was concerned, it wasn't true. She had never denied her feelings, and they had got her in enough trouble in the past . . . which was one of the reasons why she had no intention of losing her self-control again. And especially not over her boss, for pity's sake. For all she knew, Blake Adams could be a real womanizer, she thought, remembering the way the casino girls had smiled so warmly at him. And she had had enough of those to last a lifetime . . .

'Let me put you right on both counts,' she told him coolly. 'I'd prefer it if you didn't come on to me, and I definitely want you to stop – to stop – '

'Stop what? I don't remember doing anything wild enough to put that defensive look in your eyes! And if you're going to play the outraged virgin with every guy who makes a pass at you around here, Judy, you're in for a rough time.'

He stared at her thoughtfully for a moment, and before she could walk out of the bathroom with some dignity, he had pulled her close to him and fastened his mouth on hers in a light kiss from which she had no chance of escaping. One arm held her in a vice-like grip, while the fingers of his other hand raked her hair and then traced down every nodule of her spine, making her arch towards him with every touch.

He was outrageous, she fumed, once her spinning senses allowed her to think properly. He thought he could get any woman he wanted just by oozing sexuality, which he definitely had in plenty. But this was one woman who wasn't falling straight into bed with him . . .

But she realized he had let her go just as quickly. He turned on his heel to go into the bedroom, tossing her key on to the bed.

'It would be an insult to apologize for something so enjoyable, so I won't,' he said. 'And don't think I won't do it again. Harry told me you were a bit of an ice maiden, and although I don't normally take bets, he bet me I couldn't make you melt. First round to me, I think.'

He blew her a kiss while she stood rigidly, her hands clenched at her sides.

'My apartment's just across the corridor, by the way,' he went on. 'I'll call you for dinner at nine-thirty. You should be rested by then, and ready to meet a few other people.'

She hardly heard what he was saying. All she could think of was he and Harry had had a *bet* on her! Her face flamed anew when the door clicked shut behind him and she was finally alone. Round one to him, indeed! The arrogant nerve of the man! As for being an ice maiden . . . well, that might be how she appeared, and it was a useful defence when necessary, but outward appearances could be deceptive.

She touched her mouth where Blake had kissed her, feeling its softness and trying not to admit that it had been anything but distasteful.

She could still feel the hot swift pressure of his kiss. She could still feel the touch of his fingers in her hair, and the way he had traced her spine in a way that was at once seductive and possessive. Oh yes, Blake Adams knew plenty about the art of seduction, Judy thought feverishly.

But ever since her last great love affair that had ended in bitter tears and heartache, she had trained herself to be impregnable where men were concerned. She had built a wall around her emotions, and she was damned if one smart business tycoon was going to break it all down and leave her to pick up the pieces again.

Smothering a small sob in her throat, she flipped open her overnight case and defiantly took out her toilet bag. Everything she needed was already in the bathroom, but she would use none of it right now. And if this was the feeblest way of exerting her own independence, then so be it.

She ignored the shower, and instead had a leisurely soak in a fragrantly scented bath, before wrapping herself in the lemon towelling bathrobe hanging up behind the door. Finally, she pulled the curtains across the bedroom window, and lay on her bed, shutting out the world.

She awoke half-heartedly, wondering how long she had slept, and more to the point, what had dragged her unwillingly from sleep. She peered at her watch, and saw that she had been out for a couple of hours. So there was no panic, and it would be so easy to slide back into her lovely dream world.

Even as the thought came into her mind, Judy knew what had woken her. Ever since she had been a small girl, sleeping at irregular hours had produced vivid dreams. In those halcyon, innocent days, the dreams had been about fairies and elves and all the delicious trappings of childhood. Today's dream had been very different. She hadn't wanted it . . . and she couldn't forget it . . . and in those still half-conscious moments, she seemed to be reliving it all . . .

The arms reaching out for her were all too familiar, even though she had only felt them around her for the first time today. But dreams had a habit of bypassing such incidentals and concentrating on the main action. And the main action involved herself being in Blake Adams's possessive embrace, as inevitably as the sun rose each morning over Las Vegas.

They were standing close together, somewhere on a lonely, sun-kissed beach, and her toes were sinking into deliciously warm sand, and the sound of the ocean was pounding in her ears . . . or maybe it was merely the pounding of her own heart . . .

'Why did you ever think of resisting?' that oh-so-sexy voice whispered in her ear as his lips nuzzled her nape. Her nerve ends tingled at the caress, and she felt herself arching her back towards him, wanting more, wanting *him*. She was aware of every sinew of his well-honed body – and in the ways of a dream, the clothes that had hampered their contact seemed to have simply melted away, so that there was only the erotic, pleasurable touch of hot flesh between them.

'You don't know how long I've waited for this,' the relentlessly seductive voice went on. And the fantasy obliged again, conveniently disregarding the fact that they were still virtual strangers.

'I've waited for it too,' Judy heard her own voice reply. 'I feel as if I've been waiting all my life – '

'And everything that has gone before fades into insignificance – '

'Yes, oh, *yes*.'

Even the love she had thought would last for ever, that had been so brutally shattered when she discovered the painful truth that her ex-lover had betrayed her, seemed to matter little now she had found the real love of her life.

'I want to make love to you,' Blake said softly. 'Every day and every night, for the rest of our lives – '

Her senses soared as she sensed the passion in him, from every pulsing part of his body, to the love in his eyes, and she knew that her own must be dreamy with longing for him. She breathed in his very maleness, revelling in the coarser texture of his skin against hers as his kiss moved gradually downwards over her body.

They had been standing as close together as if they had been sharing the same skin, but now they were lying on the warm sandy beach, and she felt his hands circle and palm her breasts, sending the swift response to her nipples as they yearned towards him. His touch was followed by his kiss, sweet and tender, and Judy held her breath as his fingers moved gradually downwards to stroke every part of her, and it was such an effort to resist him . . .

But why resist, when this was only a dream? It was almost as if part of her was dictating the way the dream should go, the way childhood games had pandered to her own needs. But this was no childhood game, and her needs were very different, and she had been denying them for so long now.

'This was meant to be, Judy,' he whispered against her softly yielding flesh. 'I knew it the moment I saw you – '

A sound somewhere in the corridor of the hotel jerked her properly awake. She realized she was shaking, and her palms were damp. But the dream had been so real . . . and reliving it so unwillingly had made it even more real. And facing Blake in an hour or so with the memory so vivid in her mind was going to be very difficult . . .

Judy felt her eyes dilate, wondering what on earth was the matter with her to get so het up about a dream. She was made of stronger stuff than that. Once she had steeled herself, she dressed quickly, and did a careful make-up job, aware that the people Blake was about to introduce her to would be smart and sophisticated.

She turned away from the mirror, knowing that she was looking better than she might have expected, given the effects of the long flight. Her red hair gleamed, caught up at each side with silver pins, and her slender figure was caressed by the black, silver-threaded dress she had decided would be right for this first evening.

It wasn't too ostentatious, but it was still dramatically elegant and classy, which was the image she supposedly represented, according to Harry. Outwardly she was cool and composed, and she hoped that nobody could guess how her heart pounded inside . . .

She simply hadn't anticipated feeling this nervous, she admitted. And it was all because of that man, who'd had the audacity to gamble on her feelings with Harry. Labelling her an ice maiden was an added insult, and she wasn't going to forgive her agent for that one, either. She reminded herself that she had to fax him to let him know she'd arrived OK, and decided to let him wait.

Precisely at nine-thirty she heard a knock on her door, and she answered it quickly, tilting her chin as she prepared to meet the arrogant gaze of her new boss, aware that she was already acting far too self-defensively.

The man who stood at the door wasn't Blake. He wore the uniform of one of the hotel staff, and his gaze was frankly admiring.

'Mr Adams sends his apologies, Miss Hale. I'm to escort you to the Sapphire Suite, where he'll meet you.'

'Thank you,' Judy said, not sure whether to see this as a reprieve, or to be vaguely disappointed that she hadn't had a few moments alone with Blake before being thrust into the limelight. 'I'll just fetch my wrap. I'm not used to this fierce air conditioning.'

She spoke quickly, to cover her irrational feeling of nerves, not least because of that feeling of disappointment. She threw the silver wrap around her shoulders and accompanied the man to the elevator, her slim high heels making no noise on the carpeted floor.

'You're British too, aren't you?' the clerk said. 'I heard we were expecting someone from England. No offence, ma'am, but you people sure do talk pretty.'

'No offence taken,' Judy replied, feeling her lips twitch. 'Thank you for the compliment.'

The elevator whisked them down to the tenth floor, where the doorman unnecessarily announced the Sapphire Suite, and the escort let Judy out first. She had expected to see a noisy bar somewhere adjacent to the casino, but instead saw she was in an extremely sophisticated part of the hotel, where the richly coloured blue decor was subtly and dimly lit.

She entered what was loosely termed a bar, and what in reality would have done justice to the most

35

exclusive London club. Blake Adams rose from one of the tables and came towards her, and her escort melted into the background.

Blake took her hand and raised it to his lips in a continental gesture, and somehow the contrast between olde-worlde charm and the ruthlessness she had already sensed in the man had a charm of its own. She wished the thought away.

'You look stunning,' he told her. 'And I especially wanted you to meet some people before we go in for dinner. It will help you break the ice before you begin work in earnest.'

If his eyebrows gave the smallest lift as he mentioned breaking ice, Judy ignored it. It was a relief to know they weren't to be dining alone, just the two of them. There had been enough close encounters already, and with the memory of her dream still churning in her head, then the more she saw how Blake operated with other people, the happier she would be. It would be easier to get things in perspective, and to realize that his charm applied to every female in the world.

He led the way to a table where half a dozen people were seated. The men rose politely at once, and the three beautiful women assessed her appearance with glossy smiles.

'Ladies, this is Judy from England, who you'll be working with for the Spectacular. Judy, these are my top showgirls, and I'm sure you're all going to get along very well.'

Judy smiled as he introduced Laverne, Candy and Paige. But from the guarded looks in the other girls' eyes, she wasn't altogether sure of his last remark. But when she spoke her voice was as warm and friendly as she could make it.

'I'm delighted to meet you all informally like this – '

'And this is Franklin Delgado, our Dance Director, whom you'll be working under.'

Judy turned her head slowly, trying to keep the smile fixed on her face, and praying that she didn't betray the anger she felt inside. Harry hadn't told her anything about a Dance Director. She had assumed she'd be taking complete control of the choreography for the part of the show that was to be British-inspired. She'd had enough of Dance Directors in the past, whose inflated egos could undermine everything she suggested . . .

Franklin Delgado's handsome black eyes challenged her, as she had instinctively known they would. She tried to smile sweetly back at him, while feeling as if Harry had truly let her down this time.

And even though it was the last thing she really wanted, she found herself wondering for one wild, infuriating moment, if there was any way she could get herself out of this contract after all.

CHAPTER 3

Blake Adams hadn't been born into a glittering showbusiness background. His was a solid Yorkshire heritage: his grandfather had built up a vast woollen mill empire that had passed down to his father, and which was expected to be taken over eventually by Blake himself.

But his father had been his own worst enemy when it came to preparing Blake for the kind of life that was in his blood. In sending his son away to the best boarding school and then to university, he had opened his son's eyes to a very different way of life from that of rural and industrial Yorkshire.

And although such indulgence had been intended to provide him with the best that money could buy in terms of education, it had also shown Blake a far wider world that the one he was destined to lord over. Sometimes he felt he had always been meant to be the adventurer in the family, the one who rebelled against tradition and sought his own future.

When his father died and the thriving woollen empire had come to Blake, he had thought long and hard about that future, but in the end had had no hesitation in doing what his heart and his head dictated. By then he had already been living in London for a few years, and there had been no scandalized relatives to try to dissuade him, only the family lawyer, who had finally washed his hands of him.

'You can't be serious, my dear sir!' The man had been near to apoplexy. 'You want to build a gambling empire? A *casino*? And in *America*?'

He had made it sound tantamount to going to the devil.

'I assure you I'm perfectly serious, Mr Willis,' Blake retorted. 'I've been living in London for too long already to want to come back here for good, and since the inheritance is now mine to do with as I wish, I'd be obliged if you would see to the sale of the mill and all its assets as quickly as possible. I intend to go to Las Vegas in a week's time to view the location and assess the possibilities.'

At that point, the solicitor gave up. Blake was reckless and pig-headed, and in the solicitor's opinion it undoubtedly came from living in London, instead of being content to be a countryman as he was born to be. He had been away from Yorkshire for far too long.

But, just like everything Blake Adams set out to do, his plans had all gone through with meticulous efficiency. He was already a wealthy man in his own right, having been an entrepreneur in various showbusiness ventures, and dabbled successfully in the stock market. And when the Adams mill was sold to the highest bidder, its sale enabled Blake to realize his dream with hardly a ripple in his coffers.

In any case, there were other reasons for wanting to quit British shores that he wasn't prepared to explain to his lawyer, and he had set out to make the Sparkling Rocks Hotel and Casino as classy as any on the Strip.

It hadn't been his intention to find himself one of the most eligible men in town, and so far Blake had eluded getting caught in the marriage trap, although he was perfectly aware of his reputation as a ladies' man. It didn't bother him, and he didn't take any of it too seriously.

But now fate, through the unlikely shape of his old friend Harry Brady, had sent him a delightful English girl to help choreograph his Spectacular show for the next season, and he'd forgotten just how much he missed the accents from home. He surprised himself to realize how much he was looking forward to hearing Judy Hale's soft voice again.

Dinner in the Sapphire Suite dining-room was accompanied by soft, seductive music from a five-piece band, whose members were all dressed predictably in blue, as were the waiters and waitresses.

A magnificent statue of intertwined cherubs formed the centrepiece of the dining-room, and fountains of blue water sprayed continuously over and around them. It was all grossly over the top, thought Judy, but somehow it worked, as did everything in this ultra-efficient country.

The food was superb, and so was the wine, which successfully covered the need for too much small-talk. Though Judy had often wondered if all Americans took lessons in the art of continuous conversation in school, since they were all so adept at it.

Once, when Ricky had been in Washington DC, he'd visited the Capitol building, and reported to Judy how a group of pre-college kids had asked the most intelligent and pertinent questions, completely uninhibited and underawed. It was something that had always earned her admiration.

She caught Blake looking at her appraisingly. Then he leaned towards her and she quickly realized that such openness didn't only apply to schoolkids on a visit to the Capitol building.

'So what do you think of us now, Judy?'

She laughed, mildly surprised that he included himself in the 'us', when she found it impossible to include him in her appraisal of American while he still spoke in that assured British accent with the attractive Yorkshire undertones.

'If there's anything more guaranteed to make me clam up, I can't think of it! Besides, how can I tell, when my feet have hardly touched the ground yet!'

'It shouldn't take you long to decide what you think of Blake, Judy,' Laverne said. 'We're all crazy about him, and I'll take bets that you'll be no exception.'

'Judy won't be betting on anything,' Blake put in. 'She doesn't approve of gambling in any shape or form.'

Before she could answer, she saw Delgado's incredulous smile. She wasn't sure that she cared for him, nor the way the showgirls played up to him as well as Blake.

'What the hell are you doing here then, Judy, if you don't approve of gambling?'

She gave him a cool look. 'I'm here to work, the same as you, and you'll pardon me for saying so, I'm sure, but I didn't think gambling was a requisite for doing my job properly.'

She heard Blake chuckle, and knew he was enjoying this little exchange between them.

'Judy's going to be a match for you any day, Frank, and I may just look in on rehearsals to see how the sparks fly between you.'

Almost simultaneously, they both glared at him.

'I don't work that way,' Judy told him.

'God damn it, Blake, you know I don't appreciate onlookers until I've got the production under way. And it's going to be tricky enough this season – '

'With me around, you mean?' Judy asked.

His obvious irritability had the effect of calming her down, and she gave him her cool smile again. 'Don't worry, Mr Delgado, I won't cramp your style, providing you don't try to cramp mine.'

Although she kept her voice as even as possible, never in a million years had she expected to be talking like this over the dinner table, to a stranger in a roomful of strangers where she was the outsider, the foreigner.

This was their territory, but she knew that if she didn't assert herself right now, she never would. And with a swift change of attitude, Delgado began to laugh again.

'All right, kid, as long as we both know our places, I guess we'll get along well enough. And the name's Frank. Be in the Diamond Showroom at ten tomorrow morning, and I'll give you a guided tour.'

'Tomorrow's Sunday,' she reminded him.

'So who sleeps in Vegas, Sunday or whenever? But suit yourself. If you prefer to start work cold on Monday morning, it's OK by me.'

By now, Judy had deduced that every part of the hotel and casino was known by a different jewel name, and she quickly registered that of the Diamond Showroom.

'I'll be there,' she told him.

She saw Blake raise his glass to her, but what choice had she had, anyway? She was eager to absorb the ambience of the place as quickly as possible, and to know all there was to know about the sets and lighting and all the hundred and one things that the customers never knew about that went on behind the scenes to create a spectacular show.

She was here to do a job that she was damn good at, and nobody was going to put her down, however superior he thought he was. At that moment, she wasn't sure if she was thinking about Blake or Delgado.

But Judy was glad when dinner was over, and also that the evening ended with drinks and conversation, and no mention of dancing. She was becoming extraordinarily tired, and despite her earlier rest, the travel and the jet-lag were catching up with her again.

She hastily stifled a yawn, hoping nobody would see it, but it was too late, and it was Blake who gave her a sympathetic smile.

'If you want to call it a day, Judy, I'll escort you back to your suite.'

'I'm sure I can find it – ' she began, but it was as pointless as talking to the wind.

'Say goodnight, Judy,' he said, just like one of those old TV shows with George Burns and Gracie Allen, and she heard one of the girls titter.

'Goodnight, everyone,' she replied. 'And thank you for a very pleasant evening.'

With that, she swept ahead of Blake.

'You created quite a stir tonight,' he told her as they ascended in the silent elevator.

The doorman stood impassively, facing away from them, and they might have been quite alone in the mirrored, carpeted box that whisked them skywards.

'Because I'm a novelty, I suppose?'

'No. Because you're beautiful, and perhaps not quite what we expected,' he replied.

'What did you expect, I wonder?' she countered. 'Some shrewish career woman, all gaunt bones and sensible shoes, and no sense of humour?'

At the elevator clerk's discreet cough as they reached their floor, she thought shamefacedly that she was showing little sense of humour now, and not much graciousness at the compliment he had just paid her.

As they stepped out of the elevator into the corridor she turned to him contritely. 'I'm sorry. That was rude of me.'

'On the contrary,' he said, to her surprise, 'it's refreshing to have someone speak so honestly.'

She wondered if it was the nearest he would come to voicing suspicion of the way everybody fawned over him. She felt herself melting slightly towards Blake, even though she told herself it was absurd to feel the least bit sorry for someone who had everything.

'I've always prided myself on being an honest person,' she told him as they reached her door.

'Good.' Before she could stop him, Blake had put both hands on her shoulders, and then tipped her chin up to meet his steady gaze. 'Then answer my question honestly. How do you find us, Judy?'

For a moment she thought he was going to kiss her again, and she didn't want it. Not when she was so tired, and vulnerable, and far from home . . . and not when he was the one thing to remind her of it so vividly, with his voice and his charm, and his *everything* . . .

'Can I reserve judgment on that until I get to know you all a little better?' she was suddenly husky. 'First impressions aren't always the best, are they?'

And their first encounter was hardly the most auspicious, she thought, remembering the scene at LAX airport and the flight to Las Vegas. He had every right to think her shrewish after that!

He leaned forward and touched his finger to her cheek, then placed her key card in her door and clicked it open.

'Goodnight, Judy. Sleep well.'

He turned away as she went inside her room, her heart beating unexpectedly fast. It was swiftly dawning on her that American slickness combined with olde-worlde English charm could be as potent as the headiest wine.

Just before she closed her door, she glanced outside, and saw Blake disappearing into his own suite of rooms, and felt an odd sense of satisfaction that he hadn't gone back to the Sapphire Suite to rejoin the others. But it was a dangerous thought, and she rejected it at once.

She was awoken at nine a.m. by a persistent gentle knocking on her door. She hastily threw on a dressing-gown and answered it to find a man with a trolley outside.

'Breakfast room service, ma'am.'

'I didn't order this – '

'Mr Adams's orders, ma'am.'

There was obviously to be no argument. Judy watched as he spread an immaculate white cloth on the round table by her window, set out the cutlery and china with swift efficiency, and put the covered dishes on to it, together with the orange juice and the coffee pot. The final touch was a single rose in a slender silver vase.

'If there's anything else you require, just pick up the phone and ask for me, ma'am. The name's Emil.'

'Thank you, Emil,' she said faintly.

And then he was gone. She lifted the tureen lids carefully. There was a large dish of fruit, and a dish of

46

bacon and eggs and sausages and tomatoes and mushrooms. Toast and marmalade was also provided. It was far more than Judy normally ate, but the succulent smells made her mouth water, and Blake's thoughtfulness at suggesting so typical an English breakfast for her didn't go unregistered.

He had his good points, she admitted. Especially as Ricky had already told her of the huge plates of pancakes smothered in honey that he himself demolished and which seemed to be his staple breakfast diet.

The very thought had been enough for Judy to imagine the pounds piling on. She thanked heaven that her metabolism was such that she rarely gained weight, no matter how much she ate. And she'd never eat half of this feast . . .

Half an hour later, she looked in amazement at the remnants of it all. Had she really eaten so much? She would have lingered over more coffee, had she not realised with a gasp that she had better take a quick shower and dress, if she was to meet Franklin Delgado at ten o'clock.

There were clerks for everything, and you couldn't help but admire their dedication to their jobs. Judy also discovered that like all of them, the elevator clerk was a mine of information when required.

He obviously considered the entire building his domain, she thought with amusement, though she thought it must be a very boring job to be simply pushing buttons and announcing the different floors in that well-trained manner. He answered her query about his job earnestly.

'Not at all, ma'am. I get to see everybody in my job, even the stars when they come to play Vegas and perform in the Sparkling Rocks. It's very interesting.'

She supposed it took all sorts, though you could hardly have much conversation in a fast elevator that took you between floors before you hardly had time to draw breath.

'I've got an autograph book like you wouldn't believe,' he confided next.

'I'd like to see it some time,' Judy commented, by way of conversation.

'Would you? I'll be sure to bring it around in a day or so, ma'am. And here's your floor. Diamond Showroom,' he announced imperiously, even though there was no one but Judy to hear it.

She stepped outside and heard the soft whirr of the automatic doors close behind her. She had dressed simply this morning, in cream slacks and a blue cotton top. Her thick red hair was tied up in a workmanlike ponytail, which made her look younger than her twenty-four years in some ways, but which she hoped gave her a businesslike air.

She was definitely on the defensive regarding Mr Delgado, she admitted, and she tried to shake off the feeling by reminding herself that she was good at her job, and the sooner he realized it as well, the better.

She glanced along the corridor and saw the name of the Diamond Showroom backstage entrance gleaming out at her from a row of doors. On the opposite side of the corridor were a mass of doors labelled dressing-rooms, wardrobe and artistes. She opened the central backstage doors, and stepped inside the dimly lit auditorium. She was immediately transported into a remembered world of props and sets and smells. There was nothing like it, Judy thought, breathing in the mingled scents of greasepaint and sweat, and the ghosts of shows past . . .

Before she stepped through the mass of tangled wires and flexes and props, she stood completely motionless for a few moments, drinking in the sight of the vast arena and feeling the adrenaline run in her veins at the sheer size of the stage and the feeling of energy that was in the very air, both on stage and in the huge auditorium beyond the foot-lights.

'Is it all that you expected?' she heard an amused voice say from somewhere way above her as she stood with her eyes half-closed. She couldn't see anybody, and then Delgado turned on some house-lights, and she saw him in the orchestra well that was situated up high at the back of the Showroom.

'You startled me,' she exclaimed. 'And how can I be anything but overwhelmed!'

The comment evidently satisfied him, because he disappeared for a moment, and then came nimbly down some stairs and through the tables to join her on stage. He was sparely made, she saw, but with a dancer's well-muscled legs in the tight-fitting pants he wore, and well-developed muscles on his arms.

She hadn't noticed as much last night, when she was more frosty than she should have been towards him. Not that he attracted her in any way now, but she could see that he would definitely be attractive to many women.

'How come you don't have an orchestra pit?' she asked, to cover her momentary distraction.

'Because it would divert the audience's attention and take away the sense of intimacy with the dancers,' he told her. 'But you'll find that the acoustics here are so good, and arranged in such a manner, that all the music seems to come from front of house anyway.'

She couldn't help but be impressed at everything she saw. And at her obvious enthusiasm, she saw Franklin Delgado's face break into a smile.

'I got the distinct idea last night that you had expected to be working alone, Judy. Am I right?'

He was nothing if not direct. But she found she wasn't objecting to that any more. It beat being devious.

'I certainly hadn't bargained on an overall Dance Director. I'm just not used to working that way, but I dare say I'll get used to it,' she heard herself say lamely.

She knew she had to, if she wanted to keep this super job, and her first sight of this fabulous Showroom told her how badly she wanted to do just that.

He nodded without comment, becoming Mr Super-efficiency then, explaining about the rake on the stage, and demonstrating the trapezes and revolving levels on which the showgirls paraded and posed.

'We have a section of semi-nude showgirls as well as the ones who wear the more spectacular costumes. Nudity doesn't shock you, does it?' he asked casually.

'Why on earth should it? I'm a professional, Mr Delgado!'

'I just thought – well, I heard that some of you British girls are a bit prudish,' he shrugged. 'And the name's Frank.'

'I assure you I'm not a bit prudish,' Judy said, smiling at the thought. Her ex-lover certainly hadn't thought so, when they had thrashed about on his bed in his London apartment in an ecstacy of loving, night after night after night . . .

'From that dreamy look on your face, I'd have to agree with you, and I envy the guy who put it there.' She heard Delgado chuckle, and she felt her face flame.

'Don't get carried away, Frank!'

'OK. Providing you come out with me tonight. I never work weekends, so how about it? I could show you the sights, and we could have a quiet dinner somewhere away from the Strip.'

'*Is* there anywhere away from the Strip?'

'Sure there is. There's a whole city out there, with a university and all. We're not just about gambling, lady. And in case you're wondering, there are no strings attached. I wouldn't want to queer Blake's pitch.'

51

If she had been softening towards him before, Judy felt her hackles rise now.

'And what's that supposed to mean? Blake doesn't have any claim to my company – '

'Come out with me, then,' he said, and she saw how neatly she had fallen into his trap.

But maybe it wasn't such a bad idea. It would serve Blake right if he thought she really had taken a fancy to Delgado, especially in view of the insulting bet he had made with Harry Brady about melting the ice maiden . . .

'No strings?' she demanded.

'Cross my heart and hope to die,' he said solemnly. 'I'll pick you up at the front entrance at eight o'clock. Take your time in here, by the way, and put out the lights when you leave, OK?'

Before she could answer he was gone. Like any ex-dancer, which she strongly suspected he was, he was pretty nifty on his feet. She still didn't particularly warm to him, but she knew she had better get along with him. He was effectively her boss, after all. She gave a shiver, not sure which of the two men she had met was the more powerful and influential.

And then she shrugged. It was Blake, of course. Blake was the one who pulled all the strings, and could override anything that Delgado said. According to Harry, Blake could buy anything he wanted. Even people.

She didn't know why the thought entered her head right then. She only knew he wasn't going to buy her. She remained in the Showroom a while longer, but the atmosphere had subtly changed for her now. As she turned to leave, her heart jumped as she saw Blake Adams watching her from the doorway.

'How long have you been there?' she stammered.

It angered her to know how nonplussed she felt at his unexpected presence. Even more so to consciously register the fact that he couldn't see inside her head and follow her thoughts – or to know that she had just fixed up a date with Franklin Delgado. But what if she had? It was none of his damn business. But the edginess inside her wouldn't go away.

'Just a few minutes. I was admiring the rapt expression on your face. Are you always this jumpy, or do I have that effect on you? If so, I apologize.'

'I thought I was the one who kept saying sorry. You startled me, that's all. I was about to go back to my room and fax Harry as I promised.'

Just in time, she remembered it, but he wouldn't have expected it yesterday, after the long flight. She'd have a few choice things to say to him on the fax, though . . .

'Harry won't thank you for faxing him this early. It's around three in the morning in England. Besides, I called him last night to let him know you arrived safely.'

Judy gave him an exasperated look.

'You're doing it again, aren't you?'

'Doing what, for Pete's sake?' he said.

'Taking me over, as if I'm some silly little female who can't manage to do things for herself.'

'You didn't do so well at LAX as I remember.'

She glared at him and counted to ten.

'Look, Blake, thanks all the same, but I can look after myself. I'm a big girl now, and I don't need a bodyguard.'

'Nobody would dispute that.' He spoke lazily, and from the languid way he was looking her over, she knew it was meant to be a sexual compliment. At that moment, it seemed to her more of a male chauvinist insult.

'You've been away from England too long,' she said. 'Women don't take kindly to that kind of remark any more.'

She went to brush past him, and he caught at her arm.

'Then women are fools if they can't take a genuine compliment in the spirit it's meant. You're a beautiful woman, and believe me, in my business I see plenty of those. But you're something special, Judy, so don't let yourself be tarnished by any tackiness you might see here.'

He sounded so genuinely sincere that it made her feel off-balance for a moment. But she realized how quickly he could turn anything to his own advantage.

One minute he was the predator, the male hunter . . . and the next, he was the caring protector. And she didn't know which was the more dangerous for her peace of mind. She shook off his arm and moved back from him a pace.

'Thank you for the advice. Now, if you don't mind, I'm going to get that fax ready for Harry. He'll have left his machine switched over to automatic receive, no matter what time it is. In case you've forgotten, we no longer live in the Dark Ages in Britain.'

'Oh, and by the way,' she went on, 'would you put the lights out before you leave?'

She swept past him, feeling ridiculously as if she had scored a small victory by her last remark. And found herself laughing a little shakily as she went back to her suite in the elevator, realizing that she had just told her powerful and wealthy boss to turn out the lights in his own glittering Showroom.

She composed the letter to Harry on the typewriter in her room before she faxed it. She knew him well enough to speak her mind, since that was the way Harry operated too, and appreciated it in others.

'You might have warned me about Blake, you rat!' she wrote. 'Why didn't you tell me he was English, and a male chauvinist of the first order?'

. . . and a hunk, and the best thing on two legs I've ever seen . . . she pushed the unwilling thought out of her mind as she punched out the words of her letter.

'Anyway, everything's fine, although you also forgot to tell me I'd be working under a Dance Director. It conveniently slipped your mind, I suppose!

'Are you sure I'm not here just as an extra token Brit to add weight to the programme as part of the British angle of the Sparkling Rocks Spectacular?'

She read back her own words, and hoped they didn't sound too petulant and childish. But what was an agent for, for pity's sake, if not to vent all her spleen on him!

Judy grinned faintly, never quite sure what the dickens the word meant, but it sounded good enough when it fitted the mood she was in.

She finished with a flourish.

'I'll be in touch again when I don't feel so mad with you. Oh, and by the way, the theatre's fabulous. I think I forgot to tell you that. No complaints there, Harry darling!'

As she wrote the words, she felt that old familiar tingle in her veins, remembering the way the theatre had looked and smelled and throbbed with the energy of all the effort the dancers put into it, and the warmth and enthusiasm of the audiences.

And all her anger fell away, because nothing else really mattered except the work and the joy she always had in it.

But her eyes still sparkled as she fed the letter into the fax machine without changing a word. Because it wouldn't hurt Harry to know that he wasn't dealing with a pussycat here – and she had also just managed to resist telling him she knew all about his insulting bet with Blake Adams.

She wasn't going to give him that satisfaction. It would be satisfaction enough when Blake got the message that all his charm had failed to impress her one little bit and he had to admit defeat to Harry.

And she wouldn't give houseroom to the tiny thought that she could be cutting off her nose to spite her face, because after all, he *was* just about the dishiest, most charismatic man she had ever known

. . . and if they had met in different circumstances, then maybe, just maybe . . .

She dialled Harry's London number quickly, listened for the tone at the other end and pressed the start button on her fax machine.

CHAPTER 4

A short while later, her phone rang. For a second she wondered if it could be Harry already, calling back to ask what the hell she thought she was doing, faxing him in the middle of the night. Then she heard Blake's voice, as close as if he was right beside her. But since he was probably in his own apartment across the corridor by now, that wasn't surprising. The timbre of his voice was deep and sexy.

'I put out the lights as you requested, ma'am. Is there anything else I can do for you?'

Judy felt herself blushing.

'I'm sorry about that – '

'I doubt that you are, so forget it. Meet me for lunch at one o'clock in the Opal Bar and afterwards we'll look in on rehearsals for tonight's show.'

'I thought Frank didn't work on weekends.'

'He doesn't. Maggie, his assistant, takes over. How are the two of you getting along, by the way? I thought I may have sensed a bit of competitive rivalry last night.'

This was her moment, thought Judy.

'Oh, all that's forgotten now. Actually, I think he's charming, and he's asked me out to dinner this evening.'

She dearly wished she could have read Blake's mind in the momentary pause that followed. But she might have known it wouldn't faze him.

'Frank never did waste much time,' was all he said. 'See you later, then.'

The phone went dead, and it was Judy who felt ruffled. So much for thinking it mattered a toss to him who she went out with. She wondered if she needed to change her clothes for lunch, and decided against it.

She had already deduced that, in the daytime, everyone went casual. Besides, if she was going to sit in on rehearsals, she didn't want to appear looking like something straight off the catwalk.

She was whisked down to the Opal Bar, which she discovered was on the ground floor, so that her ears were assaulted with the noise of slot machines the minute she stepped out of the elevator. If this was another baptism by fire, she was getting the full force of it now, Judy thought.

As she entered the bar the raucous sounds receded, and she saw Blake sitting on a bar stool while a scantily clad girl served him with a drink.

For no reason at all, Judy felt her heart skip a beat. He really was the most terrific-looking man she had ever seen, she thought faintly, even though he wasn't conventionally good-looking in a slick Hollywood way. Now that she had detected the remnants of his accent, she recognized the rugged Yorkshire character in his face, with a determination around his mouth that could easily be construed as ruthless.

She shivered, acknowledging that it was hard to see how any woman could be immune to him when he turned on the charm. But if Blake Adams had charm in abundance when required, so had her ex-lover, she reminded herself, and look where that had got her.

'I thought you'd stood me up,' he began with a smile, and she saw that it was already past one o'clock. Her lateness hadn't been intentional, but she gave him a cool smile.

'Don't you know it's a lady's prerogative to keep a gentleman waiting?'

The minute she had spoken she wanted to cringe. It sounded so *twee* and arch, and like something out of an old black-and-white movie. She could almost imagine Celia Johnson saying it to Trevor Howard in *Brief Encounter*. Whether she had ever done so was beside the point. The comment was just so damn *British*.

But then, so was she, thought Judy, bridling at her own thoughts. And just because she was here in America and intended to enjoy the experience to the full, she didn't have to lose sight of her roots.

'Well, the lady was worth waiting for,' he said, as smooth as silk. 'So let's eat.'

She was thankful to turn to the huge menu while Blake ordered soft drinks for them both. All through lunch there was a constant run of flashing numbers on a big screen in the bar, and several of the girls were on hand to offer cards for the game of Keno.

'It's the same as Bingo, isn't it?' Judy asked.

'More or less.'

'And people actually buy these cards and gamble while they're eating?'

Blake shrugged. 'Your prejudices are showing again, Judy – and it's hardly big-time gambling. On any organized vacation trip there's usually a Bingo night for the punters, especially on a cruise. I'll bet you've had a flutter in a Bingo hall at some time in your life.'

'Actually, I haven't.'

'Of course, I forgot. You dislike gambling in any shape or form, don't you?'

She put down her knife and fork, thankful to take a moment while she wondered how on earth she was going to get through the huge tuna salad that had been put in front of her. And wishing that he didn't have this knack of making her sound so damn narrow-minded, when she wasn't.

'I do have my reasons, Blake.'

'I know. Harry told me about your brother.'

He went on eating, breaking his crusty roll into small pieces, as if totally unaware of how taken aback she was now at what she saw as a betrayal of confidence.

'Harry told you about Ricky? He had no right to do that to a total stranger – '

'Well, obviously Harry knew we couldn't remain strangers, and if you were going to come over here with a huge chip on your shoulder – no pun intended

– then I had a right to know why. Especially if I thought it was going to upset the smooth running of my operation.'

'It would never have done that. Whatever happens in my private life has nothing to do with my professional life.'

'That's what Harry told me. So where's the problem?'

The problem? *He* was the problem! Ever since they had met – God, was that only yesterday? – he had rubbed her up the wrong way, and he was doing it again.

'Don't you want your salad?' he asked mildly.

She attacked it in silence, knowing it was too good to waste. But the silence couldn't last for ever, and when she had eaten all she could she looked him squarely in the eyes.

'Just what did Harry tell you?' she said, groaning at the sizable slice of cherry pie topped with fresh cream she had recklessly ordered. She should never have been tempted . . .

'Just that your young brother's always been a thorn in your flesh and that you've had to bail him out on a number of occasions when he's got in too deeply with his gambling.'

'So do you still think I'm wrong in condemning something that can easily ruin a young person's life?'

'Of course I don't. But it's his life, and you can't live it for him. He has to make his own mistakes, just as we all do.' His voice held an odd sense of bitterness now.

'I hardly think you can have made many mistakes, with the kind of empire you've built up,' she said, simply to turn the conversation away from Ricky's problems.

'Maybe not, but we all have a past, Judy, and sometimes we're not always happy with the way things have turned out.'

Her eyes widened at what she suspected was a minor indiscretion on his part. She strongly suspected that Blake Adams only gave away what he wanted other people to know. She was intrigued, wondering what he could have done that he regretted. He had everything: money, power, success and good looks. What more could he possibly want out of life?

Anyway, it was none of her business to analyse him. There were plenty of professionals around who could do that. But she'd have a thing or two to say to Harry on the subject of Ricky the next time she spoke to him. And maybe she could find out a bit more about Blake Adams at the same time.

'Have you finished?' he said eventually. 'I told Maggie we'd be looking in on rehearsals, and she's eager to meet you. You'll love her. Everybody does – eventually.'

'My God, that sounds ominous!' She had to smile at that.

Blake laughed. His face changed so completely when he wasn't giving her one of his sardonic looks, she thought. He was almost boyish – though boyish was hardly the right adjective to apply to a man who oozed sexuality . . . but she still thought she could glimpse the boy he had once been, and as she found herself momentarily wondering about that time, she realized she knew nothing about him at all. All she knew was what she saw. And she was definitely going to quiz Harry when she got the chance.

'Maggie seems to be a bit of a harridan at first. She exacts the best out of her dancers, and she gets it. She's sharp and scathing if they don't come up to scratch, but in the end they all respect her for it, and beneath it all, she's as warm and soft as a kitten.'

Does he love her? Judy wondered. She must be really something to produce this enthusiasm, and smothered the small sliver of jealousy that ran through her veins. Just because she and Blake were both British, and shared a background the others didn't have, it was nonsense to think they would have a special rapport. He had been living in America for too long to bother about his roots. She wondered if he ever went back.

'I'm ready if you are,' she replied quickly, before the question left her lips. She didn't want to appear to be interested in him at all, even though she was almost dying with curiosity by now.

They entered the Diamond Showroom by the front entrance this time, and Judy got the full force of the extent of it. It was a huge, curving arena, and its emptiness made it seem even more vast. It was in semi-darkness, but the stage was lit with a dazzling array of lights on the team of tall showgirls dressed in leotards and work pants.

'Maggie likes to rehearse the girls this way, so that their eyes get fully accustomed to the fierce lights on stage, and the darkness out front,' Blake told her. 'Some of the acts they do can be quite dangerous, and it would be disastrous if they were suddenly blinded by the lights.'

'You're very knowledgeable,' Judy commented. 'Are you sure you never had hankerings to go on the stage yourself?'

She spoke lightly, and he laughed at the idea. But since she seemed to be suddenly very much in tune with every nuance of his voice, she could have sworn that she detected that touch of bitterness again when he answered.

'It wasn't for me, Judy. But this way I get the best of both worlds. Come and meet Maggie.'

She realized the girls had stopped dancing now, and that somebody in the front of the auditorium had stood up as they approached. And Judy got a huge shock at the sight of her. She hadn't known what to expect, but at the very least it had to be a hard-bitten woman in full command of her performers, and undoubtedly larger than life. And maybe she was, in everything except stature.

She was tiny and bird-like, with wild black hair and outrageously garish make-up. Her legs were stick-thin in the tight pants she wore, and she teetered on very high heels as she held out both arms to Blake in greeting. And there was only one person Judy could think of likening her to. She was Edith Piaf to the life.

'Blake, honey,' she shouted, in a voice like a whipcrack. And that was where the similarity to Edith Piaf ended, thought Judy. 'Is this the new gal from England I've been dying to meet?'

'This is the one, Maggie,' he said with a grin, enjoying the shock on Judy's face.

'Well, she's a good looker and no mistake,' Maggie commented after a quick scrutiny, and talking to Blake as if Judy wasn't there at all. 'But can she do the job?'

'I assure you I can, Maggie. I've had plenty of experience,' Judy put in swiftly, deciding she'd better establish herself pretty quickly if she wasn't to be discussed by these two as if she was a fly on the wallpaper. And if Maggie had been dying to meet her, she had a funny way of showing it . . .

Maggie's laugh was like scraping metal.

'Experience is great, kid, but it's how you handle the gals that counts. You take my advice and show 'em who's boss right away, you hear? And don't let Frank dissuade you from what you've got planned for the acts. He'll surely try.'

'She's already got Frank twisted around her little finger, Maggie,' Blake told her. 'He's taking her to dinner tonight.'

The woman whistled through her teeth. 'Well, you just watch out for him, honey, and remember you can always say no.'

Judy felt her face flame. Good Lord, what did they expect was going to happen from a simple dinner invitation! But then she heard Maggie chuckle, and the thin little hand was pressed on her arm.

'I'm only kidding. Frank can be as gentlemanly as you want him to be, so I'm sure you'll have no trouble. Now then, if I'm to get these gals up to scratch for the finale of this show, you'd better let me get on with it.'

As she turned away and clapped her hands imperiously, the girls lined up as if by magic, and Judy felt as if she and Blake were dismissed. She sank into one of the red velvet alcove seats beside him, feeling slightly wrung out, and fully aware of the amusement on his face now.

'Well? Didn't I say she was a character?'

'You did,' she said, her voice almost lost in the blare of music from the cassette recorder, and the clatter of practice shoes on the stage as Maggie rapped out her instructions. 'But I wouldn't have thought quite such attention to detail was necessary at this late stage. The show ends in a week, doesn't it?'

And then there would be three months with the star name of Danny Corsey blazoning out on the frontage of the Sparkling Rocks, while the International Spectacular Show was taking shape behind the scenes, and then three months of staging it. And then Judy Hale's contract would be up, and the dream ticket would be over.

'Maggie and Frank are perfectionists. There can never be enough rehearsals to make the show run like clockwork and to keep the girls limbered up. You should know all about that.'

'I do,' she said hastily, although most of her work was in the planning stage, arranging moves and sets, and showing the girls off to the best advantage in their tableaux.

Planning a theme for this particular show was the most ambitious thing she had ever undertaken. She felt the usual surge of excitement in her veins, knowing she was going to give it everything she had.

They stayed in the Diamond Showroom for half an hour, and Judy was under no illusions as to how Maggie got the best out of her dancers. She was a hard taskmaster, but it worked.

As they watched and admired, Judy noticed how close Blake was sitting to her now, even though they had this vast part of the Showroom to themselves. Despite the activity going on onstage, they might have been in an isolated cocoon of their own.

It was surely not necessary for them to be so close, but for the life of her she couldn't break away without risking his taunt that she was acting like a frightened virgin. So she stayed where she was, feeling the heat of his body against hers, and trying not to notice how seductive and pleasant it felt, and very aware that his arm had slid around her shoulder and was caressing it through the thin top she wore.

Please stop, she silently begged, *because I think I'm beginning to like it too much* . . .

'Time we left, I think,' he said finally, as if totally unaware of the effect he was having on her. But to her relief he stood up and held out his hand. She took it automatically, and they left the auditorium by one of the many side doors near the stage. At once they were in the quiet corridor, and she could only faintly hear the sounds of music from the stage. Before she knew what he was about he had raised her hand to his lips again in the gesture she found so oddly touching.

'Enjoy your afternoon, Judy. Get acquainted with the rest of my empire. I promise it's not all bad. Take a swim or a sauna if you feel like it or take a walk down the Strip. Do whatever you want while you have the chance to relax, because tomorrow you'll be thrown in at the deep end.'

As he walked away from her, his final words reminded her that she was only an employee after all, no matter how glamorous her title. And tomorrow she was going to have to present her ideas to Franklin Delgado, when she had thought she'd be having complete control of them herself.

In retrospect she knew how short-sighted she had been. Of course there would be a Dance Director. But then, this whole place was on a much larger and grander scale than she could have imagined, and she had allowed herself to be so dazzled by the opportunity Harry had put her way that she hadn't thought it through. And Harry hadn't told her everything, of course . . . certainly not about Blake's background . . . her thoughts came back to her agent as she went back to her suite in the silent elevator.

But she supposed she couldn't blame him. He'd been as excited as herself when this job had come her way, and they both knew it was the opportunity of a lifetime. She'd be a fool if she let personal prejudices and personality clashes get in the way of doing a good job in the work she loved.

And it was some tiny consolation to know she was in the same country as her brother . . . She gave a wry smile at the thought, because heaven knew where Ricky was now. The last she'd heard from him he was, in his own words, 'bumming around on the Oregon coast'. She'd looked up the state on the map, and all she knew of it was that it was the West Coast. Las Vegas was at least on the same side of the continent, but in a country as vast as America, the chances of them ever meeting was as likely as flying to the moon.

Besides, was she really so anxious for him to turn up? She just wanted to know that he was all right, but every time Ricky turned up, it meant trouble of some kind. He usually needed money and baling out from the latest scrape. Judy sighed, half-wishing she could forget him, but she could never do that. He was her brother; she loved him; and bad penny or not, she'd go on helping him. But she felt a small sense of guilty relief that he didn't know she was here in America . . .

During the afternoon, Judy explored the facilities of the hotel, enjoying the freedom of wandering around by herself. The gardens were landscaped and fragrant. The outdoor pools were surrounded by the beautiful people, the women in bikinis and the bronzed men wearing swim briefs that left little to the imagination.

The blue water looked so inviting beneath the hot sun that Judy felt a sudden yen to join them, but the mid-afternoon heat was also draining, and the effort of returning to her suite for her stuff decided her against it. Besides, she had plenty of time. She had the whole summer.

She wondered what Blake did with his free time. He must be at liberty to do whatever he liked with his time. She wondered if he had a girl-friend. She was sure he couldn't be married, or he would surely have brought his wife to meet her last evening. She found it impossible to resist her continuing curiosity about him, because among all the people she had met so far, he was certainly a novelty.

She took a short stroll down the Strip, enjoying the slightly more relaxed ambience of the daytime casinos, and studying the showtime ads, but it was just too hot for comfort, and eventually she went back to her suite at the hotel. There was another fax message from Harry waiting for her on her machine.

'Why are you so mad? I thought you'd be pleased to have a fellow Brit to work with. Blake's a great guy, so don't get yourself in a stew about it, darling. You can put anybody down at ten paces if you've got a mind to, so he'd better watch out. I'll call you some time to find out how things are going.'

It sounded just like Harry. He had a neat way of letting anybody's complaints go over his head and only seeing his side of it. And faxes were fine, but they couldn't convey all Judy's feelings . . . Before she stopped to think, she was dialling his number, knowing he always slept in on Sunday mornings. And it was morning in London now.

'Harry? It's me, Judy.'

'Do you know what time it is?' he howled.

'It's high time you got up, lazybones,' she grinned, having known him too long to mince her words. 'But never mind all that. I've got a bone to pick with you. What right did you have to tell Blake anything about Ricky? It's my personal business and not something I want all and sundry to know – '

'Now just hold on, Jude. Blake isn't all and sundry, and if there was going to be any trouble, he needed to know – '

'What kind of trouble?' She was instantly suspicious of just how much Harry knew of Ricky's movements. 'How would Blake get to know about it anyway?'

She could hear his heavy, nasal breathing now.

'It's nothing. Forget I spoke – '

'I will not! You know something about Ricky I don't, so don't mess me about, Harry. If you don't tell me, I swear I'll be on the next plane back to London,' she said recklessly. They both knew she wouldn't, but it was enough to make Harry snap back.

'He wanted to know where you were, Jude. He sent a garbled note here a few weeks ago – '

'A few weeks? Harry, how could you not tell me?' She was too upset to be angry now. Ricky had needed her, and he would have thought she'd let him down.

'The negotiations were going through for the Vegas job, that's why, and if that young layabout had put the mockers on it for you, I'd never have forgiven myself. I told him you were on tour in Europe at present, but I sent him a few quid, because I knew it's what you'd have wanted.'

'You're a prize bastard, Harry.'

She tried to suppress the tears, imagining what a slap in the face it would all have been for her brother.

'I know. But I did it for the best. You know that, don't you? I was thinking of your future, Jude.'

And your cut, you old devil . . .

'Where was he writing from?'

72

'A small place in Oregon called Seaside. He was working in some sideshow or other, but you know Ricky, and things were a bit rough, I gather.'

They must have been for him to contact her through Harry. Ricky was a fool, but he had his pride.

'Can you fax me the letter, Harry?'

'Sorry, darling. I didn't keep it.'

That was just great. Now she'd be worrying over Ricky, without a clue how to get in touch with him, or where he was. A small place called Seaside in Oregon was hardly the easiest of directions to locate.

'Look, Jude,' he went on uncomfortably. 'I did what I thought was right at the time. And I did send him fifty quid.'

She supposed she could be grateful for that. Harry was under no obligation to help Ricky, but he knew how she constantly worried over him.

'Well, thanks for that, anyway. But if he gets in touch again, you contact me at once, you hear?'

'Yes, all right. Now can I get back to bed?'

As she hung up, it was only then that she realized she'd never asked him to tell her more about Blake. It hardly seemed to matter any more.

By the time she was ready to meet Franklin Delgado for dinner that evening, Judy was trying hard to put all the worry over Ricky behind her. There was nothing she could do about it, and if he hadn't contacted Harry again, then the fifty pounds Harry had sent him had presumably got him out of whatever trouble he was in. She made herself believe it.

Frank was waiting for her in the foyer of the casino, and gave a small whistle of approval when he saw her. She wore a cream silk pant suit and several strings of gold necklaces and long gold earrings. She looked chic and elegant, and knowing that she did so gave her back the self-confidence that had slipped sideways when she'd spoken to Harry.

'You look like a million dollars,' Frank told her. 'I hope you'll approve of the place we're going to.'

'Why shouldn't I?'

He looked pretty good too, she observed, in well-fitting dark pants and cream jacket over a red shirt. They made a handsome couple, she couldn't help thinking, and half-wished that Blake Adams could see them now, just for the hell of it.

'I should have asked you if you like Chinese food.'

'I love it.'

'Good. Then you'll love the Golden Sea Palace.'

He led her towards the car park, and opened the door of a sleek blue car. Judy slid inside. It wasn't as luxurious as Blake's limo, but it was friendly and comfortable.

'The Golden Sea Palace sounds like a contradiction in terms, out here in the desert,' she grinned.

'The whole concept of Las Vegas is a contradiction in terms out here in the desert,' he agreed, laughing. 'Nothing's what it seems here, Judy – '

'Not even people?'

'I didn't quite mean that, but it's not a bad idea to step back a pace and think over what people are saying to you. There are as many sycophants in this town as in any other, and you're too nice a person to be taken in by them.'

'Thanks for the warning.'

He put one hand over hers for a moment before putting it back on the steering-wheel.

'I don't mean to sound like a lecturer, but I've lived here most of my life, and I've seen it change from a quiet little town where nothing much happened, to what you see now.'

'And you don't like it all that much, do you?' she asked in surprise, with sudden insight.

He shrugged. 'When gambling fever takes over, people change, Judy, and that's the last thing I'm going to say on the subject or this evening's going to turn into a gloomy one. Hell, I'm meant to be giving you a tour of the town, aren't I, not depressing you?'

Actually, she had warmed towards him at that moment, because for all his brashness last night, she sensed that he might half-agree with her own feelings about gambling.

But as they left the garishness and bright lights of the Strip, she realized that what he had told her was right: there *was* a whole sprawling city beyond the casinos. He pointed out the university campus, and the more sedate areas of town, before ruining the image by showing her the glittering frontage of the Liberace Museum, where all the showman pianist's memorabilia and fabulous costumes were housed.

'That's enough for one night. Let's eat,' he decided.

He drew up the car outside the Chinese restaurant with its elaborate dragon symbols and red Chinese lanterns adorning the entrance. Compared with the lights on the Strip, it was subdued, and its familiarity to the restaurants Judy had frequented in London made her feel more secure than at any time since coming here. And yet . . .

Briefly, she wondered what was wrong with her. Here she was, on the brink of a fabulous job, with an attentive man who was openly admiring but not coming on strong, and she still wasn't completely at ease.

Ricky's problems were still on her mind, of course, but it was something else too. The ambience was right, but the man wasn't. Frank was nice, but maybe he was the wrong man. At the thought, she caught herself up short, willing the image of Blake Adams out of her mind.

Just as if he could read her thoughts, Frank mentioned him as soon as they were shown to their seats and had ordered their meal.

'So what do you think of your fellow countryman, Judy?'

She looked at him blankly for a minute before realizing he meant Blake, and her face felt hot.

'I hardly know him yet,' she murmured.

'But enough to make an instant impression, I suspect.'

'Of course, but it's not always wise to trust instant impressions, is it? You have to get to know people to know what makes them tick – especially about their past, and I wouldn't presume to ask Blake anything about that yet.'

She spoke innocently, not looking at him, but she heard him give a soft laugh.

'But you're longing to know how the hell he came to be here, aren't you?'

'Not really,' she replied coolly, and then capitulated with a laugh. 'Well, maybe just a little. He's obviously well-educated, and in England you'd have probably mistaken him for a banker or successful stockbroker or something – '

Except that for Blake's persona it sounded far too deadly dull . . . and she heard Frank give an amused laugh again.

'He's dabbled in plenty of things in his time, Judy, but nothing so damn boring as all that. Not that he ever needed to do anything. His family has been in the wool trade for several generations in Yorkshire, and were worth a packet. But it wasn't what Blake wanted, and anyway, he'd lived in London for some years before he inherited the whole kit and caboodle of it, and already had a taste of show business. After his father died he could just have sat back as the new mill owner and raked in all the profits, but he had different ambitions.'

'Good lord!' Judy exclaimed. Whatever else she had expected to hear, it wasn't this.

She could see that Frank was clearly enjoying her stunned reaction to this. And Harry could have told her all of it, she was thinking, since Blake was supposedly such an old buddy of his . . .

'He sold up the entire family inheritance, turned his back on England about ten years ago, and came out here to buy up the Sparkling Rocks.'

And Judy had told him to put out the lights in his own Diamond Showroom. At that moment, it was all her whirling thoughts could take in.

CHAPTER 5

Harry Brady was nothing if not resourceful. Putting the Vegas job Judy Hale's way had been a feather in his cap as well as hers, and he certainly wasn't going to ruin both their chances of making big money by letting some snot-nosed little kid get in their way. Harry could be as affable as you liked – some would call it oily – but when it came to business, he was as hard as iron.

He felt sorry for the kid, of course, but Ricky Hale had brought everything on himself. Once, when Judy had poured out her heart to him, he'd learned how the kid had gone to pieces after their folks had died when he was only thirteen, and found his solace in the gambling arcades.

While he was totally absorbed in the flashing lights and ringing bells of the one-armed bandit machines, he could forget everything else. And that had been just the beginning.

Excited by a few good wins, and with money jingling in his pockets, he'd quickly become something of a hero among his mates, with masses of street cred. Gambling had quickly become like a fever in his blood, and once it began at such an early age, it was as difficult to stop as a runaway horse.

Harry was no saint, but he could see how Ricky Hale was heading towards big trouble if he didn't watch out. And that last garbled letter from the kid had told him much more between the lines than the actual words.

'I'm desperate, Harry. You've got to let Judy know. She'll want to help me, I know she will, so be a pal and give her my address. And tell her it's urgent, will you?'

Harry hadn't had the slightest intention of doing as the boy asked. Judy was keyed up enough, knowing how drastically her life was about to change, even if it was for the better. It was the chance of a lifetime, and this little snot-rag wasn't going to ruin everything.

To salve his conscience, and because he still had a minuscule soft spot for the kid, especially when he sounded in real trouble, he'd sent off the reply, fobbing him off and enclosing fifty quid out of his own pocket. It hardly made him feel one hell of a guy for doing so, but it was the only thing he could do.

He just hoped he'd managed to convince Judy that there was nothing seriously amiss with her brother and that he'd acted in her best interests. She needed to establish herself as the top in her field, as he knew she was, and she didn't need any niggling worries about her stupid kid of a brother disrupting her concentration.

At that moment, Judy was studying a large-scale map of the west coast of America. The state of Oregon was well to the north, and the town of Seaside was clearly marked. The frustratingly inadequate detail about the area merely said that it was a small family resort, popular for fishing vacations and seal watching.

There was no mention of gambling there, but there wouldn't be, Judy reasoned. As far as she knew – and she'd studied it carefully enough – there were only three main gambling centres in the west: Lake Tahoe, Reno and Las Vegas. The fourth was Atlantic City in New Jersey on the east coast, which she knew had once drawn Ricky like a homing pigeon.

She scanned the map again, and saw that the inland resorts of both Lake Tahoe and Reno were somewhere between Seaside and Las Vegas. But since all the states were so large, and Ricky was frequently out of money, maybe he'd never get to any of them. Maybe he'd just settle down in Seaside and be content to work the sideshows. Anything for a bit of excitement . . . it was a futile hope, but the only one she had.

And she had better get some sleep, because tomorrow morning she was going to be in the office that already had her name on the door, and had been assigned to her on the floor above the Diamond Showroom. She already had vague plans and sketches worked out for her part of the new show, and she had to present them to Frank for his approval.

That had been his last remark to her when he'd taken her back to the hotel. And it reminded her that she wasn't in this alone. The British section of the International Spectacular had to co-ordinate with the rest of it so well that the seams didn't show. She got into bed and turned out the light, trying not to think about anything or anyone at all.

'No, no, *no!*' Frank practically spat out the words. 'This is no good at all. You'll have to think again, Judy.'

She looked at him angrily. The office that she had thought of as her private haven seemed to be swarming with people, and the portfolio of her precious plans and sketches were scattered all over the desktops as Frank and Maggie and half-a-dozen other people glanced at them and discarded them.

'What's wrong with them, for God's sake?'

She bristled at once. She had choreographed plenty of shows in England, and had been highly acclaimed for her expertise, being able to see things from both sides of the fence, and not to expect the impossible from her dancers.

This, of course, was very different. The scale of the casino shows themselves were in a different league, and she forced herself to bite her tongue as Frank began to point out the flaws in her arrangements.

'The tableaux you've sketched are too tame for a start – '

"Tame?"

'Judy, I'm not criticizing the work you've done in the past. I know you come highly recommended. But you have to think big here and, so far, you're not doing so. I appreciate all your art and dance training, and these arrangements would probably do very well in a provincial British show, but not here. Our audiences demand bigger and better shows, and if the Sparkling Rocks doesn't come up with the goods, they'll go to some other show. And Blake won't like that,' he added with a gleam in his eyes.

God, he was insufferable! He made her feel like a schoolgirl on the carpet before a stringent headmaster. Who the hell did he think he was, showing her up in front of all these people . . .?

Even as the thought entered her head, she knew it was pointless to start acting the *prima donna*. As Dance Director, he had overall control of the show, and she was only a small cog in the smooth running of it. It was time to swallow her pride, and admit that the sketches that she had thought fairly ambitious, were probably small fry compared with the spectaculars that were put on here.

'I can see your point,' she muttered. 'So OK, I'm prepared to go back to the drawing-board – but I presume you don't object to the costume designs?'

She had spent ages following the lines of those she had seen in photographs and videos. The audiences must wonder how the girls ever kept on the fabulously ornate headdresses, but that was all down to the skills of the wardrobe mistress and seamstresses, and the exceptionally light fabrics they used.

'I've got no problem at all with those, honey – and you won't take all this personally, will you?'

'Of course not.' She forced a smile, still smarting inside, but too damned professional to let him see it.

'We'll leave you to get on with it then – oh, and you might cut down on the red, white and blue just a little,' he added as a passing barb.

Right now she wished she had the nerve to throw the portfolio at him, as he and his entourage moved out of the office. Cut down on the red, white and blue, indeed. What else had he expected to see for the British part of the show!

As Maggie left her office with the others, she put a sympathetic hand on Judy's arm.

'Don't let it get you down, kid. We've all gone through the mill with Frank in our time.'

A little later, while she was still brooding over the blank sheets of sketching paper on her drawing-board, there was a tap on her door.

'Come in if you must,' she snapped without thinking. 'It's open house around here.'

'Is it safe, or should I throw in my hat first?' came Blake's voice.

'Oh, I'm sorry. I didn't know it was you. I thought it would be Frank again, coming to tell me how useless I am.'

She spoke without thinking, and then, to her absolute horror, she felt her throat thicken. She'd never been so feeble as to cry over a rebuke, but it was a damn long time since anybody had questioned her work quite so vehemently, and in public too.

'Of course you're not useless,' Blake told her severely. 'And Frank has his own way of getting the best out of people.'

'By humiliating them? I've never respected anyone who does that.' And since he was obviously aware of what had happened, it was doubly humiliating.

84

'Then you'll just have to learn not to be so touchy, won't you? They do things differently here, Judy, which is why Las Vegas can boast the best and most spectacular shows on earth, and that's no exaggeration.'

'I know that. And I'm not normally so touchy,' she admitted, feeling her heartbeats slow down a little, and not even realizing what a state she had let herself get in.

It was so unlike her . . . but what with the importance of the job and the new environment, and now the added worry over Ricky ever since Harry's call . . .

'Why don't you tell me what's wrong? I fancy it's more than a little personality clash between you and Frank. I'm sure you can handle that perfectly well.'

For a brief moment, she was very tempted to tell him everything. After all, he already knew something about Ricky, thanks to Harry's indiscretion.

But she also knew something about Blake Adams that nobody had told her before last night. She knew he'd inherited a fortune from his family business, and had thrown it all up to make even more money by his own enterprise. She could definitely admire that.

But she also knew that by now he must be as rich as Croesus. So there was no way on earth that she was going to tell him that her brother was in trouble again and needed money. She had too much pride for *that*, and if Blake embarrassed her by offering to bail Ricky out, as he surely would, she would be beholden to him. Nor could she forget the ridiculous bet he'd had with Harry that he could melt the ice maiden, or some such sexist nonsense.

'There's nothing wrong,' she told him at last. 'Just put it down to belated jet-lag and getting used to new surroundings and new arrangements – and new people.'

He looked at her speculatively. His dark eyes seemed to see right through her subterfuge, Judy thought, and she told herself not to let her imagination run away with her. But her family business was her own, and nothing to do with him.

'Have it your way. But if you want to talk things over with somebody who speaks the same language, you know where to come, don't you?'

The same language! The language and moneyed background he came from was a world away from the upbringing of Judy Hale and her tearaway brother! She found herself biting her lips again as thoughts of Ricky came into her head. And without quite knowing how it happened, Blake had crossed the divide between them and drawn her into his arms.

She felt his hands caressing her hair, and unconsciously, she closed her eyes for a moment, just for the sheer comfort of knowing that someone else cared about her problems, even if he didn't know what they were. But she might have known that he would take advantage of the moment.

She felt the touch of his lips on the nape of her neck, sending shivers all the way down her spine. She made to pull away from him, but he wasn't ready to let her go so easily.

'Why do you fight me, Judy? The minute I saw you I knew you and I were made for one another. We're two of a kind here, so we've got to stick together, and besides, we make a great team, don't we?'

'I hardly think you would ever lack for company!'

As she spoke she silently wrestled with him, feeling immensely foolish at doing so.

Especially when all her instincts were telling her something very different. Telling her that she was in the arms of the most exciting man she had ever known, and it would be the easiest thing in the world to fall in love with him.

But that was what he wanted, of course. To win his bet with Harry, and to crow over her. The ultimate macho man. She wondered if he even knew the meaning of love, or if it was just the conquest that was all that mattered to him.

'Oh, but you're wrong,' he answered her comment with an odd touch of reserve. 'There are some things in life that can make anyone feel alone and an outsider, no matter how well they seem to fit in.'

There was that small hint again that something in his past had affected him deeply. Or was that all a ploy too – part of his technique, to be so intriguing? But he certainly didn't need it. His charisma alone was enough to get him anything he wanted, except for anyone strong enough to resist it. Judy counted herself among the few.

'Anyway, I know you'll still be feeling a little out of your depth,' he went on more briskly. 'So you're to join me for lunch every day.'

'That's not necessary – '

He went on as if she hadn't spoken. 'And this evening and for the next few nights, we'll sit in on the current show so that you can get the feel of it all. Once this week is over, we'll have Danny Corsey as the star attraction, and he has his own troupe of dancers and musical arrangements. His rehearsals will take place in the practice rooms, so you and Frank and Maggie will have the stage to yourselves to get the new show under way for the fall.'

His efficiency left her gasping. 'You seem to be in on everything. Doesn't Frank object to having your finger in his special pie?'

'Why should he? I'm not the kind of casino boss who's content to just sit back and rake in the proceeds. Besides, I've always had more than a passing interest in showbusiness. It's how I came to meet Harry, in fact. And why else would I have bought a place like this?'

It was on the tip of Judy's tongue to ask him to tell her more, when he spoke again.

'By the way, don't bother with dinner. We'll have supper after the show.'

Before she could argue or protest, he pressed her arm, then let her go and walked towards the door. Even while she fumed at his arrogance, there was an elegance about him that other men didn't have, thought Judy. Her dancer's eye could appreciate his supple litheness. She felt the tingle inside her veins as he turned at the door and smiled at her.

'Like I said, don't fight me, Judy. Whenever you need a friend, I'll always be around.'

It was such an unexpectedly sweet thing to say after his brash male assurance, that she felt her throat tighten. It was hard to remain completely objective about his motives when he could be so utterly charming and sincere. Unless that was all part of the big seduction scene, of course. But she didn't want to think so, whether or not it was a reckless thought.

She turned back to her work, knowing she must produce something acceptable soon, and revising her whole perception of the British theme. And acknowledging that it was a sensible idea to watch the current show this evening, if only to get the feel of Frank's work and expectations.

Going without dinner would be no hardship. As a dancer she had rarely eaten anything more than fruit and chocolate before a show, and it never bothered her to do the same now.

Within the next couple of hours she had produced some new sketches with more ambitious moves for the dancers. She knew Frank wouldn't be too concerned with seeing them immediately, as he was very much involved with the last week of his show, and producing a finale that surpassed all that had gone before.

And when she saw the show tonight, she would get even more of an insight into what was required. But it was just as important to Judy to plan her own choreography without being overly influenced by someone else's work.

'Are you feeling better?' Blake greeted her when she met him in the Opal Bar for lunch.

'Much better, thank you,' she replied, not bothering to hide the fact that she'd been so put out before.

He'd been aware of it, anyway. He was astute at sensing other people's feelings, and maybe that was part of his success with them.

'Do I have a smut on my nose or something?' he asked with a smile, and she knew she had been staring.

'That word reminds me of when my brother and I were kids,' she exclaimed without thinking. 'We used to love to watch the trains, and our grandmother used to say how lucky we were that it wasn't in the days of steam trains, because then we'd have got smuts in our eyes and we'd be sorry. I never knew what smuts were until she explained.'

She paused as Blake laughed, and she realized she had been gabbling. He was still teasing as they settled themselves in a reserved alcove table.

'You see? I always knew how refreshing it would be to have you here, Judy Hale!'

'I don't follow you — '

'Who else in this whole outlandish place could have the same kind of childhood memories as we do?'

'I hardly think we could have shared anything. I came from a very ordinary family, not — '

She stopped again, hot with embarrassment this time. Because now he would know she was well aware of his early life. She could see that his eyes were suddenly guarded.

'I see that someone's been talking out of turn. I suppose it was Harry. He always did have a runaway tongue.'

'Don't I know it! He told you about my brother, didn't he?' she retorted, not giving anything away.

'Have you heard from him at all?' Blake asked, neatly turning the conversation from himself and back to her.

'No,' she was able to say truthfully.

Harry had heard from Ricky, but she hadn't, not directly. And there was no reason for letting Blake get involved in her family affairs.

She paid full attention to the menu again, but she was seeing in her mind's eye the cheeky small boy that Ricky had been, with the big blue eyes that were a trait in their family, and the mass of carroty hair he was always trying to tame. But he had been a lovable little devil all the same, and she wondered how things could have gone so wrong . . .

'Laying ghosts again?' Blake asked her. 'The past is best left behind you, Judy, whatever it contained.'

'I couldn't agree more,' she said, more concerned with Ricky's future than his past.

He looked at her through narrowed eyes. 'You know, when you're not aware of it, you sometimes get a very alluring haunted look on your face.'

'Well, I can assure you it's not meant to be.'

He leaned back in his chair, arms folded, still studying her. Mr Macho Man again, she thought.

'I don't know why you feel the need to be so protective every time a man pays you an honest compliment. Are you so unsure of your own sexuality?'

She gasped at his blatant words, furious to think that anyone else might have overheard them. But there was a babble of noise in the Bar, and they were cocooned in the alcove.

'You've got a damn nerve,' she began, and she felt him take her hand and caress her palm as he'd done once before.

At his touch, the treacherous tingles of pleasure ran over her skin, but as she made to snatch her hand away he gripped it more tightly.

'Why do I get the feeling that someone hurt you badly in the past? Maybe so badly that you're afraid to let anyone see what a passionate woman you can really be,' he said next, in that calmly calculating way.

'You know nothing about my private life,' she responded shortly, 'and there's no reason why you should.'

And even if the ghost of Michael's betrayal did sometimes come back to haunt her, there was no way she was going to share the memories with a stranger. Especially one who had made his intentions perfectly clear. He wanted her, and if he thought he could get round her by acting as some kind of sex therapist, he could think again.

She sipped the soft drink she had ordered, annoyed to find that her hands were unsteady. Once the waitress had brought their lunch, she determinedly spoke of other things.

'I'm planning to see something of the area while I'm here. I've been looking at the brochures that were left in my room, and when I get some free time I want to take a bus out to Old Vegas. It's a kind of theme park, isn't it?'

'In a very low-key way. But if you're expecting Disneyland, forget it – '

'I'm not, thanks very much! So what's it like, then?' she went on, just to keep talking about impersonal matters.

'It's one of those places that shows what the town was like in the old days. You must know the kind of thing. We have them all over the place in England, where the streets are reconstructed with all the old-fashioned shops and so on. There's usually a blacksmith and forge, and all the usual Victorian stuff. But this being America, in Old Vegas there's also a Wild West show.'

'Why, Mr Adams, sir, just for a moment there, you sounded quite nostalgic for li'l old England,' Judy said facetiously, unexpectedly moved by the way his voice had deepened as he spoke of it.

'And why shouldn't I be?' he retorted. 'You don't have the monopoly on it. We can never forget our roots, no matter where life takes us, but that doesn't mean we can't move on. And that's the last bit of homespun philosophy you're going to hear from me. Do you want to ruin my starry image, girl?'

She laughed, thinking how very normal he could really be, when he let down his guard of being the ultimate Alpha man. It didn't detract from his charisma one bit, and she was also aware of something else.

He was a deep-thinking man, and she liked that. Even if *his* roots were considerably wealthier than hers . . . but none of that seemed to matter so much here, and that was one of the refreshing things she loved about America. She wouldn't mind betting it was something Blake loved about the country too. As she found herself smiling again, Blake demanded to know what he'd said that was so funny.

'Nothing at all. I was just having a private bet with myself, and thinking that it must be a first for me.'

'Then perhaps there's hope for you yet, once you accept that not all bets are bad,' he said.

Maybe not, except when they were all too personal . . .

Judy spent the afternoon working in her office, and was reasonably satisfied with the results. She had quickly revised her whole perception of what was required. The old image of pearly kings and queens were out, and she'd never seriously considered using that anyway, even though some of the Americans she'd met in London were almost disappointed not to see them on every street corner.

But a set piece of Carnaby Street for fashion, and Soho for a sexier theme . . . and definitely a stately home or two thrown in, if not a royal palace . . . The ideas were coming thick and fast now, and she felt the adrenaline surge through her veins as she worked. And she mentally thanked Franklin Delgado for not letting her get away with half-baked work.

By the time she decided to call it a day and locked up her office, her arms and shoulders were aching. The mental creative energy she put into the initial stages of her work was always draining, and she didn't want to see or talk to anybody for a couple of hours. So she was thankful to be whizzed up to her suite without seeing anybody except the elevator clerk.

Once there, she stripped off her clothes and tied up her hair from the nape of her neck. Then she ran an invigorating bath, and lay back in the foaming, scented water with a sigh of pure indulgent pleasure.

And the more she tried not to think about Blake Adams, the more he came into her mind.

He was such an enigma. To turn his back on the rural life he could have had, and to settle for the brash, vibrant world of a Las Vegas casino, just didn't add up. Although she could see that he would never have been happy living in any kind of backwater. His was too dynamic a personality for that.

She shivered, despite the seductive warmth of the bath water, wondering if she was being insidiously drawn into something she didn't want. Or did she? For a moment she let herself imagine what it would be like to be loved by him . . . truly loved, without the mockery that sometimes peppered his words.

Some might even call it sexual harrassment, but Judy had never thought that a man's honest admiration could be construed so stupidly. Providing it *was* honest, and not the kind of sleaze that got bandied about in the newspaper gossip columns. And in her opinion too many women cried wolf on the flimsiest pretext, hoping to cash in on the current craze.

But if the admiration was *real*, and the feelings were reciprocated, then nothing was taboo in Judy's book. She had believed it when she'd had what some would call her torrid affair with Michael – and what she had considered to be a love that would last for ever . . . and yet the love that had seemed so wonderful had faded, and she had accepted that nothing lasted for ever after all. And yet, for one sweet, wanton moment, she found herself wishing that Blake's compliments were real.

After she had finished bathing, she lay on her bed, relaxing in her dressing-gown for half an hour, and telling herself not to be such a fool. Hadn't she seen the way some of the casino girls played up to him, giving him thinly veiled invitations from their heavily made-up eyes and husky voices?

And hadn't she seen how he revelled in it? Would he have had such opportunities in the comparatively staid, countrified surroundings of a Yorkshire mill town?

She gave up thinking about it and chose some fruit and chocolate from the bowl that was always kept replenished in her room. Really, it was more like living as a hotel guest than an employee, she thought somewhat guiltily. But she had no intention of asking if she was a privileged employee, since she was enjoying the luxury so much!

At seven forty-five Blake knocked at her door. She wore a sea-green dress that clung to her figure, and her hair was held back from her face with her favourite silver combs.

'You look stunning,' he said. 'You'll have heads turning, guessing which Hollywood star I'm escorting this evening.'

'And you're mad.' Judy laughed, but was unable to resist a secret thrill of pleasure at his words.

'Shall we go?' Blake offered her his arm. 'The show starts precisely at eight o'clock.'

'Precisely?' she echoed.

'You'll see.'

As they went down in the elevator to the Diamond Showroom entrance Judy noticed, despite the short time they had known one another, how easy they could be in each other's company, providing he wasn't coming on strong. As a friend, she knew she could like him enormously. And as a chauvinist of the first order she could still find him insufferable . . .

The auditorium was almost full when they entered, and now the atmosphere was totally different from when Judy had seen it before. There was a great air of anticipation and energy in the audience that she knew only too well would just as soon be emanating back from the stage.

For a moment, as always, she felt a nostalgic ache to be one of the dancers on that stage. Dancing had been part of her life for so long, and she knew she would never lose the memory of the special electricity that flowed between performers and audience. But she accepted that now that she was on the other side of the fence, it helped in her understanding of getting the best out of her dancers.

'Our seats are this way, Judy,' she heard Blake say, and she realized she had been lost in her memories for those few brief moments.

The tables in front of all the alcove seats were lit with red candles now, and most people already had several drinks in front of them. A flunkey led Blake and Judy to a box near the stage, on a slightly higher level than the main section. It was darkly intimate in the box, and when the door behind them was closed, they were in a world of their own.

'This doesn't worry you, does it?' he asked, leaning towards her. 'These are the best seats in the house.'

'Why should it worry me? I want to see everything.'

But she had heard the smile in his voice, and couldn't help wondering how many other girls he had brought here to watch the shows. Not that she cared, of course.

At precisely thirty seconds to eight o'clock the house lights were dimmed, and a murmur of expectation ran around the audience. Shortly afterwards she dimly heard a voice saying:

'Gentleman, five, four, three, two, one' . . . and then the music began; the curtain rose to a battery of applause as the showgirls were displayed in the first tableau of the evening.

Then, as the dancers took centre stage, the topless girls flanking them stood like like perfect statues. It was all so wonderfully orchestrated and slick that Judy soon found herself completely absorbed in the show, both from the spectacular viewpoint and from her technical expertise.

The glittering, sequin-studded costumes were fabulous, and the girls could be compared with statuesque goddesses. Judy remembered the rehearsal she had seen and marvelled, as always, that the sometimes ragged performances among the leotard-clad girls could be so miraculously transformed into something so perfect and beautiful on the night.

The entire show lasted for two hours, with a mid-session interval, when coffee and wine were automatically brought to the box for Blake and Judy.

'You've obviously thought of everything,' she murmured, but secretly she was glad she didn't have to go to the bar like so many did in the interval. For her, absorbed as she was, it would have broken the continuity of this magical performance.

'And I hope you'll have an appetite for supper later,' he said casually.

'I will. Dancing always made me hungry, and I find that just watching a good show does the same. I suppose it's because I'm mentally going through it with them.'

She was speaking too fast and she knew it. But there was something about the way he said *appetite* that made her suspicious of another meaning in his words. But she was just either imagining things – or getting paranoid about the man.

CHAPTER 6

They left by a side door at the end of the show, and Judy was filled with admiration for everything she had seen. No wonder Frank had impressed on her the need for perfection. She had seen it tonight. And Laverne, Candy and Paige, the top showgirls she'd been somewhat wary about on her first evening here, had more than earned all her respect.

'Well? Did you enjoy it?' Blake said as he motioned her towards the elevator again.

'Do you really have to ask? It was breathtaking, Blake.' She spoke with total honesty. 'And I'll do my best not to let you down.'

'Good God, I never thought you would. And for God's sake don't go all humble on me. It's not your style.'

'I'm not normally,' she grinned.

'As I've discovered!'

And *she* had discovered what good company he could be when he chose to be, she thought again. They had known one another such a short while, but the rapport had been instant between them, whether it was bristly or in tune. And even though he was definitely the boss, there was no reason why they couldn't just be friends without all the sex stuff getting in the way.

But even as she thought it, she knew how foolish she was being. From the very first moment, when he had so annoyed her at LAX, the friction between them had laid the foundations of a sexual awareness that she could no longer deny.

'So where are we having supper?' she asked huskily, as the elevator came to a stop.

She glanced at the lighted number on the elevator panel, and gave a start. She had assumed they would probably go to the restaurant in the Sapphire Suite again. Now she saw that the elevator doors were sliding open at their own floor, and the clerk called out the number unnecessarily.

'You'll see,' Blake said.

She followed him suspiciously, and her heartbeats began to quicken as he pushed his key card into his own door.

Though you could hardly call it that, Judy thought, glimpsing the elegant rooms from the doorway. As befitted the home of the owner–manager of such a successful enterprise, it was a huge and lavishly furnished apartment.

'Oh, no,' she said, as he stood back for her to enter.

He gave an elaborate sigh. 'Don't play chicken with me, Judy. I've ordered supper for us both as I promised, and I thought we should both have time to talk at leisure without any interruptions.'

'We could have done that at any restaurant in town –'

'What is it with you?' he asked. 'Do you imagine that a simple supper invitation means I intend to ravish you in my own hotel? Not that the idea isn't infinitely appealing, if I may say so, but it's hardly my way.'

Wasn't it? But how could she be sure? And how was she supposed to forget the stupid bet he'd made with Harry? Without warning, she seemed to hear the echo of her brother's angry voice in her head.

Why won't you ever give me the benefit of the doubt, Jude? You always want to see the worst in me, don't you? Just because I'm not afraid to take chances, and you're content to be a stick-in-the-mud all your life!

She had seethed with anger at the time, denying everything he said, and snapping at him that if taking chances meant getting into such debt that it was going to ruin his life, then she was far happier staying as she was, thanks very much.

Besides, she was no stick-in-the-mud, and never had been. Otherwise, what would she be doing here?

'As long as it's just supper, then,' she said feebly.

'Of course. Isn't that what I said?'

She went inside the room, trying not to feel like a fly caught in a spider's web.

As she sat down gingerly on one of the silk-covered sofas, Blake picked up the phone and spoke into it. He turned to her with a smile.

'The food will be here in a few minutes. Meanwhile, let me get you a drink, and then I'll show you around.'

Judy thought she'd already had enough to drink, but as he poured her a glass of wine she took it automatically, thinking that at least while she held something in her hands he couldn't make a play for her.

God, but she sounded so feeble! She knew it, and yet somehow she couldn't stop it. And she knew that if she had ever acted this way with Michael, he'd have been out of her life in ten seconds flat.

But then, she had been besotted with Michael, wanting to please him so much, even when she knew in her heart that it wasn't really love, and that eventually he would leave her . . .

She knew now that being besotted was a poor substitute for love, and she had vowed never to let herself be so foolish again. Before she committed herself so completely to a man again, she had to know that it was love or nothing. Nothing else would do.

'Dreaming again?' she heard Blake's amused voice remark.

She smiled at him brightly. 'Not really. I was just wondering when you're going to show me round your abode.'

And then she could squash that certain feeling, for those endless moments, that he was going to be the one.

'Where would you like to begin? The apartment takes up most of this side of the floor, and I'm completely self-contained here, of course, since this is my home. Women usually like to see the kitchen first, don't they?'

'That depends on how domesticated they are,' Judy retorted. 'These days, not everyone wants to conform to the old idea of marriage and two-point-five children, and bliss in a cottage with a wifey in an apron and hubby doing the gardening and washing the car every Sunday – '

She listened to herself in horror, wondering why on earth she was saying those things. She had *never* sneered at such an image, and a career would come very far down her order of priorities when the right man came along to share her life. She had always wanted marriage and children . . .

'I should have remembered you were a career girl first and foremost, and it's just as well I wasn't about to propose at that moment,' Blake said coolly. 'I only asked if you wanted to see the kitchen – but maybe you'd prefer to see some other room instead.'

'Actually, I'd quite like to see the kitchen,' she replied hurriedly. 'Especially if you're the gadget man I suspect that you are. Though I can't imagine that someone like you ever did much cooking the way we ordinary folk did.'

It was definitely the wine making her talk in such a stupid way, Judy thought. She hadn't noticed how often her empty glass was replaced with a full one while she was so intent on the show, otherwise she would never have spoken like this, and she knew she deserved what he was saying to her now.

'Stop behaving like an inverted snob. None of us can help what we're born into. It's what we do with our lives afterwards that shapes us into decent human beings.'

'Is that another bit of your homespun philosophy?'

'No. Just common sense.'

Judy was suddenly embarrassed at the way she was reacting. Never mind his stupid bet, or the fact that she still suspected he meant to get her into bed the minute she said the word . . . but he still understood her need to find her feet in this different world. He was still a friend.

'Blake, I do appreciate the way you're looking after me,' she backtracked awkwardly.

'Think nothing of it. I'm merely looking after my investment. Now, let's have that tour before supper arrives.'

She followed him, feeling thoroughly put down, and forcing herself to take an interest in the superb view of the Strip from the windows on this side of the building.

The kitchen was every woman's dream, spotless and gleaming, and she still wondered if he ever did anything in it himself. As if he read her unspoken thought, he laughed.

'I *can* cook, you know. I'll try out my culinary skills on you one evening, Miss Dedicated Career Girl.'

'Are you implying that I can't?' she asked, smiling inwardly as she remembered the many disastrous meals she had hashed up for Ricky and herself after their parents died. But she had come a long way since then, despite the image Blake seemed to have acquired of her now.

'Honey, I reckon you can do anything on this earth that you put your mind to. You have the kind of determination that could put the fear of God into a lesser guy than myself.'

It was rare that he lapsed into Western jargon, and Judy wondered if it was done to cover his true feelings. But while his remark startled her, she knew there had been plenty of times in the past when she'd quelled an unwanted admirer with one freezing look.

'Maybe that's part of my charm,' she retorted, refusing to rise to the bait. 'OK, I've seen the kitchen, and we've agreed that I'm no domestic engineer, so what's next?'

He had a large businesslike study, she discovered, complete with computer, fax, and all the latest office equipment. He clearly liked to keep his finger on the pulse of his empire, Judy thought approvingly.

One wall of the office was completely shelved with books of every description. There were also family photos and mementoes that she suspected came from his other life, which proved his words. You could never entirely forget your roots.

'So? Is my image of the languid playboy of the Western world beginning to fade?'

'I never thought that of you,' Judy told him. 'Anyone who can make a successful business out of – '

'Out of something of which you entirely disapprove,' he finished for her. 'But isn't that tempered by the fact that it brings pleasure to so many people?'

'It can bring a lot of heartache too.'

'Only if it gets out of hand, Judy, and we keep a careful eye on our punters at the tables. Our croupiers are very experienced in sussing them out, and once they get that desperate look in their eyes the house closes down on them.'

'All right. You know your business best,' she acknowledged. 'Have I seen everything now?'

Immediately she had spoken, she knew she hadn't.

'I thought I'd keep the best until last,' Blake said. And she had no choice but to follow him into the master bedroom, with its white walls and dark blue carpet and bed coverings. It was an entirely masculine lair, she couldn't help thinking, and her instinct told her to get out of there, fast.

'Do you like it?'

'It's very nice – '

He gave an uninhibited laugh. 'God, you do my heart good with your English understatements. I've got far too used to predatory females since I've been over here.'

'That's probably because they all see you a potential catch,' she told him.

'And you don't?'

As she heard the danger signals in her head she automatically stepped back a pace from him.

'That's not what I'm here for, is it?'

'All right, I'll stop baiting you. I'll just show you the guest bedroom and then we'll go and eat.'

She followed him into the second, equally elegant bedroom, but not before she had noted the framed photograph on a bedside table in his own room. The images on it seemed to instantly fix themselves into her memory. The photo must have been taken some time ago, she thought, since Blake looked much younger and more carefree, and less aggressive that the hard-headed business tycoon he was now.

The vivacious, dark-haired girl in the photo, laughing up into his eyes, was so obviously in love with him. They were dressed formally, and each wore a buttonhole in their lapels, and there was a scattering of confetti in the girl's hair.

So was he married? Or divorced? Judy dearly wanted to know, but somehow she couldn't ask. He had commented on some of the photos in his study, but since he had made no mention of the photo in the bedroom, she assumed it was too private and personal to explain it. And if that was so, then he did have feelings after all.

Maybe she would ask Frank some time, she thought, since he seemed to have access to all that went on in Blake's past . . .

They went back to the living-room, and by then someone had come and gone, and a table was laid out with plates of smoked salmon and a dish of salad, with thin bread and butter, and a dessert concoction of fresh fruits and cream. There was also the inevitable coffee pot.

'This is hardly a light meal to go to bed on!' Judy said, although her mouth was watering by now, and the fruit and chocolate she had eaten before the show seemed a very long time ago now.

'I wasn't actually proposing bed.' Blake quickly reverted to type. 'But if you insist – '

'Of course I don't! Please don't take every remark I make as some kind of innuendo, Blake. I just meant that I'm not sure I can do justice to all this food – '

He looked at her sharply as they sat down at the table in the window, where the glittering lights of the Strip formed a glorious backdrop.

'You're not faddy about food, are you? I got the impression you enjoyed it.' His eyes wandered over her curvaceous figure that had undoubtedly gained a few pounds since she gave up dancing professionally, but which suited her far better than the gawky teenager she had been.

'Of course I like food. Doesn't everybody?'

'Not everybody. Sometimes the obsession to be fashionably thin can be as bad an addiction as gambling.'

The tone of his voice told her instantly that he was speaking personally. Someone in his past had had that addiction, and he couldn't forget it. She wondered if it was the girl in the photograph . . .

'Well, I promise I'll do my best to prove that not everybody wants to starve themselves. In fact, the sight of this little feast is making me hungrier by the minute,' she assured him, covering the small, awkward silence.

And whether or not it was the memory of some secret past that had come back to haunt him, he made no further moves on her, and behaved like a perfect gentleman.

He told her something about Yorkshire – she had never been there – and the wild, open moors, where you could walk for miles without seeing another living soul. And where you could imagine Cathy and Heathcliff emerging from around every rock, if you were romantically inclined . . .

And she told him about London, the part he wouldn't know, where she and her brother had led anything but a cushioned life, but had learned to make the best of it. And at least one of them had come up smelling of the proverbial roses . . .

'You miss him, don't you?' Blake asked

'He's all I've got, and I think families should stay close, but Ricky never saw it that way. I know he had to do his own thing, but I do worry about him.'

'You can't be his protector for ever, Judy, and I'm sure you know it. He has to go his own way and learn from his own mistakes.'

'I know. I'd just feel a whole lot better if I knew exactly where he was and what he was up to.'

And Ricky was still on her mind when she finally said goodnight, and Blake quaintly took her across the corridor and slid her key card into her own door.

'Am I allowed a goodnight kiss?' he said.

'I didn't think you needed to ask – '

She didn't mean it as provocatively as it sounded. She just meant that he'd never asked before, he'd just taken whatever he wanted.

'Then I won't.' And then she was in his arms, and the kiss was long and lingering, and Judy found herself melting into him, and holding him tightly to her. Unconsciously, her fingers gently raked the hair at the nape of his neck. She could feel every sinew of his body pressed tightly against her, and even a fool could tell that he was sexually aroused by the sudden close contact.

And then he abruptly released her.

'If I don't let you go now, Judy, I won't be responsible for my actions. And you're far too vulnerable and soft in my arms, even though I know it's only because I've plied you with far too much wine. So goodnight, and sweet dreams.'

He gently pushed her inside her own room, and as she closed the door, she leaned against it for a moment with her eyes closed. She could still breathe in the scent of him. She could still taste him. And without warning, she felt a flood of emotion, knowing how much she wanted him.

It wasn't just the wine that had made her yearn towards him. It was partly the so-gentlemanly behaviour he had displayed, when she knew only too well what a dangerous charmer he could be . . . but wasn't that what every woman secretly wanted? An impeccable escort in public, and a tiger in the bedroom . . .

Willing the thoughts away, Judy stumbled across the room, not wanting to put on the light, since her head was starting to throb. She undressed with unsteady hands. All she wanted to do was to fall into bed and sleep until morning, and not to admit that, even though she had only known him for a few days, she was already falling in love with Blake Adams.

* * *

Blake knew he was a fool for letting his feelings run away with him. But Judy Hale was nothing like he had expected her to be. He'd imagined someone as hard-bitten as Maggie. He knew only too well how hard a dancer's life could be, and how it took its toll on a person's mind and body, and somehow he'd never expected this exquisitely beautiful girl to come into his life and start to turn it upside down so quickly.

He'd never expected to find his emotions so stirred by anyone ever again. He couldn't deny that he'd had his share of beautiful women, but not since Claire had anyone else come remotely near to penetrating the barrier he'd put up against any serious involvement. He still wasn't sure if he was prepared for anyone to do that yet, not even the deliciously exciting Judy Hale.

With an impatient curse, he strode into his office and dialled Harry Brady's London number. He got the answering machine's reply, and snapped into his phone.

'I know you're there, Harry, so pick up the damn phone. It's Blake here, and we've got some serious talking to do.'

He knew that would do it. Harry was a lazy bastard, Blake thought irritably. He often left his machine on to sift his calls and ignored those that he didn't want to answer.

'I was in the bathroom, Blake,' he heard Harry's nasal voice say glibly a few minutes later. 'What's up? There's no problem with Judy, is there? Or won't she play ball?' he added with a chuckle. 'I told you she

112

was an ice maiden, didn't I? Not even your undoubted charm will melt that one, but I didn't think you'd be ready to admit defeat yet.'

'Shut up, you moron. It's not about Judy that I'm calling. She's fine, but you know I don't like my people to have anything on their minds that's going to stop them concentrating on the job.'

He heard Harry sigh. 'You mean young Ricky, I suppose. What has she told you?'

'Nothing, that's why I'm calling you. If she knew what he was doing and where he was, she'd be happier – and so would I, since I've no wish to have him turning up here,' he snapped. 'So what do you know?'

'What makes you think I know anything?'

'Come on, Harry, I know you too well. I know you've acted as some kind of guardian angel to the pair of them, incredible though I find it. So, if anybody's got a tag on where the boy is, it's you.'

'Hasn't Judy said anything?'

Blake was on to it at once. 'So you do know something. You'd better tell me fast.'

'Do you take this much interest in all your employees' welfare, Blake?' Harry taunted. 'Or is it just this particular one? Is she getting to you, boy?'

'Damn it, I've told you my reasons, so do I have to come over there and wring it out of you?'

'All right,' Harry capitulated, surprised that Blake was getting into such a stew over the girl. He hadn't acted like this since Claire, and it must be more than ten years ago now since it all ended. He'd been no more than twenty-one at the time, and nearly demented, Harry remembered.

He could hear Blake's heavy breathing at the other end of the line, and his impatience was as evident as if he was in the room. Harry went on hastily.

'OK. Ricky wrote to me a while ago asking where Judy was, in his usual panic, and short of cash as usual.'

'I thought you said he was only into gambling in a small way – '

'It might have started small by Las Vegas standards, Blake, but I think he's getting into deeper and deeper water. He needs a good shaking – or a good shrink to sort him out.'

'All Judy wants right now is to know where he is.'

'I've already told her that,' Harry retorted. 'He's up in Oregon at a place called Seaside, and he's run out of money as always. I sent him fifty quid.'

'Did you tell him she was here in Vegas?'

'No,' Harry said shortly. 'He's a jinx, and he'll ruin everything for her. Take my advice and keep out of it.'

'I'd much prefer to, but it seems as if I'm damn well in it now. Give me the last address you had for him.'

'What the hell do you think you can do? I tell you, Blake, he's bad news – '

'I don't know what I can do yet, but it's time you stopped playing God,' he snapped. 'If Judy wants to contact her brother, she should have that choice. Just as long as he keeps well out of my way,' he added, in case Harry thought he was going soft.

Harry reluctantly reeled off the address from the letter he'd supposedly destroyed, and Blake rang off.

He admitted that he never normally interfered with any employee's business, but Judy had got under his skin against all his instincts. She was as different from Claire as could be, except in one respect. Claire had been a dancer too, and headed for the big time until it all went wrong . . .

He switched his thoughts away from the painful memories and concentrated on thinking what to do about Ricky Hale. He could feel sorry for anyone getting a real taste of gambling fever, especially when he was little more than a kid.

Despite the success of his gambling empire, Blake always told his croupiers to keep a weather-eye out for those who looked as though they thought the world was going to be theirs for the throw of a dice or the turn of a card.

He punched the details of Ricky Hale's Oregon address into his computer, and threw his scribbled note into the waste-paper basket. There was no sense in worrying about it any more tonight.

Judy felt more relaxed by the next day, and Blake decided that unless she brought up the matter of her brother, he'd say nothing about his phone call. The last thing he wanted was for her to go tearing upstate to find him.

He told himself it was because of her commitment to her job, and because he was paying her, and paying her damn well. But he knew it was more than that. He liked having her around. She was like a breath of home – not that he had ever planned to go back for good. But she brought the freshness of the English countryside with her and, until now, he had never realized how much he had been missing it.

'You look rested,' he told her over lunch. 'Did you sleep well last night?'

'Yes, I did, though I think it was probably the wine that knocked me out. Apart from seeing the show, the rest of the evening is a bit of a haze to me. Except for that lovely supper, of course.'

And the sight of his bedroom, and that goodnight kiss that had stirred her so much, and started her dreaming . . .

'Frank tells me he wants to concentrate on the finale of the show for the rest of the week, so I can take some time off if I like, before we get down to the nitty-gritty. I hope you don't object.'

'Why should I?'

'Well, you are the boss, aren't you? I wouldn't like you to think I'm taking liberties just because we speak the same language – wasn't that how you put it?'

'If Frank says you can take time off, then he knows that he's doing, Judy. I leave such matters to him, and you don't have to answer to me for every little thing.'

Knowing that it sounded as if he was giving her the brush-off, he added, 'We'll both take tomorrow off, and I'll take you to see Old Vegas.'

'Oh, that's not necessary, really. I can easily take a bus. Frank says I only have to call the bus depot and arrange my ticket – '

He ignored her arguments. 'Never mind what Frank says. It's no fun on your own, and it gets a damn sight hotter the further south you go. Besides, didn't your mother ever tell you that everything's more fun when it's shared by two?'

She laughed. 'My mother told me a lot of things, but I don't ever remember her telling me that!'

'I'm telling you, then,' he said, and she couldn't miss the sudden warmth in his eyes.

Blake hadn't really thought seriously about going to Old Vegas, but why not? he asked himself. If he couldn't take time out whenever he wanted it, what was the point in owning anything? He could almost hear his father saying something vaguely similar:

If a millowner can't enjoy the fruits of his labours, then what's the point in having money? It's there to be used, lad, not to be hoarded like some damn miser.

But it had been a different matter when he'd wanted to turn his back on it and go to London. There had been a hell of a tussle then before he got his own way. And to think that he and Judy Hale had been living in the same city for a couple of years, and he'd never known it. But while Judy had still been thinking about her future career, he had become involved with Claire until tragedy struck their lives.

Soon afterwards, while he was still in a state of total shock, his father had died, and he'd had to go back to Yorkshire and sort out his life, whether he wanted to or not.

'You've become very pensive,' Judy said, noticing how quiet he had gone. He was far more complex a character than she had at first supposed, she thought, and the attractively rugged lines on his face, which came with maturity, would usually disguise a certain pain that he couldn't always hide.

'I called Harry Brady last night, and I was trying to decide whether or not to tell you,' he invented abruptly.

'Good Lord, you're not going to give me the sack already, are you?' she asked, still good-humoured.

'Of course not. But I got an address for you.'

For a second she didn't connect what he was saying. And then he saw her face redden and become so animated that it was luminously beautiful.

'Ricky – ' she breathed, and Blake found himself wishing he could produce that look on his own account. She obviously had very strong feelings for this tearaway brother.

'That's right,' he replied. 'And I hope you're not about to accuse me of interfering.'

Impulsively, she caught at his hand. 'You can interfere all you like, if it means I can find out what's happening to Ricky. Once I know he's OK I'll stop worrying about him.'

Privately, Blake doubted that. And unfortunately, he thought he knew the type only too well. Once a gambler got hooked at an early age, there was a fair chance of it lasting a lifetime.

'Was there a phone number?' she asked.

'Harry didn't say so, but you can check with the phone company by giving them the address.'

'I'll do it this afternoon. I can't thank you enough, Blake. Harry said he'd destroyed Ricky's letter. He can be a prize rat when he wants to.'

Blake could think of plenty of ways she could thank him, but this wasn't the time to take unfair advantage. Besides, she was so grateful to him now, he could shelve any thoughts of favours for the time being.

'Do you want me to do it for you?'

Judy shook her head. 'No, this is my problem, Blake, and you've done more than enough already.'

She looked at him, seeing the concern in his eyes, and a feeling of warmth flowed through her. No matter how macho he was, and how much of a chauvinistic streak he had, deep down there had to be a very genuine man.

'I'll let you know the outcome. And thank you again.'

'Just stop thanking me, will you? I'd do it for anybody. I like to keep a happy crew on my ship,' he said roughly.

And that just about brought her back to earth, before she began to think his interest was truly personal.

Judy abandoned any idea of work that afternoon. Once Blake had given her the information she needed, she shut herself in her suite and dialled the telephone company's information number, giving the necessary details, and waiting for what

119

seemed to be an interminable time before the girl answered again.

But she finally got the Seaside number in Oregon, and she dialled it quickly, aware that her heart pounded, knowing she was longing, and yet dreadling, to hear Ricky's voice. That was the way it always was . . .

'Yes? Who is it?' came a woman's scratchy voice that sounded less than welcoming.

Judy swallowed. 'I've been given this number for a Ricky – Richard – Hale. May I speak to him, please?'

There was a pause at the other end, and then the woman spoke sharply. 'Are you from the cops?'

'No! Why should I be?' Judy said, her heart sinking.

'Because the bum owes me a month's rent, that's why, and I ain't running no charity house. I'll see the little toerag behind bars if it's the last thing I do, and I ain't the only one he owes money too, neither – '

Judy slammed down the phone, her hands shaking. It was just as bad as she had feared. Trouble didn't just follow Ricky around. It was his middle name, and she had been available far too often to pick up the pieces.

But despite the fact that he was almost twenty-one now, he was still her brother, even though Harry said it was high time she let him stand on his own two feet.

Now it looked as if she would have to do just that, since she had no idea where he could have gone. He was a fool, but he was her brother, and when he'd reached out to her for help, Harry had fobbed him off with fifty pounds, she thought bitterly, all on account of her precious job and his fat commission. Knowing Ricky as well as she did, the handout would have gone nowhere.

The small hope she'd had of finding him in Oregon fizzled and died, and she felt close to crying with frustration. She had promised to let Blake know the outcome of the call, though he probably wouldn't really care, she thought miserably. In any case, she couldn't do it, not yet. She was simply too full of anxiety to speak to anyone.

CHAPTER 7

Ricky Hale had always considered himself street-smart, but he was in one hell of a mess now. He'd got in with a poker-playing crowd in Seaside, and they wiped the floor with him to the tune of five hundred dollars that he didn't have.

He'd left them his IOUs, promising to settle when the bank opened next morning, knowing damn well that he didn't have an account there, or anywhere else, for that matter. His luck was running out, and he was finally realizing it.

But he'd been born a blinkered optimist, always believing that something good was bound to happen eventually. Nobody could have a run of bad luck for ever. By the law of averages, sooner or later it was bound to change. It was just a bloody long time in coming, Ricky thought grimly.

He'd thought hard after he'd left the poker players in the back room of the saloon. He was well aware that their threats of a beating, if he didn't pay up, were all too real. He'd seen it happen too often to others. He knew he'd played himself for a real fool this time, and in a small town like this one there was nowhere to hide. So the sooner he got out of Seaside, the better.

In the middle of the night, he threw his few belongings into his rucksack and climbed silently out of his bedroom window in the rooming-house, jumping with catlike efficiency on to the back-porch roof, and into the yard below. He listened for a while, but there was no sound, and he sped off into the night towards the main highway.

From there, he'd easily hitched a ride with a trucker, going anywhere, just as long as it was away from Seaside.

'Where're you heading for, young feller?' the trucker called out as he pulled up alongside him.

'I don't have any set place to go. Wherever you're heading is fine by me,' Ricky said.

'Well, I'm due in Reno by morning, so if that suits, I'll be mighty glad of the company. It gets pretty boring travelling on these roads at night.'

'I'll bet it does, and thanks.' Ricky climbed aboard the truck, hardly able to believe his luck.

Reno! The town that claimed to be The Biggest Little City in the World, according to all the reports he'd ever read about the place, more glittering and longer established than Atlantic City, and a gambler's paradise.

Ricky had never been to Reno before, but the fact that fate had sent him on the right road had to mean that his luck was changing for the better, just as he'd always known it would. His natural optimism was reasserting itself with every mile south that the truck covered.

* * *

Judy knew she wouldn't be able to face Blake without bursting into tears, and she had no intention of doing any such thing. So she finally dialled his study extension number on the phone. When he answered, she could picture him now, busy with his papers and business affairs, and she felt suddenly embarrassed to be bothering him with her problems. He'd taken on more than he realized when he had employed her . . .

'Blake?' she said, her voice husky.

He knew at once why she was calling him. 'Did you have any luck?'

'None at all. A woman answered, and she sounded less than pleased when I mentioned Ricky's name. She said – she said he owed her a month's rent, and that she wasn't the only one he owed money to. Now he's gone, and I've no idea where. I'm sorry to have bothered you with all this.'

Knowing that she couldn't bear to hear any platitudes or sympathy, she quickly put down the phone, fighting back the tears. A few minutes later, she heard a knock on her door. She was tempted not to answer it, knowing it would be him. But he persisted, and in the end she had to let him in.

'If you hadn't answered, I'd simply have got the master key and let myself in,' he said arrogantly. 'Why are you so resistant to letting anybody help you, Judy?'

'It's not that. You've already done more than I've any right to expect, and it got me nowhere, except to be even more worried. Not that I'm blaming you, Blake. I'm very grateful, but it hasn't helped.'

'So where do you go from here? You could always get a detective agency on to it, or the police.'

'Definitely not the police! And if some snooping detective found out that Ricky had done something really criminal, he'd have to report it, wouldn't he?'

'So what's the alternative?' he said, forcing her to make a decision, while constantly wondering why he was letting himself get so involved.

'We do nothing,' she told him shakily. 'Except that I'll insist to Harry that if Ricky gets in touch again, he's to tell him to stay exactly where he is and I'll reach him. Does that sound reasonable?'

'It sounds more than reasonable to me.'

And it solved the problem of giving him the Sparkling Rocks address, and risking him disrupting everything here. He had every sympathy for Judy and the kid, even though he thought him a real idiot if he'd already got in so deeply. But he was wise enough not to say so to Judy right now.

There was a lot of truth in the saying that blood was thicker than water. It was proving true in this case, and all Judy wanted to do was to see that her brother was all right. She was the older sister, even if only by a few years. Harry had told him she'd taken care of Ricky when their parents died. He couldn't blame her for her continuing protectiveness of him, however misplaced it seemed to him.

'I'm better now,' she went on more calmly. 'And if you don't mind, I'm going to take a walk to try and clear my head, then I'll call Harry later.'

'Why don't you leave that to me? I'll be less emotional about it, and more likely to make Harry see what he's got to do. Will you trust me with it?'

'Yes – and thank you.' She agreed because she simply felt unable to protest any more. 'I don't think I could cope with any of Harry's arguments, anyway. He never really appreciated my closeness to Ricky.'

'Don't blame him for that. Harry's never lost anybody, so he doesn't know how it feels. Not that you've lost Ricky for good. Think of him as just temporarily misplaced.'

She gave the ghost of a smile, knowing he was doing his best to cheer her up. And registering vaguely from his forced tone that she wasn't the only one who had lost somebody.

Only maybe in Blake's case it hadn't just been temporary . . . but she couldn't spare a thought about that now.

Once he had left her, she changed her clothes for a cool pair of slacks and thin top, knowing it was going to be hot and humid outside. It was hardly a country-fresh atmosphere, but she needed to get away from the sterile air-conditioning of the hotel and to feel the sun on her head and whatever breeze there was in her hair.

Even if it was little more than a breeze stirred up by the volume of traffic travelling at a snail's pace down the Strip, rather than clean fresh air.

She walked for an hour, hardly seeing anything, and when she found herself at the far end of the Strip, she saw she was outside the bus depot. Without any real interest, she scanned the bus timetables, and wondered if she should book a seat to Old Vegas after all, rather than let Blake take her there. She was already becoming far too dependent on him.

But the heat of the day was making her lethargic, and in the end she couldn't be bothered to make the effort to book a trip. Besides, a ride in a luxury limo was much more inviting.

She knew she was probably taking the easy way out, but even if Blake reverted to making a play for her, he had shown a more caring side to his nature that she hadn't suspected.

Harry had told her he was a great guy, of course, but then, Harry was always respectful of somebody with money and influence. It went with the job, and it was part of his own oily nature.

What she hadn't known was that with Blake's inheritance behind him, he probably hadn't needed to build such an empire at all. He could simply have sat back and enjoyed the role of playboy. That he hadn't done so earned Judy's respect as well, even if running a casino wasn't the best choice of empire, in her opinion. But it was his life . . .

She was vaguely aware of a car cruising along beside her. She kept right on walking, not letting the driver know she had any inkling of him until she heard a voice call out to her.

'Do you want a ride, or do you intend wearing out your feet unnecessarily?'

She turned at once, to see Frank leaning out of his open-topped convertible.

'Why aren't you working?' she asked him, unable to think of anything else to say at that moment.

'I am. I needed to see some magazine ad proofs before they go to print, and I don't trust anyone else to do it.'

It might have sounded arrogant coming from anyone else, but Judy knew how important it was to have everything exactly right when it came to advertising.

'So are you getting in the car, or am I going to risk being arrested for kerb-crawling?'

He had already stopped the car, and she laughed, opening the door and sitting beside him with a sense of relief, only just realizing how far she had walked and how much her feet ached.

'I hope I haven't upset you in any way since you've been here, kid.' He glanced at her as he spoke. 'You'll learn that I soon get over my tantrums.'

'Don't worry, I understand the temperament only too well, and it never bothers me for long. I'll admit that it smarts at the time, but it usually makes sense in the end.'

'Good. I'd like to think of us as friends rather than enemies.'

'I never thought of you as an enemy, Frank!'

'No? Not even when you never expected to have to answer to somebody else when you took on this job?'

She had the grace to blush. 'Oh well, I soon got over that as well. I had to, didn't I? I'm no *prima donna*.'

'I know that. It's what's so refreshing about you, hon.'

As he spoke he put his hand on her knee for a brief moment, and she removed it pleasantly but firmly.

'I'm glad you're my friend, Frank, but I'm not prepared to be that friendly.'

He laughed. 'OK. But you can't blame a guy for trying, can you?'

'Frank, will you tell me something?' she said after a moment's awkward silence.

'If I can.'

'I may be speaking out of turn, but I really need to know. Is Blake married? Or has he ever been?'

'Not that I'm aware of. If so, he's kept it damn quiet from everybody at the Rocks!'

'Divorced, then?' she persisted, as if some mischievous devil was driving her on to know.

'As far as I know, he's never been married, but I don't enquire into his private life. Soon after he came here we'd both had plenty to drink one night, and he did say something about a fiancée back in England. But I had a hell of a hangover next morning, and I don't remember anything more. And you never heard that from me, right?'

'Heard what?' she countered. But her mind was working overtime now, wondering what had gone wrong. And she was pretty certain that the girl in the photograph with Blake had been the one.

They had arrived at the casino now, and Frank parked his car in his private parking space. As Judy got out, the blast of hot air hit her once more. There was never a happy medium, she thought. It was either blistering heat, or air-conditioned enough to freeze the proverbial brass monkeys.

But she felt calmer now than before she went out, and more able to put Ricky's self-inflicted problems into a sensible and logical perspective. If there was no way she could get in touch with him, then there was nothing she could do to help him.

She could only hope that Harry would listen to Blake, and that if Ricky contacted him again, as he surely would, he would let him know she was here. It was ridiculous. They were both in America, both wanting to get in touch, and neither of them knew where the other was. Though you could hardly compare the size of the States with tracking somebody down in England!

As she went back to her suite, her thoughts took a sudden curve, remembering Frank's visit to the magazine offices that afternoon to check on the ads for the forthcoming Danny Corsey show. What if she advertised in newspapers for Ricky Hale to contact a Las Vegas number?

But almost as soon as the thought entered her head, she knew it wasn't on. If the wrong people saw it, they'd be down here like a shot, demanding money out of her to pay Ricky's debts. She couldn't bring that trouble home to Blake, nor risk a scandal for the hotel. She was angry with herself for thinking the worst about her brother's activities, but she had a gut feeling that this time it would be really bad.

But once Blake assured her that Harry had promised to let Ricky know she'd get in touch with him the minute they all knew where he was, she felt a mite easier. From then on, she tried to put Ricky's troubles on the back burner of her mind, and to get on with her own life.

* * *

130

Blake had informed her they were taking tomorrow off and going down to Old Vegas. It wasn't a suggestion, or an invitation, it was simply an order. Take it or leave it. Judy took it.

He drove the limo himself, and she was relieved that they didn't have the uniformed chauffeur sitting up front while they behaved like company in the back.

This way, she could sit beside Blake and watch as the car slid smoothly away from the bright lights and out through the suburbs, and into the wild open country that was so incredibly near to the vibrant city.

'Impressive by its emptiness, isn't it? Doesn't it remind you of all those old black-and-white movies, with the tumbleweed rolling about the prairies and the Indians coming over the hill with their war cries?'

Judy laughed. 'You're reading me like a book! Only I was adding a bit more to it. I was remembering how a whole crowd of us used to go to the old fleapit cinema near our home every Saturday morning when we were kids, and every film star wearing a stetson and spurs was our hero.'

'It sounds like fun. We never had a fleapit cinema where I lived, and I never went anywhere with a crowd of other kids on Saturday mornings. Our place was too remote for that.'

'Poor little rich boy,' Judy said without thinking.

'Well, hardly in the way you mean it, I just didn't have much company of my own age until I went to boarding-school and then university, of course. Life got considerably wilder then, and I realized what I'd been missing all those years.'

The more snippets Judy heard about his early days, the more she knew they were poles apart. It may not have been the life of the landed gentry, but it was a far easier and cushioned life than her own.

'You've gone all broody on me again,' he went on. 'We're out to enjoy ourselves today, Judy, with no dark clouds on the horizon, OK?'

'OK,' she agreed, her eyes automatically seeking out the hazy horizon ahead, in the bluest sky she had ever seen.

But he was right. This day out was for her benefit, and she shouldn't act like a prize pig. The old childhood phrase slipped into her mind. It was something Ricky used to taunt her with when he couldn't get his own way with her. Prize pig. She gave a small chuckle and Blake glanced at her.

'Well, that's better. Whatever's triggered your memory now, I'm glad it's made you smile.'

'You wouldn't want to know – '

'Try me.'

'It's just that I was telling myself not to spoil the day and be a prize pig. It was what Ricky used to call me when we were kids. And it sounds really stupid now, and I wish I hadn't told you,' she finished lamely.

'I think it's charming. I wish I'd had somebody around to call me a prize pig when I was young. I'm sure I was, but nobody ever cut me down to size. My father was always too busy making money to bother too much about me. It would probably have done me a power of good to be called a prize pig.'

'For goodness' sake, stop it,' Judy couldn't help laughing at the way he was carrying on so seriously. 'I *really* wish I'd never told you now.'

'Why? Don't you think I like to hear about your early days? I want to know everything about you. For instance, there has to have been at least one man in your life. Nobody with your looks and personality could have got this far in life without a serious relationship at some stage.'

'Not if I'm the ice maiden Harry Brady informed you that I was,' she retorted. And she certainly had no intention of telling him anything about Michael. It was too private, and the hurt could still catch her unawares at times.

'Ah, but I no longer believe that. Not when I've had ample proof that you're a responsive, passionate woman. You couldn't hide it for ever, Judy. So tell me about your past.'

'Will you tell me about yours?' she whipped out, holding her breath.

'I've already told you. My life's an open book – '

'What about the photograph in your bedroom? The one with the pretty girl looking up adoringly into your eyes?'

And the confetti in her hair . . .

'That's one chapter that's closed,' he said shortly, and she knew she had gone too far. But this was a game that could be played by two, and she tilted her head determinedly.

'And so is mine.'

They drove on in silence, speeding over the miles, and she was relieved to see the beginnings of civilization. If that's what you could call what seemed at first to be a ramshackle collection of old buildings behind a high fence.

'Old Vegas.' Blake pointed ahead. 'Let's go and be tourists, and forget our troubles.'

She was determined to enjoy the day, despite the fact that the arid, dusty heat of the desert dried her mouth and stung her eyes. But the set pieces of the arranged shoot-outs and the sassy saloon-girl dancers were fun to watch. She was fascinated by the wooden reconstructions of the blacksmith's forge and the assay house for the gold prospectors, and the old-fashioned candy store and the bank.

There was a murky-looking jailhouse and an Indian store, and beyond the main street there was an old cemetery with quaintly worded epitaphs on the tombstones, some made of weathered stone, and others just rough wooden crosses.

'I feel as if I've just stepped on to a movie set, and John Wayne's about to come sailing out of the saloon,' Judy told him with a grin.

'It's probably more than a bit Hollywood-ized,' Blake agreed. 'But they call it an authentic replica of the West. Did you ever hear of Tonepah, by the way?'

'Yes, of course! It was a town that seemed to crop up in every western I ever saw.'

'And you thought it was a boom town, I bet.'

'And?' She half-guessed what was to come.

'It's to the north of Vegas, about halfway between here and Virginia City, and a stopping-place for bus travel nowadays. That's if you want to spend ten hours on a bus instead of taking a one-hour flight. And it's the most ornery one-horse little town in these here parts, if you'll pardon my feeble attempt at John Wayne jargon. It was never anything much, but movie directors can do anything with the right props. And it had the desert all around it, so it was an ideal setting for God knows how many Westerns.'

'And Ricky and I always thought Tonepah was a really huge place! You've disillusioned me now.'

He laughed. 'I believe in saying it like it is, ma'am. Now let's go and get some real Western tucker.'

He was in such a good humour now, and she was getting to like him more and more. She resisted putting a deeper meaning into her feelings about him. She had already told herself it wouldn't do. Once this job was over, she'd be back in England and she doubted that their paths would ever cross again. And she wouldn't admit to the pang she felt about that either, telling herself she couldn't really have fallen in love so soon, and it was fatal to trust her emotions to the kind of philanderer Harry had intimated him to be.

Though she couldn't always trust Harry's words . . .

They had lunch in a large wooden building, where the steaks were big and juicy, the baked potatoes were the size of melons, and the fried onions and red peppers were crisp and mouth-wateringly tangy. The whole atmosphere was nostalgically old-time. The plates were metal, the mugs were tin, and you collected your eating irons from a table loaded with cartons of ketchup, and your coffee from huge tin pouring jugs.

The girls and guys who served up the food wore check shirts and jeans, stetsons and cowboy boots. There was loud saloon music playing the whole time, and Judy was totally charmed by the whole place. It was just like being transported to the OK Corral, she told Blake . . .

'Has Frank ever thought of using this Western theme idea in one of his shows?' she asked, when they'd been escorted to their table, knowing that he surely must have done.

'I believe that's one of his ideas for the new show. Your arrangements will be totally British, and we're having a French and several other European sections, as you know. But I think Frank's quite keen on a Wild West theme, providing we give the customers plenty of what they really come to see.'

'And what's that?' Judy said, her mouth already watering at the thought of tackling the huge steak on her plate now.

'Girls, of course. Girls, girls, and more girls, topless and glamorous. It's what Vegas is all about, Judy. We give them the most beautiful girls in the world. And before you say that's completely sexist, we all know damn well that it is. But you'll never change human nature, no matter how politically correct you profess to be.'

She had to agree with that. Besides, in her book nothing was taboo if it was tastefully done. And what was wrong with nudity, for pity's sake? You were born naked, and anybody with a beautiful body had every right to be proud of it . . .

'And what's going through that gorgeous head of yours now?' Blake asked, sitting opposite her at the

136

wooden table and looking at her sardonically. 'You're not going all prim on me, are you? If so, you've come to the wrong place.'

'Of course not. I've been in this business too long for that. I was agreeing with you, actually.'

'Well, notch one up to me, then!' he grinned.

Judy gave all her attention to the marvellous meal then, thankful he couldn't really guess what had been on her mind.

But the very thought of a beautiful body had made her think only of him. He had the lithe, virile body of a very sexy man, and for those moments she had been imagining him as she had once seen him in a dream . . . slowly and tantalizingly stripping off his clothes, and revealing that strong, muscular, tanned body to her alone . . .

'More onions, ma'am?' she heard one of the cruising waitresses say, and the moment was gone.

But she thoroughly enjoyed the day out, and even though she had learned nothing about the thing she dearly wanted to know from Blake, and couldn't seem to ask, at least she knew a little more about him than before.

It wasn't all fun being rich and isolated, she admitted. No wonder such kids went on the wild side when they went to university after such a lonely existence.

But she still didn't know anything about the girl in the photo, and she knew she had been snubbed when she broached the subject. Whoever she was, she had clearly meant something very special in Blake's life, and he meant to keep it private.

She made up her mind not to pry any more, and hoped she would be able to keep up her good intentions. And by the time they got back to Vegas in the late afternoon, she was more than ready for a nap, and then to take room service dinner and spend the evening watching television.

The Danny Corsey show was destined to be a wild success. It was his first time in Vegas, and Frank told Judy that a large number of hotels had been trying to book him for months. It was the Sparkling Rocks that had finally got him after his New York summer season, to everybody's delight.

During the early hours of the following Monday morning, once the current show had been put to bed, the electricians would set to work dismantling the dazzling advertising displays that had been there for the past three months.

And within hours the array of lights outside the Sparkling Rocks casino would have changed, and be blazing out Danny Corsey's name in metre-high lights. Judy had heard of him, of course. Who hadn't? He was one of the old style of singers, in the Perry Como-cum-Andy Williams mould, and he must be well over sixty years of age if he was a day.

But one of the things Judy had always admired about American fans was that they were unfailingly loyal to their favourites. And Danny Corsey was still big and blonde (even if it was less than natural these days), rugged and beautiful. He had a larger-than-life presence on stage that was undeniable. And when he sang his midnight-blues type of romantic songs, every woman in the audience believed he sang them to her alone.

During the past week, and since the trip to Old Vegas, Judy had checked out some of the shows in the other casinos. It was obviously the usual thing for solo singers to come down among the audiences and shake everybody's hand and sing a few bars especially to each person. It was over the top, it was sometimes almost embarrassingly personal, and it was always a terrific hit.

She was sure that Danny Corsey would do exactly the same, and knew that the older ladies in particular, would love it.

When she was introduced to him, he took her hand and raised it to his lips. It wasn't so different from the way Blake had done it, but this time she felt an urge to snatch her hand away. It wasn't that he was oily in the way Harry was oily. It was just that in the flesh there seemed to be nothing behind those surely-too-richly-blue contact lenses.

She said as much to Blake when they met for lunch later.

'That's because all his energy goes into projecting himself on stage. He's an incredible act to watch, and he gives it everything he's got when he's swanning around the ladies in his audience. I don't mean that disrespectfully, because they love it. But it seems to me there's nothing left over for his private life.'

'How very perceptive of you!'

'Not really. I've just seen it happen before, that's all. And since he's always been a bit of a loner, I guess it suits Danny to be so obsessively single-minded. He's happy enough with his touring entourage and his adoring fans. That's fine at his age, and I know he'll go on until he drops. It's when that kind of obsession hits somebody younger and takes over their life, that it can turn sour.'

'Are you speaking personally?' she dared to ask.

He seemed to get her properly into focus then, and she knew with absolute certainty that he had been somewhere in his past, to a place she didn't know, and where he had no intention of letting anyone in.

'I was just making a general observation,' he said.

And she knew damn well that he wasn't.

'Do you want to see Corsey's first-night performance with me?' he went on.

'I certainly think I should. I'm eager to see what this paragon has got that makes so many women rave over him.'

Blake laughed, and the small tension between them was lifted. 'Just don't expect any Tom Jones gyrations, that's all. Our Danny's a little too stiff in the joints for that, though he'd be furious if he thought anybody suggested it.'

'Then I won't. But in other words, he's got an ego of gigantic proportions, right?' Judy guessed.

'You could say that, but when you know you're the best, it's understandable, isn't it?'

Looking in on his first rehearsal, Judy wasn't altogether sure that she liked the real Danny Corsey. He had demanded that this first one must be in the

Diamond Showroom to ensure that he got the full effect that he wanted from his minions.

He was scathing with his musicians and frequently swore at them. Judy didn't like his brusqueness with the lighting engineers, and she could tell that his demands for flattering spotlights wherever he moved among the audience were going to stretch even their ingenuity to the limit.

After a while she slipped out of the auditorium without him even being aware that she was there. In any case, there were already plenty of admiring people at his beck and call, including his PR girls and his manager, and also some of the showgirls who weren't rehearsing that afternoon.

'What did you think of him, Judy?' the girl called Paige fell into step with her as she went towards the nearest elevator. 'He's quite a doll, isn't he?'

'I know he's got a great voice, but he's not really my favourite. I've never seen him perform live, of course.'

'You'll be converted as soon as you do. My Mom heard him years ago, and she's got all his old show posters and had all his old forty-fives converted to CDs. I think she's got every one he ever recorded, and that's some collection.'

'Wow,' Judy murmured, hoping she sounded impressed, and wondering what size house Paige's mom must have.

'See you tomorrow, then, Judy,' the girl said now. 'We start rehearsals at ten a.m., don't we?'

'On the button,' Judy agreed cheerfully, trying to disguise how suddenly nervous she was about the whole thing. She knew her ideas were good, and Frank had approved the second set of sketches she'd been working on all week. So there was no reason on earth for her to feel nervous . . .

CHAPTER 8

The next weeks were very hectic ones for Judy. She needed to establish herself with the dancers and all the backroom boys and girls associated with staging a new show. There were always hiccups when somebody new came on the scene, and she had little time to worry about her brother's problems.

In fact, as far as Ricky was concerned, she made herself believe that no news was good news, however misguided her assumption so often proved.

But as she threw herself into her work, she came to have a new respect and admiration for Frank's methods, and was relieved to find she had a healthy rapport with Maggie. The girls too, once they realized she knew her job backwards, responded to whatever she wanted from them. The whole show had to co-ordinate, and the separate parts had to merge into one another, while still retaining their own identity.

Judy knew that an International Spectacular wasn't new in Las Vegas. Other casino showplaces had staged them, but it was a first for the Sparkling

Rocks, and as always, Blake wanted and expected his show to be the best.

But the work was tiring, mentally and physically. Like the good choreographer that she was, Judy never put her dancers through any routines she couldn't do herself. But the new show was taking shape well by the time the opening was little more than a week away. And Judy had begun to feel more than ragged with all the effort she had put into it in these past three months.

'Do you like horses?' Blake asked her abruptly, the weekend before Danny Corsey's show was due to close.

She looked at him, a little startled. 'If you're thinking of including a Wild West theme in the show, it's a little late for that, and I don't think Frank will take kindly to it – '

'I wasn't thinking about the show. I just asked if you like horses, that's all,' he retorted.

'Well, there weren't too many horses in the streets where I grew up, so I don't really know,' she hedged drily. But presumably there would have been some in the horse-riding Yorkshire countryside of Blake's background.

'We'll go and see some tomorrow then. There are some people I'd like you to meet, and I'm sure you can do with a break away from here before the new show begins.'

She looked at him in some annoyance. He was dictating to her again, and she was prepared to argue. 'I'm not sure I want to spend Sunday at

144

some rodeo or other, if that's what you had in mind – '

'Why must you always jump to conclusions? A rodeo is not what I had in mind, anyway. Some friends of mine own a ranch and I'm invited to Sunday brunch. It's always open house, and I thought you might like to see how other folk live around here. Las Vegas isn't all about glitter and glamour, despite the image it likes to present. So what do you say?'

It sounded such a refreshing idea that she stopped prevaricating at once. 'I say yes – if you're sure your friends won't mind me tagging along uninvited.'

He grinned. 'Actually, they're dying to meet you, so be ready about noon, and wear something casual. Nobody stands on ceremony at the Coopers'.'

He was called away on his pager then, and Judy stared thoughtfully after his elegant figure as he wove his way in and out of the crowded casino. She wondered suddenly if he ever hankered over the kind of lives these ranch friends lived. Living in a proper home, rather than an undoubtedly luxurious apartment on top of the job, must sometimes be appealing. It wasn't the same as putting down roots, though, and could never be compared with a real family home.

But she had thought this was just a casual invitation, until his throwaway remark that his friends were dying to meet her. She couldn't think why, unless she was considered a bit of a novelty to them because she was a fellow Brit.

It didn't worry her, anyway.

* * *

By the time she got up on that brilliant Sunday morning, she realized how much she was looking forward to visiting someone's home, and getting away from the tacky heat of the Strip, if only for a few hours. The Las Vegas casinos were wild and wonderful, and the hotels were the ultimate in luxury, but in no way could they be called homely.

In the three months that Judy had been here now, life had been really hectic with all the rehearsals for the new show. But it wasn't as if she didn't also enjoy a more normal kind of life as well.

She had been out on various occasions with Frank or Blake or one of the show-girls on a shopping spree, but until now, she had never really stopped to think how much she missed the comfort and relaxation of being in a real home.

Not that she imagined the Nevada ranch would be anything like the small, cramped house in London in which she and Ricky had grown up! *That* had hardly had room to swing the proverbial cat, let alone relax. But it had been home, all the same.

That morning she dressed in an easy pair of blue jeans and a soft checked shirt. Casual gear was what Blake had decreed, and she hoped he had really meant it. She met him in the hotel foyer at noon and to her relief she saw that he was similarly dressed. And far from detracting from his wealthy owner aura, it enhanced his ruggedly outdoor appearance, and had plenty of female heads turning his way, as usual.

'The newcomers here probably think you're a movie star, dressing downmarket for the sake of anonymity,' Judy spoke mischievously and without thinking as they walked towards the limo that had been brought round to the canopied entrance.

'I like the sound of that remark, madam,' he grinned, as he opened the limo door for her and then slid behind the steering-wheel on the other side.

'What remark? That you could be mistaken for a movie star? Oh Lord, I didn't mean to swell your ego, but I might have known it would,' she returned with a mock groan as the car glided smoothly away from the hotel.

'You didn't.' He laughed. 'No, I meant the way you referred to other people as newcomers. You obviously don't think of yourself that way any longer.'

'Hardly. I've been here three months now, so that qualifies me for residency, I think, however temporary. Although I remember that Frank once asked me if I thought I could live here permanently, and I rather surprised myself by saying that I thought I could probably adapt to it.'

She spoke teasingly, just making conservation, and she wasn't fishing for an invitation to stay on when her second three months were up. But she didn't miss the way Blake's hands tightened on the steering-wheel at her words.

'You've been seeing quite a lot of Frank lately, haven't you?' Blake said as they headed south, away from the Strip and the residential area of the city, and out towards the desert.

'I can hardly avoid him in working hours, but we've also been out together on a number of occasions. I like him, but we've established firm ground rules between us. We're friends, and nothing more. Is that what you wanted to hear?'

She didn't have to qualify it, and she was half-annoyed with herself for doing so. Remembering Blake's bet with Harry, it might have been a good idea to let him think there really was something going on between herself and Frank, but she couldn't be bothered with such guile.

Petty attempts at arousing jealousy had always seemed pointless and immature to her, and she couldn't forget the many times Michael had done it, almost to the point of cruelty, before it had finally dawned on her that his taunts about his exploits with other women were all true.

She quickly turned her thoughts away from Michael before they became maudlin.

'Sunday brunch is quite a big thing out here, isn't it, Blake? I've seen it advertised all over the place.'

'It certainly is, and I hope you didn't eat much breakfast. Ginny and Kyle always put on a huge feast as if they're expecting a cast of thousands. I hope you like kids too,' he added as an afterthought.

Just like a man, he hadn't thought to mention this before, Judy thought. 'Of course I do. How many are there?'

'Bobby's ten and Zoe's just seven. She's my god-daughter, so obviously I take a special interest in her. And what do you find so amusing about that?' he asked, sensing her smile.

'It's just that whenever I think I know you, you come out with something that surprises me, that's all. Somebody with a goddaughter sounds quite human, and not just a casino figurehead hell-bent on getting richer all the time.' She paused for breath. 'And now I've really insulted you, haven't I?'

He laughed out loud. 'Good God, no! It's refreshing to have somebody saying just what they think. That's the way I was brought up, in case you've forgotten. Plain-speaking Yorkshire no-nonsense was the order of the day in my family. They said what they meant, and meant what they said. But I'm glad you think I'm human after all, and not just a moneymaking machine.'

'Now you're laughing at me,' she protested, but more than thankful that he hadn't taken offence at her comments. It would be a shame to let anything spoil this lovely day.

'Well, that beats crying, doesn't it?'

And she had done her share of that, thought Judy. But as they sped towards the wilder open country now, flanked by the blue-hazed mountains, she knew she was happier than she had been in a very long time. She had the job of her dreams . . . and the man of her dreams sitting beside her . . .

'The Cooper place is in front of us now,' Blake said a little later, pointing ahead.

In between the vast stretches of open desert scrub, they had passed a number of very comfortable homesteads between Las Vegas and here, and Judy could see the huge fenced area ahead of them now.

149

There were horses grazing in their corrals, and the whole panorama was pastoral and serene, and as far removed in essence from the brashness of Las Vegas as it was possible to be. As they approached, they drove through wide wrought iron gates with elaborately entwined initials of C and R, depicting the Cooper Ranch.

At the end of a winding driveway, the long, low, brick-built building in the centre of all this splendour was also a world away from any homely family house Judy might have imagined. It was *Dallas* and *Dynasty* all rolled into one . . .

'I never expected to see anything like this. It's simply beautiful,' Judy felt bound to say, while the extent of it took her breath away.

And so it was. Anyone who lived here surely had it all; the hot sun and the endless blue sky, and the wide open spaces where you could breathe unpolluted air.

There could be total peace and privacy out here, and yet they were within less than an hour's drive from one of the hottest, brashest, most exciting places on earth. And Judy admitted to herself now that Las Vegas was all of that too, but that since she had been here she had inevitably come under the spell of the place.

As they approached the building, Judy saw the two children running out to meet them, and when Blake stopped the car, he leapt out, swinging the small girl up in his arms.

'How's my best girl today?' he asked with a smile.

'All the better for seeing you, daddy Blake,' she squealed in response, and Judy guessed that this was a ritual greeting between them.

He was so free and easy with her, she thought in some amazement. And maybe if things hadn't gone so wrong between him and Claire, they would have been married by now and had a home and family of their own like this one.

She still didn't know what had happened to break them up, but it must have been something devastating. She couldn't imagine the very macho Blake Adams being the kind of man to let go of someone he loved without a very good reason. She pushed the unwelcome thought out of her mind as she saw Blake put down the child in his arms and turn to her, drawing her into their circle.

'Judy, come and meet Zoe and Bobby.'

The boy showed the mild interest of a ten-year-old. 'Is she your real girl, uncle Blake?' he asked.

'She just might be, you cheeky young monkey!'

Judy half-expected Zoe to show some jealousy at the smile in his voice, but after a moment or two she put her hand into Judy's and looked up at her hopefully.

'When daddy Blake called to tell us you were coming, he said you might teach me to dance after we've had our brunch. So will you?'

Daddy Blake assumed far too much . . . and it was obvious now that these people knew all about her, and that this had been far from a casual invitation. She had been expected . . . but Judy knew better

151

than to dampen a child's enthusiasm, and she rose to the challenge in Zoe's eyes.

'It takes years to learn everything about dancing, Zoe, but I'll certainly teach you a few basic steps.'

She gave a high-pitched giggle. 'You talk a bit like daddy Blake. It's funny.'

Bobby spoke more loftily. 'No, it's not. It's because they both come from England, dope. We're all going there for our summer vacation,' he told Judy importantly as they began to walk towards the house.

'Are you?' Judy was full of interest now. 'Which places are you going to be visiting?'

'I don't really know yet. Everywhere, I expect!'

Judy and Blake exchanged amused glances as they went into the house, which was cool and air-conditioned. They went through the open French windows to the back yard, where the patio furniture was shielded from the rays of the sun by large umbrellas. A burly man dressed in Western gear covered by a striped apron was cooking steaks on a barbecue. The succulent smell made Judy's mouth water at once.

'Ginny, they're here!' he yelled, and turned with a smile to greet the visitors.

'Pay no attention to Ginny's lateness,' he told Judy cheerily. 'It's nothing personal. She was late for our wedding, and she was late delivering the kids, so I guess she'll be late for her own funeral.

He laughed at his own joke, and beckoned Judy nearer. 'Come on out here, honey, and let me take a good look at you.'

152

He did exactly as he said, inspecting her as if she were a prized possession, and then he nodded his approval.

'Yep, Blake, old buddy, I reckon you've found a winner here all right. She's a real beauty, so don't forget to invite us to the weddin'.'

He laughed again, clearly not expecting anybody to take him seriously, even though Judy's heart had leapt at his last words and she didn't dare look at Blake. But she could hardly take offence at Kyle's big, bluff, uninhibited manner. He was one of the world's naturals, saying exactly what he thought, and able to let any censure pass right over his head. No wonder Blake felt so at ease with him.

And Ginny was nothing like she had expected. Any thoughts of *Dallas* and *Dynasty* sophistication flew out of Judy's head as the large, buxom woman came out from the kitchen, red-faced with pleasure at seeing Blake.

'Well, it's about time you got here with this lovely lady you've been telling us about. We began to wonder if she existed at all. You just keep him in line, Judy, honey, and don't let him spend all his time with his dull old accounting books. I keep telling him there's more to life than making money,' she added, as if she and Judy had known one another for years.

Judy had no idea what Blake might make of all this, linking them together so neatly. And he'd hardly take kindly to the thought of any woman keeping him in line! But the longer the extended brunch went on, and the mountains of food kept coming, she realized he was able to relax more naturally with this family than she had ever seen him. Out here, away from the pressures of his real life, he was a very different Blake Adams from the hard-headed businessman she knew.

'Will you come and see my pony, daddy Blake?' Zoe asked eagerly, once Judy had shown her the promised dance steps, and she had struggled to master them.

'Of course I will. You just try and keep me away.'

They went off with Kyle and Bobby, and Judy offered to help clear away the dishes, but Ginny would have none of it.

'You're company, Judy, and besides, we have a girl coming in later to see to it all. What's the use of having money if you can't pay somebody else to do the chores? Anyway, I want to show you over the place.'

Judy didn't argue. She had never been in such a lovely house in her life. The views from the main bedroom were especially breathtaking, surrounded as they were by mountains and desert. And to the north in the far distance, Judy could just make out the faint, shimmering buildings of Las Vegas.

'It's beautiful, Ginny,' Judy told her, half-enviously.

'I'm glad you think so. I keep telling Blake it's time he moved out here and raised a family of his own, instead of pouring all his energies into that gambling empire of his.' She paused. 'You knew about Claire, I suppose?'

'I've never asked – '

'Then he's the one to tell you all the details if he wants to, and I shouldn't be talking out of turn. But she was a dancer too. Not like yourself, though. Claire was a professional ballerina and dedicated to her career. She'd never have fitted in here the way you do.'

Judy gave a nervous laugh, startled by these revelations, and hardly noticing Ginny's last remark. 'I wouldn't let him hear you say that!'

'Oh, he heard it often enough in the past, though we never talk about it these days. But we've known him too long to mince words with him. When we sell up, we'd dearly like to think it's Blake who buys us out, and we've told him so.'

'You're not thinking of leaving here, are you?'

'Didn't Blake tell you? It's no secret, and you'd have got to know about it eventually, anyway.'

Although her mind was still full of the scraps of information Ginny had told her about Claire, Judy thought suspiciously that she was being far too casual as they went down the curving staircase to the spacious sitting-room below. Especially at the breezy way Ginny was talking now.

'He's called this place his second home for long enough, and any time he wants to get away from Vegas he comes here. Kyle and me think it's high time he moved out here instead of living in a miserable apartment. What kind of life is that for a man? Blake needs a wife and kids, which is why we're so delighted he's met you, Judy.'

'He's not thinking of marrying me!'

155

Ginny laughed comfortably, easily brushing the protestation aside. 'That's not the way it's looking to us, honey. He's never brought anybody out here to meet us before, and he always said we're the nearest thing to family he's got now. Besides, anybody can see he's crazy about you.'

'Will you stop!' Judy began to laugh too, though she was starting to feel embarrassed at the way this conversation was going. And she hardly thought Blake would be pleased to know how his life was being so cut and dried by his old friends.

As for calling Blake's luxury apartment a miserable place to live in – well, that certainly didn't apply, unless you were an out-and-out homemaker like Ginny. And it wasn't hard to see where her priorities lay.

By the time the others had come back to the ranch house, she had managed to get Ginny to talk about the Coopers' summer vacation in England, and made suggestions about various places they should visit. Zoe was full of excitement and climbing all over Blake, and he certainly seemed to revel in it. The casino girls wouldn't recognize him now, with his hair all tumbled and his face so relaxed, thought Judy.

'Are you going to marry Judy, daddy Blake?' Zoe demanded.

Judy felt her face go hot as Blake laughed. These kids had certainly inherited their parents' blunt way of speaking, she thought.

'I haven't asked her properly yet, so I can't answer, honey,' he said lightly. 'But I'll be sure to let you know if she relents enough to say yes.'

This was crazy, thought Judy, avoiding Blake's mocking gaze and helping Ginny to hand round mugs of coffee. People shouldn't make fun about making marriage proposals.

Marriage was meant to be taken seriously . . . and she didn't want to think that it was only because she wanted it that way that she was in danger of feeling ridiculously upset at the child's innocent question and Blake's blatant reply.

As for wanting it . . . without warning, she knew instantly just how much she *did* want it to be true, and it had nothing to do with being affected by this lovely home and all the love and happiness that was radiated in it.

It was far more basic than that. She wanted *him*, in every sense of the word. And it was a feeling she had better try to keep strictly under control.

'So, what did you think of the Coopers?' Blake said lazily, as they began the drive back to Las Vegas.

'I liked them enormously.'

'Good. They liked you too. I hope you noticed you especially got Zoe's approval.'

Judy wouldn't rise to the bait. Instead she said, 'I can imagine that her opinions are quite important to you. She's a sweetie, and you're obviously very fond of one another.'

'She's the nearest thing I've got to a daughter of my own,' he said simply.

Judy wondered if he was thinking about Claire at that moment, and the life that could have been. Now that she knew a little more about the girl, she fully appreciated how obsessive an ambition dancing could be, especially that of a professional ballerina.

Maybe Claire hadn't been prepared to give up such an adulated and strenuous life for the less frenetic one of wife and mother . . . although she had met more than a few women who would dispute that the one was any less fraught than the other. Blake and Claire had presumably met in London, long before he came out here . . . so the question of Claire spending her life on a ranch in the Nevada desert would never have applied. She realized she couldn't stop thinking about the girl now, no matter how much she tried.

'From your prolonged silence I imagine you're thinking what a lousy father I'd make. Am I right?' Blake challenged.

'Actually, I think you'd make a very good one. You and Zoe got on marvellously together, and you fitted in with their family so well. So why didn't you tell me they were selling the ranch, and you were thinking of buying it?' she finished, before she could stop herself.

It was a question that she knew now had been bugging her ever since Ginny had told her. Not that she thought he had any obligation to tell her of his plans, but for a darker reason. She had begun to wonder if this visit to the ranch had been a kind of test in reverse to her own conclusions about Claire.

To see if Judy Hale was secretly a homemaking person, about to flit off with the first eligible man who asked her. Or if he could rely on getting any extra pounds of flesh out of her, if he considered extending her six months' contract.

She knew she was thinking in crazy terms, because why should he care . . .?

She suddenly noticed he was stopping the car. They were miles from anywhere, and once the engine was turned off, they were surrounded by the desert silence, and they might have been the only two people in the world.

'I haven't decided yet. Besides, I wanted your opinion on the place before I asked you to marry me,' he said bluntly.

Judy gasped. It was hardly the most romantic of proposals, and yet she could almost believe in its sincerity because of the very measured way he had said it. But it set all her nerves on edge, all the same.

'You must be joking -- '

'I never joke about serious matters, and nor do I say anything I don't mean. As you already know, I come from good Yorkshire stock, where we say what we mean and don't beat about nonsensical bushes.' Even as he spoke, Judy could hear the undertones of that Yorkshire background become more pronounced in his voice. 'So what's your answer?'

'Of course I can't marry you!'

'What's to stop you? You're not already wed, as far as I know, and neither am I.'

So far, he hadn't touched her, and Judy felt a growing sense of distress. If only he had swept her in his arms and vowed undying love . . . but he was a plain-speaking Yorkshireman, who didn't say things he didn't mean . . .

'We don't know each other well enough,' she managed to say at last.

'Good God, woman, I knew enough about you the minute I saw you,' he said roughly.

She couldn't tell what he meant by that. Their first meeting had been anything but easy, and she still remembered how she had thought of him as Mr Macho Man. She still did, and he was doing nothing to dispel that feeling.

'So what do you want to know about me?' he said, when the silence lengthened.

She spread her hands awkwardly, feeling like an intruder, prying into something very private that was never meant to be exposed to public view. But somehow she couldn't stop herself.

'Well, it was just the photograph I saw in your bedroom. I couldn't help wondering at the time if it was a wedding photograph. But it's your business.'

She felt her face burn again. Of course she had damn well thought it was a wedding photo, seeing the confetti and the button-holes. And she knew she was going to great pains to avoid mentioning Claire's name, since he probably wasn't aware that she knew it.

'We've come too far for any of that nonsense, and maybe I want to make it your business,' Blake said bluntly. 'The girl was Claire. And yes, it was a wedding photo.'

As she gasped, he went on speaking. 'We were chief bridesmaid and best man at a friend's wedding, and rather saw it as a practice run for our own, scheduled for six months' time. That was when Claire's contract with the company came to an end.'

'You've lost me. What company was that?' She willed him to tell her everything now.

'She was a very talented ballerina, and incidentally, Harry Brady was her agent too. Everybody said she was headed for the big time, and Claire knew it too.'

There was something in the way he used the past tense so deliberately that told Judy there was disaster to come. She knew enough about rigorous dance training to know how obsessively it could take you over when your heart was set on becoming the best. And Blake had hinted once before that he knew all about obsession.

'So what happened?' she asked quietly.

'Not long before her present contract expired, she was offered a fabulous role in a new musical ballet. It meant putting our wedding plans on hold, but that wasn't important. We were already living together in London, much to my father's disapproval, naturally. What did matter was how the demands of the role affected Claire, even before rehearsals began.'

Judy found herself wondering if he had ever confided in anyone during all these years – except to Frank, during that one night of incoherent drunken misery, that he couldn't even remember properly. But she made no comment. She just sat quite still in the car, trying to make herself as invisible as possible, and knowing that she was no more than a sounding-board right now.

'Claire became totally and irrationally obsessed with her weight. She was always so slight a breath of wind could have knocked her over, but the costumes for the new show were going to be skin-tight and far more revealing than she'd ever worn previously. She began to imagine every part of her was fat, when it was anything but that.'

'My God, you're not telling me she became anorexic, are you, Blake?' Judy exclaimed.

'I wish I wasn't, but the more I told her she was imagining things, the more she'd deny it. She changed out of all recognition. Whenever I tried to help, she'd scream that she'd never forgive me if she lost the part because I tried to get her to eat properly, instead of toying with a couple of carrots and celery sticks for dinner.'

'And did she lose the part?'

'She lost far more than that.'

For a moment, Judy didn't follow him, assuming that they had broken up because of Claire's attitude, and that he refused to take any more of it. But then she saw the frozen look on his face, and drew in her breath as he went on grimly.

'By the time they took her into hospital it was far too late. Once you get on that downward spiral the body has no defences or reserves to get you out of it, no matter how many drugs they pump into you. She died a couple of months before my father, and while I was still in a state of total shock I was summoned back to Yorkshire to sort out his affairs.'

He suddenly seemed to realize Judy was there, sitting silently in the passenger seat of the limo.

'I'm so sorry,' she murmured. 'And I promise I'll respect your confidence in telling me.'

'It all happened a long time ago,' he spoke more briskly, and his face relaxed again. 'So now you know all there is to know about me, Miss Hale, what's your answer to my question?'

She stared at him uncomprehendingly, her mind still totally involved with all he had been saying.

'What was the question?' she asked vaguely.

'Will you marry me?'

CHAPTER 9

Judy's head spun for a few moments. How could she possibly answer, or take him seriously? She was still too caught up in Claire's tragedy, especially since she had never expected to hear anything of the sort.

But she knew he must have loved Claire very deeply, which went a long way towards her understanding of why he never allowed any other woman to touch his emotions in the same way, and kept them all at arm's length.

She understood, because she had felt the same after Michael. But in her case she had opened up her heart to close friends, in a way that she suspected men never did, and the telling had acted as a kind of catharsis.

It was that old macho image again, she thought, that would never let them admit to any weakness in their psyche.

After a few minutes' silence, Judy spoke slowly. 'Blake, I do appreciate all that you've told me – '

'And one of these days you can tell me your dark secrets. Fair's fair, isn't it?'

'Fair's fair,' she said huskily.

'So? Will you marry me or won't you?'

She was filled with a mixture of emotions at that moment. Here was the love of her life, almost agressively demanding that she gave him an answer, and yes, it had to be the most unromantic proposal she could ever have imagined. She couldn't think why he had even done it. And how could she possibly say yes, after all she had just heard about Claire!

Unwittingly, she had chosen completely the wrong time to ask him, and now she knew it. It effectively blocked her from giving him the answer she would dearly love to do.

'You can hardly expect me to give you a reply on the spur of the moment,' she said, almost angrily. 'It needs thinking about – '

And why on earth had she said that, when, if she had any sense, she shouldn't even consider it at all!

'I've been thinking of nothing else for weeks,' Blake told her drily.

'Would you really go this far to win a stupid bet with Harry?' she asked, her mood changing, and needing to quell the suddenly charged atmosphere between them. And she could see by the gleam in his eyes now that he was as arrogant as ever. It was something of a relief, because she couldn't bear to think that this proposal was made just for convenience. Blake had decided he needed a wife . . . and she fitted the bill . . .

'Nobody, not even Harry, would make me propose marriage unless it was what I wanted.'

'But why me?' she said, trying not to weaken.

'Why do you think?'

She couldn't stand much more of this. She took a deep breath, and challenged him unblinkingly.

'Look, if this is a serious proposal, I've said I'll think about it, and I will. But you've got to give me time.'

'I'll give you two weeks.' He spoke as unemotionally as if he had just offered her a take-it-or-leave-it job in the casino. 'But remember what I told you. A Yorkshireman always says what he means, and means what he says.'

But he hadn't told her he loved her, Judy thought numbly, as he started the car again and headed towards Las Vegas. And even if he had, she wouldn't have believed him, no matter what solid Yorkshire values his father had instilled in him – which made her decision whether or not to accept his proposal all the more poignant, because she meant what her heart said too. She had always believed in doing what her heart dictated, but it had never involved sharing a man with a memory.

It was ironic that Harry sent her a fax the next day.

'No news from Ricky, kiddo, so let's take that as a good sign. This is just a quickie to wish you luck with the new show. I imagine that you and Blake make quite a team. Bye now, and I'll get back to you soon.'

Judy could see right through his artfulness. Now that she knew about the bet between the two men, Harry would do his best to link her with Blake. And she certainly didn't intend telling him that Blake had proposed to her, which she was beginning to find more and more bewildering.

For a few moments she had even been tempted to play right into his hands by pretending to fall for him, agreeing to a marriage and then backing out, just to watch him fall flat on his face. But even as she thought it, she knew there were two reasons why she would never do it.

One was that she could never play fast and loose with his emotions, after what he'd told her about Claire. And the second was that she loved him. She admitted it to herself, even if she had no intention of admitting it to him.

And she still couldn't quite believe he had truly got over Claire, even after all this time. It was a hell of a long time to be carrying a torch for someone, but if it had lasted that long, it was going to be very difficult for anyone else to put it out. And maybe it would be wrong to even try.

She faxed back a brief note to Harry, preferring that to getting into a lengthy phone conversation with him.

'Everything's fine here. The show looks as if it's going to be a great success, and Blake's OK. I really like Frank too, and we've been spending a lot of time together lately. Don't read anything into that, but watch this space!'

She added a few more innocuous remarks, and smiled as she fed the letter into the fax machine, knowing Harry would read plenty into the comment about Frank. It would just serve him right to let him think she was more interested in the Dance Director than Blake. Two could play at his game.

She hadn't bargained on Harry responding so quickly, but when her phone rang shortly afterwards, it was to hear him saying he'd better warn Blake that his legendary charm was slipping . . .

'Don't you do any such thing,' Judy warned. 'There's nothing going on between Frank and me, other than friendship, and I aim to keep it that way.'

'And between you and Blake?' he asked slyly.

'I believe you know that Blake's heart is still elsewhere,' she said at last.

She heard Harry's low whistle at the other end.

'So he's told you about Claire, has he? You may not know it, kid, but that's a first. He never speaks about her to anybody any more, not even me. No, if he's decided to confide in you, that means something special, take it from me.'

She swallowed. 'Well, I'm not interested in competing with a memory.'

'How could there be any competition, for God's sake? Claire was a lovely girl, and a talented dancer, but she was a pale waif compared with you. And she's gone. Any sane man would prefer a real live girl with some delicious meat on her bones – '

'You're really tacky, Harry,' she told him in disgust. 'And if you're going to be so tasteless, I'm hanging up.'

'All right, but remember what I said.'

'I certainly won't.' Then she had to ask, 'Harry, you're *sure* you haven't heard from Ricky lately?'

'I'd tell you if I had. Blake made it clear I was to tell him the minute he contacted me – '

'Don't tell Blake. Tell *me*!'

'Yeah, of course. Anything else on your mind?'

She fumed. He had called her, not the other way around, yet she could hear the impatience in his voice now.

'Not a thing. Goodbye, Harry.'

She hung up. He could be the most impossible man, and it was only because he'd always acted as an unexpectedly sweet father confessor when she needed it, and had had no one else, that she continued to be his client.

She felt a sliver of unease, remembering that he knew all about her affair with Michael and how devastated she had been when they broke up. He knew all about Michael . . . and he knew about Claire . . .

She hoped Blake would forget her promise to tell him about Michael, but she couldn't help wondering if Harry had already said something about it to him. Indiscretion was Harry's middle name, along with crass tactlessness, and a few choice others. But in the end she gave up worrying about any of it, and any of them.

Since arriving in Reno, Ricky Hale had scrutinized all the relevant free newspapers and brochures in his motel room until he found the ad that he wanted. The one that asked no questions. He'd made up his mind about what he was going to do now, and nobody was going to stop him.

For once, he was glad his sister wasn't around, screaming at him that it was the worst thing in the world he could do, and any fool knew that. If Judy were here, she'd stake him, anyway. But even Harry, that wily old agent of hers, would probably tell him he was going to the dogs, and that the only person who ever got rich through going to a loan shark, was a loan shark.

But since the pair of them were always saying he should grow up and not rely on Judy for handouts any more, he was going to do exactly that.

He swaggered out of his cheap motel, whistling tunelessly, and hoping he looked a damn sight more confident than he felt. He had to make the guy believe he was a good risk. And so he would be. Once he had a wad of dollar bills to play with, he knew his luck was going to be in. He could feel it, and his fingertips were already itching to feel the cool chips in his hand. Reno was going to be his salvation.

The loan shark's office was in a seedy part of town, down a narrow street that was little more than an alley. It didn't look any too savoury, but it was one of the very few that advertised loans of any amount with no fuss and no interrogation.

Ricky had never been to a place like this before, and he took a deep breath before pushing open the door. He was almost sorry he had done so as the rank smell of stale cigars rose to his nostrils. A few minutes later a man dressed in an ill-fitting, sober black suit came through the bead curtains from a back room, wreathed in cigar smoke. He looked Ricky over quickly, then waved him to a chair, while he sat on the other side of a paper-strewn desk.

'Mornin', young feller. What can I do for you?'

'I'm here about a loan.'

'Well, sure you are, otherwise you wouldn't be in my office,' he smiled easily. 'So how much do you want, and what collateral can you offer?'

Ricky stared at him in dismay. 'Collateral?'

'Security, boy. Don't you understand plain English? I thought that was a Limey accent.'

Ricky ignored the jibe. 'The ad didn't say anything about putting up security. It says you offer no-questions-asked loans on a fixed rate of interest over generous repayment times.' He recited the ad exactly.

'So it does. But it all depends, see?'

'On what?'

The guy leaned forward, his easy manner gone, his hooded eyes narrowed and penetrating. To Ricky's heightened senses, he suddenly seemed to get bigger, like a watchful vulture hovering over him, ready for the kill. He wasn't normally fanciful, nor afraid of anything, but at that moment he could believe anything of this guy.

'On whether or not I think a client is a sound investment, sonny.' The loan shark was sharper now. 'I need to see proper returns on my money, and I ain't no charity organization. So what do you intend to do with a loan, should I enter into a contract with you?'

'I didn't expect to come here and get the third degree, for a start – ' Ricky felt so crushed he was almost ready to leap up and scuttle out now.

171

The guy shrugged. 'Take it or leave it. If you can't tell me what you've got in mind, then it's no deal. I've seen enough of you kids throwing all your money into the casinos. Not that I give a damn about that, except for getting the interest payments back. Now, if you should be thinking of getting an automobile, say, or something sensible, I might waive the idea of collateral. In that case, you'd sign on the basis of compound interest repayments, on account of the added risk I'm taking on you.'

Ricky could see right through him now. Mentioning collateral was just a way to make the clients panic. Any fool could see Ricky Hale had nothing to put up for security, except for the crumpled clothes he stood up in.

But he could also see that he'd been going to get the loan all along. He breathed easier and spoke recklessly, knowing the guy had given him an opening, as he'd probably calculated. It took one to know one, he thought, grudgingly acknowledging the man's cunning.

'That's just what I do want it for. I need a car to get me to and from work. Once I get wheels, I'll be in business, and the repayments will be no problem.'

The loan shark's mouth gave a small smile.

'OK, so here's the deal. You start repayments in two weeks, and you sign a contract to that effect. I'll need your name, address and signature. There's no limit to the amount, but you'd better understand the meaning of compound interest, and read the small print carefully before you sign.'

'Oh, and boy,' he added warningly as Ricky scanned the document that was pushed towards him, 'I've got my own methods of ensuring that you live up to your commitments. *Comprendes*?'

He cracked his knuckles in such a farcical Mafioso way that Ricky almost laughed out loud. But as he read the details on the contract, he knew the interest demanded was extortionate. But by now he was so high on the thought of having money in his pockets, and the way it was going to turn his life around, that he was ready to sign anything.

Hell, he'd been lucky playing poker in Seaside, and even the miserable slots had paid out in the roadside cafés on the way down to Reno. He was filled with optimism. He signed his name and other details with a flourish, and went away with five-thousand dollar bills in various denominations, the most he'd ever had in his life.

And the guy had put a new idea in his head now. It would be good to feel the power of a car beneath him. So the first thing he did was to go around to a used-car lot and bought an old banger for seven hundred dollars, paying half down, and the other half in easy instalments.

He could have looked big and settled it all, but why get rid of so much all at once? The car was OK, even though the engine rasped and the exhaust smoked. It still made him feel one hell of a guy as he drove around town, then back to his motel for some black coffee and to collect his breath.

He spent an hour planning his moves before he set out for the casinos, knowing it was going to be no more piddling slot machines from now on. He felt far too lucky for that. It was the roulette tables and the big time.

Even so, by the time he'd been in Reno a month, Ricky could hardly believe his luck. Everything was going his way on the roulette tables. He was well up on the money he'd got from the loan shark now, and once he was on to a winning streak, he was confident that he couldn't lose.

He began putting down larger and larger stakes, and his favourite numbers were still paying out. He'd settled the first of the interest repayments on his loan, and on the car repayments. He was making money hand over fist, and the loan shark regarded him with renewed interest when he boasted of the fact.

'I like to see my clients hitting the big time, boy. You want to borrow some more, you just say the word. Same conditions applying, of course,' he spoke casually, blowing his usual cloud of cigar smoke into the air.

'I hadn't thought about borrowing any more, but hell, why not, when I'm on a winning streak!' Ricky bragged.

Common sense told him he shouldn't need it if his luck continued to hold, but common sense didn't play much part in his thinking these days. There was no reason why he shouldn't bet even higher stakes. The sky was the limit when you were winning, and he'd be able to settle the loan shark's debts in one fell swoop, without having to pay out any more of the bloody extortionate compound interest.

Yeah, he'd borrow more and gamble bigger. He'd been on the losing end for far too long, and it made him feel a hell of a guy to have an envious crowd standing around him now that he was raking it in. The way the blood pumped around his veins every time the pile of chips was pushed his way was better than anything. Better than sex.

Before he stopped to think twice, he was signing a new contract for another five-thousand-dollar loan. By now, he knew that even that was small-fry stuff compared with some of the stakes the well-heeled guys, with their solid gold jewellery and fat wads, were gambling every night. He wanted to be in their league. To win big, you had to gamble big, and Ricky Hale was out to make a killing.

He'd played in a dozen Reno casinos now, but the tables in the one he favoured most were extra busy that night, and he couldn't get to his lucky one.

But since he was starting to think of himself as invincible, he told himself it didn't matter. He didn't know the croupier, either, which was a pity, as he'd already established a rapport with his usual one.

As a breed, he didn't care for most of them. But they were in business to cater for their clients' needs, and when the new croupier looked him up and down in his crumpled clothes as if he was dirt, Ricky felt his blood boil.

'You're in the wrong place, kid,' the guy grunted. 'We play for big stakes here.'

'So what makes you think I don't?'

The guy shrugged. 'Have it your way, but don't say I didn't warn you. What're you staking?'

His eyes flickered as Ricky took the rolls of chips from his inside pocket, and he became slightly more attentive.

The dice rolled, and the roulette wheel spun round. And within half an hour, Ricky was raking it in again, and a crowd had gathered. Several young women were placing their chips alongside Ricky's now, hoping to share his luck.

The hovering presence of the casino manager decided him when he'd had enough at this particular table.

'Sorry, ladies.' He smiled at the two young women. 'That's it for now, and I'm cashing in my chips.'

'So are we, honey, and then we'd like to buy you a drink,' one of them said. 'It's thanks to you that we've done so well tonight.'

'Sure, why not?' Ricky decided it was time he had some fun, and he didn't have to live like a monk, especially now that he had money to burn. 'Why don't we have something to eat as well, and see what develops?'

He didn't think this was as hilariously funny as they seemed to find it, but he wasn't objecting to being thought of as a great guy.

'You British are so cute,' the second woman gushed. 'I could listen to you all night.'

'Play your cards right, and you just might,' Ricky grinned. 'Not that I guarantee I'll be doing much talking.'

That started them off laughing again, and once they had cashed in their chips they all went off towards the nearest bar, arm in arm.

Ricky couldn't have said what woke him. It could have been the metallic sound of tin cans rattling down the windy alley. Or the scream of police sirens somewhere in the night. Or the howling of a tom cat. Whatever it was, the minute he lifted his head, he knew he wasn't in his own bed at his motel. Nor did his head feel as though it belonged to him any more. It was ten sizes too big for his brain, for a start, and his tongue was ten sizes too big for his mouth.

He moved cautiously, wondering where the hell he was, and how he had got there. Then he realized he was lying in a gutter, and that there was something warm and sticky on his cheek. He knew instantly that it was blood.

He'd been done over . . . and if he hadn't been doing so well in the casinos lately, he'd have thought that the loan shark's heavies had done it, just to remind him of his debts. But there was no need. He was quids in . . .

A sudden feeling of nausea swept over him, as his disjointed thoughts focused on the two women who had fawned over him, standing him a meal and a good few drinks.

And no doubt spiking them, he thought sickly now. He felt frantically in his inside pocket where his wad of bills should be, and there was nothing. He felt a wild rage, and then suddenly convulsed, and spewed right then and there in the gutter. Knowing how such people worked, he guessed now that the women had been part of a gang, and the bastards had cleaned him out. He'd taken most of his money to the casino that night. There was only a small amount left at his motel, and he'd have to begin all over again.

Swaying, his head near to bursting, he staggered to his feet. He had a job to read the name of the alley, and when he did, he had no idea where he was. It was only the general glow of light in the sky that told him the general direction of the casinos, and he limped his way back to his out-of-town motel by following it.

Jesus Christ, he thought irreverently. Talk about following the light of a bleedin' star . . . but if he hadn't thought that way, he knew he'd have come closer to crying than at any time since he was a kid.

He spent three days holed up in his motel room, afraid to go out, and wondering what the hell he was going to do. He'd lost virtually everything, and the loan shark would be baying for his blood very soon. The car dealer would be breathing down his neck as well, but the amount he owed on the old banger was like a flea spit compared with the massive interest and capital he owed on the loans.

He couldn't possibly get hold of that kind of money, short of highway robbery, and he hadn't sunk that low yet. All he'd done, since his luck had finally run out, was to sit and drink coffee and watch inane gameshows on TV. Either that, or he idly scanned through the freebie magazines he picked up from the motel rack when he collected his coffee from the machine, wondering if he could find the details on some scam or other that somebody else had tried . . .

He had just about decided that the only thing he could do was to try to skip town and hitch a ride to anywhere, when one of the showbiz weeklies caught his eye, if only for the sight of the gorgeous showgirls depicted on the cover, and the dazzling centrespread showing more of them.

He looked at the ad sourly, deeply resenting the lucky devils who could afford to stay in such places where these big shows were put on. He'd seen them often enough, dripping in diamonds and wearing enough gold to pay off the National Debt. But he wasn't so far down that he couldn't appreciate the pics of the girls, and registering the name of the hotel where this big new show was apparently creating a sensation.

The Sparkling Rocks in Las Vegas . . . Ricky's small spark of interest faded, because he was never likely to get there. But because he had nothing else to do, and the gameshow on the TV in the corner of his motel room was more asinine than usual, he forced himself to read the write-up of the show that had just opened.

An International Spectacular was nothing new, but the paper had made something of the fact that the hotel owner was British, and that the show owed a good deal of its success to a young British choreographer, and Judy's name suddenly leapt out at him.

Ricky's heart began a rapid jungle dance as he read on quickly, and then it beat so fast he thought he was going to keel right over. And it was a good few minutes before his muddled brain could accept that what he was reading was true.

'My God,' he croaked out loud. 'Jude's been in Las Vegas all this bloody time and I never knew it. And that bastard Harry Brady palmed me off with fifty measly quid, just so he didn't have to tell me.'

For Judy, the show was the success of her dreams. She was still in a state of euphoria when she returned to her suite on the final night of the first month. Praises were still ringing in her ears, and she found herself hoping Frank and Maggie didn't think she was taking too much of the credit.

Her phone rang, and she ran to answer it, thinking it was probably Blake inviting her to his apartment for a nightcap – and preparing to say no. All she wanted was to sleep . . . and she spoke shortly into the receiver.

'Is that you, Jude?' she heard a thick male voice say.

For a moment she stared at the phone, unsure of the identity of the cracked voice at the other end. It certainly wasn't Blake. It was some crank, she decided furiously, and any minute now she was going to hear some obscene message. She was about to slam down the phone when the voice spoke again.

'Jude, it's me. Ricky.'

Her heart leapt, and she sat down heavily on the bed, feeling as if her legs wouldn't hold her up much longer. She gasped out a reply.

'Ricky, for God's sake, where are you?'

'Jude. I need your help desperately,' he blundered on. 'Can you get some money to me, and fast?'

Judy's heartbeats began to slow a little, recognizing the mixture as before. She knew she should harden her heart right now. Living and working in the gambling environment, she had been able to deal with her initial revulsion to it.

But there were gamblers and gamblers, and Ricky was a silly little fool who didn't have the sense to walk away while there was still time . . .

'I mean it, Jude. They're after me, see?'

'Who's after you? Talk sense – and where *are* you, anyway? And how did you know how to find me? Have you spoken to Harry recently?'

She flinched as she heard him practically scream into the phone then. 'For God's sake, don't start giving me the third degree and playing the big sister with me now! I haven't been in touch with anybody. I saw the ad for your show in a showbiz rag, and I couldn't believe you were over here all the time. That bastard Harry conveniently forgot to tell me, but I need you badly, Jude.'

'Just calm down a minute and talk sensibly,' she snapped. 'How can I help you if I don't know what's wrong, and I don't even know where you are? So start at the beginning.'

'I'm in Reno, and I'm in a hell of a lot of trouble, and you're the only one who can get me out of it, Jude.'

'How much?' she said brutally.

He didn't answer for a few seconds, and when he did, he was almost belligerent. 'Promise you won't go berserk, then. But if I don't pay up what I owe, I'm going to be scraped up off the sidewalk by some heavies any day now – '

'Stop exaggerating, and tell me what you need,' she snapped again. 'And I'm not promising anything yet.'

He spoke in a stammering rush, because he was still only just realizing what a bloody awful mess he had got himself in.

'Fifteen thousand dollars at a pinch, but twenty would be better, then I could get the hell out of here and back to England. And I'd never bother you again, honest!'

The amount he mentioned took Judy's breath away. When she could speak, she shouted into the phone.

'Are you mad? I don't have that kind of money, and you can't possibly be in debt for that amount. Even I know that no casino will let you run up IOUs to that amount – '

'But loan sharks will.'

Dear God, she thought, *this can't be happening, and not even Ricky could be that reckless . . .*

'I'm telling the truth, Jude. I've been a fool, and I know it. I was on a winning streak and I thought I couldn't lose, so I started betting heavier and heavier. By the time my luck ran out, I'd borrowed more, and then some professional casino dolls conned me out of my winnings, and I got done over for the rest, and everything began to fall apart. I'm begging you to get me out of this, Jude, and I swear I'll be through with gambling for good.'

She could hear the rising hysteria in his voice. Her heart ached for him, but she had heard it all before, and it was always going to be the last time.

'Jude?' he went on hoarsely. 'I'll be here at the Sandiman Motel for as long as possible, unless I have to move on in a hurry. Don't let me down, Jude. You're my only hope.'

The phone went dead, and Judy put down her receiver with shaking hands. He hadn't even thought to give her the motel phone number, but she could find that easily enough.

And then a mad rage took hold of her. How on earth was she going to find twenty thousand dollars in a hurry? She was well paid, but she hadn't been living the life of a nun since coming here. She had bought clothes and souvenirs and been to shows, and apart from that and normal living expenses, the bulk of her salary had been paid straight into a bank account in England for when she returned home.

But there was one person who could help out. She couldn't bear to ask him, and she never would have done for herself. But for Ricky's sake, she'd have to swallow her pride and ask Blake for a loan until she could get the funds back over here.

Crossing the corridor, she knocked at the door of his apartment, and he showed complete surprise as he let her in.

'Well, this is an unexpected honour. To what do I owe such a pleasure?'

'Can I come in? And please don't mock me, Blake. Ricky's just called. He's in serious trouble and he needs help.'

As she said the words, to her horror all her stoicism vanished, and she found herself shaking uncontrollably as he steered her to his sofa and sat beside her, holding her cold hands tightly while she fought to hold back the tears.

'Tell me,' he ordered gently.

CHAPTER 10

Judy couldn't speak for a moment, and then she blurted everything out at once, the way Ricky had.

'He's in Reno and way out of his depth. He's been to a loan shark and borrowed money, he's been ripped off by some women, and then been mugged for the rest of his money. He's asking me for twenty thousand dollars, because if he can't start paying up soon, he says he's in danger of getting scraped up off the sidewalk. I'm not sure I believe everything he says – '

'Then you'd better believe it,' Blake retorted.

Judy looked at him with frightened eyes, 'Tell me the truth, Blake. Would it really be as bad as he says?'

'It would. And if he tries to skip town, he'll have no chance, because they'll be on his tail quicker than blinking.'

She licked her dry lips, hardly realizing how she was clinging on to his hands now.

'Blake, I have to help him, and you're my only hope. I don't have that kind of money. I can get a good part of it from my bank in England, but that will take time, and from what you say, Ricky doesn't have time. So I've got no choice but to ask you to lend me the money for the time being.'

It humiliated her to ask, and when he didn't answer at once, she felt physically sick, wondering if she had gone too far. Why should he help her brother? He would have seen enough reckless gamblers in his time not to care what happened to one young man who was no concern of his.

'I'm sorry. I should never have asked,' she muttered, her shoulders drooping.

'Don't be bloody silly. Of course you should have asked. But there's no way we can get there tonight. We'll fly up to Reno in my private plane in the morning and sort things out.'

Judy looked at him in disbelief, even while her heart suddenly soared with hope. Private plane? She knew nothing about any private plane, but then, she was constantly learning new things about him.

'Do you mean it?' she asked huskily.

'You should know by now that I never say things I don't mean. But there's a condition.'

'Condition?' she echoed. But as soon as she saw the determination in his face, she knew. And she backed away from him at once, shaking her head.

'Blake, no. Not even you would blackmail me into marrying you in exchange for helping Ricky out – '

'I'm not blackmailing anybody. I've already asked you to marry me, and it's time you gave me your answer. As soon as you say yes, I promise we'll fly up to Reno first thing tomorrow morning with the money.'

It was still blackmail. He was forcing her hand, and they both knew it. She lifted her chin, thinking quickly.

'If I say yes, I have a condition too.'

She saw his mocking glance. It said, *What possible condition could she have, when he held all the cards . . .?* She went on before she could change her mind.

'If I agree to marry you, you have to know it's solely on Ricky's account, and my condition is that nobody else knows of it. Not Ricky, or Harry, or the Coopers, and certainly nobody in the hotel! I don't want to give people a false impression about our relationship, nor arouse anybody's jealousy in thinking I've come over here and married the boss in so short a time. You must see that's what could happen.'

'Agreed,' Blake said.

She looked at him suspiciously. 'You agree?'

'Providing that at the end of your time here, we make a proper announcement.'

'We may decide by then that what we want is a quickie divorce,' she replied smartly, desperate to continue finding whatever objection she could.

'We may,' Blake agreed again. 'In that case, no harm will have been done, will it? Now, I've got some calls to make, and so have you. Ask Marcie on reception to find you the number of Ricky's motel, and tell him we'll be there about midday tomorrow. Be ready to leave around eight in the morning.'

She felt as if she was being dismissed, and she didn't know how to thank him, or if she really felt like doing so. She still felt as if she had been coerced into accepting his proposal, and that he'd taken unfair advantage of her.

But in making her own condition not to tell any of the hotel staff, she was also making sure she wouldn't be moving into his apartment. She had every intention of keeping to her own suite, even if she did have to honour the proposal once they had got Ricky off the hook.

She could hardly sleep that night, wondering if she had done the right thing, yet knowing she had done the only thing she could. But Blake wasn't getting all his own way, whatever he might think, and it was the only comfort she had.

She was ready before eight o'clock next morning, jittery and anxious after a quick breakfast of fruit and coffee in her room. Blake knocked on her door and nodded briefly before they went down in the silent elevator and out to his waiting limo. It was going to be the strangest journey of her life, Judy thought, and she still didn't know what state she was going to find her brother in at the end of it.

They drove to the airport, and out to the strip where Judy could see the dozens of private planes lined up. When they had parked the car, Blake sorted out the necessary documentation at the control centre before escorting Judy to a plane that looked as though it took no more than six people.

She eyed it uneasily. She didn't mind flying, but this one looked extremely flimsy compared with the big jumbo jets she was more used to.

'Don't worry,' Blake told her, seeing the way she chewed her lip. 'It's the safest way to travel, and I've never lost a passenger yet.'

If it was meant to calm her, it wasn't doing it, she thought. It would take more than that on this crazy day, but as she took her seat beside him and strapped herself in, she started talking quickly to take away some of her nervousness.

'How long will it take to get to Reno?'

By now the plane was already bumping out towards the runway, and Judy tried to hide her apprehension.

'An hour or more, depending on altitude and wind speeds,' he answered.

'Is that all? Then why did I have to tell Ricky we wouldn't be there until midday?'

'Because we have a wedding to go to first.'

Judy stared at him, her heart jolting. But she should have known he'd make sure he got his part of the bargain before she got hers. She couldn't speak for a minute, and as she felt the plane leave the ground, she knew that the customary lurch in her stomach wasn't only due to that.

'What did you expect, my sweet? That I was going to risk you welshing on your promise as soon as you knew your brother was out of danger?'

She was outraged at the very suggestion. 'If that's what you thought, then you can't think very much of me!'

'On the contrary. I think a great deal of you, and if I put things badly just then, I apologize. I just wanted to be sure the bargain was well and truly sealed, and since you'd put your own condition on it, this seemed the best way to go about it.'

Judy glared at him. 'I don't know what you mean by that.'

'Don't you? Well, since you want nobody else to know about our plans, we could hardly get married in Las Vegas, where I'm well known, could we? And a big church wedding was definitely off. So I called a wedding chapel in Reno last night to make the arrangements, and they're expecting us at ten-thirty this morning.'

His gall took her breath away. He was determined to marry her, and there wasn't a damn thing she could do to stop it now. And it was all so very different from the way it could have been . . . should have been. Without warning, she felt the sting of tears in her eyes, and she looked away from him quickly, hoping he hadn't noticed it. When he put his hand briefly over hers for a moment, she knew that he had.

'I'm not an ogre, whatever you might think of me, Judy. I won't put any undue pressure on you, especially if you're still thinking about somebody else – '

'I'm not,' she said, choked.

'So how important is the guy you left behind in London – compared with your career, shall we say?' he went on remorselessly. 'And before you ask, Harry hasn't told me anything, but I know the signs. I've been there, remember?'

It was the craziest time and place to be having such a discussion, soaring over desert scrub almost as soon as they left the bright lights of Las Vegas behind them, and headed north. But if Blake was beginning to believe that she thought her ambition for a brilliant career was more important than a fulfilling relationship with a man she loved – just like Claire – then he couldn't be more wrong.

'It's not like that at all,' she told him, too honest not to put the record straight. 'Michael and I were finished months before I came here, and he doesn't mean anything to me any more. He hasn't done so for a long time.'

'But you would have married him?'

'Of course I would – if he hadn't been married already. And, although we were living together, he was cheating on *me* as well. There's nothing more to tell, and I don't want to talk about it any more. Michael's history.'

And it was nothing as tragic and dramatic as his affair with Claire. It was just a sordid little story of a married man playing around . . .

He said nothing, but concentrated on his flying, while Judy gazed down at the speeding ground below and tried to take an interest in the swift contrast of scene now that the glittering casinos were well behind them. Anything was better than remembering why they were here at all, and that she was going to marry Blake Adams before seeing her brother.

The wildly beautiful desert landscape, with the sagebrush rolling about in the breeze, made her think of every Western movie she had ever seen, and she murmured as much to Blake.

'You'll soon get tired of it,' he commented. 'There's nothing much between here and Reno, except for Tonepah, and you'll see what I mean about that when we fly over it.'

When they did, she felt a ridiculous stab of disappointment, because it fell so far short of a place that the old movies had depicted. The few shabby-looking buildings below, seemingly in the middle of nowhere, made her admit that Hollywood could produce miracles of illusion.

It all served to divert her mind from the real purpose of their morning flight. But the nearer they got to Reno, the more agitated Judy became. Not on her own account, but on Ricky's. What if they were already too late, and the thugs had already tracked him down since he had called her? Her hands were damp, trying not to imagine the consequences.

'Blake, these heavies, as Ricky called them. They don't actually kill people, do they?'

Reassure me. Tell me anything. Tell me lies.

'It has been known. Try not to think about. There's nothing you can do about it, and we're doing all we can – '

'Telling me not to think about it is just about the daftest thing anybody ever said to me,' she snapped. 'How can I help thinking about it? It's all I *can* think about!'

'Then try thinking of something else,' he went on ruthlessly. 'Think about tonight being your wedding night.'

Despite the tone of his voice, she couldn't miss the meaning in the words, and she turned away, her face flaming. Because if he thought for one minute that this was going to be a proper marriage, he was in for quite a shock. She had no intention of moving in to his apartment, and whether he realized it or not, he had scuppered that idea by agreeing to her demand that the marriage should be kept a secret.

It would hardly do either of their reputations any good for the hotel maids to see one unused bed in her suite, and one very well-used bed in Blake's apartment . . . she became aware that she was suddenly breathing faster, and that he mistook the reason for it.

'I see the thought is not entirely unpalatable to you,' he said, more arrogantly.

If he expected an answer, she simply couldn't give it, knowing that if this had been a proper marriage, she could think of nothing more wonderful and right than spending her wedding night with the man she loved. As it was . . .

A slight change in air pressure caused the plane to dip slightly, so that Blake had to give all his attention to righting it, and as the buildings of Reno were fast coming into view, the emotional tension of the moment was gone. Within a short while then, they were landing, and he was turning off the engine.

'Blake, you know how much I appreciate all you're doing for Ricky, don't you?' she blurted out.

'But . . .?' he responded to the tension in her voice.

'But what if he starts doing the same thing all over again? Sometimes I think it's an endless spiral – '

And if that happened, she would have gone through this farce of a marriage for nothing.

'He won't, because I've no intention of throwing money away.' She heard the hardness in his voice then. 'There'll be conditions for him too, and he'll have to stick to them.'

She hoped Ricky would realize that Blake was no soft touch, and she respected him for it. But as they left Reno airport in a hire car, she gave up thinking about it, knowing there were more immediate things to think about. Like the little matter of marrying Blake Adams.

They reached the wedding chapel early, and waited in an anteroom while a previous couple went through their ceremony. Judy could hear their responses and then the strains of their wedding music very clearly. It might not be a church wedding, but those other two were marrying for love, and she felt a sudden shame at their own reason for being here.

If it wasn't for Ricky . . . She felt Blake's hand tighten around hers as they went through the necessary paperwork with the clerk, and knew it was far too late to back out.

At the appointed time they went through to the wedding chapel, where two witnesses were waiting to join them. It was all so farcical . . . and yet, as she heard the words that were to bind her to Blake, for however long, Judy's throat filled, and her responses were every bit as low and emotional as that other bride's. Anyone, listening to her, would believe she was truly in love . . . as she was.

She felt Blake slide the heavy gold ring on to her finger and hold it there as he repeated his vows. She had no idea where or when he had got the ring, but since he seemed able to organize anything he wanted with the minimum of effort, she felt too light-headed to question it.

'You may kiss the bride,' she heard the registrar say, and she dutifully turned her face towards Blake. She hadn't promised to obey, but she could at least honour this moment.

As she looked up at him, she couldn't fathom the expression in his eyes, but she automatically responded when he took her in his arms and kissed her for the benefit of the onlookers. And then it was all over, and they collected the wedding certificate and went out of the chapel as another couple was preparing to move in.

'It's a bit like production-line marriage, isn't it?' Judy murmured, more upset by the whole procedure than she had expected to be, and hardly knowing what else to say to this man who was now her husband.

'It's none the less real to those who want to make a commitment. You don't need all the trappings of a big fancy ceremony for that, even though I suppose it's a useful way of telling the world,' Blake added practically.

'Then since we've no intention of telling the world, as you put it, maybe in the circumstances this way was best for us, after all,' she retorted, not wanting to let him think for a moment that a fancy ceremony with all the trappings was what she had always dreamed about.

They got back into the hire car, and Judy had to fight back the tears. The heavy gold ring felt cold and unfamiliar on her finger, and after a moment, she pulled it off and handed it silently to Blake.

'You'd better keep this. It's rather a giveaway, isn't it?' she said, trying to be cool and unemotional.

'I'd rather you kept it,' he told her brusquely. 'It's yours for as long as you want it, no matter whether you wear it or not.'

Judy bit her lip as he started up the car engine. Their next stop was the Sandiman Motel, and the reunion with her brother. Despite all her anxiety for him, it wasn't one that she relished, and her nerves were very much on edge at wondering what they were going to find once they got there.

'Why did you marry me, Blake?' she asked in a low voice. 'What possible reason could there be? I won't demean you by suggesting it had anything to do with that bet with Harry. I think you've got a little more integrity than that – '

'Thanks. A compliment at last.' But as he glanced at her, he saw the distress on her face, and his voice became more mellow. 'Maybe I married you because I love you. Did you ever consider that?'

'Not really,' she muttered. She was pretty sure he lusted after her, but that wasn't the same as love.

'Then I won't say it,' Blake retorted. 'Take another look at that street map and give me directions, will you?'

It took a while to find the Sandiman Motel, which was even shabbier than Judy had expected. There was peeling paint on the doors, and a creaking sign that advertised cheap rooms. As they got out of the car, the oppressive midday heat hit them.

The guy at reception took a while answering Blake's persistent bell-ringing. He looked at them boredly.

'You wanna room? Twenty dollars for a kingsize, twenty-five for two beds,' he said, with little interest.

'We don't want a room,' Blake told him shortly. 'We're looking for Ricky Hale. What's his room number?'

The guy looked wary. 'What's it to you? Are you the cops? If the kid's done something wrong, he can just sling his hook. I might be prepared to stall anybody who came looking for him, but I ain't sticking my neck out for no kid who's in trouble with the law – '

'We're not the cops. And this is for your trouble.' Blake flung down a ten-dollar bill, and the guy whipped it up so quickly it was almost like a sleight of hand.

'Room sixteen,' the guy grunted. 'Around back, halfway down the second line.'

They found the room, but when they knocked on the door, there was no answer, and Judy felt renewed fear that they were already too late. Anything could have happened under cover of darkness, and she was pretty sure that the guy at reception was the type who would shut his eyes and ears to anything that didn't concern him.

'Call out and tell him who it is,' Blake ordered. 'He's probably too scared to come to the door until he's sure.'

Judy leaned her face against the door. 'Ricky, it's me, Judy. Open up, *please*.'

Very slowly, the door opened a chink; once he was sure who it was, Ricky took off the chain and drew his sister inside. Blake followed and shut the door firmly behind them.

'Jude, thank God,' Ricky croaked, and as she held him in her arms she could feel him shaking uncontrollably against her. When he finally moved away, she could see how thin and gaunt he looked. She was shocked by his appearance.

'Who's this?' he asked suspiciously, looking Blake over.

'This is Blake Adams, the owner of the Sparkling Rocks Hotel where I work in Las Vegas. Didn't I tell you he'd be bringing me here?'

She was becoming more alarmed by the minute, realizing that he didn't seem able to concentrate on anything for more than a minute or two. For a few frantic seconds she wondered if he was on drugs, but she decided against it. You needed money for drugs, and it was obvious to anybody that Ricky didn't have any.

'When did you last eat?' Blake asked.

Ricky looked at him resentfully. 'Yesterday, I think. Or maybe the day before. Hell, I don't know! What difference does it make? That's not what I need – '

'Ricky, don't talk that way. Blake's here to help you,' Judy snapped. 'I've brought some fruit with me, and you're to eat some, and then we'll talk. We all need some coffee too – '

'There's a vending machine near the reception office,' he said sullenly.

Blake took charge. 'I'll get it, Judy. You two need to talk. And try to get some sense into him, if you can.'

'Who is that guy?' Ricky almost snarled when he and Judy were alone. 'He's got a bloody lot to say for himself.'

'I told you. He's my boss, and you'd better listen to what he has to say, Ricky, because a lot depends on it.'

He didn't say anything more as she gave him the bag of fruit she had thought to bring, and watched silently as he wolfed it down. She could hardly compare the once-bright, intelligent boy he had been with the hunted and pathetic figure he was now.

'You are going to help me, aren't you, Jude?' he said at last, when Blake had brought the three plastic cups of coffee back to the room.

'Blake's going to help you,' she told him firmly. 'It's out of my hands, Ricky. I couldn't possibly get hold of the kind of money you were asking for – and how you could have got yourself into such a terrible mess – '

'Let's leave out the lectures for now, Judy, and get down to business,' Blake put in as her voice began to rise.

He might be feeling a certain envy at the closeness that obviously existed between the brother and sister, even while she was so despairing of him, but he knew this wasn't the time to be thinking about that. And the sooner he got things sorted out here, and got back to his own environment, the better he would like it. He looked hard at Ricky.

'So let's talk. You're in debt to this loan shark for an extortionate amount of money and his heavies are breathing down your neck and threatening you with extinction if you don't pay up. Have I got the picture?'

Judy gasped. He sounded so hard and callous, and Judy could see that Ricky didn't care to have his problems so brutally outlined by a stranger. She didn't like it either, but everything Blake said was true, and Ricky had to face it. If he didn't change his way of life quickly, he probably wouldn't make it to his next birthday.

'You've got it,' he grunted.

'All right. So if I'm going to get you out of this mess, there's going to be a price to pay. You don't get anything in this life for nothing, and you're not going to be a millstone around your sister's life for ever.'

'Who the *hell* do you think you are?'

Judy held her breath. Blake could so easily go back on his promise not to tell anyone of their marriage, just to reinforce the connection between all three of them. He didn't even glance at her as he answered.

'I'm a businessman who's got no intention of losing the best choreographer I've had in a long time, just because some stupid kid has got into debt and is in danger of being wiped off the face of the earth.'

Judy gasped. He sounded so ruthless and so cold – and as if he really meant exactly what he said. As if he had no feelings for her at all, except for keeping her under contract for his precious show.

Her face burned with fury, still protective of her brother's feelings, but to her amazement she could see a spark of respect in Ricky's face now. Plain speaking from a stranger had evidently reached a part of his brain that she couldn't.

'So what are the terms?' he growled.

Blake continued in that cold, unemotional voice. Judy felt as if she hardly knew him any more, but she recognized that this was the business tycoon speaking, the one who was so brilliantly successful in everything he did and always got what he wanted.

'I'm not a charity, but I'm prepared to pay off your debts as a loan to Judy, who will pay me back in due course. Since I'm sure you'll want to spend a little time together, you'll come back to Vegas with us for a few days, but no longer. And if I get a whiff from any of my staff that you've spent so much as one red cent in the casino, you'll be sent packing. After a few days, if I find I can trust you, you'll fly back to England, where you'll agree to undergo a course of therapy for your addiction. I'll be getting in touch with Harry Brady to organize it with a Harley Street chap.'

'There's no need to involve Harry. I can do it myself – '

'But you won't, and I will,' Blake said calmly. 'That's the deal, so take it or leave it. And if you don't agree with any part of it, Judy and I are walking straight out of here, and you won't get a penny.'

Ater a few moments when she felt as if the atmosphere was electric between the two men, Judy saw her brother's shoulders slump, and he nodded slowly.

'You win. I've got no real choice, have I?'

'None at all,' Blake said pleasantly.

Judy hated him at that moment. She knew he had done all this for her, and she should be grateful. And so she was, but the humiliation she had seen on Ricky's face was almost enough to wipe out any feeling of obligation.

But it seemed as if Ricky wasn't going to feel humiliated for long. He was recovering with disgusting speed, Judy thought now, as soon as Blake said they were going immediately to the loan shark's office to sort things out.

All the same, she didn't miss the way Ricky glanced all around him before he got into Blake's hire car, as if he was still scared out of his wits that he was being watched. It wouldn't hurt him to be scared, she thought rebelliously, not if it pulled him up short to appreciate how near to disaster he had come. And if he had to seek professional help, as Blake insisted, maybe this time he could kick the gambling habit for good. She had to believe it.

They drew up at the seedy little office Ricky knew well by now, and Judy saw how he cringed back in the seat for a moment before getting out of the car. Even now, he was terrified of what might happen to him, but was clearly relieved when Blake told him curtly to stay quiet and let him do all the talking. They went inside, and the loan shark's eyes narrowed as soon as he recognized Ricky.

'What's all this? If you're bringing reinforcements to extend your loan, you're out of luck, sonny. I warned you what was going to happen if you didn't start paying up – '

Blake broke in sharply.

'We don't want a further loan. I'm representing the boy, and I want to see his contract, and every detail of the current amount he owes before you see a penny back.'

'Who the hell are you? If you're his lawyer, it cuts no ice with me. Everything's legal, and you don't see nothing until I'm assured that I'm getting something out of this young bucko. I ain't obliged to show you my records, neither – '

'And I say that you are, or you'll find yourself under investigation. And if you threaten him again, or touch him in any way, I'll have this place closed down so fast your feet won't touch the ground,' Blake snapped.

The guy gaped at him, clearly unsure just what authority he had. Judy knew he was calling his bluff, but to her relief, the guy wasn't taking any chances. He yanked open a drawer in his desk, and pulled out a large file full of accounts and details of repayments. Judy felt sickened, thinking of all the gullible people who came here. Kids like Ricky . . .

He threw down the relevant pages, and Judy saw Blake's mouth tighten as he scanned them quickly.

'You're a bastard,' he rasped. 'There's not a chance of anybody repaying to this extent.'

'I don't ask any of them to come here. I provide a service – supply and demand, that's all. And if that's all you've got to say – '

'It isn't,' Blake said coldly. 'Show me the contract.'

'How about showing me the dough?' The guy was suddenly more wary. 'How do I know this ain't all a set-up?'

'It isn't,' Judy broke in before anybody else could speak. 'Ricky's my brother, and we're here to get him out of this mess, so please do as we ask.'

After Blake's belligerence, maybe it was her softer voice that had the desired effect. Whatever it was, the guy said no more as he got out Ricky's signed contract, and Blake went through all the documents, trying not to show his disgust. The compound interest demanded was unbelievable, and so was the fact that Ricky had gone back for a further loan after the first one. Despite his business, Blake had never had to get personally involved in the results of gambling before, and it sickened him now as much as it did Judy.

While the loan shark waited watchfully to see what was going to happen next, Blake drew out a large roll of large denomination dollars from an inside pocket. The guy's eyes bulged as he began counting them out, but before he could touch any of it, Blake's hand slammed down over the bills.

'I'm prepared to settle this debt in full when you tear out all the relevant pages from your records and hand them and the contract over to me.'

'Like hell I will!'

'Then here's a taster on account, and you get the rest of it when you comply. Otherwise, you'll get nothing, and I'll see you behind bars for extortion.'

As he pushed a few of the bills across the desk, Judy prayed that he wasn't going too far. He was gambling now, on his voice and his authority, but she should have realized that he knew all the tricks. Once the loan shark had seen the wad of dollars almost in his hands, he was ready to agree.

Within seconds, it seemed, the accounts pages and the contract were handed over to Blake, who tore them into little shreds, set fire to them, and dropped them in the waste-paper bin. And only then did he push the remainder of the money across the desk, with a warning in his voice.

'Now we're quits. You never saw this young man in your life before, and you're never going to see him again.'

Judy couldn't get out of the fetid little office quickly enough. If Blake hadn't handled it the way he had . . . they owed him so much, and Ricky awkwardly tried to thank him.

'Forget it. Just keep out of trouble from now on, and do us all a favour,' Blake retorted. 'And remember that if it wasn't for your sister's concern, then some fine morning you'd probably have been found cut up into little pieces. Word would soon have got around that you'd lost every red cent – '

'Blake, for heaven's sake, hasn't he been through enough?' Judy gasped. 'He's promised to give up gambling – '

'Well, let's make sure about that when he spends a few days with temptation at the Sparkling Rocks, shall we?'

CHAPTER 11

They settled the motel bill and headed straight to Reno airport. Ricky seemed hardly able to say anything for a long while, since events had taken him over so quickly, and it was hard for him to believe he was really out of the wood. Judy tried to jolly him up as they made their way to the plane.

'You can sit in the co-pilot's seat if you like. I'm just going to close my eyes until we reach Vegas again. I've had enough excitement for one day.'

It should have been the happiest day of her life, and in some ways, it was the worst. As if getting married in such a hole-and-corner way wasn't enough, then the hateful experience in the loan shark's office . . . and if Ricky was still feeling down, Judy's spirits were getting lower all the time.

But, unbelievably, she realized he was getting perkier as the flight progressed, and asking Blake all about handling the controls of this little plane.

'Don't even think about it,' she heard herself say sharply. 'I wouldn't put my life in your hands if you were the last person on earth.'

The words were out before she could stop to think, and she heard Ricky answer just as sharply.

'I don't blame you for that, Jude, but you could at least give me a chance to prove myself. Blake's more civil to me than you are now.'

She could have told him it was because Blake didn't know him as well as she did . . . or because Blake had coerced her into marriage on account of saving Ricky's neck, and had got his own way yet again . . . but she clamped her lips tightly together and said none of it as the flight progressed.

As they neared Las Vegas they could see the glittering lights ahead of them, and Judy hoped it wouldn't start Ricky's fingers itching again. He was talking far more like his old bouncy self now, and she found herself praying, too, that he wouldn't let Blake down.

'We'll find you a room as soon as we get to the hotel,' Blake told him casually as they began the descent into Las Vegas airport.

'That won't be necessary,' Judy spoke at once, hiding her flicker of triumph at keeping this mini-trump card up her sleeve all this time. 'I'd prefer it if Ricky shared my suite. It's a long time we've seen one another, and we've a lot to talk over, and he can sleep in the small dressing-room.'

She dared Blake to object, but how could he? She expected him to honour their agreement, which meant he was hardly going to speak up now and demand that his wife shared his apartment, as he had every right to assume. Except that Judy had already insisted on her own condition. Nobody was to know

207

about their marriage for the foreseeable future. How long that situation was going to last, she wouldn't even consider, nor how difficult it might be to carry out.

She heard the coldness in his voice as he replied.

'If that's what you want, then naturally, I'll agree to it. What do you say, Ricky?'

'Whatever Jude says is OK by me.'

And he was only too eager to please, no matter who was pulling the strings, Judy thought.

She smothered any small sense of guilt she felt at knowing she was deserting her husband on their wedding night. But if co-habiting certainly hadn't been part of the bargain, neither was an occasional nocturnal visit to his apartment, or vice versa. And Ricky's presence in her suite was effectively going to clamp down on that idea. In any case, she had never agreed to a marriage solely of convenience, nor put it into those exact words, but that was the way it was going to be, no matter how dearly she would have wanted it otherwise.

In any case, she told herself she had no need to feel guilty over anything. She had married Blake under duress, and she had every intention of paying him back every penny of Ricky's debt, no matter how long it took. This was never meant to be a normal marriage, and there was no way she was going to pretend that it was.

But much later, lying in bed alone, with Ricky in the small adjoining dressing-room, she felt the sweet, treacherous longings inside, picturing how very different this night would have been for two people who truly loved one another.

This was surely the strangest wedding night anybody had ever had. Her husband, whom she loved, was in his apartment across the corridor of this luxurious hotel, and she was alone, restless and frustrated, while her feckless brother slept peacefully in the room next door.

For a wild moment she wondered why she had made her own stupid condition about the marriage, and if she was being extraordinarily stupid in not taking all that life had to offer for once. Even if it only lasted a while, and she behaved as recklessly as any gamblin' man . . .

She didn't know how long she had lain awake, tossing and turning, and trying not to imagine whether or not Blake was lying sleepless too, when she became aware of the sounds coming from the dressing-room. For a moment her heart stopped, and then, as she recognized the sounds, she slipped out of bed quickly, tying her dressing-gown around her.

At the adjoining door, she hesitated, wondering if she should ignore it after all, but she knew it was impossible. How could you ignore someone you loved, who was weeping as if his heart was breaking? He was still her young brother, no matter how many times he had abused the relationship.

She opened the door quickly and sped across the room, kneeling down beside the bed and taking him in her arms.

'Ricky, don't. It's all right now, really it is.'

'You don't know what it's been like, Jude,' he choked out. 'There were even times when I thought the best thing for everybody would be for me to end it all – '

'You musn't say that!' But she was appalled to realize how low he had got.

'It's true, though. You don't know what it's like to reach rock bottom. Nobody does, until they've been there. I had nothing, and I owed everything. That bastard meant what he threatened, Jude. If you and Blake hadn't come to Reno when you did, I probably wouldn't be here now. Time had run out on me,' he finished on a sob.

'Well, you're here now, and nobody's going to do anything to you. You've got to think positively from now on, Ricky, and look forward to the rest of your life. And you've also got to admit that you need help, and to accept it.'

While he was in a receptive mood, she knew she had to persist, even at the risk of making him lash out again. But it seemed as if he had seen the sense of it at last.

'I'll do it, Jude. And by the way, Blake is far more of a man than that rat Michael. So what's between the two of you?'

'Not a thing,' she answered steadily. 'He came to my rescue when I needed it, and we should both be grateful to him for that and not let him down. Right?'

'Right,' he agreed. 'Listen, I know it's late, but I'll never be able to sleep. The bed's too comfortable for a start, and I'm too used to staying alert half the night for obvious reasons. So I don't suppose there's any coffee going, is there? And you can tell me about this new show of yours.'

'To stop you thinking, I suppose?' she retorted lightly, since he'd never shown much interest in her work before.

'You know me too well,' he said.

So if the wedding night had begun strangely, it ended even more strangely, with the two of them in her sitting-room, poring over the sketches for the costumes and the dance routines, until Judy could hardly keep her eyes open. Finally, she just had to go to bed.

'You may not be tired, but I'm shattered,' she told him. 'We've both had enough soul-searching for one night, and I'm taking you shopping tomorrow.'

'What the hell for?'

'For some decent clothes. I'm not having my brother walking round the hotel looking like a slob. I've got my reputation to think of – and Blake's,' she remembered to say.

'Oh, yeah. So does he really own all this, Jude?'

'All of it.'

He gave a low whistle. 'He must be loaded, then.'

'Maybe he is, but don't let it go to your head, Ricky. He's my boss and nothing more. What he did for you was a favour to me, but it was strictly business, and I'm going to be paying him back as soon as I can.'

As she repeated what she had already told him, she hoped she had finally got the message across to him. She certainly didn't want Ricky to have any inkling that her relationship with Blake was anything more than strictly business . . . And at last she went to bed, feeling completely drained, and slept until morning.

* * *

She ordered a late-breakfast room service for them both. By the time it arrived, they had both showered and dressed, and Judy introduced her brother to the waiter.

'Luis, this is my brother, Ricky Hale. He's going to be staying here with me for a few days.'

'It's good to meet you, sir,' Luis answered, as smooth as ever and showing no surprise.

Judy hid a smile. The waiter was so spruce and immaculately dressed, like all the hotel staff, and Ricky was . . . well, still Ricky. His hair was long and dishevelled, and his denim jacket and jeans had seen better days. But all that was going to change, Judy thought determinedly. Today they were definitely going shopping.

After breakfast, she called Maggie's office to say she would be unavailable for the rest of the day.

'Is everything OK, Judy? When you and Blake disappeared like that yesterday, we wondered what was going on.'

Judy looked at the phone blankly for a few seconds. For one wild moment she wondered what Maggie would say if she said what was actually in her head right then.

We flew off to Reno and got my brother off the hook with a loan shark. Oh, and while we were there, Blake and I got married . . .

'Judy, are you still there?' she heard Maggie's voice again, and she answered quickly.

'Sorry, Maggie, I was involved in some paperwork. I'm fine, but I've got my brother staying with me for a few days, and we're going shopping today, that's all.'

And hearing Maggie's surprise as she commented that she was looking forward to meeting Judy's brother some time, she realized how she had neatly sidestepped telling her anything about their whereabouts yesterday.

The less she was reminded of it the better . . . even though she knew how futile that was. In her purse was the constant reminder of the gold wedding ring Blake had placed on her finger, wrapped in tissue paper inside its box. In any other circumstances what had happened would have been a whirlwind, fairytale romantic affair . . .

Even marrying in a twenty-four-hour-a-day wedding chapel in downtown Reno had been far less tacky than Judy might have imagined. Even without the dress and the flowers and the photographs, there had still been dignity and solemnity and beauty about the ceremony that she couldn't deny. Even with the farce of it all . . .

'Jude, are you OK?'

Ricky's face came into focus then, saying almost the same words that Maggie had said on the phone. She forced a smile.

'Of course I am. Yesterday was a bit of a shock to my system, though, and I won't forget it in a hurry.' And if they were both thinking of different things at that moment, that didn't matter, either.

'I know, and neither will I,' he told her, more crestfallen than she had ever seen him. 'I really messed things up for you this time, didn't I, Jude? Landing you with my massive debts and all. But once

213

I get home I'll get a job and pay you back as much as I can, I promise.'

She nodded, knowing that whatever kind of job Ricky got, it was going to take years for him to pay her back what he actually owed her.

'We'll get by,' she said instead.

He couldn't leave it there, though. 'But you won't want me hanging around here for too long, will you? I don't want to be an embarrassment to you – '

'You heard what Blake said. We both want you to stay for a few days. You need time to readjust after your ordeal, and the best place for that is with people who love you.'

He gave a snort. 'I can't imagine that guy loving anybody. He's as ruthless as they come.'

Judy didn't look at him then, knowing only too well that Blake knew all about loving somebody. He had loved Claire so much . . . and when Judy had asked him why he had married *her*, he had professed, in a throwaway manner, that he loved her . . .

It had probably been said because Mr Macho Man thought it was the kind of thing a woman wanted to hear. She hadn't believed it then, and she didn't believe it now. But in her heart, all she wanted was for it to be true.

'Blake's been the best friend you'll ever have, and don't you forget it,' she told Ricky evenly. 'I couldn't have got you out of this mess without him.'

'You're not falling for the guy, are you, Jude?' Ricky asked, more perceptive than usual at her tone of voice and the empty look in her eyes at that moment.

214

'Good lord, no!' she said in all honesty. She wasn't falling for him! She had done that long ago . . .

'That's all right, then. I wouldn't want him to have any kind of hold over you on my account.'

'I promise you he doesn't. We went into a business arrangement concerning you, and the less we pick it over now, the better. You've got to put it all behind you, Ricky. And if we're going shopping today, let's get a move on before it gets too unbearably hot to breathe outside.'

To her relief, he seemed ready to forget any suspicions about her relationship with Blake. The last thing Judy wanted was for him to think she had been blackmailed into marriage.

Having planned to take part of the day away from the hotel, Judy was relieved that she saw nothing of Blake before they left. She and Ricky spent the morning well away from the Strip, exhausting all the big stores and arranging to have the packages delivered to the Sparkling Rocks Hotel, since there was no way they could carry them all back.

'I don't need all this stuff,' Ricky protested, by the time they were in a downtown coffee bar for a breather. By then he was wearing a new pair of jeans and checked shirt, and looking decidedly tidier and more alert than he had been yesterday. 'This casual gear's OK, but I've got no intention of being dressed up like a dog's dinner – '

'That sounds like one of Granny's old sayings,' Judy grinned. 'But you just listen to me. It's only for a few days, and when you leave here and go home,

215

you can dress any way you like. But while you're here, you're not going to let Blake down – nor me. Do you think I want people to think I've got a gypsy for a brother?'

Or a gambling addict, she added silently.

'All right, I give in. But am I allowed to take a look around Vegas by myself, or do I have to have a bodyguard with me at all times?' he challenged her.

'I don't know. Do you?'

She saw his face redden. 'I know what you're thinking, Jude. Once I'm let loose, I'll be in one of the casinos and back to my old tricks. But I won't. For one thing, I don't have any money, and I'm not asking for any.'

'Well, that's a first,' she replied, trying to ignore the lump in her throat at the determination in his voice, and praying that *this* time, he really meant it.

And she had to trust him. She left him with a few dollars for cab fare if he needed it, and went back to the hotel by herself.

'I hear that Blake took you out to the ranch, Judy,' Maggie remarked that afternoon, when they were well into rehearsals. 'You don't know how privileged you are. He keeps his private life very private, and none of us knows all that much about him, even after all this time. Except maybe Frank, and he's as close as a clam when he wants to be,' she added resentfully, making Judy smile. Maggie loved a bit of gossip.

'I'm not saying Blake doesn't know exactly what he's doing, mind, by being so mysterious about his past,' Maggie went on, relieving Judy of the need to comment about the ranch visit. 'He's got his head screwed on all right, and it certainly intrigues all the girls who'd like to get into his bed and catch themselves a rich husband.'

'God, you're a cynic, Maggie,' Judy laughed.

'You need to be, kid, didn't you know?' she agreed, taking no offence. 'I'ts a cut-throat world in this business. Maybe things aren't the same in li'l old England, but out here, it's every gal for herself.'

'But you're still as soft as butter underneath, aren't you?' Judy grinned.

'Maybe, but don't you dare let anybody know it. Anyway, let's get back to the point. Don't tell me Blake hasn't made a play for you yet. The fact that he took you to meet these Cooper folk is quite something. None of us has ever met them.'

'It was no big deal. He probably just wanted company for the day, that's all, and took pity on a fellow Brit far from home.' And in making light of it, she sounded really pathetic, Judy thought in annoyance.

'Well, if you believe that, you'll believe anything,' Maggie retorted.

She was right, of course. Why would Blake Adams ever need to be short of company? Although, she also knew that the higher you rose, the lonelier you could be. It happened to kings and princes . . . and it was just about the feeblest thought to apply to someone like Blake.

But the thought lingered. Nor could she quite forget that special look in his eyes when he'd had Zoe's adoring arms cuddling him. Given the right

217

circumstances – and the right woman – Judy had had a glimpse of the family man he could be.

'We'd better get back to work,' she said quickly to Maggie, knowing she was in danger of letting the dreams get in the way. 'And I want to spend some time in wardrobe to check on those replacement Soho costumes. I have a nasty feeling that the new sheer fabric is going to be far too revealing, even for Las Vegas.'

'Honey, nothing's going to be too revealing for our audiences,' Maggie said drily.

Judy knew that she was probably right. Maggie had been in the casino, cabaret and show business long enough to know what the customers wanted. Besides, what did it matter about flimsy costumes when there was always a section of topless girls in every show!

It was only the more prudish-minded who could call them blatant. Their step-routines were always stately, and about as non-provocative as Mom's apple pie. Mostly, they provided no more of a static backdrop than if they were part of the scenery. They were just there to be admired, or ogled at, whatever your preference.

It was the showgirls who performed the set tableaux, with glittering costumes and towering, feathered and jewelled headdresses, that made the audiences gasp and applaud the loudest. But it was a comparatively small section of the company who did the most energetic and daring dances that produced the most excitement among the performers and audiences alike.

The show was already well into its run now, and was a rave success. It was reviewed as a spectacular extravaganza, but there were still costume changes to be made to bring it up to Judy's satisfaction, and she didn't want the adapted Soho costumes to be unnecessarily sleazy. Especially as she was introducing a new mood in one of the sequences.

It would be danced beneath muted blue lights to the haunting strains of 'Streets of London', *à la* Fred Astaire and Ginger Rogers. And she was especially pleased that Blake, as well as Frank, had approved of the various small changes she wanted to bring in during the show's run. She had wondered how that would go down with Frank, especially.

But Maggie was forever telling her that Frank was so besotted with her now that he'd agree to anything she said. Judy was sure it wasn't true; nor did she want it to be true, because it was a complication she could well do without. Since their first scratchy moments, there was a free and easy friendship between them now, and she was thankful she had got through to him that there was unlikely to be anything else.

She didn't see anything of Ricky until much later, by which time he produced the same amount of money she had given him earlier in the day, saying he hadn't even used it on cab fare. She gave him a quick hug, almost embarrassed by his eagerness for approval.

'You don't have to account to me for everything, Ricky, and tonight I want you to join me and Blake to watch the show. It's a special night, as it happens. We're a third of the way through the run, so there's a party afterwards. You'll get to meet a lot of people. It doesn't worry you, does it?'

'Not if some of the gorgeous girls I've seen around the casino are going to be there.'

Judy laughed. Ricky was back on form. And she was glad he was around to share the box with her and Blake that evening. She hadn't been alone with him since their marriage, and the thought of it was suddenly making her nervous.

'You've been avoiding me,' he murmured in her ear later, when they had taken their seats in the Diamond Showroom.

By now, Ricky was leaning eagerly over the side of the box, taking in everything, and Judy and Blake were out of earshot in the general hum of noise.

'I've been working this afternoon, and took Ricky shopping this morning so that he wouldn't disgrace you – '

'And apart from all that, you've still been avoiding me,' he stated. 'There's no need, Judy.'

She didn't know how to answer him. What did he expect? As far as everybody here knew, they were the same as they had always been. He was her boss, and she was his employee. They had never lived in one another's pockets before, and nothing had changed – except for the marriage certificate in his possession, and the wedding ring in hers.

'Please don't pressure me,' she murmured. 'You agreed to my terms.'

'And you agreed to mine, which didn't include behaving like a monk towards you – or any other woman, come to that.'

She looked at him sharply as the lights in the auditorium began to dim. 'What's that supposed to mean?'

Although he spoke quietly, she could hear the arrogance in his voice as he taunted her. 'Well, since we're not married as far as the rest of the world is concerned, there's nothing to stop either of us having a fling with someone else, is there? Unless you want to change your mind about making a formal announcement, of course – '

'I don't,' she said furiously, turning away. And nor could she bear the thought of watching him with someone else . . . but now she had a strong suspicion that he intended to do just that. Just to make her mad.

She gave all her attention to the beginning of the show then, thankful that her professional interest allowed her to become totally absorbed in it. It also helped to push away the thought of seeing Blake flirt with some other girl, and being unable to do a thing about it, since no one would think it was any of her business.

It was childish to taunt her with such a thing, she thought contemptuously. It wasn't worthy of him, and maybe he hadn't meant it seriously. But if he had . . . Judy's eyes suddenly sparkled. If he had, then two could play at that game, and it would just serve him right . . .

But it could be a dangerous game to play, especially with someone like Frank, who would need very little encouragement to overstep the bounds of friendship. And by the time the show was over and most of the company had been drawn into the party atmosphere of the Sapphire Suite, she had already decided not to lower herself to Blake's level.

As she took a glass of champagne from a tray, she eyed Ricky with some relief, seeing him already surrounded by some of the showgirls, who were appreciating the novelty of a new face and another British accent. And he was certainly enjoying good company and a better way of life. Hopefully, it was going to rub off and keep him sane.

Blake certainly did things in style, she thought, eyeing the mountains of food at the party that would surely never get eaten. There were dishes of caviare and other delicacies, great mounds of strawberries and creamy desserts.

She hadn't seen him make any kind of move on any of the girls, so perhaps his flirting threat was no more than a tease. But Frank was getting more than a little high on champagne as the late evening progressed, and Judy decided to keep well away from him. But inevitably he caught up with her.

'I hope you're going to give me a goodnight kiss tonight, baby,' he slurred, and she felt his clammy hands reach for her bare shoulders in the strapless black evening dress she was wearing. He had somehow manoevred her into a corner and pinned her to the wall. But he was so unsteady now that she managed to slide out from under him, and in seconds he was the one propping up the wall.

222

'You've had enough kisses already from the other girls, Frank,' she teased.

'Don't be stuffy, Judy,' he protested. 'Or I'll start to believe it's true what they say about you English girls.'

'And what's that?' She knew she shouldn't ask, but she had said it before she stopped to think.

'They say they're nothing but teasers. When it comes to the point, they put on that icy front that freezes a man off quicker than blinking. You're not like that, are you, honey?'

Judy froze then, wondering furiously if Blake could possibly have let slip Harry Brady's stupid name for her. Ice maiden . . . she was mortified to think Blake had mentioned it to anyone, and surely he wouldn't have . . . but she couldn't be sure, and Frank was grinning at her so lecherously now that all she wanted to do was to get away from him.

'Excuse me, please,' she croaked out, uncaring whether Frank slid right down the wall or not . . .

'What are you scowling about?' she heard Blake's voice ask close beside her. 'This is a party, and you're supposed to be enjoying yourself like your brother.'

In the crush of people, she hadn't caught sight of Blake for a while, and her heart leapt as always, seeing how terrific he looked in a tuxedo. Any man could wear one and look good, but when he also had flair and elegance, he looked like a million dollars. But she was in no mood to feel kindly towards him now.

'How many people have you told about the ridiculous nickname Harry gave me?' she hissed.

223

He stared at her as if she was crazy.

'None, of course. What do you take me for? And who's been talking out of turn to make you think I have?'

His curt reply made her feel foolish at once. It had been a spur-of-the-moment question, and this was neither the time nor the place to ask it at all. Besides, she had to agree with Maggie's comments. Blake never went in for idle gossip, and he never spoke about personal matters to anyone else. Certainly not his own, unless he chose to, and not hers.

'I'm sorry,' she muttered, even though she found it galling to apologize. 'It was just something I heard, and I probably took it the wrong way. I shouldn't have blamed you for it.'

He looked at her thoughtfully before he agreed. 'It seems to be a habit with you. But what makes you think I believe it any more? I know that beneath that cool exterior there's a very sensual woman just longing to get out.'

'Blake, please – ' she said, glancing around them quickly. But everyone else was enjoying their own slice of the party, except Frank, who had finally called it a day.

'Please what? Stop fighting me, Judy. Don't you know you're the most desirable woman in my life?'

'Oh?' she answered him flippantly. 'And how many others have you got in line?'

'None. I'm already spoken for, remember?'

She didn't want this intimate conversation. If he was flirting with her now, she knew she could get to like it far too much. She glanced around, looking for

Ricky. He was her buffer, and she knew she must be mad to think of needing a buffer to keep her away from her own husband.

'If you're looking for your brother, he and some of the girls have gone off to another party,' Blake told her casually. 'It's Candy's birthday, and they'll all be gone for the rest of the night. I told Ricky not to disturb you – if he comes back at all tonight.'

'You shouldn't have done that, Blake!'

'Why not? He's a man, Judy, not a child, and you've got to let him go. Besides, it gives us a chance to be alone.'

'I think all I need is bed,' she muttered.

'I can arrange that too.'

'That's not what I meant,' she said angrily.

'All right, then we'll have a nightcap in the apartment, or black coffee if you prefer. And I'll sit six feet away from you and never touch you – unless you ask me to.'

CHAPTER 12

Judy opened her eyes slowly. She was filled with a feeling of sleepy, Sunday morning well-being. The bedroom was still dark, and she stretched langorously with a contented sigh, knowing she needn't stir until noon if she chose. No one would disturb her unless she rang for room-service breakfast . . .

She suddenly froze, sliding her hands down the length of her body and realizing she was naked. She often slept that way in summer, but here, the air-conditioning usually had her snuggling into a nightie before the night was through.

But it was surely morning now . . . still somewhat disorientated she slid out of bed and groped for the robe at its foot, tying it around her shivering body and padding across to the window to draw back the curtains. She stood stupidly for a moment, staring out at the view that was dissimilar from her own. Staring out at the view from Blake's bedroom window . . .

'Oh no,' she groaned. 'I didn't – did I? *Did* we?'

If they had, it had been either so uneventful that it wasn't worth remembering, or with the help of the alcohol at the party, she had simply blanked it out.

She looked down at the unfamiliar dressing-robe she wore now. Silky, green striped, a man's dressing-robe. Blake's robe. The thoughts came and went in her head in short, staccato bursts. She was his wife, but even so, this hadn't been meant to happen. And, agonizingly, she couldn't even remember whether or not she had enjoyed it.

Or if she had agreed to it . . .

The suspicion that Blake could have taken advantage of the situation and forced her against her will wasn't welcome. But she dismissed it at once. Whatever he was, he was no rapist. Anyway, could a man be accused of raping his wife? She knew she was pushing away the memories as long as possible by these crazy thoughts, because in her heart she knew it had been wonderful . . .

And she was gradually remembering being scooped up in his arms, winding her arms around his neck and kicking off her shoes as he carried her off like some erstwhile sheikh in the desert . . . He had said he wouldn't touch her unless she asked him to, but she was intoxicated by the wine and the party, and his nearness . . . and it had all been so inevitable to make this their delayed wedding night . . .

The hazy recollections were becoming sharper now. He had lain her gently on his bed, and as his fingers had sought the fastenings on her dress, she had helped him. Slowly at first, and then feverishly as the hunger for each other overtook them both. His body had been warm and hard against hers, and she had been soft and compliant and welcoming. And he had been everything she had ever wanted . . .

'Oh, God,' she whispered now, closing her eyes tightly, as the treacherous memories came rushing back, and it seemed that every part of her tingled and throbbed, reminding her of just how incredible it had been.

She had felt so cherished, so loved. More loved than she had been in her life before. He was more gentle than Michael had ever been, yet more passionate too. And if that hadn't been love, she didn't want to question it.

She glanced at the clock on the bedside table and saw that it was ten in the morning, and she was alone. She shivered again, knowing she had to get out of here. She prayed that Blake wasn't still in the apartment. She couldn't face him right now. She dressed quickly. Maybe no one would even raise an eyebrow at seeing a woman in an evening dress in the morning, in this twenty-four-hour-a-day fun palace, but she certainly didn't want wanting anyone to see Miss Judy Hale creeping out of Blake's apartment . . .

She bit her lip, because she wasn't actually Miss Judy Hale any longer, but Mrs Blake Adams. But nobody else knew that, and it certainly wasn't her style to sneak out of a man's apartment at ten in the morning in last night's evening dress . . . She took a deep breath and pushed open the bedroom door, her head held high.

There was no one else in the apartment. There was only a breakfast tray covered with a white cloth near the sitting-room window, and a prominent note beside it.

'I couldn't bear to wake you since you looked so peaceful and angelic.'

Angelic? Remembering ever more acutely now how they had made love so wantonly and erotically, Judy doubted the accuracy of the word. She read on quickly.

'Have a good breakfast. Ring for more if you want it. I'm tied up all day, but I'll see you for dinner. And by the way, Ricky got back OK.'

There was no word of love, no endearments. Maybe that was best. Maybe endearments would have seemed just as false and farcical as this bizarre note to a lover. But to Judy's heightened senses, it was cold and insensitive. It suggested that he couldn't get out of there fast enough.

And her cheeks burned, wondering if she had been such a fool after all. She had told him about Michael, and he had seemed so understanding, because *he had been there*, and yes, she knew now that she had wanted to stay with him, to feel the comfort of his arms around her. A man who wanted her . . . she could have stopped it at any time, but she hadn't. She had wanted it too much to.

So, despite all that he had said, if he was privately crowing now over winning his bet with Harry, she was just as much to blame for allowing it to happen. Without wanting to admit it so blatantly, even to herself, she ignored the breakfast, found her evening bag on the sofa and rushed from the apartment, opening her own door with shaking hands and closing it quietly behind her.

Within minutes, she had stripped off her evening clothes and was standing under a steaming shower, knowing that however long it took, she could never wash away every memory of that magical night she had shared with the one man she knew she could love for a lifetime.

But later, feeling more sensible and awake, she defiantly ordered and ate breakfast in her own room. Making love had always made her ravenous, and the very thought embarrassed her now as she tried to think more rationally.

So what if she and Blake had made love? People did it every day, and if it was the original sin, then she couldn't think of a more pleasurable one. It wasn't even a sin in the strictest sense, since they had made their wedding vows. She should simply put it down to experience, play it cool, let him see that it had amused her as much as she presumed it had amused him. In the words of the song, it was 'just one of those things' . . . and 'this had definitely been a lovely way to spend an evening' . . . the words kept going round and round in her head like a litany, and she couldn't stop them.

She had got far too steeped in the slushy old romantic songs Danny Corsey had been belting out for the past three months, she thought despairingly. And then she gave a start as Ricky came sleepily out of the dressing-room, begging for coffee, apparently completely unaware that neither of them had been in the suite all night, and groaning that he intended staying in bed for the rest of the day.

Judy spent the rest of the morning unnecessarily revising details of some of the routines for the show, knowing they were as near-perfect as she and the performers could make them, but needing to get her mind back to workaday things.

But thoughts of Blake kept intruding, as she had known they would. She remembered his hands, holding her, caressing her . . . she remembered his mouth kissing her, tasting her . . .

She had been starved of love for too long, refusing to let it into her life again. But in one long, blissful night she had lost all her inhibitions, and abandoned all thoughts of modesty. He had brought her back to life as surely as if he had been the Prince to her Sleeping Beauty.

As the crazy thought entered her mind, she thought she must be going out of her head to be getting so dreamy about him. She had to remember that this was all a game to him. He had offered her marriage to save her brother's neck, and she had accepted in the same spirit, but on her own terms. Not that they had stopped him . . . but to preserve her sanity, she had to pretend that it was all a game to her too.

After a while, she knew she couldn't concentrate on any of her sketches and dance routines. She simply wasn't seeing them, and she had to get out of her suite. She needed noise and action to clear her mind of the insidious realization that she was lost now, hook, line and sinker, and life would never be the same again.

Ten minutes later she was in a place she had vowed never to be. Sundays made no difference to the lure of gambling. The casino was alive with weekenders, the slot machines tumbling out coins in joyous abandon, bells ringing everywhere. There was excited shrieking whenever anybody won, even if it was only a few dollars.

Judy stood behind a couple of large, blue-rinsed ladies working adjoining machines as if their lives depended on it, and watched them for a while. Their scarlet-tipped fingers dripped with diamonds, and they were obviously wealthy, yet they played the quarter machines as if they didn't have a dime to their names, and were noisily ecstatic when their winnings rattled into their plastic pots. It was mesmeric to watch.

'You waitin' to take a turn on this machine, honey?' one of the women asked Judy.

'No, thank you. But do you mind if I watch? I'm not putting you off, am I?' she said hastily.

'Watch all you like, hon. Maybe you'll bring me luck,' the woman chuckled, turning her attention back to the whizzing icons on her machine.

As if by magic, three jackpot figures appeared in a line, and it seemed as if the whole machine leapt into life. Flashing bright lights on the top of it spun around at speed, and the usual bells were accompanied by crashing music.

The woman clapped her hands, then hugged her friend, while Judy stood bemused, not sure what was happening.

'Have you won?' she asked, seeing that nothing else seemed to be happening. Except that a small crowd was gathering around them, and as they seemed to think she was part of the threesome, she began to feel conspicious.

'Sure thing, hon,' the woman shouted now, her voice and manner becoming louder in her excitement. 'Only the blessed jackpot, that's all! I reckon you did bring me luck. Now where's that darling manager boy?'

Judy started to back away, as somebody behind her hollered in her ear that winning any jackpot meant the machine had to be opened and re-set, and the winnings were then confirmed and paid out by a casino official at a pay-out desk. And since the winner looked very much like a seasoned slottie, and knew what she was talking about, Judy guessed that the Sunday-morning official would be Blake. Presumably he would have been paged by now to come and congratulate the winner.

Judy looked around desperately, and saw him coming their way. He didn't see her at once. He was too busy smiling and chatting to one of the casino hostesses with her tray of drinks and her come-on eyes. To Judy it seemed to say it all. He simply couldn't resist it, and since no one knew they were married, there wasn't a damn thing she could do about it. She looked away at once, her face burning, wondering why she had ever come into the casino at all.

As she made to push through the small crowd that had gathered, the winning lady grasped her arm.

'Oh, don't go, hon. Me and Martha are regulars here, and I want to tell our cute Mr Adams how you brought me luck with that fancy accent of yours. I can tell you're a Brit, same as him. On vacation, are you? I'll introduce you. He's got an eye for pretty girls.'

On and on she prattled in that loud, penetrating voice, and Judy knew Blake must have overheard most of it. He smiled indulgently at the woman.

'Stop your wicked matchmaking, Mrs Faraday. Anyway, the lady and I are already acquainted,' he told her, with wild understatement, thought Judy. 'Now then, are you two threatening to break the bank again?'

'It'll be a long time before anybody does that to you, darling boy,' the woman gushed.

God, she was actually making up to him, Judy thought in amazement, and she hid a smile. She must be a well-preserved eighty years old, and she was what Harry would have called a game old bird, and while there was life, there was hope . . . and if she didn't stop thinking in these ridiculous clichés, Judy knew she was in danger of becoming as cynical as he was.

'Hey, honey, why don't you stick with us and I'll stake you to a few dollars? We could clean up in this li'l old casino,' Mrs Faraday said now, still chuckling at Blake.

'Yes, why don't you, Miss Hale?' Blake asked innocently. 'You look as if you could do with a bit of excitement.'

'I think I've had enough excitement in my life for a while,' she replied, knowing he would know exactly

234

what she meant. 'So please excuse me, ladies – and good luck.'

'She does talk real pretty,' she heard the woman say behind her. 'I always did love a British accent, which is why I love yours, Mr Adams, honey.'

Judy escaped, smothering a laugh as she glimpsed the almost desperate look on Blake's face as the woman and her companion closed in and took him in charge. He had left the machine re-setting to one of his staff now, and was presumably going to escort Mrs Faraday and her friend to collect their winnings.

But from the way each woman had her arm linked firmly in his, it looked very much like the other way around. One up to the ladies, Judy thought.

But for her, it had been a sobering experience to see how the other punters crowded round, some envious, some downright aggressive as they complained that the two women had hogged those two machines all morning.

They must have spent a fortune in quarters, and all for whatever size jackpot they had got. It had still made them ecstatic. But however much it was, Judy had no doubt it would all be fed back into the machines again. It was frightening.

She didn't want to think of such an obsession and relate it to her brother. She tried not to be censorious, but it was the hardest thing in the world not to be, knowing what a fool he had been with his gambling craze in the past, and praying that he was finally seeing sense.

If he was once tempted again, she thought there would surely be no hope for him, and she wondered uneasily about the wisdom of Blake's idea to invite him here to stay here. It would surely have been far better to put him straight on a plane for England. But then she wouldn't have seen his nerves begin to unravel in her supportive company. She had to believe that Blake was experienced enough to know what he was doing.

Judy realized she had wandered through the rows and rows of slot machines that were getting busier now as the day progressed, but the far end of the casino was considerably quieter. The roulette and blackjack tables were here, and most of them were covered up during the early part of the day.

Only a very few were opened at this hour, to cater for the serious gamblers who simply couldn't keep away. She smiled at one of the croupiers she recognized, waiting for customers behind her baize-covered table.

'You're having a quiet morning, Ellie,' she greeted her.

The girl smiled. 'It won't last, but it's nice to take a breather. A couple of my regulars are getting married today, and the whole Hawkings party will be coming here later to celebrate.'

'You mean they're having their reception here? That's news to me – '

'No!' Ellie shook her head. 'They've decided that instead of taking a regular honeymoon they're going to celebrate with all their friends by having a big gambling spree. They've promised to start off here, but then they're moving on to the other casinos. It's like you people call a pub crawl, only in this case I guess it's a casino crawl.'

She grinned at her own joke. To Judy, it all sounded so awful that she couldn't let it go at that.

'I think that's terrible! What a waste of money!'

'It pays your wages, honey,' Ellie said drily.

'Oh, I didn't mean to criticize what you do. I just can't imagine giving up the thought of exchanging a honeymoon for a night in a casino, that's all.'

'Yeah, well, I see what you mean by that, but the two of them have been together for a long while now, so I don't suppose they worry about all that. The weddin's' just a formality to please their folks.'

'Where are they getting married?' Judy asked out of politeness, feeling she had to show some interest, even though the reality of it sounded so appalling to her.

Ellie glanced at her watch. 'At the Golden Bells Wedding Chapel along the Strip, I believe. If you're interested, you could just catch them. It's scheduled for two-fifteen.'

'I might just do that out of curiosity. Wedding chapels like this don't exist in England,' she said.

She had no intention of doing any such thing, and nor did she want to think about weddings and honeymoons. Until Michael had dropped his bombshell on her, she had fondly supposed that they would get married one day . . . they had been together a long time too, and a legal piece of paper hadn't been important to them either. It was only later that she knew it hadn't mattered a damn to Michael at all.

She left the casino through the far entrance, avoiding the hectic sounds of the slot machines, and the gimlet eyes of Mrs Faraday and her friend. She had no wish to be a good luck charm for anyone.

Outside, she stood uncertainly, wondering which way to go. The Sparkling Rocks was in a prime central position, and she headed north again, relishing the sunshine and pushing all thoughts of Blake and last night out of her mind. And reminding herself that she should know better than to read anything significant into what had happened between them.

A taxi cruised along beside her.

'You want a cab, lady?' the guy called out. 'It's a long walk for those pretty feet, and you'll be doing plenty of standing around in the casinos.'

'No, thanks. And I'm not going to any casinos.'

'Why not take a ride then, and see the sights?'

The guy still cruised alongside, clearly refusing to take no for an answer for as long as possible. And after a few more minutes' indecision, Judy gave in.

'All right. You can take me to the Golden Bells Wedding Chapel,' she snapped, and the taxi door was opened almost before she could draw breath.

As she sat inside, and the cab chuntered along the Strip, she was still wondering why on earth she had said it. It was no more than a focal point in a day in which she still felt unsettled and disorientated. Ellie had put the idea in her mind, and she was acting on it. And if that made her a wimp with no thoughts of her own, then a wimp she was.

'Here you are, lady,' the driver said eventually. 'You sure this is where you wanna be? I'd have thought a classy dame like yourself would have wanted a big-scale weddin'.'

'Thanks for the compliment – I think,' she muttered, not bothering to tell him she wasn't the one getting married. She thrust his fare into his hand and didn't wait for any change. She wasn't going to get it anyway, she thought, as the guy sped off to look for some other fare.

The outside of the wedding chapel was painted in garish blue and gold, and the sounds of muted music could be heard from inside. She saw a small group of people coming outside, and all of them, including the bridal pair, were dressed in Western outfits, and Judy hastily stood to one side.

Another group was drawing up in a white limousine, and as it was almost two-fifteen now, she presumed this was the wedding party Ellie had meant . . . and then her eyes widened.

The girl who stepped out of the limo wore the kind of wedding-gown that must have cost the earth. It was encrusted with *diamanté* and pearls, and wouldn't have looked out of place in Westminster Abbey. Her headdress was a glittering tiara that certainly hadn't come out of Woolworths.

She was a stunningly beautiful girl, and the sight of her was so unexpected that Judy couldn't think straight for a minute. The groom was dressed in a formal tuxedo, along with most of the small party of guests.

'You coming inside?' she heard a voice urge beside her, and along with another passer-by, Judy found herself propelled inside the wedding chapel.

She knew what to expect now, but although the ceremony was as brief as hers and Blake's had been, she couldn't deny that it was beautiful, and for a very special reason. The couple exchanging their vows and gazing into one another's eyes were so obviously in love . . .

She swallowed the lump in her throat, suddenly needing to get out of there and breathe some fresh air.

She was near the casinos at the far end of the Strip now, and she went inside the first one, just to clear her mind of what-might-have-beens. But the sight of that wedding had really got to her more than she had expected.

She ordered some coffee in the casino coffee bar, glancing around and trying to take an interest, and comparing it unfavourably with the Sparkling Rocks. This one was smaller, and brasher, and if any casino could be called classy, it was Blake's. But then, he'd had the money to plough into it, and it was obviously drawing clients who appreciated luxury accommodation and attention to detail, and had plenty of money to spend. She forced herself to think in cynical terms, to take her mind off the bridal couple in the wedding chapel.

Later, she took another taxi back to the Sparkling Rocks. The day was getting hotter, and she couldn't face the long walk back down the Strip. She entered by the roulette entrance again, and was completely taken aback to see the entire Hawkings wedding party now surrounding Ellie's table.

Judy hadn't expected them to be doing their casino crawl still wearing their wedding outfits, but from the way it was drawing a crowd, she knew it could only be good for business wherever they went. Everyone would want to touch the bride for luck . . .

She turned away, and she found Blake walking straight towards her, and her heart leapt.

'How are you?' he spoke quietly, taking her by surprise.

'I'm fine! Why shouldn't I be?'

He looked steadily into her eyes, just as if he could see behind the brittle façade. Just as if he could read her mind at that moment and know that she was thinking that however tacky she had always thought a Nevada wedding chapel to be, as long as the couple concerned were in love, it didn't matter a damn. Even if it did take no longer to get a divorce than it did to get married . . .

'I'm just going to congratulate a couple of our regulars who got married today,' Blake told her.

'I know. Ellie told me. In fact, I was there. It was – interesting.'

She heard herself making aimless small-talk because, suddenly, she didn't know what to say to him. How did you react to a man who had made passionate love to you the night before, and who looked at you warily now, as if he thought you were about to denounce him in public!

She knew she was completely overreacting, but it was hard not to when he seemed so remote, and so businesslike, when she knew just how passionate and loving he could be.

'Interesting,' he commented. 'Well, that's one way to describe it, I suppose. And after all the money the

Hawkings families have put into today, I hope they get some returns on their investment.'

'And I thought I was being cynical! Anyway, with the type of honeymoon they're having, the only people to get rich will be the casino owners.'

They were a little way away from the noisy end where the Hawkings party was whooping it up now. They were temporarily in an isolated world of their own among the rows of silent, covered roulette tables.

'So what kind of honeymoon will suit you?'

Judy flushed at the mocking question.

'*If* the question ever arose, I'd want something a good deal more romantic than going from casino to casino!'

'In case it's slipped your beautiful mind, the question's already arisen. And I'm asking it again.'

'My answer is about as serious as the question,' she retorted, wondering how they had ever got into this discussion.

She moved away from him and walked quickly through the casino without seeing or hearing any of the jangling slot machines. It was crazy to feel upset by a light-hearted question, no matter how provocative.

But then, she had just seen two people who loved each other get married in such an unexpectedly moving ceremony in the most unlikely place she had ever imagined. She had let her own foolish dreams into her head, and she could do without Mr Macho Man Adams goading her into saying things she didn't want him to hear.

Where *would* she want to go for a honeymoon, anyway . . .? Certanly not here. Anywhere away from here, and away from people. Judy couldn't imagine anything worse than having all those people breathing down your neck, when all you wanted to do was to be alone with the man you loved. Somewhere romantic and peaceful, and away from the rest of the world . . .

She was so caught up in the thoughts that she only dimly heard a voice speaking to her as she passed reception.

'Miss Hale, I've been calling your room for the past half-hour. There was a call for you from a London number. I have it here, and the gentleman left a message for you to call him back.'

She hardly needed to look at the number on the piece of paper the girl was handing to her. It was Harry's number, as she had known it would be. And she wondered at once if Blake had thought to call him or fax him about Ricky! It seemed unbelievable to think that everything had happened yesterday; events had overtaken them so fast since then that she hadn't even given Harry a thought.

Once in her suite she almost flew to the phone, and yelled into it as she heard him answer.

'Harry? Has Blake given you the news about Ricky? I know I should have done it myself, but everything happened so quickly. Anyway, in case you don't already know it, Ricky's all right, and he's here – '

There was the usual interminable few seconds' wait across the Atlantic before he replied, but when

243

he did, the careful way he chose his words told her that he was fully acquainted with everything.

'Blake's already called me with the details, Jude, and I just want to say that if he wants a roof over his head when he returns home, Elsie's offered to put him up for a while until he finds something more permanent. You know what a soft spot she always had for him.'

'That's really kind of her.' Judy was extraordinarily touched by his secretary's offer.

'And I'll get on to the Harley Street man Blake mentioned right away. The sooner the better, I imagine.'

'Yes, you're right,' Judy said slowly, hoping desperately that Ricky wouldn't go back on his promise to seek help.

But with Elsie's motherly eyes on him, she doubted that he'd stand much chance. Especially if Harry was also looking out for him. Without any compunction, she decided to cash in on his good nature while he was in a benevolent mood.

'Harry, you do know how important it is for my peace of mind that Ricky's all right, don't you? And before you say it, I know he's a man and all that, but if I'm to carry on working over here – '

She didn't need to say any more. The last thing Harry would want now would be for her to blow her contract, and his fat commission with it.

'Don't worry about a thing, Jude. I'll look after him as if he was one of my own – '

'Yes, well, don't overdo it.' She grinned into the phone.

'Oh, and Jude – you'd better fax over the details of his return flight once Blake's arranged it. There's no sense in fixing up doctor's appointments for the kid until we know when he's coming back. But I gather it'll be pretty soon.'

'I guess so. And since Blake seems to be arranging everything, I'm sure he'll let you know as soon as possible.'

She didn't know why it irked her so much that Blake was so efficient. Ricky was perfectly capable of arranging flight times for himself, and she was even better. Instead, Blake was seeing to it all. Blake wasn't only taking her over, he was taking over the whole damn lot of them, it seemed. She should be grateful, but she wasn't, even though she knew how churlish it was to think that way.

And of course he'd want to get Ricky away from here as soon as it was convenient. It had been so easy, last night, for him to get her to stay in his apartment. No one had been aware of it, and although Ricky was staying in her suite, even he had been oblivious to the fact.

It would be even easier for Blake to continue his relentless seduction once her brother had gone back to England, and Judy wasn't sure how long she was going to be able to resist what her heart really wanted.

CHAPTER 13

Two days later Blake checked the accountant's monthly casino and showtime figures with less than his usual feeling of satisfaction. He and Judy had managed to avoid one another very neatly all that time – or rather, she had been avoiding him, he thought in annoyance, preferring to spend all her spare time with her brother.

But the Sparkling Rocks was enjoying a spectacular run of success with its new show now, and he knew that, between them, Frank, Maggie and Judy had worked miracles and were getting rave reviews. He believed in praising his staff, and he knew he should be feeling on top of the world, but there was a nagging feeling of unrest in his soul.

He had always prided himself on getting the best, and the hotel had an enviable reputation for quality in all areas, but he could never have anticipated that the best in his life would come in the delectable shape of Judy Hale. And he couldn't forget what had happened on the night of the party nor did he want to – but because of the circumstances, it wasn't giving him the pleasure he knew it should.

He had cursed the ridiculous bet he'd made with Harry Brady a hundred times, and even more, he'd cursed taunting Judy with it. But in the beginning it had been no more than the kind of competitive game he and Harry had always played, and which he invariably won, he thought arrogantly.

But he wasn't winning now. He recognized that the tables had been well and truly turned on him.

It was true that there had been very little seduction needed on his part. Judy was his wife, and she had gone far more willingly into his arms and his bed than he'd had any right to expect after the way he'd got her to marry him. But a night that had begun at a late-night party had ended more passionately than even Blake had anticipated.

He truly hadn't intended it to happen. Not then. But, slowly and surely, Judy Hale had also grown more important in his life than he had intended. Long ago, he had decided that the idea of giving all his love to one woman had died when Claire had died. He hadn't even wanted to love again, and was prepared to take his pleasures when and where he chose.

However calculating and selfish that was, he had persuaded himself that such a decision staved off the hurt that came when love died. And he knew that in that respect, he and Judy were very much alike, for she had done the same thing after her affair with the unknown Michael had ended.

But such cold calculations didn't take account of emotions and feelings and longings . . . and the fact that during these last weeks, while their show was getting such ecstatic reviews everywhere, and they should have been celebrating together, Judy had barely given him the time of day when she didn't have to.

And it had driven him wild – until the night she had come bursting into the apartment with the news about her brother.

He knew damn well she had only agreed to marry him to save Ricky's neck, and Ricky had been a complication that he had easily been able to deal with. But for the first time in his life, Blake Adams was feeling remorse because of that one wonderful night they had spent together, and he didn't care for the feeling. It also got in the way of the memories of Judy's lovely, responsive body lying in his arms.

He rang through to her suite that afternoon, knowing she was there. He had to have it out with her, if only because the situation was becoming impossible. He no longer felt in control of his emotions or his life. In weeks, rather than months, her time here would be up, and all he could see was a bleak future without her. Unless he did something radical about it, like telling everyone about the marriage – and he knew that wasn't on.

'Can you come to the apartment, Judy?' he asked abruptly. 'I want you to see the monthly figures for the show.'

'I'll take it as read, now you've told me.'

'Damn it, woman, I want to make my peace with you,' Blake snapped into the phone. 'Can't you recognize an olive branch when you see one?'

'Oh, is that what this is?' She was suddenly enjoying making him squirm. Maybe most women would have played along with him, and been delighted to take one night of bliss as the doorway to a heavier relationship, but she wasn't most women. One-night stands weren't for her. But she had no intention of letting him think it had been so all-important to her either – even if it was.

'If you're not in here in two minutes flat, I'm coming over to get you,' he told her curtly.

'Well, since you're the boss, and that sounds like an ultimatum, I'll be there right away – sir.'

She put down the phone gently, resisting the urge to hurl it across the room. Ricky was still asleep, and she had no intention of waking him. Plenty of sleep was obviously what he needed now that his traumas were behind him.

She watched the second hand on her clock until it had registered one minute and fifty seconds, and then she walked across the carpeted landing, and knocked on the door of Blake's apartment.

'Exactly on time, I believe.' She hoped she sounded calmer than she felt. 'Just like a good employee should be.'

She was amazingly nervous at being here, but since he was calling the tune and paying her salary, she didn't have much choice. And she could hardly accuse him of sexual harassment, knowing how willing a partner she had been . . . and she couldn't dispute the fact that she *was* his wife . . .

Blake called to her to come in, saying the door was on the latch. She registered the very Englishness of the comment, since there were no visible latches on these electronically operated doors.

He was standing by the window, looking out, and just for a moment Judy had the extraordinary feeling that he looked vulnerable and alone. It was just as she had once said. The higher you rose, the lonelier you could be. The feeling faded as soon as he turned to her, his arms folded.

'I wanted to congratulate you on your part in the success of the show.' He spoke almost without expression.

'So you said, and I'm pleased, of course, but it hardly needed a command appearance for you to tell me that, did it?'

He smothered an expressive oath. 'Damn it, Judy, why must you always hold me at arm's length?'

If this is love, he has a strange way of showing it, she thought. But of course it wasn't love. It was no more than a sexual challenge. He was a gambling man, and she had better remember it. But then she wilted slightly.

'I don't remember always holding you at arm's length,' she muttered. For one night that had been more spectacular than any showtime, they had been as close as if they shared the same skin.

And she couldn't forget it. No matter how much she tried, it seemed as though the images became more sharply defined in her memory. It wouldn't help to dispel the tension that always seemed in danger of flaring up between them. For that reason, she knew she had to avoid being in his sole company as much as possible. Thank God he had arranged their wedding in Reno and not here, where everyone would expect them to act like normal newlyweds. And just as quickly, she knew how bitterly she regretted what had almost amounted to a shotgun wedding . . .

She was quiet for so long that he took her silence as contempt, and his voice mellowed.

'Look, Judy, about what happened between us – '

'Oh? Did something happen?' she countered, wide-eyed and innocent.

'You know damn well it did, and don't tell me it didn't mean as much to you as it did to me!'

'I know what it meant to you. It meant you won your bet with Harry, and you could report back that you'd melted the ice maiden – that *was* your phrase for it, wasn't it?'

'Good God, what do you take me for? Of course I haven't reported anything to Harry. And I forgot the stupid bet long ago. I wish I'd never mentioned it in the first place.'

'So do I,' she muttered. 'Now, was there anything else, or was I sent for simply to discuss something so unimportant?'

He looked at her without speaking for a moment, and then he shrugged.

'I don't believe you would ever think of making love as being unimportant. You're capable of much deeper feelings than that. But we'll let it pass for the moment. And, yes, I also wanted to show you the latest reviews in case you hadn't seen them. We made the front page of *Showbiz Weekly*. My actions aren't all subterfuge, whatever you may think.'

She took the magazine he held out to her from the pile on a side table. No, she hadn't seen it. She was almost shocked to think how little interest she had had in following up the reviews. Now that the show was going so well, her part in it was superfluous. They could manage very well without her.

It was a thought that had come to her more than once during the sleepless hours of the night. The situation between herself and Blake was in danger of becoming intolerable, even if no one else knew of it but themselves.

And if she insisted on a quickie divorce when her contract expired, what then? Another opening, another show in some other town . . . But she wouldn't think about that. She would do a Scarlett O'Hara and think about it tomorrow . . . or tomorrow or tomorrow . . .

She gazed at the photos on the front page of *Showbiz Weekly*. The beautiful showgirls were pictured in their fabulous Soho costumes that Judy had thought far too risqué at one time, even for Las Vegas.

But she had to concede now that Maggie had known what she was talking about. The costumes were just perfect, and she couldn't deny a thrill of pleasure, knowing she had been responsible, in part, at least, for the success of the show.

'You're mentioned again. Turn to the centre pages.'

She automatically opened the magazine to the centre spread. The feature was a marvellous piece of publicity for the Sparkling Rocks. There was a montage of the various dance sequences on the centre pages, and along the foot of the page were the smiling faces of Frank, Maggie and herself. There was a brief bio beneath each one, acknowledging the importance of the Dance Director and choreographers.

Judy felt undeniably pleased. She was used to having a brief mention in the programme pages, though she doubted if people ever took much notice of anyone but the stars of a show. She didn't normally get her photo included, and she was definitely flattered, and curious.

'Where did you get the photo?' she asked Blake at last, knowing she had to say something.

He was as smooth as ever. 'I got Harry to send me one in case we needed it for publicity purposes at any time.'

'Well, I'm delighted we got such good reviews. Can I keep this copy? I'd like to read the feature in my own time.'

'Of course. Oh, and by the way, Ricky's flight home is fixed for Thursday. I'll let you know the details later,' he added, as if he was just as anxious to be rid of her now.

As she escaped to her own suite Judy's heart jolted at his words, but she had known that Ricky's departure was inevitable. It was crazy. She longed to be with Blake, but the tension between them was almost palpable now. They had crossed a barrier over which they couldn't return, and life was going to be even more difficult here from now on.

Keeping their marriage a secret was only the tip of the iceberg, and she bit her lip as the word came into her mind. There were times when she'd thought she and Blake could be so compatible, and *had* been. And she missed it.

She concentrated on reading the *Showbiz Weekly*, and had to agree that the reviews couldn't have been better. Whoever the mag's critic was, he was overflowingly gushing in his praise, not only of the professionalism of the show itself, but of those behind the scenes. And that included Judy Hale.

The critic emphasized her Britishness, and how she had brought it so stunningly to the public in her routines for that part of the show. He finished by reporting that of course, he was an Anglophile at heart, so Judy Hale could do no wrong in his eyes. She blew him an imaginary kiss.

Her next thought was that Harry had to see this. She rang down to reception, knowing there would be dozens of copies of the mag strewn about the casino, and asked for one or two to be sent up to her suite. Not for anything would she knock at Blake's door again.

Minutes later a bellboy knocked on her door and handed her a pile of the magazines. They never did things by half here, she thought drily, thanking him.

Then she called Harry.

'I thought you'd like to know we've got rave reviews again, and I've even had a proper mention with my photo included,' she said.

'That's great, kid. I always knew you were headed for the big time. Didn't I tell you?'

'You did, Harry. Do you want me to fax the pages to you, or put a copy of the mag in the mail?'

'Both,' he answered predictably. 'And now you can tell me what's wrong.'

'There's nothing wrong! What should be wrong?'

'Come on, Jude, I know you too well, and I can hear the strain in your voice. You should be on cloud nine if the reviews are as good as you say. And you haven't mentioned Ricky yet. You're not still worrying about him, are you? I tell you, now that Blake's taken him in hand, he'll do all right. Blake's a pretty good psychologist, and if he thought it was a good idea for Ricky to stay in the hotel, it will be. Baptism by fire, and all that.'

Judy latched on to his words. Even though it seemed that Blake was always coming out whiter than white in Harry's view, anything was better than letting him suspect there was real friction between them – or anything else.

'Of course I'm worried about Ricky. Aren't I always? But he does seem to be more relaxed now,' she admitted. 'In fact, if I don't get him out of of bed soon, this entire day will be gone. Oh, and apparently his flight home is booked for Thursday. I hope he'll be OK when he finds out!'

She heard his heavy sigh, and knew he wasn't convinced that she was as relaxed as she made Ricky out to be.

'Jude, you don't need this. Leave him to sort out his own problems, if he's still got any. And get the exact flight times over to me as soon as possible. Elsie's already fussing over the thought of having him to stay, and driving me crazy with her nesting instincts.'

Judy had to laugh at that, knowing where Elsie's nesting instincts would have taken her, if Harry hadn't been such a confirmed and crusty old bachelor.

'I'm sure you're right, Harry, and I'm an idiot,' she agreed, trying to inject a lighter note into her voice. 'What would I do without you?'

'With your credentials, you'd probably get along very well. But since I don't aim to let you go, you'd better forget I said that.'

She laughed, her spirits lifting. Despite all, it did her good to talk to Harry. He could be foxy and ruthless when it came to business deals, but she knew he cared about her.

She was still smiling when she put down the phone and carefully cut out the relevant pages of *Showbiz Weekly* to fax to him. She fed them into the machine and sent them through.

Next she packaged up two extra copies and called out to Ricky that she was going out, deciding to take a walk to the post office with them rather than using the hotel mailbox, and needing some air.

'Oh, Jude,' he called back. 'I may be out for the rest of the day. That's OK, isn't it? I've got a date with one of the casino girls, and we're taking a drive somewhere.'

'Of course it's all right! You know you can come and go as you please.'

She hesitated for a moment, because after Thursday everything would be changed, and he'd be on his way back to England. But she didn't want to burst his bubble by telling him yet. She'd leave that until later – or let Blake be the harbinger of his own news.

She left him then, feeling relatively free of her own commitments now, even though she still liked to be on hand to check that the dance routines were still as she wanted them. There were still rehearsals to oversee, but the girls were such dedicated professionals they rarely put a foot wrong.

She was in the post office paying the cost of mailing the magazines when she heard a female voice behind her.

'Why, Judy, how lovely to see you again!'

She turned in surprise, and then her face broke into a smile as she saw Ginny Cooper's red face beaming at her. She certainly wasn't a movie-star beauty, but Ginny had the kind of warmth in her face that money couldn't buy.

'It's lovely to see you too, Ginny, but I didn't expect to see you here! What are you doing so far from home?'

Even as she said it, she knew the distance from the Cooper ranch to here was nothing in terms of the travel most Americans did. They thought nothing of making a two-hundred-mile-or-so round trip for dinner.

'Oh, we come in once a month for grocery shopping. Kyle's somewhere around town,' she answered vaguely. 'He's gone to the travel agency to fix up our trip to Europe. The kids are so excited about it, you wouldn't believe.'

'I'll bet they are. Say hello to London for me,' Judy told her with a smile. Though she knew at once that it was a pointless remark to make, since she might well be back there before the Coopers!

'Do you miss it, honey?'

Judy thought for a split second. It didn't take any longer than that to answer.

'Not really. I love it here, and even the climate doesn't bother me too much now that I'm used to it, and I love the people – and my job, of course.'

'Yes, well, that sounds like a pretty good list of credentials. But don't let Blake work you to death. He thinks of nothing but work, and it's time he thought about his real life a bit more. I thought you two were getting along pretty well when you came out to the ranch, by the way, so when are we going to see you both there again?'

Judy kept her voice as expressionless as possible as she spoke. 'I don't know, but you shouldn't go reading anything special into our visit, Ginny. As you said, Blake thinks of nothing but work.'

'Well, maybe that's what I said, but it wasn't entirely what I meant. And he's never brought anybody out there before. Kyle still hopes he'll buy us out. Blake needs to put down some roots, instead of spending all his time in that old hotel of his. What kind of life is that for a man?'

Judy hid a smile. Ginny was the most uncomplicated woman she knew, and a hectic showbusiness life was something she simply couldn't comprehend. She spoke lightly.

'I don't imagine anybody will have any influence on changing Blake's way of life except Blake himself.'

'Or the right woman,' Ginny put in neatly. 'Don't ever think that it won't happen, even to the best of men.'

She persuaded Judy to join them for coffee and then lunch, and for all the money that they undoubtedly had, they met Kyle at a hamburger bar and sat on stools at the counter. The whole decor of the place was in the fifties style, with an old jukebox blaring away in the corner. At any minute Judy expected to see the High School kids from *Happy Days* come through the doors and to see Fonzie slicking down his hair.

She was totally charmed by the sheer nostalgia of it all, and sometimes she thought she could easily start to believe that the whole of America was one delicious theme park.

'You and Blake are to come on out to the ranch some time soon, you hear?' Kyle told her, when they had finished lunch. 'I'll call him and arrange things.'

'Well, don't be surprised if he declines, at least at present,' Judy spoke quickly, hoping she didn't sound ungracious. 'We're terribly busy with this new show, as you've probably seen in the papers. And I've got my brother staying at the hotel for a while too.'

'We never read the showbiz pages.' Kyle shook his head. 'Ginny and me are too busy living in the real world to bother with all that stuff.'

'We've never even set foot inside Blake's hotel,' Ginny added, confirming what Maggie had told Judy. 'Kyle and me don't care for all that phoney baloney, no offence, hon. But it's nice to hear that you've got your brother staying. Maybe you could bring him out some time too.'

259

'Well, he's only been here for a short visit, and I think he'll be going back to England in a few days,' she told Ginny with a forced smile.

But the pair of them were incredible, Judy thought. They even seemed to think as if they were carbon copies of one another, but they were such nice people, in the best sense of the word, and she had an enormous amount of respect for them. In the middle of all this glitter and razzmatazz, they were the sanest people she knew.

And they had obviously brought up their children the same way, since a trip to Europe to visit all the famous places was going to be the highlight of Bobby and Zoe's year.

'Well, I suppose I should be getting back now,' Judy said reluctantly, though she didn't have any real need, and Ricky seemed far more disposed to occupy himself with the off-duty girls now than to spend every minute with his sister.

It was how it should be, and since she knew the girls never wasted their money in the casino, Judy was highly relieved that he'd turned his attention to healthier pursuits.

'Why don't you come on out to the ranch with us now for the afternoon?' Ginny suggested. 'You look kinda peaky, Judy, and some fresh air will do you good. Kyle will run you back when he picks up the kids from school. They both have after-hours classes today.'

She didn't ask him about the plan, but she obviously didn't need to, knowing he'd be agreeable to anything she wanted. And before Judy could think of any reason why she shouldn't go with them, they were standing up and brushing the crumbs from their clothes and taking it as read.

'That's settled then,' Kyle was saying now. 'Ginny will be glad of the company, and the two of you can jaw as much as you like. Zoe's a great kid, but Ginny can do with some grown-up female company from time to time.'

And if Judy suspected an ulterior motive in pumping her about how likely it was for Blake to buy the ranch, she chose not to think of it. It would be an unexpected trip, and she wasn't answerable to anybody.

All the same, just in case Ricky got back before she did and started wondering where she had got to, she called the hotel from a phone booth, and left a message at reception that if anyone wanted her, she would be out of town for the afternoon. Other than that, she didn't see any reason to let anyone know exactly where she was going. Especially not Blake. The Coopers were his friends, but by now, she felt that they were her friends too.

The nearer they got to the ranch in Kyle's station wagon, the more cheerful and relaxed Judy felt, even though it was an odd way to feel, considering Kyle's driving. He drove at breakneck speed, and Ginny frequently shouted at Judy to hold on to her seat. They were a crazy, wonderful couple, she thought, and so lucky to be so much on the same wave-length.

But they weren't fools, despite the almost hillbilly image they seemed so happy to cultivate. She doubted that they would ever change, no matter where they went. London didn't know what was in store for it . . .

Kyle roared the station wagon to a halt in front of the ranch house, and Judy climbed out, admitting a small feeling of relief at having survived it.

'I keep telling him he's missed his vocation,' Ginny told her. 'He shoulda been a racing driver.'

It was the only hint of affectionate criticism Judy ever heard her make about him.

'You can sit out on the patio for a spell if you like, Judy,' she said next. 'Or you can sit in the kitchen and talk to me while I make some chocolate cookies. They're Bobby and Zoe's favourites. I always make a batch for the weekend.'

'Oh, I'll sit and talk to you. I haven't come all the way out here to act like the lady of the manor.'

'Good. And you can tell me all about this job of yours, and when you plan to give it up and get married and raise a family with Blake like proper folk.'

Judy laughed out loud. She had already deduced that when Ginny Cooper wanted to know something, she came right out and asked the question. And because she was so plain-speaking, she expected a plain, straightforward answer.

'You're a crazy woman, Ginny! And I don't know that I'll ever want to give it up. It's all I ever wanted to do. Although that's not strictly true, of course. I was a dancer and I loved it, but then I changed direction and I'm very happy with what I do now.' She neatly ignored any idea of raising a family with Blake.

262

'Then that answers one question, doesn't it? If you can change direction once, you can do it again, and of course you'll want to give it up eventually.'

As she went on, Ginny was already whizzing ingredients in a food mixer as if there was no tomorrow, and raising her voice above the whirr of the machine. 'It's not normal for a woman to spend all her time teaching other folk how to dance when she could be teaching kids of her own. Look how much Zoe enjoyed it when you were here last time.'

'Oh, well, maybe that's what I'll have to do when I get too old to co-ordinate the strenuous show routines. I enjoyed showing Zoe her steps, and I could always start up a dance school to teach young children the rudiments of dance,' she added, with no real thought behind the words other than to stop Ginny prying too deeply into her movements.

She daren't let slip for a moment that she and Blake were already married. And married in every sense of the word . . . if Ginny once knew the truth of it, Judy knew she'd be planning all kinds of celebrations, and probably inviting them out here for their honeymoon . . .

Ginny stopped whizzing her cookie mixture for a moment and looked at her. 'Say, that's a great idea, Judy. In between having kids of your own, of course.'

Judy had to remind herself that she was still talking about her vague remark about starting a dance school, but thankfully, there was no stopping Ginny when she was on a crusade. She enthused on and on about the sense of it, and Judy let most of it pass over her head, not taking any of it too seriously.

But by the time Kyle drove her back to Las Vegas and dropped her off at the Sparkling Rocks in the late afternoon, she had to admit she felt more exhausted than if she'd been instructing a class of beginners all afternoon. And it wasn't all due to Kyle's erratic driving. Ginny Cooper just had that effect on people.

Ricky was slumped in front of the TV set in the suite, looking less than pleased, and before she could say a word he had started grumbling.

'Where've you been, Jude? I've been back an hour, and nobody knew where you'd gone, not even Blake.'

'I don't have to report to Blake about the things I do in my spare time,' she told him crisply. 'And what's wrong with you? The last time I saw you, you were raving about all the girls you fancied around here. Spoilt for choice was the way you put it, I seem to remember.'

Ricky scowled. 'A fat lot of good any of it's going to do me after Thursday, isn't it? They'll still be here, and I'll be six thousand miles away.'

'Oh, I see. Blake's told you, has he?'

'So you knew already, did you? Why didn't you tell me?' He was ready to put the blame for his displeasure on anybody, and she had been his nearest and dearest for too long . . .

'Now just you listen to me, Ricky,' Judy said keenly. 'We both know what the plans were for you, and Blake only invited you here for a few days so that you could get yourself sorted out, and to arrange things with Harry. I'll never forgive you if you throw Blake's kindness back in his face now.'

'I still think there's something between you and that guy,' he changed tack.

'Well, there isn't, and there's not likely to be, so you can get the idea of having a rich brother-in-law right out of your head.'

But of course he already had that, had he but known it, Judy thought.

'You think I'm going to slip back into my old ways as soon as I'm out of here, don't you, Jude?' Ricky asked suddenly. 'You still don't trust me, do you?'

'Yes, I do – '

'Then give me some proper money instead of the piddling schoolboy pocket-money amounts you've been doling out, and let me loose in the casino for a couple of hours,' he challenged.

She looked at him silently, and after a few moments she took some bills out of her purse and thrust them at him.

'Enjoy yourself, Ricky,' she said quietly.

She watched him stuff the bills into his jeans pocket and go swaggering out of the suite. Once he had gone, she wondered frantically what the hell she thought she was doing, in practically giving him *carte blanche* to make the most of the little time he had left here in Las Vegas by spending it in the casino.

And she simply couldn't resist wandering down there herself a little later. She wasn't spying on him, she told herself. She just had to know.

He was lounging near one of the roulette tables on the edge of a noisy crowd. Judy's heart sank, recognizing the croupier as one of the girls Ricky was keen on. And if he wanted to prove himself a big spender to her, Judy had just given him the means to do it, she thought sinkingly . . .

She suddenly heard Blake's voice close by.

'Are you keeping tabs on our boy?'

'Are *you*?' she countered, annoyed to think he might have followed her.

'I'm just doing my job, ma'am, but in case you were worried, he's just waiting for Annie to finish her shift.'

'So you *have* been watching him!'

Blake shrugged. 'I've got quite a stake in that boy, remember. But before he catches sight of us, I suggest we go and have some tea and leave him to it. And you can tell me what you've been doing all day.'

'Fine. And you can tell me what Ricky's reaction was when you told him he was being sent home on Thursday.'

She didn't mean it to sound like censure. She had known it was coming, and she had also begun to realize that the longer Ricky was around, the more fraught her nerves were going to be on his account.

Now that he was over his fright from the loan shark, he had definitely found his self-confidence and self-esteem again, and Judy was more than thankful for that.

But the thought that he might go the other way – become so cocky that he thought he could just have a small flutter and no harm done – that was something else. And Blake had put all that temptation in his way, knowing the risk.

'Trust him, Judy,' she heard him say now, as they walked through the crowded rows of slot machines. 'And trust me.'

CHAPTER 14

She didn't see Ricky again until late that evening, and she wouldn't let herself wonder what he might be doing. When he came back to the suite around midnight, she was just making coffee, and offered him some at once.

'Thanks, Jude, and here's your change. Annie and I went to the movies and splashed out on a meal afterwards, but there's still quite a bit left.'

He couldn't resist the slight taunt in his voice as he tossed the dollar bills on the sofa. Judy picked them up and gave them right back to him.

'Keep it. You've still got a few days to go, so if you need any more, just ask.'

'As long as it's for all the right reasons, yes?'

'I never thought it would be for anything else,' she retorted lightly, knowing that she had, and that he probably knew it too.

To her surprise he came and put his arms around her shoulders and spoke with rough affection.

'Remind me to tell you you're the best sister any guy could ever have. Or have I said it before?'

'Occasionally,' she grinned, remembering the many times she had heard it when he was desperate for cash.

'Yeah, well, Blake impressed it on me even more when he told me I was going home on Thursday,' he said, moving away from her. 'He said if I ever let you down again, I'd be answerable to him as well. I tell you, Jude, that guy's got far more than a passing interest in you. Big Brother's got nothing on him!'

And you don't know just how true that is, thought Judy.

On Wednesday, Harry's secretary called Ricky especially to tell him she had a room all ready for him in her flat, and he wasn't to worry about a thing.

'Elsie's going to smother me,' he groaned to Judy when the call ended, but she could tell he wasn't altogether unhappy at the thought of some easy living.

'Did she say whether Harry's fixed up some appointments for you?' she asked him delicately.

He nodded. 'All in hand. And don't worry, between the lot of you I'll get myself straightened out.'

'It's what you want, isn't it?'

He gave her a wry smile after his small outburst. 'You know it is, Jude. And Blake knows it too. He really rapped into me that afternoon, and I guess it took somebody with a shrewd insight into human nature to dump me right in the middle of temptation the way he did. But it worked.'

All the same, Judy was glad in many ways when Thursday finally came. Once Ricky was on the

Harley Street man's readjustment programme, as Blake called it, she knew she would feel far easier in her mind.

They both took Ricky to the airport for the early-afternoon connection flight to his onward one at LAX. Judy hugged him close, trying not to get tearful at the last minute, but knowing that this was a momentous step for him.

'You call me as soon as you're settled, you hear?' she told him fiercely.

'Don't worry. Elsie won't let me forget.'

Blake shook his hand and wished him well, brushing aside his clumsy last-minute thanks.

'We've done all that,' Blake said briefly. 'All you have to do now is to get on with the rest of your life.'

They watched him go, and it was a wrench, Judy admitted. But he looked so very different now from his haggard appearance at the Sandiman Motel in Reno that she knew she would be eternally thankful that Blake had been there to pick up the pieces.

She was quiet on the way back to the hotel, and he didn't try to jolly her along. At least, not at first.

'You've done what you had to, Judy. You've let him go.'

'I know,' she muttered.

'And you've got a life too, remember?' he went on remorselessly. 'And at the end of your contract here, it'll be make-your-mind-up time on a more personal matter.'

She flinched. 'I'm in no mood to think about that now, Blake.'

'Just make sure you think abut it some time soon, then. I've begun to have serious thoughts about buying the Cooper ranch, and it's far too big a spread to have all to myself.'

Her heart jolted at the thought of that lovely place, but she wasn't going to let him guess it. 'You never give up, do you!' she said instead. 'First you blackmail me into marrying you to save Ricky's neck, and now this.'

'There are other reasons,' he told her. 'But as you always seem to doubt everything I say, it's hardly worth mentioning them.'

And this was hardly the place to profess undying love, Judy thought scathingly, as the limo wove in and out of the downtown traffic, even if he had meant it.

But he never said things he didn't mean . . . or was that all a line too? There had been a time when she had never been so sceptical, but that was before Michael had let her down so badly, when she had believed everything he'd said to her without question as well. She was far cannier now.

'So what are your plans for this evening?' he asked, when they reached the hotel.

'I don't know yet – '

'Then I'll see you for dinner after showtime.'

He didn't wait for a reply, and she thought how typically arrogant that was, assuming that she had no other plans. It wasn't her night backstage, anyway, or Frank's, but Maggie's. The three of them had worked out a satisfactory schedule now that the show was well into its stride, and each of them

271

had one night in three on duty, while the other two took time off.

There was a message from Frank on her answering machine in her suite. It was like manna from heaven, she thought, as she heard what he had to say.

'I guess you'll be feeling lost without your brother around, Judy, so how about a night out on the town tonight? There's a new roadhouse just opened that we could try out, with an adult revue dinner show.'

She called him on his pager, and when he answered she told him she'd be delighted.

'That's great, Judy – and you won't object to the odd drag act, will you? It's a pretty risqué show, I'm told.'

'I've seen drag acts in London, Frank,' she said drily. 'I doubt that there's anything there that will shock me!'

And she had no intention at all of letting Blake know her plans until the very last minute. Since they were both presumed to be unattached, they were both free to see other people, and anyway, Frank was just a friend.

She pushed a note under Blake's apartment door to say she had another engagement and wouldn't meet him for dinner, just before she went down in the elevator to meet Frank in the foyer. He was certainly a snappy dresser, she thought, as he opened the passenger door for her to slide inside.

They would be at the roadhouse in about half an hour, he told her, depending on the traffic. He was a confident driver, and Judy tried to relax, telling herself there was absolutely nothing to worry about in her life any more. Ricky was on his way home to be taken care of in every sense, and Blake was going to be kept resolutely out of her mind, for this evening, at least.

'You're quieter than usual, Judy,' Frank commented. 'I know your brother will still be on your mind, but if you're regretting this evening, we could always go somewhere else if you don't fancy the thought of an adult revue.'

'I'm not in the least worried about it, Frank, and I'm fine. Just laying a few old ghosts, that's all.'

'Old ghosts should be put to bed and then forgotten,' he told her. 'Otherwise they'll just carry on haunting you.'

'It's not always as easy as that, but I know you're right, and thanks for the advice.'

And wasn't that just what she always told herself . . .?

'Any time, ma'am.'

Almost before she was aware of it, she realized that his right hand had moved to cover her knee while the other one rested easily on the wheel of the automatic.

'Come on, Frank, you know the rules,' she said edgily, not bothering to remove his hand herself, and assuming that he would merely laugh and take the hint. He didn't. He squeezed a little harder, and moved his hand a little higher, and she felt a frisson of annoyance.

'*Frank!*' She was sharper now, and it took effect.

'OK, OK, but you can't blame a guy for trying. You give out all the right signals, honey, whether you know it or not.'

'I do not! Not if you compare me with Laverne and Candy and some of the other girls in the show – '

'When they're on stage, that's what they're paid for. And anyway, Laverne's a slut,' he added, making Judy gasp at this unexpected crudity. 'You don't want to take any notice of anything she says to you. She'll have every guy in the place who doesn't come on to her painted blacker than hell.'

He laughed when she remained silent.

'As a matter of fact, Laverne and I understand each other very well. If she steps out of line with me, she's out of the show, and she knows it. We've had our moments, though, and I'm not denying that some of them have been pretty good. Hell, some girls get their chances by being nice to the Dance Director. You must know that, honey, even in England I'm sure it goes on.'

'Maybe it does, but it doesn't work that way with everybody. I also know damn well that the girls have to succeed on talent, otherwise the shows would flop.'

'Talent's what I'm talking about, babe,' he said drily.

From the small slur in his voice, Judy suddenly knew he must have been drinking long before this outing started, and his words were loaded with innuendo. And she remembered how he had tried it on with her on the night of the party. It hadn't been a serious come-on, though, and she suspected he had quickly forgotten it. So had she, until now.

She closed her eyes for a moment and clenched her hands. She didn't need this, and she didn't want it.

All she wanted was a pleasant evening away from the hotel, and that was all he had been offering. Or so she had thought.

When something was bugging her, she had never been one to hedge about, as even Harry had found out more than once. If something needed to be said, it needed saying quickly.

'Look, Frank, if you've got the wrong idea about me, just because I said I'd come to this revue with you, you can forget it. And maybe we'd better turn back right now – '

'For God's sake, you're not going to turn all puritan on me, are you? OK, so I fancy you like crazy. So do half the guys in the cast – at least, the ones that aren't fancying each other – so what's wrong with that? You're not going to tell me Blake hasn't come on to you either.'

'What is this?' She was full of suspicion now. 'Some kind of contest to see who makes out with the new girl?'

She'd never thought about it before, and it was more upsetting than she realized to think it might have happened that way in the beginning. But Blake making out with her because of a silly bet with Harry was one thing, and she knew what Harry was like. He'd bet on anything, but at least they were continents apart, and she didn't have to see him.

The thought of Blake and Franklin Delgado doing the same thing, and maybe comparing notes, was unbearable. But the minute she thought it, she dismissed it. She knew enough about him by now to know that Blake had more integrity than that, even if Frank didn't.

'You're hardly the new girl any longer, babe,' Frank was saying now. 'But you've got one thing all wrong. I don't go into competition with other guys. I don't need to.'

The sheer arrogance of it took Judy's breath away, but she clamped her lips together and refused to rise to the bait. But Frank, whom she had thought so amiable, and her friend, was turning into somebody she didn't know any more, and she didn't like what she saw.

And if he thought he knew her pretty well by now, he didn't. He didn't know the real Judy Hale at all. He didn't know how her heart had been frozen after Michael's betrayal, or that she was already in love with someone else . . . without warning, she felt her throat tighten, catching her breath on a small, ragged sob.

As Frank glanced at her she knew he must be aware of how tense she had become. This evening, which had begun with such free and easy promise, was turning into something of a nightmare before it had properly begun. She knew she was probably overreacting, but she couldn't stop the feeling.

He spoke more uneasily now. 'Hey, I'm sorry, if you think I'm coming on to you like the lowest form of life. You're such a doll I sometimes forget to treat you like an English lady. And that's meant to be a ham-fisted compliment, in case you thought otherwise.'

She forced her voice to be light, but there was still far too much arrogance in him for her liking.

'Then I thank you for that. I think.'

This time his free hand covered hers for a second only.

'So are we friends again?' he mocked.

'We were never anything else,' she said deliberately, and as he laughed, she hoped he realized she meant it.

'All the same, I don't know why you should think it's impossible for two people who work together to be more than friends,' he went on, confirming her thoughts. 'Anyway, here we are at the roadhouse. So do we continue the evening, or do I drive you back?'

Judy spoke coolly. 'I haven't come all this way just to go straight back again. Besides, I'm curious to see what's considered so risqué in this town that I haven't seen before.'

She had to admit that there was little in the adult revue that was remotely shocking. A couple of the drag acts wouldn't have raised an eyebrow in a London nightclub, and some of the so-called comedians were trying so hard that their humour was more infantile than risqué.

She managed not to tell Frank she'd heard plenty that was just as bad outside any big comprehensive school in south London. Ricky had come home with some choice words and jokes in his teenage years, and had had to be curbed pretty hard.

But she laughed in all the right places. She wasn't a prude, and if the acts were second-rate, the seafood and steak supper was excellent. What the place lacked in finesse was more than made up for by the superb food. And if Frank was drinking steadily, she tried to ignore it.

As soon as they got back in the car in the almost deserted car park, she discovered her mistake. Frank reached for her at once, pulling her roughly towards him, and she felt his hands roam all over her, octopus-like.

'For pity's sake, Frank, stop it!' she gasped. 'Aren't you capable of taking no for an answer?'

'In my job I've met plenty of girls who say no when they mean yes,' he slurred. 'Why should you be any different?'

Judy wrestled with him silently, starting to feel ridiculous as his drink-sodden breath reeked into her face, and his fumbling hands kept missing their target.

'Because I'm not one of them,' she snapped. 'I've told you enough times already, and I've no need of your help in getting a job or keeping it. Stop making a fool of yourself, Frank, and don't ruin our friendship.'

'Oh, come on. You know as well as I do that a good choreographer is hard to find. I only have to say the word and I'm sure Blake will let you stay on as long as you like.'

She pushed him away from her with an effort, pulling down her skirt and clamping her knees together.

'I don't *need* all this, Frank, so either you stop it this minute, or I get out of this car and call a cab to take me back to Las Vegas,' she said crisply.

She saw him scowl, but she thought he was beginning to realize at last that she meant it, and she pushed home her advantage.

'Don't spoil it for me, Frank. I enjoy your company while you're behaving yourself, but I don't play these kind of games, not with you or anybody else.'

'OK, I'm beginning to get the picture,' he muttered.

'I hope you are. Now can we please get going?'

To her relief he started up the engine and drove back to Las Vegas at speed, despite the amount he'd been drinking. She said goodnight to him thankfully, reasonably sure he wouldn't remember too much about what had happened by the next morning, and vowing that she wouldn't go out alone with him again. For all his promises, she knew he couldn't be trusted when he'd been drinking.

But she put him out of her mind as she went up to her suite, thinking instead about Ricky, and inevitably, about Blake. There was an answering note from him under her door, and she couldn't help thinking this was a bizarre way for a married couple to behave. But they were far from being any normal married couple. She read the note quickly.

'Enjoy your night on the town. See you tomorrow.'

It was cold and unemotional. He obviously didn't care that she was out with another man, and if she had been trying to prove something in letting him know she wasn't being tied to any imaginary apron strings, she knew she had failed. In any case, he knew Frank better than she did, and he probably hadn't seen him as any threat, especially since he knew she could stand up for herself perfectly well when necessary.

But as she prepared to go to bed that night, she felt lonelier than she had in days. It was almost impossible to think about what had happened in so short a time. She had found Ricky again, and Blake had come so magnificently to his rescue. And she had become Blake's wife, in a temporary marriage in a Reno wedding chapel that she had virtually insisted was in name only. But Blake had had other ideas . . .

She snuggled down beneath the bedcovers, trying to close her mind to the memory of the night she had spent in his apartment. But the imagery of them together, of lying in his arms in his bed, was so overwhelming at that moment that it might have been written in letters sky-high, comparable with all the glittering lights in Las Vegas . . .

She was desperately tired, but no matter how she tried, Judy couldn't sleep. Her thoughts kept returning to Blake, no matter how much she tried to resist it. Wishing they could recapture the feelings she truly thought they had shared on that one night when it had seemed so right for them to be together . . . and knowing that the sooner her contract came to an end now, and she went back to England to reorganize her life, the better.

Just as if Blake was reading her mind, he suggested over dinner one evening that once her contract came to an end, she should stay on for at least a few days as his guest.

'We both know why I can't do that – '

'No, we don't. It seems a very sensible idea to me. You'll need to relax, and the arrangement for our next star billing is the same as we do every year. You once told me how much you like country and western music.'

'Yes, I do,' Judy said. And she would have liked to see the show with the female country and western star she most admired. But there were plenty of excuses she could make to resist the idea of staying on as Blake's guest. Surely he must see how impossible that would be!

'Anyway, I have to go home. I shall want to see how Ricky's getting on, and to see if Harry's got anything in the pipeline for me – '

Blake was clearly prepared to argue. 'Since when did an independent woman like you ever let an agent rule her life?'

'He doesn't rule it. He guides it.'

'Well, maybe I'll come back with you when you leave,' he went on, to her dismay. 'This place can run perfectly well without me for a while, and it would be good to see Harry again. And to check on our mutual investment.'

He meant Ricky, of course. But Judy was too horrified at the thought of him accompanying her to London to think about that for the moment. She couldn't bear the thought of him prolonging their time together just to torment her.

Besides, by then, they would have come to some kind of decision about their marriage. In her mind, there was none to make. It had been done for a purpose, and it had to end. And she wouldn't let herself think how the thought of it twisted her heart. She sounded strained when she spoke.

'And you also want to let Harry see how united the two of us are, I suppose? It won't work, Blake, because I'd make sure he didn't read anything special into your visit.'

He changed direction with the ease of a chameleon. 'I'll bet you would. And maybe I wasn't serious about coming to England, anyway.'

'Good. Because I assure you I don't need nurse-maiding on a transatlantic flight – '

'You didn't do so well just getting here from LA, if I remember rightly,' he retorted. 'But you've got plenty of time to think about staying on for a while. And of course, if you decide you've got to leave, you'll be guest of honour at the show's final-night party.'

The thought didn't thrill her as much as she knew it should. It would be heartbreaking enough, saying goodbye to all the friends she had made . . . and to him . . .

'I'd rather not have any big fuss made about it, Blake. I'll probably get all weepy and make a fool of myself – '

'Then stay.'

'I can't,' she said simply. 'And you really must excuse me now. I'm tired – '

'What you need is something to relax you – '

'If you're going to suggest a massage, don't bother.'

He laughed at her immediate bristling. 'I wasn't. But why don't you use the indoor pool for a while?

It's out of bounds to the customers and staff alike at this time of day, as you know, but the security man will give you a pass key, and you won't be disturbed. It will help you unwind.'

She stared at him, sorely tempted. 'You mean it? Nobody else is likely to be there?'

'I've told you. Leave it with me to organize it with security and take as long as you like.'

It was too tempting to resist. When they parted company, Judy went to her suite for her bikini and towel, and then took the elevator down to the lower ground floor where the indoor pool was housed. It was quite silent now, as Blake had said, except for the low lights that were always left on, and the security man inside his little office nearby. As soon as he saw her, he stopped reading his newspaper and smiled.

'Evenin', Miss Hale. Mr Adams told me you'd probably be coming down. The pool's all yours, so just let me know when you're leaving, OK?'

'Thanks, I will,' she replied.

He unlocked the door to the themed pool area that resembled a South Sea island resort, with artificial palm trees and thatched umbrellas over the bamboo tables and chairs. The pool water was an impossibly emerald green and the ceiling was a cerulean blue with fluffy white clouds adorning it. Normally, there was Hawaiian music playing softly from tapes in the background. And even as Judy registered the thought, the seductive strains of the music were being piped through for her benefit.

She slipped off the shirt and jeans she wore over her bikini now, but feeling more relaxed by the minute, she acknowledged that Blake had been right. This was just what she needed. As she slid into the blissfully warm water, she closed her eyes, almost able to imagine she was on some island paradise, and she had swum several leisurely lengths of the pool before opening them properly again.

When she did, it was to see Blake sitting on the edge of the pool, watching her. He was already wearing swimming briefs, and his broad chest and limbs were tanned and very strong. She was so startled by the sight of him that she trod water angrily.

'This is an underhand trick, if I ever saw one!'

He laughed lazily. 'Why is it? When I decided I needed unwinding as well, I couldn't think of a better place to do it – or better company. Do you object?'

She could hardly do that, since it was his hotel and his pool. She didn't have to stay here with him . . . but why shouldn't she? Why let a clash of personalities get in the way, and spoil what had become so very pleasurable?

'You can do what you like,' she said, twisting away from him and swimming to the far end of the pool.

Within seconds he had reached her. She was a strong swimmer, but he was stronger. He caught her in his arms and she couldn't get away from him. His legs were entwined in hers, and his face was no more than a breath away.

The tang of the chlorinated water was in her nostrils and her mouth, and she could see the pearls of it on Blake's face and hair. And then she couldn't see anything more as his mouth claimed hers in an almost brutal kiss. Her eyes closed, and her arms clung to him as they trod water.

A moment later, Judy came up gasping, trying to wrench away from him, but he was still too strong for her, and he kept her in the circle of his arms.

'When are you going to admit that we're a match for one another?' he asked her calmly.

'Never,' she said between clenched teeth. 'You constantly play with my feelings. You forced me into marriage, and although I admit it didn't do Ricky any harm to stay here, I was anxious for him every moment. And you said I would have this pool to myself.'

She finished lamely, because his fingers were stroking her back now, and she was still pressed so tightly against him that she could feel every sinew of his muscular body. And what she felt was telling her very surely that he desired her. She felt an answering throb of desire deep within herself, and willed it away.

'Please don't do this, Blake,' she whispered.

Somehow they had moved to the edge of the pool, and her back was against it now. There was nowhere she could go . . . and he was cupping her face in his hands now, and there was seduction in his eyes and voice, and every other part of him.

'Judy, for God's sake, we're married,' he said, almost harshly.

'But not as far as anyone else knows, and I mean to keep it that way. I don't know why you thought it necessary to go to such lengths, anyway.'

'Because I love you, and everything about you – '

'Oh, I don't think so! You're still playing games!'

She wouldn't let herself believe him. Now that he was pretty sure she meant to end this marriage as soon as possible, he obviously thought he was going to make the most of this marriage while it lasted.

'When you know me better, you'll know that I never play this kind of game, Judy – '

'Well, I won't be around long enough to find out, and the sooner you get the divorce proceedings under way, the better I'll like it.'

Unbelievably, she saw him shake his head. 'We agreed that no decisions would be made until the end of your time here, and you've still got six weeks to go.'

'And you mean to persuade me to change my mind in that time, do you?'

His arrogant reply shook her. 'I may decide it's not worth the chase after all. I gather you had a hot date with Frank the other night, and what's right for the goose is all right for the gander, if you'll pardon the crudity. You keep insisting that nobody knows we're married, so you can hardly object if I'm seen to look around for pastures new, can you? I've never been a saint in that department.'

She ignored the annoying thought that Frank had evidently been speaking out of turn. It hardly mattered compared with the rest, and Blake's meaning was perfectly clear.

She simply didn't know how to answer, but she wasn't going to back down on announcing their marriage, or to beg him not to do this . . . In the end, he made the decision for her.

'I see it doesn't make any difference to you, my sweet, so let's leave it there, shall we? Enjoy your swim, and don't forget to let security know when you're ready to go.'

With that, he swam away from her, and within minutes he had picked up his towel, given himself a cursory rub with it, then wrapped it around himself, and left her alone.

Judy spent another fifteen minutes swimming up and down the pool until she was exhausted. She didn't want to think of what Blake had said. She didn't want to think of him wining and dining someone else – or what might occur later.

He was *hers*, she thought fiercely, and she loved him, and yet she seemed to be doing everything she could to push him away from her. She couldn't understand her own feelings any more, but far from feeling relaxed now, she was as jittery as she had ever been.

She got out of the pool and went into one of the little cubicles to dress, trying to make her mind a complete blank before returning to her suite to try to sleep. And trying even harder not to imagine Blake with some other girl, only too eager for his favours, while she, who wanted and needed them, and had every right to them, had thrown them back in his face.

But surely he hadn't really meant what he said? As she lay in the darkness, more upset by his arrogant statement than she knew she had any right to be, she began to question his words.

All right. He had inherited the bluntness of a Yorkshireman, who said what he meant, and meant what he said. But those were just words. He had left the rural Yorkshire life many years ago, and he was very glib with words. If only she could be sure it wasn't just to prove that he could get any woman he wanted – and that Judy Hale had proved to be the biggest challenge of all.

But you could never be sure. She had been so sure with Michael, and it had all ended in disaster. For all that, she had never meant to live like a nun for the rest of her life, and any relationship was a bit of a gamble. But this one between her and Blake had certainly had more than its fair share of that. The endless questions went round and round in her head with no hope of finding a satisfactory answer.

CHAPTER 15

During the next few weeks, Judy phoned Ricky several times, and learned that he was perfectly happy at Elsie's flat, and that there might be some job prospects in the offing soon.

'And what about the other business?' she asked him carefully.

'If you mean am I going for treatment, you needn't be afraid of saying it, Jude. I've seen the Harley Street man a couple of times, and he's sure he can get me sorted out. So you can stop worrying.'

'I doubt that, but it's good to hear you so cheerful and positive,' she said thankfully.

'I am. Oh, and give my love to Annie, will you? Tell her I'll write sometime, but it was never my strong point.'

Judy smiled at that. 'Don't I know it!'

'So how's Blake – and the show?' he went on, making normal chitchat.

'He's the same as ever, but you've reminded me that I'd better stop talking, as I'm due in rehearsals pretty soon.'

Really, it was no more than a useful excuse not to be drawn into any discussion about Blake, and hearing what a good bloke he was – according to Ricky . . .

But in these last weeks, Judy discovered that Blake had meant what he'd said at the pool that night. He was as polite and attentive to her as ever, but the regular dinner dates were dwindling now, and more and more often she discovered he was otherwise engaged.

It was Laverne who told Judy what was going on. Since Laverne had never been as friendly towards Judy as most of the other showgirls, she couldn't hide her liking for passing on a bit of malicious gossip.

'I reckon you've lost your lover-boy, Judy,' she told her during a break in rehearsals.

'I wasn't aware that I had a lover-boy,' Judy said mildly. 'And I hope you're not referring to Frank –'

'I'm not. Frank tries it on with every new face around here, but it was pretty obvious he wasn't going to get anywhere with you. He's not your type. You'd go for the more sophisticated, tycoon kind of guy.'

'What's your point, Laverne?' Judy was becoming exasperated by the way she was hedging about.

The other girl's eyes gleamed. 'Well, I heard it on good authority that Blake has been seen around town, squiring one of the croupiers from The Riviera. It looks as if your fellow Brit's getting tired of having you around, Judy.'

'It doesn't matter a damn to me what Blake does with his time,' she snapped. 'And you should know better than to spread such gossip around here, Laverne.'

'Oh, yeah? And methinks the lady doth protest too much, if I've got the quote right.'

'You have, and I don't. Now, why don't we get on with what we're supposed to be doing?'

But it didn't do her ego a power of good to know that Laverne had undoubtedly got it right. Blake had warned her that he was going to do exactly as he pleased from now on.

He was squiring somebody else around town, as Laverne so charmingly put it, and there wasn't a thing Judy could do about it. She just had to grit her teeth and pretend that it didn't matter a damn to her.

But as the days drew on towards the final weeks of the show, the situation was becoming unbearable, and she knew how thankful she would be when they could end it all, and she could go home. She presumed they would have to fly up to Reno to get the divorce, in order to continue the secrecy. It was a thought that filled her heart with sadness, knowing it could all have been so different.

But Blake seemed to be making it clear now that he was his own man, and that he had had enough of the annoying Judy Hale. On the occasions when they still had dinner together, she dearly wanted to ask him what he did on the nights she didn't see him. But her pride certainly wouldn't let her ask, and he didn't offer any explanation.

He hardly needed to, Judy seethed, when Laverne was always ready to supply any information, true or false, given half a chance.

It was late one night when her phone rang, and she had been in bed for some while. She picked up the receiver and answered it listlessly, still half-asleep.

As she heard Ricky's scared voice at the other end, her heart plummeted, because he sounded so much like he had that other time, when he'd called her from Reno.

'Ricky, what's wrong?' she said, instantly awake.

'It's not me,' he managed to choke out. 'I'm OK, Jude.'

'Then is it Elsie? What's happened, for God's sake?' She sat up in bed, switching on her bedside light and feeling her heart beat rapidly. She was fond of Elsie, and would never wish her any harm, but guiltily, for Ricky's sake, she also prayed that nothing had happened to her.

Even though she knew she was thinking selfishly, she knew that anything that disturbed his frame of mind now could only be bad news.

She heard a mumble of voices at the other end of the line, and then she heard Elsie's voice, as loud as ever, if more quavery than usual.

'There's nothing wrong with either of us, Judy. It's Harry.'

'*Harry!*' Harry was as tough and wiry as couch grass, the type who would go on for ever, or so Judy had always thought. 'He's not ill, is he?'

But even as she said it, she knew something had to be very wrong for them to be calling her in the middle of the night, even though it was still late afternoon in London, she calculated rapidly.

'Harry had a stroke during the night, Judy. He's in St Mary's Hospital in intensive care – '

'My God!' Judy whispered, hardly able to take it in for the moment. 'What are his chances?'

'They still haven't confirmed how serious it is yet, but we know the next twenty-four hours are the critical ones. If he gets through those, there's every hope – '

Judy could hear the break in Elsie's voice. She had been in love with Harry for years, even if he'd never been able to see it. But Harry being dangerously ill reminded Judy of how mortal everyone was. She ran her tongue around her dry lips.

'You weren't the one to find him, were you, Elsie?' she asked, almost certain of the answer. Who else would have found him, if not Elsie?

'He was late coming into the office, and when he didn't answer his phone I went round to his flat to remind him of two appointments that day. I have a key,' she added vaguely, 'and when I saw him I thought he was dead at first. He'd fallen out of bed and knocked his head, and he was badly bruised. I sent for the ambulance, and they took him away – '

She ended on a sob, and Judy could sympathize with her. Harry wasn't the handsomest of men at the best of times. Harry with a stroke and a battered and bruised head couldn't have been a pretty sight. She tried not to imagine it.

'Elsie, you've got to think positively. If you hadn't been there, it could have been far worse. You've got to keep remembering that, do you hear?'

'I know. You'll pass on the news to Blake, will you? And there's no point in any of us calling the hospital until the twenty-four hours are up.'

Judy agreed, and put down the phone slowly. But she had to tell Blake, and it couldn't wait until morning. She rang his number quickly, praying that he'd be there. For all she knew, he might be out on the town again . . .

'Yes? Who is this?' he snapped into the phone.

For a second, Judy couldn't speak, and then it all came out in a rush.

'Blake, I'm sorry to disturb you like this. I've just had a call from Elsie in London. Harry's had a stroke, and he's in hospital in intensive care – '

And that was as much as she could say before she choked up. Harry had been her agent and her friend for a very long time now, and she listened to herself, mentally writing him off, and it was too much to bear . . . She replaced the phone clumsily and put her head in her shaking hands.

Within the next few minutes she became aware of the rapping on her door, and then she heard Blake's voice outside.

'Judy, open the door,' he ordered.

'I'm all right,' she croaked.

'I didn't ask if you were all right. Let me in.'

She had never promised to obey him . . . but she did as she was told now, if only to have the contact of another person. He could have used his pass key . . . but as she opened the door to him, he came inside and took her in his arms at once.

'I don't suppose you've got any brandy, so I've brought some to lace our coffee,' he said practically. 'And then perhaps you can calm down and tell me more coherently what's happened to Harry.'

'I've already told you – '

As he felt her begin to shake, he made her sit down while he filled two mugs from her instant coffee-maker, lacing them liberally with brandy. Judy didn't care for the taste, but when he instructed her to drink, she obeyed him again.

'Now then, what did Elsie say exactly?' he asked.

She repeated what she knew about the first twenty-four hours being critical, and then what was really in her mind spilled over.

'And if he does recover, what will he be left with? Loss of speech, paralysis? You know Harry as well as I do, Blake. Can you imagine what it would be like for him to be disabled or dependent on other people for everything? Knowing him, I know he'd rather be dead.'

Her voice ended on a sob. Harry was no relative of hers, but she loved that impossible old rogue. She didn't know it happened, but she found herself clinging to Blake, and he was comforting her like the Dutch uncle she had always considered Harry to be.

'Don't write him off yet. He'll come through, if I know Harry,' he said roughly. 'We just have to pray that he'll make a complete recovery.'

'I can't imagine you praying for anything,' she mumbled, once her shaking had subsided a little.

'Oh, but I do. Frequently,' he replied, and folded her into him. She didn't ask what he meant. Now wasn't the time, anyway. All her thoughts and energies were concentrated on willing Harry to recover.

'It's time you went back to bed, sweetheart,' she heard Blake say some while later, when she shivered with cold, despite having his arms around her. But she had become so disorientated she had no idea how long they had been sitting close together on the sofa.

'I think you're right,' she murmured, but when she stood up she stumbled a little, and said the first inane thing that came into her head. 'Sorry. That's the effect of the brandy. I never could take it.'

Before she could say anything more, he had scooped her up in his arms and carried her into her bedroom. She had hardly bothered to register that he was only wearing the silky, green striped dressing-robe she remembered, or that she had sped to the door clad only in her nightdress. But she registered it now, as he turned back the bedcover and lay her down inside it, and then slid in beside her.

'Blake, you can't do this. Not now!' she mumbled, wondering how anybody could be so insensitive. Didn't he know how distraught she was over Harry . . .? Couldn't he comprehend that this was the most despicable time for him to take advantage of the fact . . .?

'What do you take me for?' he said harshly. 'If you insist on it, I'll put a pillow down between us to prove that my intentions are strictly honourable tonight. But I don't think you should be left alone to brood, and since we both want that old schemer to get well, maybe our combined wishes will somehow get through to him.'

It was clear he wasn't going to take no for an answer, and by now Judy was feeling too light-headed to give it. She gave a small sigh as his arms went around her again, resting her head against his shoulder, and after a long while, she eventually fell asleep to the steady rhythm of his heartbeats.

When she awoke, she was alone, her thoughts flying immediately to Harry. She was startled to find how late she had slept into the morning. The brandy must really have knocked her out . . . The next minute Blake appeared with a mug of coffee for her. He was fully dressed in his normal daytime attire, and had evidently used his pass key to come back to her room this time. He sat on the edge of her bed and answered her unspoken questions.

'No, I didn't take advantage of you, and no, we can't phone for news of Harry until this evening. Now, I suggest that you get up and take a shower, then order a belated breakfast, and go to work.'

'Work! How can I think about work?'

'Because it's what I'm paying you for,' he said. 'And it'll stop you thinking too much. Believe me. I've tried it.'

He leaned forward, and his unexpected kiss took the sting out of his words.

'Keep smiling,' he went on more gently. 'In the law of averages, we're all due for a miracle some time in our lives. This will be Harry's.'

'You can guarantee that, can you?'

'No. I just intend to believe it.'

Judy tried to take comfort from his words, though she knew life didn't work that way. Even so, you had to cling on to whatever hope you had. And he was right about one thing. Mentally, she *had* already written Harry off. She lifted her chin and spoke more resolutely.

'All right, so life has to go on, however trite that sounds. Perhaps you'd let Frank know I'll be reporting for work before lunchtime. And please pass on the news about Harry so that I don't have to – will you?'

As he agreed, she couldn't help thinking how crazy it was that Blake should be acting as her messenger. He was the boss, the all-powerful owner of this entire mega-building, and right now she had to admit that he seemed genuinely concerned that she shouldn't fall apart.

She couldn't even raise an atom of cynicism in thinking that it was for the sake of his show. They both knew Frank and Maggie could deal with these last rehearsals perfectly well without her. But if Blake was concerned about her, then he was human after all, and not just a money-making machine, and it was the one thing in these last terrible hours that put any warmth back into her.

Then, professional as ever, she remembered there were a few changes to be made in one of her special routines, since one of the girls had broken a toe and had to be replaced.

In all honesty, she had never felt less like working, or facing people. The job that she loved so much suddenly seemed so trivial compared with the drama going on in St Mary's Hospital, Paddington.

Her nerves were all on edge by the time she finally reached the rehearsal room. She reminded herself that none of these people knew Harry, but Blake had obviously told Frank and Maggie by then, because when Frank saw her appear he squeezed her hand for a moment in unspoken sympathy, but his voice was crisp and practical.

'Good. Now let's get down to work,' he told her, and she nodded, thankful that he hadn't peppered his words with unnecessary platitudes. From Frank, especially, she just couldn't have stood it.

Everybody said that work was a panacea, and Judy knew the truth of that. She got through the day, knowing it was stupid to dwell on what might be happening six thousand miles away.

There was nothing she could do about it in any case. She had toyed briefly with the thought of taking a plane home and rushing to Harry's bedside, but she had dismissed it as soon as it entered her mind.

She was only one of his clients, after all. She wasn't family, even if she had felt like it for so long. But a fine thing it would be if all Harry's clients turned up on the hospital doorstep. Actually, she thought with a weak grin, Harry would love that. It would make him feel like royalty.

Blake insisted that she ate dinner with him that evening, and that they sat in on the show together. She hardly saw any of it, nor heard the wild applause from the capacity audience. It was so much less important than Harry . . .

'You've got to stop this, Judy,' Blake ordered later.

By then, they were sitting in one of the quieter bars and on their third pot of coffee. Not that she

needed it to keep awake. She was simply too tense to
go to bed.

'Stop what?'

'Staring into space and imagining the worst.
Didn't your mother ever tell you that thinking of
something positive can make even the blackest day
seem brighter?'

'Thanks, but I can do without your attempts at
philosophy right now!' And she quickly revised all
her charitable thoughts about him.

'Well, at least I've goaded you into a response. I
began to think I was sitting here all alone – '

'We're all alone in the end, aren't we?'

She looked into the cup of coffee she didn't really
want, and bit her lip. She was spouting philosophy
now, and she couldn't think why the hell she had said
such a stupid thing. She felt Blake's hand briefly
cover hers.

'You don't have to be alone tonight, Judy. In fact, I
don't think either of us should be.'

'My God, you're pushing it, aren't you? I appreciated your being there last night, Blake, but if you
think you can make up to me when I'm feeling so bad
about Harry – '

'And if you think I had anything else in mind but
keeping each other company for mutual support,
then you don't know me at all. Harry was my friend
long before you ever knew him, in case you've
forgotten. He was Claire's agent too.'

She began to feel that she didn't know him at all.
He kept sending her off-balance. For all that she had
been blinded and prejudiced by his arrogance when

they had first met, he had already shown her that he could be vulnerable. Just as she was.

'You really mean what you said about being together just for mutual support and company? No strings attached?'

'Not one,' he promised.

Whether it was foolish or not, the thought of not being alone for the next few hours was too much to resist. They went up in the silent elevator, and when he opened the door of his apartment he stood back and waited for her to go inside.

The sound of the alarm clock Blake had set for two a.m. woke Judy with a start. It would be six o'clock in the evening in London, and well past time to call the hospital for some updated news.

She was alert at once, moving away from Blake beneath the bedcover. They had shared his bed, but nothing could have been more innocent, since they were both still fully dressed. She had insisted on that, but she couldn't deny the deep comfort of having his arms around her.

She followed him to the sitting-room and sat with her hands clasping her knees while he dialled the hospital number and asked for information on Harry. It seemed like an endless wait, and then she saw his face relax.

'So does that mean he's likely to make a full recovery?' she heard him say.

After a few moments he spoke again.

'But he's in no immediate danger, and his speech isn't impaired at all?'

Judy hardly dared to credit what she was hearing, but after a few more exchanges Blake put down the phone and turned to her. He looked as if he had shed a lot of years in the last few minutes, and she knew how important Harry was to him too.

'You can relax, Judy. He's not out of the wood yet, but his symptoms were complicated by the concussion from his fall. The stroke wasn't as bad as they feared, and although he'll be advised to take it easy for a while, there's no reason why he can't continue to live a normal life.'

'Well, that'll be a twist. He's never done it before!'

As the joking words left her lips, her mouth trembled, and she felt as though she was about to collapse in a heap on the floor. It had all been too much . . . too much . . .

She became aware of Blake holding her up. She slowly raised her face to his and felt his lips on hers, and then she was clinging to him and kissing him, and wanting him . . .

'Blake – ' she began.

'Calm down. But if we don't both get some sleep, we'll both be like a pair of rag dolls tomorrow.'

'I'll go back to my room then – '

'You'll do no such thing. You'll get undressed and put on my robe, and then we'll go back to a warm bed and get some sleep, and your honour will be quite safe.'

It was a bit late for that, Judy thought . . . but he had honoured his words last night, and as she began to protest again, he put one finger on her mouth and spoke quietly.

'I won't let you be alone for the rest of the night, Judy. No matter what that hospital nurse told me, you'll still be imagining the worst, won't you?'

'How did you know?'

'I know the way it goes,' he said, and she knew he was thinking of Claire at that moment.

He led her to the bedroom, and she was too weak with relief to argue any more. She undressed quickly while he was in the bathroom and put on his short, silky robe.

A few minutes later, he appeared in a bathrobe, flipped off the light, and got into bed beside her. His arms folded around her, and he murmured against her hair.

'You see? Prayers do get answered.'

And she could get to like this, she thought weakly . . .

She wasn't sure what time it was when she awoke next. Blake had left a table-lamp switched on in the sitting-room, and there was a sliver of light showing beneath the bedroom door. It was enough to let her see the outline of his face, and listen to his deep and rhythmic breathing.

For several moments she lay watching him lying so still beside her. There was something oddly moving about watching somebody sleeping. All the worry lines disappeared, and people looked far more vulnerable than when they were awake.

Without thinking, she traced her fingers softly around the contours of his face, and on an impulse she leaned forward and touched her lips to his mouth. She couldn't be sure whether or not he was actually awake, and it hadn't been her intention to waken him. But with the contact, his arms instinctively closed around her more tightly, drawing her close to him beneath the cocoon of the bedclothes.

His lips were still on hers, one hand moving up behind her head to hold her, and she became aware of the other one edging down to caress the silky fabric of her robe, and sliding it inexorably upwards. He felt her tense at once, and his voice was a mixture of arrogance and seduction.

'Are you really going to tell me you don't want this, Judy? We've been all through this before, remember?'

'But you promised – '

'I know what I promised. And I won't do anything you don't want me to do.'

The words seemed to hang in the air, and Judy's throat was so dry she couldn't speak. She wanted him desperately. She wanted his love and commitment, and to feel a part of him, and she didn't dare to ask how deeply his feelings for her really went. But oh, this wasn't fair . . .

Her relief that Harry wasn't about to die was a cause for celebrating, yet she recognized that even that wasn't nearly as overwhelming as the need she felt for Blake right now. And what better way was there to celebrate anything than to be in her lover's arms . . .? Her husband's loving arms . . .?

Slowly, she brought her hand round to the front of his body and slid it inside his bathrobe. His heartbeats were as wild and uneven as her own. She could feel the warmth of his skin beneath her fingers, and the touch of his hand was moving inwards on her thigh, tracing her, easing her apart. She could feel his tongue caressing hers, and the burning need in her then had nothing to do with thoughts of Harry.

Her agent was furthest from her thoughts as she gasped with pleasure at Blake's touch, and the sweet, remembered familiarity of his kisses that began at her mouth and moved slowly downwards over every tingling part of her.

Any thought of resistance was fast disappearing in her hunger for him, and his for her. She needed him so much . . .

'You can still stop me if you must,' Blake whispered.

But how could she, when she was already opening up to him, arching towards him and drawing him into her moist, welcoming warmth? She ached for him, and there was nothing on earth that would make her deny it now.

A long while later, still wrapped in each other's arms, she murmured tentatively that they should get up, or the entire hotel staff would be wondering what had happened to them. Privately, she would have been content to lie here all day, but it was hardly the done thing, especially for someone in Blake's position. And especially if any of the hotel maids were to come and find her in the apartment.

It was farcical. As his wife, she had every right to be there. But for the first time since they had made love, Judy knew a sense of embarrassment. She didn't want him to think of her as cheap, ready to jump into bed with him at the least opportunity . . . or whenever she decided she had teased him for long enough . . .

'Blake, I really do think – '

He tipped up her chin, forcing her to look at him. 'You think too much. There comes a time when you've got to stop thinking, and do what your heart tells you to.'

But as Blake turned away from her now, she knew she had somehow broken the spell. She watched him as he walked with elegant, naked grace across the room and pulled back the curtains. Feeling oddly embarrassed again, she looked away to the place where the laughing photo of him and Claire had been. Her heart leapt as she saw that it was no longer there.

She dressed with shaking hands and let herself out of his apartment while he was still taking a shower. Once in her own room, she realized how fast her heart was beating now. So the photograph in Blake's bedroom was missing. She tried to think logically. It could be just because he was sensitive to her feelings on that score – or towards any other woman he had invited here, come to that.

If so, Judy thought, then why hadn't he removed it before? Unless no other woman had been important enough for him to do so, until now.

She worried that she was in danger of reading more into it that was really there, because it was what she wanted to believe. For a moment she let herself dream, and the dreams included seeing herself at the Cooper ranch, not as a visitor, but as the wife of the new, dynamic owner . . .

The phone rang in her room, bringing her out of her dreams with brutal swiftness. She was almost too scared to pick it up, knowing it was unlikely to be anyone in the hotel needing her at such an early hour, and dreading that it might be a call from the London hospital.

She didn't recognize the voice at the other end of the phone for a moment. It sounded thicker than usual. Then it registered.

'*Harry?*' she gasped.

Her mind was completely disorientated for a few seconds. She couldn't rid herself of the ghastly imagery that Harry had died and that disembodied waves across the ether were continuing to tell her to *give it all you've got, kid.* And then her heartbeats settled down as she heard his chuckle on the line, and it was definitely the Harry she knew.

'Of course, *Harry.* What did you expect? I'm not ready for kicking up the daisies yet, girl.'

'Oh, Harry,' Judy said softly, knowing she had thought exactly that. 'We were both so worried – ' She linked herself and Blake together without giving it a second thought.

'No need, kid, even though the dragon of a nurse here ain't going to let me use this phone for very much longer. I just wanted to let you know I'm OK, and I'll be up and running again before you know it.'

'Don't you dare! You just do as you're told, you hear?'

But she was smiling as she put down the phone, because he had sounded so much better than she had dared to think he could be. He wasn't quite the old Harry, but he wasn't ready to quit the world yet, and he'd give old Nick a hell of a run for his money before that day came.

Even as she thought it, it was as just if she could hear Harry saying the words in her head. It was just the kind of nonsense he would say, and believe it too. He always did think he was immortal. He wasn't, any more than any of them were, but maybe believing in something strongly enough was halfway towards getting it.

She was back to thinking about Blake again now, and she called him quickly on the internal phone to tell him about Harry's call. He must be still in the shower, she decided, and left the message on his answer machine.

'Don't bother replying to this message, Blake. Let's just be thankful that some prayers are answered after all.'

She hoped he wouldn't read anything personal into that remark. Even though several of *his* prayers had been answered recently, and hers too . . .

After only a few more days, and endless phone calls between herself, Elsie and Ricky, it became clear that Harry's minor brush with old Nick, as he was predictably calling it now, was over. And Judy realized that her time in Las Vegas was drawing to an end far more swiftly than she could have imagined.

Six months had never gone so fast, and they were six months that had changed her life. Success in her professional field had never been in doubt. The added bonus was her enjoyment in working here, to be so compatible with the way of life, and hardly to miss England at all. It still surprised her at times to know how easily she had become acclimatized.

But now she knew Harry was well on the way to recovery, she felt she was entitled to enjoy life again. It had been a far more traumatic time than she had bargained for, and if she thought she had successfully shelved all the capacity for deep feelings and emotions she had ever had, she knew now how wrong she was.

They were always there, ready to be brought out whenever they were needed. They had surfaced in her anxiety for Harry, and even more so in her love for Blake. No matter what all the pundits said, there was a limit to how much of your inner self you could plunge into work to the exclusion of all else.

Eventually, you were what you had always been. In Judy's case, it was a warm, passionate woman, the one that Michael had once known, and the one that Blake had re-awakened. She was honest enough with herself to know it and accept it.

CHAPTER 16

There was only a week to go now for the International Spectacular to finish, and for Judy's contract to come to an end. The country and western people were already moving in their equipment for their own rehearsals, and pretty soon now she was going to be redundant. Surplus to requirements . . . and she had already decided that on the Sunday after the show ended, she would insist that that was the day she and Blake must fly up to Reno and get the divorce.

No one need know about it immediately, she reasoned, any more than anyone had known about the wedding. If he felt he needed to keep up the pretence for a while after she had gone home, that would be up to him. Just as long as she could get away as soon as possible once it was all finalized.

She would be under no personal obligation to him after that – except for the little matter of Ricky's debt, Judy reminded herself! But he had already told her that any thought of repayments could wait until later.

She knew exactly what he had meant by that. If she stayed married to him, the debt would be wiped out. It was emotional blackmail again . . . and Judy was just as determined that the debt would be settled in full once she made the necessary arrangements with her bank in England, even if she had to take out a loan herself to do it.

The irony of it didn't escape her, but she wouldn't let herself think in any other terms. Now that it was nearly all over, all she wanted was to go home. She had an odd feeling of being in limbo now, but she had never really felt married, except on those few occasions when she admitted to herself that nothing could have felt more right. But she tried not to dwell on those.

There were frequent phone calls to and from England, sometimes with Ricky, and sometimes with Elsie. It was Elsie who rang that night, and Judy could hear the excitement in her voice.

'I've got good news! Harry's being discharged at the end of the week. They're telling him to take it easy, of course, but you and I both know they might as well ask pigs to fly. I shall do my best to keep his work load down as much as possible, and that's not going to be easy!'

'But you'll love mothering him, all the same,' Judy replied knowingly.

She sensed Elsie's hesitation. 'Oh, I don't deny that, even though Harry will want none of it. All the same, I'm sure this little setback has shaken him more than he realizes. He could do with a bit of cheerful news to give him a boost.'

'Such as hearing that Blake and I got married, for instance?'

Because she had been thinking so much about it recently, the teasing words were out before Judy stopped to think what she was saying, or how literally they might be interpreted. She had to hold the phone away from her ear as she heard Elsie's shriek of excitement.

'Oh, how marvellous, Judy! I can't think of a better welcome-home present to give Harry. He'll be thrilled – '

'Hold on a minute, Elsie. I didn't say it was true – ' but she might as well have been talking to thin air, as Elsie seemed to be gabbling to someone in the background.

'Will you listen to me a minute?' she finally yelled.

'Sorry, my love. Ricky's just come in, and I couldn't resist letting him know right away. I'll hand you over to him for a minute.'

Before Judy could say another word, she heard her brother's chirpy voice.

'So you finally did it, did you, Jude? I always knew it was going to happen between you two. Didn't I tell you?'

'Ricky, for Pete's sake, listen to me,' she almost snapped into the phone now. 'It's not like you think, and in any case it's not going to last – '

He was suddenly suspicious. 'Oh? And what does that mean? It doesn't have anything to do with that other business, does it? You know what I'm talking about.'

'Not a thing,' she lied. 'But I'm not so sure now that it was such a good idea, after all. I didn't have time to give it proper thought, that's all.'

'You mean he swept you off your feet and all that stuff?'

Judy closed her eyes, wishing she'd never been so reckless as to let the words slip out of her mouth. She hadn't meant Elsie to take the marriage as a fact. She had just meant that even the *possibility* of it would give Harry a boost . . . and that had been a big mistake too, since the last thing she wanted was for Harry to get wind of it at all. What a mess she was making of things, she thought helplessly.

'Something like that, I suppose,' she told Ricky now. 'Look, let me speak to Elsie again, will you?'

'OK. I was just going out anyway, for a job interview, no less. Wish me luck – oh, and congratulations, Jude.'

She gripped the phone cord, knowing she had brought all this on herself. But before Elsie could go on burbling away at her, Judy knew she had to put her right.

'Elsie, please listen to me, and don't go overboard about this. In fact, Blake and I are both beginning to think it was a mistake, and that we acted too hastily. Anyway, it's as easy to get a divorce over here as it is to get married, and it will probably have happened by the time you see me.'

Elsie's voice was full of outraged indignation. 'Oh, Judy, you can't mean it! I always thought you and Blake would get along well, and I know Harry thought so too.'

'Promise me you won't let him know any of this,' Judy said sharply. 'I shouldn't have said anything at all, and the last thing I want is for Harry to know anything about it. I mean it, Elsie. It's very important to me.'

She was aware of the delay in replying while Elsie was digesting this strange request.

'It seems to me there's more behind all this than you're telling me,' she said at last. 'But it's your business, Judy, and of course I'll respect your wishes, though it'll be hard not to tell Harry. He'd have loved all the details.'

I'll just bet he would, Judy thought, as she finally replaced the phone. Harry would have wanted to know every detail of the where and when, and once that became common knowledge, Ricky would know that the wedding had taken place on the day they went to Reno. And two and two would very quickly be put together.

There was never a more apt truism, she thought, than the warning: 'O, what a tangled web we weave/ When first we practise to deceive.'

And how often it all came unravelled . . .

Ricky came out from his job interview later that afternoon, feeling pretty chipper. It wasn't a certainty that he'd get it, and he'd got the usual spiel that there were other interviewees to see, but he was fairly optimistic. And his sister's surprising news on the phone had been good too, even if she hadn't sounded exactly over the moon about it.

But that was Jude. She was always more cautious in giving away her feelings now than she used to be.

Except when she was mad with him, he grinned. He paused outside a newsagent's shop, and on the spur of the moment he went in and bought a wedding congratulations card.

It was pretty slushy, and not really his style, but hell, it wasn't every day your sister got married to a big tycoon. He wondered if Annie had known about it, but since he owed her a letter as usual, he couldn't blame her for not passing on the news. She would have expected him to know, anyway, but he decided to call her very soon to make his peace.

And since he was in the Paddington area, and not far from the hospital, he thought he'd steal a march on Elsie too, and go and give old Harry the surprise of his life. After all, Jude was his sister, and he had a right to spread the news. He wasn't going to say anything about her daft remark that it was a marriage that wasn't going to last, though . . . In any case, Blake was far too macho a bloke to stand for that . . .

Blake was taking a tea break in his apartment that afternoon when his phone rang. He had to hold the receiver well away from his ear as he heard Harry's voice.

'Hold on a minute,' he yelled back. 'I can't understand a blessed thing you're saying, and you'll be in danger of bursting a blood vessel if you're not careful.'

But he could tell that Harry was clearly back on form and feeling immortal again.

'Good God, I'm not worried about a little thing like that! But you're a sly devil and no mistake, and didn't always say that you and Jude were made for each other?'

Blake started, wondering what the old goat was getting at now. He was a great one for stirring things up, and maybe he thought that now Judy's contract was nearly over, he had better put on some pressure.

'What are you getting at, Harry? And from the sound of your voice, I presume you're feeling better – '

'Good enough for them to be letting me out of this cage at the end of the week, thank God. What I'm getting at, Blakey boy, is the little fact that you and Judy got married and never even told me. Afraid that I well and truly won my bet in fine style, I suppose! But I wasn't so near to death's door that I couldn't appreciate that kind of news!'

'Who the hell told you?' Blake said flatly.

His mind whirled, trying to think. It wasn't Judy, for sure. And nobody else knew. She had been so damn insistent on that, and he'd agreed to go along with her wishes – for the time being. So how else could the news have got out? He wasn't well enough known in Reno for his name to have prompted a mention in a local rag, and anyway, the wedding was weeks ago now . . .

'You're not going to deny it, are you?' Harry demanded.

'No, I'm not denying it – ' In any case, it seemed pointless to do so now.

Harry chuckled. 'Well, young Ricky seems quite pleased to have you for a brother-in-law. He's just been here and spilled the beans, though I must say

I'd have expected you or Jude to do the decent thing and tell me yourselves. But I guess you wanted to keep me on a string as long as possible, right?'

'Something like that,' Blake retorted. 'Harry, it's great that you're going home, but you just take it easy, or you'll be right back in hospital again. I'm sorry I can't talk for longer, but I've got a business meeting in ten minutes, so I'll have to go – '

'Oh, sure. I understand all about business before pleasure. Well, give Judy my love, and tell her I want to talk to her *soon*!'

And he wasn't the only one . . .

As soon as he had hung up, Blake marched across the corridor and rapped on Judy's door. There was no reply, and he immediately remembered she had gone out. He had invented a business meeting simply to get away from Harry's chatter, and he needed to see Judy *right now*.

The more he thought about it, the more angered he became. She was his wife, but she'd refused to let anyone know, until *she* decided the time was right. He should never have accepted her terms, and realizing it was neither a pleasant nor a familiar feeling for Blake Adams.

It was much later before Judy returned to the hotel, carrying several packages of shopping from the more exclusive dress shops. She'd spent far too much money, knowing it was little more than comfort shopping, the way some people turned to food when their minds were so unsettled. Only in this case, it was a hell of a lot more expensive . . . but she had a stunning new dress to wear at the last-night party here that was going to bolster up her confidence . . .

She answered the impatient rapping on her door with an exclamation of annoyance, and was almost pushed aside as Blake stormed inside.

'Well, do come in!' she said sarcastically.

But her eyes sparkled. Blake in his dangerously seductive mood was far more difficult to deal with, than in whatever had caused this belligerent one. Then she noticed how dark with genuine anger he looked, and she felt less certain of herself.

'What's wrong?' she asked more carefully, knowing that of course there had to be something wrong.

It couldn't be to do with Harry's illness, or Blake would be far more concerned than he looked at this moment. So it had to be something she'd done, but for the life of her she couldn't think what it was . . .

'You think you're so clever, don't you, pulling all the strings any way you want them?'

She stared at him, not understanding. Her feet ached, and she would dearly like to kick off her shoes, but that would give him far more of a height advantage over her, and right now, she had the strongest feeling she was going to have to defend herself. She tilted her chin defiantly.

'Are you going to explain that remark? If I've done something to upset you, at least let me know what it is – '

'We had an agreement, and it was at your insistence that I went along with it. If you intended to break it any time you chose, you could have let me in on it before I got such a garbled phone call from Harry.'

Judy felt her heart sink. Blake wasn't the kind of man to tolerate things going on behind his back. And if Harry had called in the way Blake implied, it could only have been about one thing. And Elsie had *promised* . . .

'Elsie,' she muttered sickly.

'What's Elsie got to do with it?'

'Well, wasn't it Elsie who told Harry we were married? I presume that *is* what you're talking about – '

'Of course it is, but Elsie had nothing to do with it. No, I gather you decided it was time to tell your brother the news. I suppose the two of you had a good laugh at my expense over the way you'd managed to keep it a secret all this time.'

Judy felt as if every bit of colour left her face. Too late, she remembered now that Ricky had been about to go out while she had been talking to Elsie, and making her promise to keep the marriage a secret from Harry.

Ricky hadn't stayed in the flat long enough to get the message that Harry wasn't to know, and he must have gone to the hospital to tell him, sure that it would cheer him up. Judy sat down heavily on the sofa, feeling that if she didn't, she would fall down.

'Blake, it wasn't like that!' she whispered. 'You've got to believe me.'

'That's rather an optimistic statement, isn't it?'

She bit her lip, knowing he had every right to feel that way. Why should he believe her? But she had to explain.

'I don't even know how it happened,' she said, spreading her hands helplessly. 'I was talking to Elsie on the phone, and it slipped out as a kind of teasing remark that something like hearing we'd got married would cheer Harry up. I don't even know why I said it, and I certainly didn't mean her to take it as a fact, but she picked up on it at once. And then, well, I couldn't deny it.'

'You mean you were reluctant to add one more lie to all the rest?'

'That's not fair, Blake! And of course I never expected Ricky to go and tell Harry. I'm really sorry.'

And if he couldn't see how upset she was becoming, then he had no feelings for her at all. But his attitude was totally bewildering, and she hadn't expected his anger at having their marriage known to three people on the other side of the world.

Except, of course, that Blake would have wanted to do the telling himself. To crow to Harry that he'd won his bet in a far more spectacular way than the agent had expected. That had to be it.

He looked down at her for a long moment before he sat beside her without touching her. And she wondered how two people who had once been so close in body and spirit could be so distant now.

'I'm well aware that you're sorry I persuaded you to marry me,' he said, making her heart twist. 'But it was your brother who blew it, and there's nothing we can do about it now. I gather he's not too displeased. Nor will Harry be, and Elsie's head will be filled with moonlight and romance by now. So where do we go from here?'

'Nowhere. Nothing's changed,' she said huskily. 'I'm still leaving when the show's over, and before I do we go to Reno on Sunday to get the divorce as we agreed. Nobody here has any idea of what's happened, and I see no reason why it shouldn't stay that way.'

She found out how wrong she was when she awoke on the following day, after a night that was haunted by dreams and nightmares and indecisions. She had made many mistakes in her life, and perhaps the most stupid one of all was not acknowledging to the world that she had married the man she loved. It all seemed too late now to make amends.

She didn't hurry over her morning shower, and she was enjoying a second cup of coffee when someone knocked on her door. With a heavy sigh, she went to answer it, knowing that if she didn't, Blake would simply use his pass key. But it wasn't Blake who stood there.

As soon as she saw the bellboy, almost hidden behind the enormous basket of flowers, she gaped in disbelief.

'Congratulations, ma'am, and all the best for your future happiness,' the boy said with a wide smile.

She didn't have to guess his meaning, and although Judy took in the elaborate floral arrangement with an answering smile, the smile cracked as soon as she closed the door behind him. It had to be Blake who had done this, of course. And if the bellboy knew, then probably everyone did. The hotel grapevine spread gossip faster than a bush fire, and if this was Blake's idea of paying her back, by letting everyone in on their marriage without telling her he was going to do so . . .

She was tempted to throw the card that came with it straight into the bin, but she couldn't resist ripping it out of its little envelope to read the message he had written.

'With all love to two of the nicest people I know. Be happy. Harry.'

The minute she read the words, Judy's eyes stung with tears. No matter how wily he was, or how he tried to manipulate people, inside that stubborn chest beat a heart of fool's gold, at the very least. And she must be going softer in the head than usual to be having such dozy thoughts about the old rogue.

Someone else knocked on her door almost immediately. It was like Victoria Station here, thought Judy. And then Maggie came in, shrieking into her ear.

'Is it true, Judy? Well, of course it is,' she answered herself. 'The whole place is buzzing with the news, and we got it on good authority. Good luck to both of you, hon, though you certainly kept it in the dark, even to the pretence of keeping this suite going. I still don't know how you managed it, with the whole town knowing who Blake is.'

'He told you, I suppose,' Judy put in, when she finally drew breath. 'Do you want some coffee?' she added, just to keep herself busy.

'Yes, I'd love some, and no, I haven't seen him yet today. Not that that's so surprising in the circumstances. No wonder the two of you have been sleeping in late, if you get my meaning, especially if you've been commuting across the corridor for however long it's been.'

Judy interrupted her chuckle before she could start asking for dates and places. 'We did our best to keep it quiet, so how did you get to hear about it, Maggie?'

The hotel flower shop in the foyer, maybe. But although Harry's message would probably have been faxed to them, there was nothing on it to specifically say it was a wedding congratulation, or who the two people involved were.

'Annie from the casino – you know, the girl your brother was seeing – has been been telling everybody after he called her in the early hours of this morning.'

Ricky again! It seemed as though he was responsible for everything. But she knew she couldn't really blame him. She just hadn't thought to warn him to keep it strictly to himself, the way she had told Elsie. And Ricky obviously approved of the marriage. Maybe by telling everybody, he even thought he'd help his sister to start thinking the same way . . . he'd want the best for her, and he'd clearly thought the best was Blake.

No, she couldn't blame Ricky. If it was anybody's fault, it was her own. And Maggie was still prattling as she accepted her mug of coffee.

'Most of the girls think it's all very romantic. But you should have told us you and Blake were getting married,' she scolded mildly. 'We'd have had a bridal shower for you. It's not too late, of course, and I mean to get it organized.'

'Oh, Maggie, please don't! We don't go in for all that in England – ' She stopped, knowing how

323

ungrateful and snobbish that sounded. But there was no stopping Maggie now.

'You're not in England now, babe, and you'll have a bridal shower, whether you like it or not,' she said, laughing. 'But maybe we'll leave it until next week after the show ends, when we'll all have more time for a hen party, and you can get out a list of the things you'd like.'

Judy didn't want anything at all. It was distressing her more by the minute as Maggie went on and on, and any minute now she was going to ask where she and Blake were going to live, or if she'd simply move into his apartment now.

That would certainly simplify the wedding list, Judy thought, almost hysterically. And it gave her an inkling of what to say next.

'We haven't even decided on that yet, since it all happened so quickly,' she heard herself say, just as if this was a regular discussion about a whirlwind romance. 'So perhaps it would be best if you left the shower until a later date, when we know exactly what we'll be doing.'

'Well, OK,' Maggie nodded. 'Don't leave it too late though, or it'll take away some of the excitement. And I've got to hand it to you, hon.'

'What do you mean?'

'Well, I always thought you English gals wanted the whole wedding bit – the church and the white dress and all that mushy stuff – but I guess when you find the right man, none of that matters in the end, does it?'

Thankfully, she didn't pursue it further, and it was a great relief when she left. Judy felt weak by then, knowing she would have to face this kind of thing from now on.

Everyone around here would be seeing it as the wedding of the year, and there was nothing she could do about it. She didn't want to leave her suite, but she could hardly stay where she was all day, and if she did, she was sure her phone would never stop ringing. She picked up her purse, and went across to Blake's apartment.

'Things are happening,' she said flatly. 'The entire hotel is aware of our marriage – '

'So I've discovered.'

'And I know it wasn't you,' she went on. 'Ricky called Annie, and I suppose she naturally assumed it was OK to mention it. You'll be sorry you ever set eyes on him – '

'I won't, but we'll let that pass.'

'Harry's sent flowers.' She was almost hysterical now at the farce of it all. 'Maggie's talking about arranging a bridal shower, but I've managed to put her off, at least for the immediate future, but it looks as though we're going to have to face up to all the good wishes for now.'

'You mean until you run out on me, and I make the divorce announcement, is that it?'

'None of this was my idea, Blake, and you know it. I didn't plan to marry you, and if it hadn't been for Ricky – '

'I agree that he's got a lot to answer for, but let's forget about him. And since you seem to have an answer for everything, what's your next move?'

Slowly, Judy opened her purse and drew out the heavy gold wedding ring. 'Well, people will be assuming that it was a marriage made in heaven, even if we know it wasn't, so I suppose I had better wear this – '

'That has got to be the most ungracious acceptance of a wedding ring ever heard,' he said coolly. 'But I accept your reasoning, so let's put it back where it belongs.'

Before she could think what he was about to do, he had taken the ring from her hand and for the second time he pushed it on to the third finger of her left hand. Then he lifted her hand to his lips for a moment, before turning over her palm to kiss the soft inner flesh. He spoke more softly.

'It doesn't have to be like this, Judy – '

She pulled away. She couldn't bear to prolong this.

'I think it does. I'll go along with the pretence of being the loving wife for the next few days, but after that, it's over. I mean it, Blake. I can't – I just can't – '

'All right. But you do realize you'll have to move in here now that it's all out in the open?'

She felt her heart beat more quickly. She should have been prepared for this, but she hadn't. There had been too much going on since yesterday to think about it too deeply.

'Providing I can have the second bedroom,' she stated. 'And I'll still keep the suite for business purposes.'

He gave a short laugh. 'Still making conditions, I see. But why not? It's not far to walk between bedrooms – '

'Blake, *please*!' Couldn't he see how tense she was, and that she wanted none of this? It was all getting far too complicated . . .

He went on relentlessly, 'Shall we move some of your stuff over now, or shall we go down and face the music as a united front?'

She took a deep breath. It was such a sad way to think of greeting people as a married couple and receiving their good wishes and congratulations. But it would have been a shock to everybody here, and she knew it had to be done, and once it was over, perhaps they could be a little more relaxed.

'Let's go and face the music,' she said huskily.

It was true that everyone loved a wedding, no matter where they lived, and people seemed to love the fact that these two had apparently skipped off secretly and got married right under everyone's noses.

As they went through the casino and the various bars and suites, Blake kept her arm firmly linked in his, so that the wedding ring was prominently displayed. It made Judy feel distinctly uncomfortable, feeling that she was deceiving all these people who were wishing them well.

'Smile, darling,' Blake said, close to her ear. 'You're supposed to be the happy, blushing bride, remember?'

She couldn't be as jocular as he was. 'I'll admit that I'm the bride, and the mess we've got ourselves in makes me blush all right – '

He didn't relinquish his hold on her arm as they left the casino and took a breather in the hotel grounds. 'Is it so very distasteful to you to be married to me, then?'

'It wouldn't be if this was a proper marriage,' she retorted. 'And don't get the wrong idea from that. I just mean that if you and I had been different people and met under different circumstances, then maybe . . .' She was floundering and couldn't seem to stop.

'But we're not different people. We're us, and you can hardly deny that we're compatible in every way. So give me one good reason why this marriage couldn't work.'

'You give me one good reason why it could!'

'I've already done that. I've told you I love you, and I think I've proved it in a hundred different ways. Or rather, twenty thousand ways – '

Judy stopped walking, and her voice was bitter.

'You see? That's one very good reason. I would always remember how you tricked me into marrying you in Reno before you got Ricky out of trouble. You just couldn't do the one thing without the other, could you?'

'Maybe I just wanted to be sure of you.'

'You mean you couldn't trust me to honour my agreement, and you thought I'd find some way to back out of it, if wasn't already a *fait accompli*, is that it?'

He turned to her, and she couldn't read the expression in his eyes, but she knew he was angry.

'I never thought any such thing – and why do you never trust me to mean what I say? Haven't I told you – '

'I know what you've told me. You're a good Yorkshire lad who says what he means and means what he says.'

'Exactly. So why can't you believe it?'

It seemed to be stalemate as they stared at each other, and Judy couldn't help thinking how bizarre it would look, had there been anyone close enough to hear them. They were two newlyweds who couldn't seem to stop bickering over whether he truly loved her or not. Maybe he did, and maybe he didn't. What was certain was that they had to go through with this now, for just a few more days. She took a deep breath.

'I guess we'd better stop this, at least in public, if we want to keep the image of the happy married couple intact.' She couldn't even smile at that. 'People will think we're having our first fight.'

'Hardly the first, but I couldn't agree more,' he said at once. 'So do we call a truce on all our differences, and concentrate on acting out our allotted roles?'

'How formal you make it sound! But yes, we do. And if we weren't getting such arch smiles from everybody out here now, I'd suggest that we shake on it. But that would be even more formal, wouldn't it?'

'Especially when I'd far rather kiss you.'

Before she knew what he intended, he had tipped up her face to his and kissed her, to the delighted applause of the little group of elderly hotel guests approaching them.

Judy felt suddenly reckless, knowing that these were the games they would have to play in public. As long as she remembered that they were actors playing their parts, and it was all for show, maybe it wouldn't be too difficult . . .

And for one of them, at least, it wasn't entirely acting, she thought, as she kissed him back rather more fervently than he might have expected.

CHAPTER 17

'There's one thing we must do right away,' Blake told her.

They had finally got away from all the congratulations and good wishes, and returned to the apartment for a quiet half-hour to recover.

They had had an especially hard time disentangling themselves from all the people in the show who could hardly contain their surprise, and had applauded them loudly when they appeared in the rehearsal room.

Frank's reaction had been the most predictable of all, Judy thought, whispering in her ear under cover of the general ballyhoo that she'd got the biggest prize after all.

She was aware that he'd never *quite* forgiven her for freezing him off the way she had, but as she turned to another wellwisher, she simply dismissed him from her thoughts.

'What do we have to do right away?' she asked Blake now, slipping her feet out of her shoes as she liked to do whenever possible, and curling up on the sitting-room sofa in the apartment without giving it a thought.

'That was something worth seeing,' Blake commented, diverting her attention.

'What was?'

He nodded towards her bare feet. 'The way that comfortable little action made you seem so at home in here, as if you really feel that you belong.'

'I'm just getting into the part,' she reminded him. 'And Blake,' she added, more warningly, 'you're not going back on our arrangement, are you? Separate bedrooms, remember?'

'I can hardly forget it. And I never go back on a promise, whether I like it or not.'

'So what is it that we have to do right away?' she went on, wanting to get over this far too personal a conversation, and wondering if he was ever going to tell her. She watched as he made them both some coffee and handed her a mug. This was still very much his preserve . . .

He spoke more authoritively. 'Now that the secret is well and truly out, somebody's sure to tip off the reporters pretty soon, and I'd far rather Ginny and Kyle heard it from us than read about it in any local rag.'

Judy didn't think her own wedding would have stirred up that much interest. She was still a comparative newcomer here, despite her part in making the Spectacular such a success. But Blake was something else, she conceded. Blake was the wealthy and charismatic owner of the successful Sparkling Rocks Hotel and Casino, and he was a *somebody* in this town.

'Are you proposing that we go out to the ranch and tell them?' she asked, thinking at once that it wouldn't be a bad idea to get away from the hotel for a few hours until all the immediate excitement had died down here.

And then she remembered Elsie's reaction to the news. If that had been so palpable from six thousand miles away, what on earth was the exuberant Ginny's going to be like?

'Could you really stand it?' Blake grinned, as if he could read her mind. 'No, I think it's best if I call them, but I wanted to suggest inviting them all here for dinner and to see the show this evening as our guests. Do you approve?'

She felt absurdly pleased that he was asking her opinion and she agreed at once. By the time they got here, the initial impact of the news would hopefully have calmed Ginny down a little . . . But she asked him to wait until she had finished her coffee and gone back to the suite while he made the call.

There were still times when all the lies and subterfuge caught up with her, and she couldn't bear to listen to him telling his friends and making it all sound so real.

'That's fine,' he said coolly. 'And while you're there, pack up everything necessary for you to move in here. I'll arrange to get the suite serviced once you're done, and then the Coopers can stay there overnight.'

He thought of everything, Judy thought, even to neatly arranging it so that she couldn't sleep in her own suite tonight if she wanted to.

And she knew she was going to have to move into the apartment now, unless there were going to be a lot of raised eyebrows among the service staff, about the strange habits of two Britishers who didn't spend their honeymoon nights together. But they could think what they liked about separate bedrooms. Royalty did it, so who were they to argue . . .?

She was smiling at the thought as she went back to the suite to begin organizing her things. Once there, she let out a long-drawn breath. It seemed as if she had been holding it in for ever. She caught sight of her reflection in her mirror, and felt a stab of surprise.

Without doubt, this morning had been as weird as any morning could be, having to receive all the good wishes of the people who knew her and Blake, and she had fully expected her colour to be heightened by it all.

What she hadn't expected was for her to look as ecstatic as any new bride was supposed to look. Her colour was high, but her eyes were blue and sparkling, and her mouth looked as if it had just been kissed. So it had been, even though it was some time ago now, but the memory still lingered, and so did the touch of Blake's mouth on hers. She touched her fingers to her lips, remembering how spontaneously she had responded.

And then she turned away abruptly, opening her wall closets and starting to remove her clothes on their hangers, ready to take everything into Blake's apartment. It was only for a few days, she told herself, little more than a week at most, and she wouldn't let herself think how full of tension those days and nights might be, knowing she was sleeping in the adjoining bedroom to the man she loved.

The rest of the morning was spent in removing the things she needed and leaving the rest neatly boxed, so that the maids could come and service the suite. It would be assumed that she would still be using the computer and fax equipment, so her desk was left virtually as it was, as an indication that someone worked here.

Rehanging all her clothes in the closet in Blake's second bedroom felt weird too, but at least she didn't have the piquancy of hanging her dresses next to his suits. The task kept her busy, and stopped her from thinking too much how all her careful planning had begun to get away from her, and that Blake was calling the tune. And if she hadn't made that one reckless remark to Elsie, none of this would be happening now.

The Coopers were due to arrive around seven o'clock, and they would all eat dinner after the show, despite the hour being quite late for Zoe. But Judy guessed that excitement would keep her awake more effectively than anything else.

By then, she and Blake had changed for the evening. Knowing the Coopers weren't formal people, neither of them had dressed ostentatiously, and Judy hoped she wouldn't betray the nervousness she felt. Acting a part for strangers was one thing. For people with whom she worked, it was more of an ordeal. But for these people who knew Blake so well, and were enchanted that he and Judy had got married secretly despite all her earlier protestations . . . that was something else.

The minute Blake opened the door of the apartment to them, it seemed as if the whole world burst inside. It wasn't, of course. It was just the Cooper family. But the Cooper family *en masse*, brimming with excitement over the news they had heard, was something to be experienced.

Judy was clasped in Ginny's embrace, while Kyle seemed to be practically fighting off his wife to do the same thing. Bobby was quieter as befitted a boy of his age, but Zoe was leaping all over Blake now and asking when the babies were going to be arriving, sending Judy hot with embarrassment at the artless questions.

'You'll have to forgive her, Judy,' Ginny shouted above the general din. 'She's been watching a schools' programme on TV about babies, and she thinks that now the wedding's over, it'll happen overnight.'

Dear God, thought Judy, if a seven-year-old child was going to be watching for signs of babies from now on, what chance did she have from the rest of them? It had never even occurred to her until that moment, either, that people might be putting two and two together on account of their hasty marriage, and making a potential *three*.

'Not all couples have babies right away, Zoe,' she told her, as soon as she could extricate herself from the Cooper parents. 'And certainly not the minute

336

they get married. It takes a long time for a baby to grow – '

'Oh, I know all about it,' Zoe said importantly. 'It takes months and months. But I've worked it all out, and it could come on my birthday next year – '

'I think you'd better forget all about it for now, sweetheart.' Blake was hardly able to contain his laughter at the outrage on Judy's face that she was trying hard to conceal.

He put his arm loosely around her waist, well aware of how tense she was becoming, despite her efforts to the contrary. He kissed her cheek and she steeled herself not to move away. 'In any case, married people like to have some time together on their own before any babies come along.'

Zoe scowled with disappointment, and he spoke quickly to Judy before there could be any more probing questions.

'Why don't you put some coffee on, darling? Unless Ginny and Kyle would prefer a cocktail?'

But he knew them too well, and cocktails could wait until they were all seated in one of the best booths in the Diamond Showroom. Judy turned away to do as he asked. It was obviously assumed that she was already settled in here, and from the pleased smiles on the Cooper faces at the way things had turned out, she knew she couldn't disillusion them.

There would be time enough for all that later, she thought, feeling an undeniable pang in her heart. But she squeezed Blake's hand in a vice-like grip before moving towards the kitchen.

'Right away, darling,' she said sweetly. 'You see how domesticated he's got me already, Ginny?'

She spoke mockingly for Blake's benefit, but she should have known that Ginny Cooper was the wrong person to address in that way. She heard the woman chuckle, and through the hatchway of the kitchen, she saw her glance at her husband and give a firm nod.

'That's just why we were so pleased when Blake called us up and invited us here tonight. We'd have come in to town tomorrow, anyway, but this gives us the chance to say what we wanted to say to two very special people.'

Judy's hand froze over the coffee maker. At that moment, she felt as though she was being drawn further and further into a mesh from which there was going to be no escape.

'We're really keen to sell the ranch, as you know,' Kyle went on now. 'And now that you're married, Blake will want to put down proper roots and establish a home for his children, so we're prepared to offer a handsome deal on the property. A *really* handsome deal,' he emphasized.

'Besides which, Blake honey, you know how much we always wanted you to have it,' Ginny added.

'And we can come back to the ranch for visits, daddy Blake,' Zoe shouted gleefully.

Good God, they even had the kids involved in all this, Judy thought, aghast. Not that Bobby had much to say on the subject. Ten-year-old boys weren't so interested in homemaking as the little poppet jumping all over Blake on his sofa now.

338

And Judy could see how he was loving it . . . It didn't matter a damn to him that he was the successful and wealthy owner of this entire mega-building. Right now he was daddy Blake, caught up in the chubby arms of his goddaughter. He was made for a proper home, and kids . . . and she knew she was on rocky ground, just thinking about it.

'We haven't got around to thinking about our future plans yet, Kyle,' she said swiftly, before Blake could say a word. 'In fact, Blake swept me off my feet so fast, I haven't had time to think about anything very much – '

Ginny chuckled again. 'You don't have to explain a thing to me, honey. And why would you be thinking about anything but your husband right now? We shouldn't even be here at all, muscling in on your honeymoon – '

'Oh no, that's perfectly all right, and we wanted you to share in our happiness.' Aware of her slight hesitation before saying the word, Judy knew she was scarlet with embarrassment at the interpretation Ginny was putting on her words.

This domestic little scene had been none of her making, and quite how Blake accomplished whatever he wanted, she would never know. But there was one thing he wasn't getting. She was going to make sure of that.

She heard Blake showing them all quickly around the apartment now while she prepared the coffee, and soft drinks for the children. Then Ginny came to offer help, taking the tray out of Judy's hands.

'It'll all be new to you, honey,' Ginny said softly. 'But believe me, you're the best thing that ever happened to Blake, and I just wanted you to know it. He's been on his own for far too long – and I hope I'm not talking out of turn. I assume you know all about Claire by now.'

'I know he must have loved her very much,' Judy murmured, saying the words that could twist a knife in her heart. 'He kept their photo in his bedroom all these years.'

'Did he? But now he's got yours.'

Unaware of the way Judy started, she went on. 'You know we're not party folks, Judy, and we've never even been here to the hotel before, strange as that may seem to you, so it was nice that Blake gave us a quick look around the apartment just now. And your photo is just beautiful.'

In an instant Judy knew what had become of the photo Harry had sent over, the one that had been used in the showbiz rag. Feeling ridiculously touched by the other woman's romantic idealism, she made the excuse of needing a tissue, and fled to Blake's bedroom to take a look. And there it was.

In pride of place, in the frame that used to hold the photo of Blake and Claire, was her own smiling photo. She had always thought the photographer had somehow captured a particularly intimate look in her eyes, and Blake must have put it there for the Coopers' benefit.

The door opened behind her, and she whirled around at once, still clutching the framed photo in her hand. Blake came towards her.

'It's lovely, isn't it?'

'It would be, if it meant anything to you to have it here. And the idea that we're now living here cosily together is only for show. The minute the Coopers leave, I'm going back to my suite,' she added recklessly.

'No, you're not, darling.'

She looked at him in shock. 'You have no right – '

He took her hand in his, and caressed the gold ring on her finger.

'This gives me the right, remember? Whatever you think, I hadn't bargained for having the news of our marriage broadcast until I was ready for it, but now that it's out, do you think I'm having my staff spreading the gossip that Blake Adams and his wife don't share the same apartment?'

'You can't do this,' Judy whispered. 'You promised – '

'I promised to love and keep you, as I remember, and all the other bits and pieces – '

'And you mean to keep me,' Judy said bitterly. 'Until Sunday, anyway.'

'And besides,' he went on relentlessly, 'I've already had the Coopers' overnight bags taken to the suite. It's far too late to change anything.'

They heard hammering on the door then, and Zoe's shrill voice was yelling at them to come out. Judy pushed past Blake, her head held high. She was still learning how implacable he could be when he set his mind on anything. She was fuming inside, but if the Coopers thought her face was unusually red as

341

she came out of the bedroom with her husband, well, this was her honeymoon, wasn't it . . .?

There was still some time to go before they needed to go down to the auditorium, and a little later, Kyle looked at her thoughtfully. She had just finished telling Bobby a bit more about London, and assuring him that he must certainly visit the science museum, since he was becoming so interested in all things scientific.

Kyle wasn't the brightest of men when it came to working out women's thoughts, and with Ginny he never needed to. She was as uncomplicated and transparent to him as glass, and he liked it that way. But Judy was different. She hid things, he thought intuitively.

'So now that you've had time to catch your breath, what are your thoughts about moving out to the ranch, Judy? You must have some,' he asked, never one to waste words when something needed to be said.

'You musn't rush her, Kyle,' Blake put in before she could answer. 'I've rushed her far too much already, and we'll have to discuss it thoroughly in private. But you can say that we're definitely considering it.'

'Well, don't keep us waiting too long. You'll never get a better deal on a property.'

'I know that,' Blake answered with a smile.

Not that such a detail mattered to him, thought Judy. What did saving a few extra thousand dollars, or even millions, mean to a man who already had everything? It hadn't concerned her that she was married to an extremely wealthy man, because in her eyes, if you didn't marry for the right reasons, then you had nothing at all.

But as he smiled at her now, she went through the motions of being the loving wife, reacting in the way he obviously wanted her to react. She had made a bargain with him to play along with the game. And so she would. For now.

And she wouldn't think about tonight, when she would no longer be able to go to the sanctuary of her own suite. Blake had taken care of that.

The International Spectacular had more than lived up to its name, and it was nearing its final few performances now. The Cooper family, coming from out of town, weren't theatregoers any more than they were party folk, and they were clearly as overwhelmed by the fabulous costumes and intricate dance routines, as the attention to detail in the various national displays and tableaux.

'It was truly marvellous, Blake,' Ginny told him when it was all over, and they had finally left the auditorium and taken their seats for dinner in the restaurant. 'I've never seen anything like it, and you must be very proud.'

'Of course. And I'm especially proud of my beautiful bride for bringing such class to it all.'

'You know I was only a small part of it,' Judy protested. 'Any choreographer could have done what I did. It's the dancers who bring it all to life.'

He raised her fingers to his lips. 'You Britishers always underestimate yourselves,' he drawled teasingly, anticipating the remark from one of the others.

As they laughed, Judy thought how easy they all were with one another. She admitted that even she was more relaxed now, and she knew how much having the Cooper children around contributed to that. It somehow diffused the intensity of this whole evening.

Bobby had been more than interested in the showgirls, Judy thought with amusement, and Zoe declared that her new ambition was to be a dancer, and that after they had moved into their new home out east, she was going to visit Judy at the ranch all the time for more lessons.

'Maybe you could start that dance studio that you once mentioned, and give instruction to young hopefuls,' Blake suggested, under cover of the general chatter. 'There's plenty of space there.'

'I'm not likely to do it, since I won't be living there,' she answered him beneath her breath so that the others couldn't hear.

Not that the idea didn't have its charm . . . for an ex-dancer wanting something different, but still to be involved with the work she loved, it would be less frenetic than working with an entire company. It could be a delightful mixture of family life and still keeping her fingers – and toes – on the pulse of her old life. She realized where her wayward thoughts were going, and quickly ignored them before she let herself get carried away by the idyllic thought of it.

Besides, why should she want anything different? This was her life, and she saw no reason to change it . . . At that moment she saw Maggie cross the restaurant, alone as she so often was, and she gave a sudden shiver. Maggie had a dynamic personality, and was always surrounded by people in her working life, but at the end of the day, she was still alone. Judy knew she wouldn't want to end up like that.

'Giving it a second thought?' Blake asked, just as if he was reading her mind again in that infuriating way.

'Not even a first,' she replied.

But Ginny had obviously been mulling over the idea in her mind ever since their visit to the ranch, and she had caught his earlier remark, if not Judy's reply.

'It would be ideal for you, Judy. One of the barns could easily be turned into a studio, and you could be doing a service for the starstruck kids whose only ambition is to perform in Las Vegas. You really should think about it.'

'You really should, darling,' Blake said mockingly, raising his wine glass to her.

They lingered over dinner awhile, but finally Ginny made pointed hints to Kyle that it was time they all hit the hay. Zoe was finding it hard to keep her eyes open now, but once they had reached their floor, Judy realized that the out-of-town Coopers were the kind of people who didn't quite know how to end an evening.

In particular, they seemed reluctant to disappear into the suite until they had seen Judy safely inside

Blake's lair. She couldn't think of it in any other terms at that moment.

As the small talk looked destined to stretch into embarrassing inanities, Blake spoke firmly.

'I'd ask you in for a nightcap, Kyle, except . . .'

His deliberate hesitation seemed to galvanize Kyle into a decision. 'I reckon you've had enough company for one day, old buddy. You've given us all a great time and all you'll be wanting now is to have that little gal all to yourself.'

'Besides, these two babes are falling asleep, and Zoe should have been in bed long ago – ' Ginny added, nudging him.

She ignored the howls of protest from Bobby and Zoe, who had obviously wanted to prolong the time spent with their favourite uncle. But, unbelievably, Judy saw that they were all waiting at the open door of the suite until Blake had opened the apartment and waved them goodnight.

'It's worse than having a maiden aunt checking up on you,' she told him with a shaky smile. 'Not that a maiden aunt would send me so willingly into a man's apartment, of course.'

She found herself talking too fast, and Blake took her in his arms and kissed her lightly on the lips.

'But I'm not just any man. I'm your husband, so what are you so afraid of?'

Of you. Of me. Of betraying how much I love you, and regretting how I've pushed you into this impossible situation. Of everything . . .

'I'm not afraid of anything.'

346

'Good. Because you've no need to be. I'm not about to ravish you.'

'Aren't you?' she asked faintly.

'Are you disappointed?'

'Of course not. Maybe just a bit surprised, that's all.'

He spoke sardonically as he move away from her. 'Why? Because I know how to behave like a gentleman, despite all you might think to the contrary?'

'Not exactly,' she murmured.

Not for the world was she going to admit to him that her surprise came from the obvious. She *was* his wife, no matter what the circumstances, and this strange day, when they had both played their parts to such good effect, had almost let her believe that it was all real. That they had both married for love, and that it was going to last for ever . . .

She had also believed that now that they were here together like this, Blake would definitely take advantage of it all. And even if she hadn't consciously thought that far ahead, she knew with instant certainty that she would only have put up a token resistance, if any . . .

'You can use the bathroom first,' he was saying calmly now, 'and I'll see you in the morning.'

She turned away from him, before he could see the darkening desire in her eyes. She had brought all this on herself, and to her heightened senses it seemed that he was as good as telling her now that he didn't want her after all.

Much later, lying sleepless in her solitary bed, she could only think how near, and yet how far away he was. If she had been a different kind of woman, the kind who took whatever life offered, and to hell with the consequences, she would probably have simply gone to him right now.

Her ex-lover had spoiled all that for her, she thought bitterly. Michael had taken away all her self-esteem, and it had taken an enormous effort for her to claw her way back to sanity, vowing that no man would ever hurt her that way again.

She was still far too full of stubborn pride to take chances now. So stubborn . . . but that was the way she was. She turned her hot face into her pillow and tried to sleep.

To her relief, the Cooper family had to leave early the following morning. Kyle couldn't stay away from his beloved property for too long, and Judy wondered mildly how he was ever going to live without it. It was their business, but leaving that lovely ranch and all those wide open spaces for an eastern city life bore no comparison. Any more than it would compare with living and working in London . . .

They all met for breakfast, and it was obvious that they wouldn't linger over morning goodbyes, which was a huge relief to Judy. She couldn't have borne too many more of the coyly knowing looks from Ginny, after the honeymoon night she and Blake had supposedly shared.

By now, Judy's feelings had become almost aggressive, thinking that he was behaving in a most unnatural way towards her. She was highly suspicious of the fact that he wasn't hassling her in any way. She had definitely expected him to take advantage of their enforced intimacy now, she admitted.

But the sudden consideration was bewildering. She had honestly been prepared for him to come to her bedroom during the night, and he hadn't.

He *was* being the perfect gentleman, she thought in annoyance, at a time when she wouldn't have minded a bit of sweeping off her feet. It was no longer a case of not knowing her own mind. She simply couldn't fathom out his.

She stared at her breakfast bacon and eggs and hash browns as if they were the most important items in the place, wondering how on earth she had become such a philistine. One minute she was determined to keep Blake at arm's length, and the next she longed to be a part of him. She couldn't have it both ways, and she knew it.

She was glad when breakfast was over, and there was the usual bustle of parting. Kyle put in a final word as the family prepared to leave. Their baggage had already been put in their car, which was now beneath the front canopy of the hotel, and Kyle leaned out of it for a final word.

'Don't forget now, Blake. I've told you my offer on the ranch, and I'll expect to hear from you very soon.'

'You've got my word on it,' Blake told him. 'I'll be in touch within the next few days.'

They waved them off, and Judy was glad that at least they could stop the pretence of being a happily married couple in front of them. They were such honest people that it made their own deception all the more embarrassing.

'What's going on in that beautiful head of yours now?' she heard Blake say.

'Nothing much. I was just wondering how you're going to get out of buying the ranch, when they've even got Zoe putting the pressure on you,' she retorted.

'Oh, I'm sure I'll think of something. Don't I always?' he answered, more in his usual arrogant style.

And she couldn't argue with that.

CHAPTER 18

The wedding congratulations card from Ricky arrived a couple of days later. Judy stared at it, unable to stop the smarting in her eyes. It was so unlike him to have bought a card at all, let alone a blatantly romantic and sentimental one like this. She was tempted not to show it to Blake at all, but they had received so many others by now that, in the end, she showed it to him without making any comment.

'It's a good thing someone in the Hale family is taking this marriage seriously, isn't it?' was all he said.

She bit her lip as she joined him for their regular room-service breakfast, thinking that he seemed far more able to take this sham of a marriage in his stride than she was. He didn't seem to appreciate the strain of it all, as far as she was concerned. It had been difficult enough to spend that first night in his apartment with their agreed conditions, especially under the Coopers' indulgent eyes.

But by now she was finding it more and more frustrating to remain saint-like and unaffected by the

351

fact that her husband was sleeping in the next room each night, no more than a few feet away from her, and seemingly content to stay there.

But tonight was the very last night of the International Spectacular, and for Judy it was going to be a bittersweet relief when it all came to an end.

'I couldn't go on like this indefinitely, Blake,' she was forced to say once she had put Ricky's card on one side along with all the others. 'I feel more and more embarrassed everytime I leave the apartment and have to face people. I've never been comfortable with deceit.'

'Most people would consider it more deceitful to pretend we were married when we weren't, wouldn't they?'

'You know very well what I mean. It's having to be this close, living in one another's pockets, when we're not – and everyone naturally thinks that we *are* – ' She floundered.

'Making love, you mean?'

She spoke carefully. 'What I mean is that everyone naturally thinks that this is a normal marriage, and we know very well that it's not! I'm not comfortable with any of it.'

He reached across the breakfast table and caressed the back of her neck beneath the fall of her hair.

'There's nothing in the rules that says we can't make it a normal marriage. You only have to say the word.'

'I know I do,' she snapped. 'And the word is no.'

She hardly thought he could be so passionately keen to make it a normal marriage in the biblical sense, since this was the first move he had made towards her in days. She twisted away from the fingers that were still caressing her neck, shivering as always at his touch.

Until these last months, she had never imagined that her brother's addiction to gambling could have such a far-reaching effect on her own life. If it hadn't been for her aversion to everything about it, she might even have been able to take the silly bet between Blake and Harry in her stride.

As it was, she had never been able to. But this was no longer Ricky's hang-up. It was hers . . .

'Then it looks as if we're stuck with one another for the time being, doesn't it?' Blake said at last.

She made herself believe that if he could sound so blasé about it, he obviously didn't care about her that much. She was a trophy, and no more. To imagine that he was really in love with her would be to enter the realms of fantasy.

There was more truth than people realized in the old saying that love for a man was a thing apart, while for a woman it was her whole existence . . . or something like that. She had made it her whole existence once, with Michael, and she was trying so hard now to put it into the same separate compartment of her life that Blake seemed able to do.

'I've got something for you,' he told her, more briskly. 'And I'd particularly like you to wear it tonight.'

She knew he was referring to tonight's party. It was going to be an extra-special one this time, since they would all be congratulating the newlyweds, as well as celebrating the end of a wildly successful show.

'Blake, I really don't need anything.' She started to get up from the table, not wanting any frivolous gifts from him.

'Stop arguing, woman, and stay right where you are. I swear I never heard anyone argue as much as you do!'

She sank back in her chair as he went into his bedroom. A few moments later he returned with a small jeweller's box in his hand, and Judy's heart began to thud dully. Whatever it was, she didn't want it, and if it was no more than a bribe to continue with this farce, then she wanted it even less.

He sat beside her and slowly opened the lid of the box. As if mesmerized, she drew in her breath at the beautiful sapphire and diamond ring inside that she knew at once must have cost a fortune. The fact that he *had* a fortune didn't make her any more receptive to accepting it.

'Blake, it's beautiful, but you must know I can't take it. It's far too much!' she burst out.

His reply was arrogant. 'Nothing is too much for my wife, so don't deny me the pleasure of putting it on your finger.'

Before she could say another word, he was holding her hand with the gold wedding ring on her third finger, and sliding the sapphire ring alongside it. He kissed the back of her hand and then her palm in the quaintly old-fashioned way he had done before. But his voice was light when he spoke.

'Now we're officially engaged as well as married. I'm just sorry it didn't happen in the correct order, ma'am.'

Judy was more moved by the gesture and the words than she wanted to be. But every time she thought she knew him, he did something totally unexpected.

When he had mentioned a gift, she had thought it might be a necklace or a bracelet, neither of which could be construed as overly significant, however personal. But a ring was different. In any other relationship, this would be a definite commitment.

'Then I'll be happy to wear it at the party tonight if that's what you want, Blake,' she murmured.

He gave a barely concealed oath beneath his breath.

'Damn it, woman, I don't just want you to wear it for one night. I want you to wear it always. It's yours.'

She didn't know what to say to that. All the fight had momentarily gone out of her, and in the end she simply thanked him and rushed to the bathroom for her morning shower.

She didn't need to work that day – nor ever again, she thought, feeling somewhat disorientated at the thought. Her contract officially ended that day. But once she had dressed in slacks and shirt, she left the apartment and wandered down to the rehearsal rooms, where Maggie was putting some of the girls through their last-minute paces.

At least here, surrounded by the sights and smells and the vibrant atmosphere that she knew so well, she could stop thinking of all the other problems in her life. Which was just about the craziest way for any woman to be thinking about being married to the man she loved, Judy thought ruefully . . .

Maggie came to join her a few minutes later, and she caught sight of the sapphire ring at once. It was hard not to do so, and it had seemed too much like throwing back Blake's generosity to remove it, whatever his motive in giving it to her, and so she hadn't. Or was that simply the story she was telling herself. . .?

'My God,' Maggie exclaimed, grabbing hold of Judy's left hand and turning it all ways so that the flawless, brilliant jewel caught the light. 'That's some sparkler and no mistake. Blake's really gone overboard for you, kid.'

Judy laughed uneasily, knowing that her conscience had already dictated that she must give the ring back to him once the divorce was final. It was the most beautiful thing she had ever owned, but she would never feel truly entitled to it.

'I think you could rephrase that remark, Maggie! He simply decided that since we'd rushed into it all so quickly, I needed an engagement ring to make it look legal and proper, that's all.'

'That's *all*? When a man buys a woman a ring like that, it's more than just for show, kiddo. He'll be putting a ring through your nose next.'

Maggie chuckled at her own joke, but Judy thought wryly that Blake had virtually already done that, and in her mind there was no escaping the fact.

'Are you all set for the party tonight?' Maggie went on. 'I suppose you've bought a wonderful new dress for it, seeing as it's going to be an extra-special occasion?'

Judy ignored the last part of the remark, but talking about clothes was at least on safer ground, knowing that Maggie was something of a clothes fanatic.

'I have bought something special, as a matter of fact, but you'll have to wait until tonight to see it,' she teased.

'Oh, well, that's OK,' Maggie retorted. 'Whatever it's like, I know you'll look stunning in it. With those fabulous blue eyes and that delicious red hair, you always do.'

For no reason at all that either of them could think of, Judy gave her a quick hug.

'Thanks, Maggie. You don't know what confidence that gives me,' she said huskily.

Maggie looked at her in some surprise. 'If anybody's going to be lacking in confidence tonight, it certainly won't be you, kid. Not when you're wearing the catch of the town's ring on your finger!'

Mercifully, she was called to the stage then, and Judy could concentrate on watching how the last-minute dance adjustments took up all her attention. But if Maggie thought she was super-confident, then she couldn't have been more wrong . . . but even as she thought it, she knew she would have to act that way . . . she must act her heart out tonight, no matter how much it cost her.

The dress she had bought especially for the last-night party was a dramatic black cocktail dress. It was sleek and sophisticated, and she wore no other jewellery but her wedding ring and the dazzling engagement ring.

Even if she still didn't feel easy about flaunting them, since this wasn't a real marriage at all, she couldn't deny the surge of pleasure at her own appearance. And when she emerged from her bedroom, Blake was waiting. He studied her for a few silent minutes, and as always her heart throbbed, and her skin tingled at his intense look. And then he kissed her gently on the cheek.

'You look like a million dollars,' he said simply.

When they arrived in the Sapphire Suite, the party had already begun, and they were greeted by an involuntary round of applause from the rest of the company. Everyone wanted to congratulate them again, on the success of the show, as well as the marriage, and finally Judy found herself next to Frank.

'You look like a princess tonight, babe. And this is decision time, isn't it?' he said, startling her.

'What do you mean by that?' Surely he couldn't have any idea of the true situation, she thought distractedly.

He was well into the party mood by now, Judy thought, and remembering other times, she determined that this small encounter wasn't going to be prolonged, if she had anything to do with it. He went on breezily.

'Well, you'll have to decide how long the honeymoon's going to last before you leave your new husband and go home to sort things out. In case

Blake's not too keen to go back to the old country with you, and you need company on the trip – '

Judy laughed, ignoring the irony of his remarks.

'You never give up, do you, Frank!'

'Not until they bury me six feet under. And now that you've broken my heart by marrying Blake, that might not be so far away,' he said mournfully.

'Stop fooling, Frank, and if that's what you think, which I doubt, then just remember that now I've married Blake, I've removed the competition for you, haven't I?' she added mischievously.

He laughed again, saying that she knew him too well, before he moved away to start chatting up somebody else.

Judy smiled, watching him put his usual technique into action. Frank would never be short of female company, and as she turned away to receive more good wishes and requests to show off her engagement ring, she instantly forgot him.

She knew the ambience of an end-of-show party so well, when everyone's adrenaline was at the highest pitch, and the successful reviews in all the papers and showbiz mags were as sweet as the wine of the gods to everyone concerned.

But this party had an added piquancy because of their own situation, even though she often lost sight of Blake. She was fêted along with Frank and Maggie on account of the show's success, and Judy didn't want her own news to dim the excitement of that. Tomorrow it would all be over, but tonight belonged to all of them.

The party had been in full swing for several hours when the lights in the Sapphire Suite were dimmed, and a fanfare of music rang out. And then the thing she had half-dreaded happened, and there was nothing she could to stop it, as a huge wedding cake was wheeled out, followed by a host of gift-wrapped parcels that would be taken up to the apartment for her and Blake to open at their leisure.

It embarrassed Judy so much she didn't know whether to laugh or cry. It could all have been so wonderful . . . and so it was . . . and everyone was so generous . . . she reminded herself that if she ever had to prove herself as an actress at all, now was the time.

To her horror, she saw that Blake was preparing to make a speech now, and drawing her to stand beside him.

'On behalf of my wife and myself . . .' he began ritually, before pausing for the cheers to die down, 'I want to thank you all, not only for what you've given us tonight, but for making Judy so welcome here in the past six months. Neither of us knew things were going to turn out this way, nor that finding myself a brilliant choreographer for the show was going to result in my finding a beautiful bride as well.'

He leaned towards her and kissed her cheek, using it as an excuse to whisper fiercely, 'Smile, can't you? You're not about to go down with the *Titanic*.'

Judy smiled dutifully, though it was hard to stem the tears at that moment. Then, when everyone had toasted the happy couple, she realized that they were calling for her to say something as well. She just couldn't do it . . . and for one wild, blistering moment she wondered just what would happen if she denounced Blake here and now, in front of them all . . . but she knew she couldn't do that either. Not when he had done so much for Ricky.

And Blake was holding her very tightly in the circle of his arm right now. Just as if he was aware of every damning thought in her head . . .

'Hold on a little longer, love,' he whispered more gently.

She nodded and took a deep breath, knowing she had gone into this with her eyes wide open, and if she wasn't as accomplished an actress as some of the company here, she had to go through with it.

'There's nothing I can say except to thank you all for being so warm and welcoming, and for the privilege of letting me share in the success of this wonderful show. As for taking Blake away from you – well, that was something I'd never anticipated doing either, and of course I haven't really done that! He belongs here, and always will.'

She couldn't think what else to say that wasn't going to sound just as inane and fatuous, but it was enough to please everybody, and she didn't need to say anything more.

She seemed to spend the next hours answering queries as to how it had all happened so quickly, and neatly avoiding actually telling them anything. She was becoming remarkably adept at lying, she thought bleakly.

Laverne was treating her with slightly more respect now that she was the boss's wife, and even made a thinly worded apology for any misunderstandings

361

she might have given Judy about Blake being interested elsewhere in recent weeks.

'Obviously, I was completely wrong about that, Judy, and I suppose it was just a blind, the same as when you went out with Frank a few times,' she said sweetly, not quite able to keep the habitual barbs out of her words. 'You and Blake wanted to keep us all guessing until you sprung it on us.'

'Something like that,' Judy nodded, thinking how easy it was to let people surmise whatever they liked, and just go along with it. By now, there must have been a dozen different suggestions, times and places circulating, as to the true details of the marriage, but neither she nor Blake had confirmed or denied anything.

'So what's next? Are the two of you planning on hearing the patter of tiny feet in the near future?'

Laverne's little bombshell was so much like the uneasy thought about people's reactions that had entered Judy's mind more than once that she retorted quickly, 'Not unless I start up a children's dance school, which is something that could be very useful around here.'

It wasn't the answer Laverne had expected. 'And what does Blake think about that?' she said, clearly taken aback.

'Why don't you ask him?' they both heard Blake say behind them. 'But I'll save you the bother, Laverne,' he added, putting his arm around Judy's shoulders. 'Whatever my beautiful wife wants to do is all right by me. Just as long as she's happy, then I'm happy.'

'How sweet. I kinda thought you'd want your wife to be sitting up for you with the slippers by the fireside, like they did in all those old British movies. I didn't expect you to have quite such progressive ideas, Blake.'

'Well, that's because you never knew the real me, isn't it, honey?'

And that seemed to put her firmly in her place, thought Judy. If she had ever tried to imply that she and Blake had had something going for them, he'd effectively snubbed her.

But she'd had enough of Laverne by now, and she turned thankfully when Maggie joined her and Blake. The party had been going long enough, thought Judy, and some people were either getting maudlin or scratchy, or ridiculously high on champagne and adrenaline by now.

It was already well into the early hours of the morning, and from the way her own head was spinning, Judy guessed there would be plenty of hangovers among the rest of them. As she stifled a yawn, Maggie spoke teasingly to Blake.

'Isn't it time you took your lovely wife off to bed? In fact, I can't think what the two of you are still doing here, when you must have far more interesting things to do.'

'That's just what I've been telling her ever since we arrived,' Blake said.

Judy ignored that, and they slipped out of the party quietly, but once in the elevator, she had to lean heavily against Blake, otherwise she knew might not have been able to stand upright. It wasn't even the amount of wine she had drunk, since she thought she had been careful not to overdo it. But tiredness and intense emotional feelings were finally catching up with her.

'I was sorry the elevator ever had to stop,' Blake said, as they went towards the apartment door. 'It was very enjoyable having you cling to me as if you meant it.'

'Don't start reading anything into it,' she muttered, with a horribly nauseous feeling sweeping over her now. 'I'm so tired I'm almost dead on my feet, and all I want to do is sleep.'

'I wasn't actually suggesting anything else,' he commented. 'Do you want me to put through a wake-up call, or shall we just wait until we wake up naturally tomorrow?'

Judy's head had begun to ache far too much by now for her to work out what he meant by all of that. 'It's already tomorrow, isn't it?' she murmured. 'And why bother with a wake-up call, anyway? The show's over.'

She stopped abruptly, feeling the most enormous rush of emotion at the finality of the words. The show was definitely over, in every sense of the word.

'Don't tell me you've changed your mind about going to Reno?' Blake said, and Judy registered that he was still irritatingly far more alert than she was. 'I'm happy to go along with that idea, if you are – '

'No, of course I haven't changed my mind.'

But, even though she found it almost incredible to believe, she *had* temporarily forgotten it.

In all the excitement of tonight, the congratulations and the wine, and the euphoria surrounding the whole company, how *could* she have forgotten the fact that tomorrow she and Blake were going to Reno to get a divorce?

The reminder of it was as sharp as a blow right between the eyes. She didn't actually reel backwards from it, but the sick sensation inside made her feel as if she had.

'Then since there's no reason to get up any earlier, I'll arrange for a wake-up call for one p.m.,' Blake went on calmly, just as if it didn't matter a damn to him now that there was no going back on their plans. 'And I suggest that you go to bed right now, before you fall asleep where you are.'

She did as she was told, moving like an automaton away from this man who was her husband, and who seemed to care so little for her any more.

Unless he was already thinking of a way to save face when the eventual news emerged that the marriage hadn't been destined to last after all.

In an instant, all the heady excitement of this magical evening threatened to fizzle away, because she simply couldn't see what the future was going to hold. And all her emotions were too fragile and too mixed up to think logically about any of it. Once in her bedroom, she undressed quickly with shaking hands, thinking what a mess she had made of her own life, when all she had wanted to do was to help her brother. It wasn't fair. It wasn't damn well fair.

She awoke to the weird sound of something sizzling nearby; when she managed to open her eyes a fraction, it was to see the glass of frothing white liquid beside her bed. She felt as if she had been asleep for barely ten minutes, and she couldn't bear the light in her eyes.

Someone had pulled her curtains back a little to let the glare of sunlight in, and she groaned, unwilling to face another day. She closed her eyes tightly again, and wriggled down beneath the bedcovers.

'That's going to do you no good at all,' came Blake's aggressive voice. 'Sit up slowly, and take your medicine.'

Judy gritted her teeth. How dare he be so wide awake when she was feeling like death . . .? He had been at the party just as long as she had. He had undoubtedly drank more, and eaten more, and here he was, already dressed and ready to start the day . . . at least, she presumed that he was . . .

She raised her eyelids another chink and shifted the bedcovers a tiny bit. Yes, he was looking as dashing as ever, perhaps even more so in the casual clothes he wore when he wasn't on official duty in his domain. And she was feeling increasingly belligerent towards him, knowing she was at such a physical and moral disadvantage by comparison.

'Will you please sit up?' he ordered again. 'Otherwise I might just have to force-feed you with this disgusting stuff.'

'What is it?' But she sat up very slowly as he dictated, knowing it was the only way. If she moved too fast, she was afraid the room would simply gyrate all around her. *And people got this way for pleasure?* she couldn't help thinking.

'Never mind what it is. Just drink it down while it will do you the most good.'

She did as she was told, feeling the bubbles tickle her nose as she swallowed the entire glassful in one go. It wasn't disgusting at all, and she wondered vaguely if the rest of the company were taking hangover cures to clear their heads this morning too . . .

'Right. Now I suggest you get up and take a shower, and by then we'll have some brunch sent up – '

'No, thanks! I couldn't eat a thing, Blake!' The very thought of it made her feel like throwing up.

'Believe me, it's the best way of curing you – '

'You're not suggesting that this is a hangover, are you? You know I don't drink that much – '

'I know all about that, but the excitement of the party and everything else probably provided the rest. You'll be fine with some food inside you. Now, can you manage to get out of bed by yourself, or do I have the delightful prospect of carrying you to the bathroom?'

He was relentless, she fumed, and he obviously didn't intend taking no for an answer. And it occurred to Judy that he was avoiding any mention of where they were going that day.

'Of course I can manage!' she said, throwing off the bedcovers as he made a determined move to do just as he said.

She glared at him, and then she followed his interested gaze. She had stripped off her clothes so quickly last night – or was it this morning? – and simply fallen into bed. Now that she realized she had nothing on, she idiotically snatched her dressing-gown to cover herself, as coy as a Victorian maiden.

'I'd have thought it a bit late for such modesty,' Blake remarked. 'But since you're sure you can manage, I'll leave you to it.'

To her relief he went out and left her to make her own shaky way to the bathroom. Half an hour later, she walked into the sitting-room. The shower had roused her full awareness, and the stabbing headache she had woken up with had dwindled considerably by now.

She was well aware of the benefits of eating food to ward it off still more, although she was sure she would only be able to manage toast and marma-lade. She was so thankful Blake hadn't ordered anything cooked . . . and she needed coffee, of course. Lots and lots of black coffee . . .

'When are we supposed to be leaving here?' she asked.

'Whenever we're ready, but I have a few arrange-ments to make first. I'm sure you can find something to do, though I doubt that there'll be very much activity among the rest of the party-goers yet.'

'I don't feel like company, anyway,' Judy said fervently. Especially when what they were planning to do today was looming ever nearer. 'But I think I'll go back to the suite for a while and sort out a few things in my desk.'

'Fine. In about an hour, then.'

She watched as he left the apartment, leaving her feeling more alone than she'd felt in months. And knowing that she only had to say the word, and all this could be so different . . . and yet she had to admit that she was starting to wonder if things could really be changed after all.

Perhaps, after all, they had come too far down the wrong road, and certainly Blake's attitude today fell far short of the various ways he had acted towards her before. There was no hint of seduction or tenderness. It was as if he had decided at last that the sooner he, too, got out of this entanglement, the better. And she couldn't blame him for that.

But even if the thought of it bruised her pride and tugged at her heart, she wouldn't accept that she had ever blown hot and cold towards him. She had always been honest in telling him that this couldn't work, and she had meant it – at the time.

It was just so ironic how many people seemed to think that they were made for each other. Ginny and Kyle, of course . . . Harry and Elsie . . . Maggie . . . the casino girls who saw it as such a romantic affair . . . even her own cynical brother . . .

And there was one other person who knew it too, if only she would let herself admit it. But she wouldn't, and she couldn't, because today was the day she and Blake were getting divorced.

CHAPTER 19

Judy spent an aimless few hours trying to get her thoughts together, sorting out the rest of her clothes, and going through everything in her desk with a view to clearing it. She presumed Blake had business of his own to attend to, and was no doubt leaving messages with his staff to say he would be away for the rest of the day. She hadn't seen or heard anything of him since she returned to the suite, and she went through the rooms slowly now, remembering how happy she had been here, and wishing it didn't all have to end.

But she squared her shoulders resolutely. In the words of Scarlett O'Hara, tomorrow was another day, and Judy had been through enough of those tough other days in her life to be able to cope with this one.

But when she heard Blake's pass-key opening her door, her heart leapt, knowing there was no turning back now . . .

'Are you ready?' he asked without expression.

She nodded, and went towards the door without a backward glance. It was always better to end things that way. *Never look back* was another of her own favourite sayings, even if she couldn't always trust herself to abide by it.

She had a light jacket slung around her shoulders now, knowing it would be colder in the plane than in the heat of Las Vegas. And she couldn't help thinking of the last time they had flown to Reno, when her thoughts had been in such turmoil over Ricky . . . and she admitted that she owed this man so much. If only he hadn't extracted such a price from her . . .

Blake's car had been brought round to the front of the casino, and she slid into the passenger seat beside him. He was obviously driving them to the airport himself, and she couldn't think of a single thing to say to him.

She forced herself to project her thoughts ahead. To going home. To seeing Ricky. To chasing Harry up for a new job, or seeing what he already had in mind for her. Meeting new people, new challenges, new shows . . . it was her life, and yet there was no sparkle in her thoughts of it.

She found herself twisting the rings on her finger, and remembered with a little start that she hadn't intended to wear them any more. She had kept them on while she went through the hotel for the sake of appearances, but she could hardly take them off and thrust them back at Blake now. Everything was getting too complicated for comfort, she thought, closing her eyes against the bright glare of the sun.

'Nearly there,' Blake said, and she realized she had had her eyes closed for longer than she thought. Last night was obviously still catching up with her.

He drove to the airport area where the private planes were lined up for their executive owners. And she had a strange feeling of *déjà vu*. This had all been done before . . .

'There's a holdall in the trunk of the car with a couple of thick jackets in case we should need them later. It could be very cold by the time we fly back – or it may be more convenient to stay overnight and fly back tomorrow.'

But he spoke far too blandly for it to have been a last-minute idea, and Judy was suspicious at once.

'I don't trust you – ' she began.

'Then it's time you started. Have I ever let you down in any way?'

She couldn't argue with that. He had been the best friend she had ever had, and Ricky's too. And he had been so much more than a friend.

'I'll go along with that,' she admitted quietly.

'Then trust me now.'

When they left the car he had the holdall over his shoulder, and Judy followed him numbly to the plane. She felt in a state of limbo, but she almost welcomed it, because it meant she didn't have to think too deeply of where they were going, and why. She strapped herself into the co-pilot's seat beside Blake as he started up the engine.

'I seem to remember telling you once before that we're not about to go down with the *Titanic*, and I'm saying it again now. Cheer up. This is what you want, isn't it?'

It was a rhetorical question, and as she gave him the briefest smile, which was all she could manage,

Judy thought he was far too busy with the controls on the plane to heed her lack of response. The roar of the engine saved her the necessity of saying things she didn't mean, anyway, and almost as soon as they had taxied along the short runway, they were airborne.

Almost at once, Judy realized that unless she was going crazy, the sun was on the wrong side of the plane. Which meant that instead of heading in a northerly direction to Reno, they were heading south. She spoke sharply.

'What's going on, Blake? I know this isn't right.'

'You intend to be leaving here soon, and before you do, you really shouldn't miss seeing one of the great sights of the area,' he said, as calm as you like.

'Are you turning into a tourist guide now?' she snapped, her nerves too fraught to cope with any of this. 'Turn this plane around at once – '

But she was was unable to stop her mouth twitching at the absurdity of what she had just said. It was as crazy as something out of the Keystone Cops . . .

'Do you really want to go back to England without seeing the Grand Canyon?'

His words took her by surprise, but she couldn't deny she felt far more than a spark of interest. Ever since she had come here, she had been promising herself a visit to the Grand Canyon. It had been very much on her one-day-soon agenda, but the show had taken up most of her time, and then other events had taken over to the exclusion of everything else. But she wasn't letting him get away with this lightly!

'You've got no right to do this without asking me. It's virtually kidnapping – '

'Since when could a man be accused of kidnapping just by taking his wife on a trip?'

'When you're the man, and I'm the wife,' Judy retorted. 'And what about Reno? I'm not changing my mind, Blake, and we surely can't do both trips in a single day. How long will it take to reach the Grand Canyon, anyway?'

She was even more suspicious now, because even with her inexpert knowledge of the terrain, she knew that the two places must be many hundreds of miles apart. And this was only a small private plane . . .

He gave her a similar reply to the one she'd heard on the trip to Reno, using pilot's jargon.

'A lot depends on wind conditions and air pressure, but it'll be well inside a couple of hours, and it takes a bit of viewing. The Canyon's more than two hundred miles long and four miles wide, so it's not something to be toured in a hurry. It's at its most spectacular at sunset, and that's what I really wanted you to see.'

'My God, you really have missed your vocation, haven't you? Are you quite sure you never wanted to be a tour guide?' She spoke mockingly to cover the undeniable thrill at the thought of seeing that vast natural phenomenon she had only ever heard and read about.

When he didn't deign to answer, she turned away from him, knowing there was nothing she could do about the situation now – she was totally in his hands.

She looked down as they soared skywards and away from the city, her heart lurching slightly as the desert scenery seemed to fall away beneath them.

Everything about this part of America was majestic, she admitted, and it was easy to fall in love with it. As perilously easy as it had been to fall in love with Blake.

'Are you feeling more relaxed yet?' he asked her later, when neither of them had said a word for some time.

She kept her voice cool. 'I'm fine. Though why you're bothering with this trip I can't think. Or is it all for show, because people would think it a romantic thing to do?'

The thought came to her immediately, and when he didn't answer, she decided that his silence was more significant than words. It all pointed to the fact that he didn't really care about her at all, regardless of the fact that he had once professed to love her.

But she steeled her heart against such lies, and gave up worrying about personal feelings as the vastness of the scenery gradually began to unfold before her. She had always heard that the Grand Canyon was awesome, but once it was ahead of her, she knew that words could never do justice to the multi-coloured layers of strata, the soaring mountains and fantastic rock formations, and the plunging chasms that descended down to the winding Colorado River a mile below.

And who was reacting like the typical tour guide now? she asked herself, but freely accepting that it was impossible to do otherwise. It wasn't until they they entered the first of the magnificent panoramas that Blake spoke again.

'It takes your breath away, doesn't it?'

It did more than that. It made her giddy, and she felt a very insignificant part of the universe.

'It also makes me feel that when you see something like this you wonder why people make such a fuss over petty matters. Not that they'll seem so petty once we get down to earth again,' she added, in case he thought she was weakening. 'But you do get a different perspective on things up here.'

'That's one reason why I love flying,' Blake told her. 'No problems can touch you, and you're as free as the birds.'

And just like the birds, they too were up here alone, with this huge, cavernous canyon below them. They were so small, so dependent on man-made machinery and a pilot's skill. Without thinking, Judy drew in her breath and clasped her hands together as a shiver as keen as a premonition ran over her skin. Blake glanced at her and spoke firmly, just as if he was reading her mind.

'There's no need to worry. We'll get down safely, if that's what you were thinking. I've never lost a wife yet.'

'I didn't think you'd ever had one before,' she said quickly, feeling the need to be sparring with him again, if only to allay the sudden irrational fear she felt.

'I didn't. Nor did I ever think I would want to marry anyone after Claire died. Not until now, that is.'

In any other circumstances Judy felt that she should have been affronted or annoyed that he'd brought Claire's name between them, and then added what was almost a little aside.

Even if this vastness of space made it somehow seem the right place to speak of such things; to mention them with love, and then let them go . . . and in her nervousness she knew she was in danger of letting herself get too emotional, and seeing things that weren't there . . .

The sun was getting lower in the sky now, and Judy could see at once what was meant by the changing face of the rock strata as the sunlight and shadows played over them. Sunset would transform it into a truly magical place.

'Didn't the Hopi Indians live here once?' She forced herself to remember something she had read up about the Canyon before coming to America.

'They did. How would you fancy being an Indian squaw up here, living on your wits and at the mercy of the elements?'

'I wouldn't, thank you very much,' she said smartly.

'Pity. I thought we might try it — ' he reverted to his old mocking tone.

'And if I thought you had any such stupid intentions — ' she broke in.

'You'd do what? Open the door of the plane and jump out? I wouldn't advise it, sweetheart. It's a long way down!'

Automatically, she looked directly downwards to the dizzily yawning chasm below, already full of dark shadows, and she turned on him, her heart beating sickly.

'You had no right to frighten me like that.'

'I had every right to show you one of nature's wonders — ' his voice had become steely and arrogant now '– and a husband has a right to take his bride anywhere he pleases on their honeymoon.'

'*What*? Well, if you think I'm going to be the little subserviant wife, and go along with your schemes – '

'Good God, do you think I'd ever want a wife like that? But right now, I'd be obliged if you'd stop arguing, and let me get on with the job in hand. Flying can be a dangerous business if you don't give all your attention to it.'

She clamped her lips together, knowing it was impossible to stop his plans now. But if he considered this side trip to view the Grand Canyon a so-called honeymoon, stuck in a small plane miles from anywhere, she certainly didn't!

After a while, gingerly looking through the window of the plane again, she saw that it was more than dusk now, and that the light had almost gone. The spectacular blood-red sunset had come and gone so fast, and it would surely be unsafe to be flying through the canyon in the dark, so perhaps she should be grateful that they were presumably going to land in some tourist area for the night.

The whole thought of this deliberate kidnapping, no matter what Blake called it, incensed her so much that she simply refused to ask. But tomorrow morning she would insist that they flew right up to Reno at first light, and do what they had supposedly set out to do.

Moments later she heard Blake swear beneath his breath, and immediately she was aware of the plane's engine spluttering.

'What's wrong now?' she asked. 'This isn't a car, so don't tell me we've run out of petrol or anything stupid – '

'I'm going to have to put her down.'

From the tone of his voice she knew at once that this wasn't a joke. They were in real danger, and the Canyon plunged hundreds of feet below them. They were going to die . . . a scream began to well up in her throat and then she felt his hand squeeze her knee for a second.

'Don't give in to panic yet. We're above a plateau and with reasonable luck and a prayer we'll land safely enough.'

His words did nothing to allay her panic, and she was praying all right. And then the engine died completely, and they seemed to coast down towards the ground in the darkness.

Judy closed her eyes, terrified that they were going to crash, but somehow the plane bumped its crazy way along the ground and then came to a stop. And it wasn't true that all your past life flashed before your eyes at the moment of death, she found herself thinking hysterically, seconds before she turned to Blake in a fury.

'If this is another of your crazy plans, landing us miles from anywhere, you can just get us out of here right now. And if not, then you'd better radio for help, because I've no intention of sitting it out here all night.'

He ignored her accusation and spoke coolly. 'I could say you've got no choice, but there's always a chance we can find a deserted cabin on this plateau. There are a number of them scattered around. If so, we can certainly make ourselves more comfortable than sitting it out here. Incidentally, the radio's out too, and I'll need daylight to fix it. You can try it, since you'll naturally not take my word for it.'

She snatched it from his hand, but no matter how many times she flipped the switch, it was completely dead.

'I told you this was kidnapping, and this just confirms it, doesn't it?' she raged, more upset than she let him see.

'You could call it that. I'd prefer to call it an unexpectedly romantic way to spend a honeymoon. Face it, my sweet. There's nowhere to go, so let's make the best of it and see if we can find some shelter for the night.'

'I'd rather stay in the plane – '

'Well, I wouldn't.' Blake was more assertive now. 'The temperature will soon drop rapidly, and I've no wish to die from exposure. Once we find shelter we can build a fire and keep warm, and the fire will keep any stray wild animals or rattlers well away.'

Judy shuddered at the thought, but she looked at him with deep suspicion now.

'And what a surprise it will be to stumble across one of those deserted cabins, won't it?'

'Amazing. So let's put on our thick jackets and go outside and be pioneers.'

She couldn't believe that all this was pure coincidence. And now she knew exactly why he'd brought the two thick jackets. She couldn't shake him, and she couldn't shame him. He had the upper hand and he knew it, and this forced landing was all a ploy to delay the inevitable divorce. Saving face, she thought again, if only for one more day . . .

But since she didn't want to stay here all alone in this wild, untamed place where, she was already starting to realize, the silence was unbroken and infinite, she had no option but to step outside the plane with him.

She got a swift sense of how bleak a wilderness it really was when Blake switched on a powerful flashlight, and she shivered at once as the keenly cold air hit her. At least he'd been right about that, and she huddled into her thick jacket as he spoke more briskly.

'Since I don't want you dying of hypothermia, the sooner we move and get a fire going, the better.'

'Even in the open?'

'I doubt that there'll be any need for that.'

She spoke bitterly. 'I didn't think so. So when are you going to stop pretending that you didn't plan this all along? And that the plane's engine cutting out never put us in any danger at all?'

When he didn't answer she wondered fearfully just how long he intended to keep her here as his virtual prisoner.

'Start walking and keep close to me,' he ordered, his arm around her and holding on to her tightly.

She did as he said, not wanting to let him know how very scared she was. The terrifying thought that there might be rattlesnakes in the area was enough to curl her toes and dry her mouth, and despite the flashlight's beam she couldn't even tell if they were on a proper path or on rough ground. The sky had darkened so rapidly that she couldn't make out a thing beyond the pool of light in front of them, until a dark shape loomed up ahead, and Blake pushed open the door of the ramshackle cabin they had reached.

'This is our honeymoon destination, I suppose?' she asked, close to tears, because everything was so different from the way it should have been. 'It's hardly the Ritz!'

'It doesn't need to be. But I presume you would prefer it if I didn't carry you over the threshold?'

'You're damn right!'

He kicked the door shut behind them and struck a match to light the oil lamp on the table in the middle of the one large room. At once it was lit with a rosy glow. The cabin was far cleaner than Judy would have expected, and there was a vase of fresh flowers on a side table.

It was just as though the place had been prepared for a visit. There was a large bed with clean bedding at one side of the room, and the fireplace was laid with paper and sticks, and would only need a match put to it as well. She whirled on Blake, all her suspicions confirmed now.

'We didn't have to force-land here at all, did we? This was all planned beforehand, and you never intended to take me to Reno today – '

He no longer bothered to deny it. 'Are you objecting? You're still my wife for the present, at least, and can you think of a more romantic place for a honeymoon? Everything we need is here. There's food and drink in the cupboard, and we'll soon have a warm fire – and we have each other.'

Judy forced down the lump in her throat at the sweet seduction of his words as he put a match to the fire. She watched as it blazed into instant life. It was every bit as perfect as a woman's romantic heart could wish. But she still couldn't forgive his methods.

'What I object to is being tricked!'

'And I object to your continual refusal to admit that we have what we both want.'

She stared at him mutely, knowing what he meant. He wanted her, whether love was involved or not. And she . . .

'Are you hungry?' he asked, less aggressively. 'It'll have to be a cold meal, but the coffee will soon heat up on the spirit stove, so just relax.'

It really was a bit like pioneering, Judy allowed herself to think . . . but she also wondered if she was really cut out for a rugged wilderness life in the way Blake seemed to be. It might not compare with the wilds of Yorkshire, but she knew by now that he was the type of man who could fit in anywhere. And he had almost certainly checked out this place already.

Maybe he had even brought someone else here . . . but even as she thought it, she rejected it, if only because she simply didn't want to imagine it.

The fire warmed the room very quickly, and they were able to shed their jackets before they ate a silent meal, and drank the welcome coffee and a bottle of wine. And Judy knew that the very isolation, and the crackling, sensual warmth of the wood fire were all helping to relax her taut nerves.

Resolutely, she reminded herself again that there wasn't a single thing they could do about the situation until morning. There were no curtains at the window, and the night was inky black outside now, with no sign of the moon or stars. She had to make the best of it, but she would have plenty to say about Blake's trickery once they got out of here . . .

'I'll keep the fire banked up, but I suggest we hold each other close to keep warm,' he said predictably. 'There's no point in wasting that inviting bed.'

'I'd rather stay right where I am, thanks.'

He got up from his chair and walked towards her purposefully, pulling her to her feet.

'And I would far rather spend the night with my wife in my arms.'

Judy's felt her heartbeats quicken crazily. 'Even if you had to force me?'

'But I wouldn't have to. Would I?'

She felt his hands slide down her arms, and her skin responded and tingled as always at his touch. She realized she was dizzy with the effects of altitude, but it was more than that. She was also dizzy with the wine, and with his nearness, and she could no longer deny it. And she was his wife . . .

There was a sudden ferocious noise outside, reminiscent of all the demons in hell being let loose. It shook the cabin and made Judy's heart leap with fear. Thoughts of wild animals of the prehistoric kind surged into her mind, and she found herself shaking from head to foot. She leapt into Blake's arms as the roaring sounds crashed and rattled unabated, and with them came jagged flashes of blue light that lit the sky through the uncurtained window. Its brightness penetrated Judy's tightly closed eyelids and had her petrified with fear as she clung to him.

She was sure that whatever it was was about to split the cabin in two, and in an instant her nerves were in shreds. She buried her head against Blake's chest, knowing that it was only his supporting arms that were holding her up, since her legs seemed to have turned to jelly.

He had to shout in her ear then, not only to penetrate the violence outside, but to get through her shocked senses as well. 'It's all right, Judy, it's only an electrical storm. They can be terrifying, but they're usually fast and furious and then they're over. You're quite safe.'

She still shuddered against him, finding no comfort in his words. She was never normally afraid of storms, but she had never encountered anything like this before. It was like a concentration of all her worst nightmares as the thunder echoed and roared through the Canyon, its sounds magnified and thrown back a thousand times, while the lightning splintered down through the sky in jagged spears of blue and yellow.

'How can you be so sure?' she almost sobbed. 'If the lightning struck this cabin it would go up like a tinderbox, we'd disappear in smoke and nobody would ever know we'd been here at all.'

As her vivid imagination soared, she felt his voice vibrate against her shaking body as he gripped her tightly.

'Nobody's going to disappear in smoke, sweetheart, and I'd do anything rather than let anything harm you. I know it's frightening, but believe me, it won't last long.' He hesitated and then went on. 'And despite the way it looked when we landed on the plateau, we're not that far from civilization. There's a tourist look-out post and restaurant less than a mile away from here, and people do know we're here.'

Even in the midst of her fear, Judy felt her sickeningly fast heartbeats stop for a moment and then race on. She tried to get out of his embrace, but his grip was too strong for her. But she could draw up her hands and beat against his chest in a fury at knowing the truth of it.

'Don't you know you've scared me half to death? And now you tell me we're close to civilization. I hate you for doing this, Blake!'

'And I love you,' he said angrily. 'I've loved you from the moment you came into my life, though I must admit I didn't always see it that way – and you're hardly the easiest person to love, with that fiery temper of yours – '

She jerked up her head, wondering if she was still imagining things. Her emotions and her nerves were still in a turmoil, but the way in which Blake had just told her he loved her was something that only a fool could disbelieve. And she was no fool. Her hands had become still now, her palms resting against his chest, and she could feel his heartbeats too, as rapid and uneven as her own as he went on talking in that low, still angry way.

'Don't you know I'd have gambled anything to make you my wife and to keep you here? I'd give you anything to make you stay – including the Cooper ranch – and by the way, that's already taken care of –'

She found her own shaky voice at last. 'I don't need bribes to make me stay, Blake. There's only one thing I need.'

As she spoke, she realized that the violence of the storm had lulled a little, and that perhaps it was truly going to be over as quickly as it had begun.

But even as she thought it, a vicious clap of thunder seemed to split the air right above the cabin, and she was clinging to him again. And this time she made no protest as he drew her down to the bed beside the softly crackling fire, and cocooned them both inside the blankets.

'What is it you need?' he asked softly, his fingers caressing her cheeks and smoothing her hair.

The words she spoke were only tokens, because her heart was telling her all that she yearned to know.

'I need to believe that you really do love me, and that this isn't just a pretence.'

'I love you more than anything in the world, but you don't have the priority on needs. No one should have to settle for a one-sided love, and there's something I need to know too. Why did you agree to marry me?'

After such sweet words, he shot the question at her so suddenly that she almost flinched.

'You know why! It was on account of Ricky, and I'll be eternally grateful for what you did – '

'I don't want your gratitude. I want more than that.'

'All right, then! I married you because I love you – '

It was the first time she had said it to him, and it no longer felt as though she was giving him a victory. It had never felt more right.

'Then what the devil were we going to Reno for?' Blake said softly. 'Two people who love each other as much as we do should stay married, shouldn't they?'

Before she could give him the answer they both wanted, a brilliant flash of lightning lit the cabin once more, and Judy found herself thinking fleetingly that not even a gamblin' man could have foreseen a violent electrical storm in this wild and lonely place at such an opportune time.

And a careless bet made between old friends was the furthest thing from her mind as her husband's arms reached out for her ever more hungrily, and his kiss on her eager, waiting lips promised all the love in the world.

THE EXCITING NEW NAME
IN WOMEN'S FICTION!

PLEASE HELP ME TO HELP YOU!

Dear *Scarlet* Reader,

As Editor of *Scarlet* Books I want to make sure that the books I offer you every month are up to the high standards *Scarlet* readers expect. And to do that I need to know a little more about you and your reading likes and dislikes. So please spare a few minutes to fill in the short questionnaire on the following pages and send it to me.

Looking forward to hearing from you,

Sally Cooper

Editor-in-Chief, *Scarlet*

QUESTIONNAIRE

Please tick the appropriate boxes to indicate your answers

1 Where did you get this Scarlet title?
Bought in supermarket ☐
Bought at my local bookstore ☐ Bought at chain bookstore ☐
Bought at book exchange or used bookstore ☐
Borrowed from a friend ☐
Other (please indicate) _____

2 Did you enjoy reading it?
A lot ☐   A little ☐   Not at all ☐

3 What did you particularly like about this book?
Believable characters ☐   Easy to read ☐
Good value for money ☐   Enjoyable locations ☐
Interesting story ☐   Modern setting ☐
Other _____

4 What did you particularly dislike about this book?

_____

5 Would you buy another Scarlet book?
Yes ☐   No ☐

6 What other kinds of book do you enjoy reading?
Horror ☐   Puzzle books ☐   Historical fiction ☐
General fiction ☐   Crime/Detective ☐   Cookery ☐
Other (please indicate) _____

7 Which magazines do you enjoy reading?
1. _____
2. _____
3. _____

And now a little about you –
8 How old are you?
Under 25 ☐   25–34 ☐   35–44 ☐
45–54 ☐   55–64 ☐   over 65 ☐

cont.

9 What is your marital status?

Single ☐   Married/living with partner ☐

Widowed ☐   Separated/divorced ☐

10 What is your current occupation?

Employed full-time ☐   Employed part-time ☐

Student ☐   Housewife full-time ☐

Unemployed ☐   Retired ☐

11 Do you have children? If so, how many and how old are they?

_____

_____

12 What is your annual household income?

under $15,000	☐	or £10,000	☐
$15–25,000	☐	or £10–20,000	☐
$25–35,000	☐	or £20–30,000	☐
$35–50,000	☐	or £30–40,000	☐
over $50,000	☐	or £40,000	☐

Miss/Mrs/Ms _____

Address _____

_____

_____

Thank you for completing this questionnaire. Now tear it out – put it in an envelope and send it, before 28 February 1998, to:

Sally Cooper, Editor-in-Chief

USA/Can. address
SCARLET c/o London Bridge
85 River Rock Drive
Suite 202
Buffalo
NY 14207
USA

UK address/No stamp required
SCARLET
FREEPOST LON 3335
LONDON W8 4BR
Please use block capitals for address

GAMAN/8/97

Scarlet titles coming next month:

DEADLY ALLURE Laura Bradley
After her sister's murder Britt Reeve refuses to let detective Grant Collins write the death off as an accident. Britt suspects that the murderer could be someone with family ties, and soon she and Grant find themselves passionate allies in a race against time . . .

WILD FIRE Liz Fielding
Don't miss Part Three of **The Beaumont Brides** trilogy! Melanie Beaumont's tired of her dizzy blonde image. She's determined to show everyone that she can hold down a proper job. And if that means bringing arrogant Jack Wolfe to his knees . . . so much the better!

FORGOTTEN Jill Sheldon
What will happen if Clayton Slater remembers who he is and that he's never seen Hope Broderick before in his life? And Hope has another problem . . . she's fallen in love with this stranger she's claimed as her lover!

GIRLS ON THE RUN Talia Lyon
Three girls, three guys . . . three romances?
Take three girls: Cathy, Lisa and Elaine. Match them with three very different guys: Greg, Philip and Marcus. When the girls stop running, will their holiday romances last forever?